THE DA...
PILOT

Julien Evans

Steemrok Publishing
Chesham, England

steemrok.com

CHAPTER 1

In the computer room in HMP Stensfield, a Category B prison near Braintree in Essex, there were only three inmates hunched over their keyboards. February was still a week away, but the almost spring-like weather had enticed many of the others outside, making the most of their temporary extra freedom. Occasionally shouted obscenities from the football pitch touchline drifted through the bars of the partly opened windows. C wing were playing E wing. The quality of play would be agricultural and the referee's work unenviable. The match was not yet half an hour old. At the moment the score was goals nil, broken noses one, knees-in-groin two and threats of grievous bodily harm . . . too many to count.

The men in the computer room paid no attention to the mayhem outside. One, only just twenty, was destroying aliens on the planet Zordon 3. Another, a fragile veteran known to the other inmates as Oscar Wilde, was writing love poems to his partner on the outside.

The third man looked about forty, well built with straight black hair beginning to grey. People who didn't know better took the permanent hint of a sardonic smile that played on his face as a token of warmth. If they looked closely at the dark eyes they would get a different message. Those same eyes were now staring at the monitor in front of him. The page heading was 'Tax Regulations for Foreign Residents in Aruba.'

None of the three men heard the warder come in. The young man and the old man were too engrossed in their labours and the dark-eyed man was seated well away from the others and from the door.

'Hello Maurice,' said the warder as he approached.

The prisoner showed no reaction. 'What do you want?'

The warder looked around to make sure the others were out of earshot. Through the window came the muffled cry 'Kill the bastard!' The warder drew up a chair and sat next to the prisoner.

'We never finished our conversation the other day.'

'Yes, we did,' said the prisoner, still looking at the screen.

Warder Harry Ford smiled. It was the smile of a poker player about to show his opponent four aces.

'We both want a quiet life, don't we?'

Maurice Holmin, convicted murderer, at last looked at the warder. He returned the smile but the dark eyes were still cold.

'It's too quiet in this shit hole, Harry.'

'Hey, come on,' said Ford. 'Things aren't so bad. Keep your nose clean and you'll be out in less than ten years.'

Holmin nodded. 'Yes, you're right. Less than ten years.'

He had nearly got away with it. The defence claimed that the victim had somehow got tangled up in a rope that had been attached to the tow-hook on Holmin's car as he sped along at ninety. But a traffic surveillance video recording turned up showing the defendant tying the rope to the victim's ankle before he started the car. The plea was changed to guilty. The charge of speeding was dropped.

'So, I'm just asking that we renegotiate the consultation fee.'

The smile vanished from the prisoner's face and Ford was momentarily alarmed. Then reason got hold of him again and brought to his mind the information that would guarantee his safety. Maybe in the silence that followed the prisoner was following the same line of thought.

'Alright, how much?'

'I'm not greedy, Maurice, as you well know.'

The smile returned to Holmin's lips but not to his eyes.

'How much?'

'Another five.'

The prisoner nodded. 'Okay.'

Ford smiled back and mentally breathed a sigh of relief. Holmin had agreed more quickly than he expected. Maybe he should have gone for twenty grand instead of ten. The data was obviously very important and it was to the warder's advantage that Holmin did not know exactly how much Ford knew about it.

It was purely by chance that Ford had come across the information. As one of the designated Computer Room Supervisors he was responsible for checking the browsing history of inmates using the computers to make sure they had not bypassed the system filters which prevented them from accessing websites deemed unsuitable by the authorities. It was also the job of the CRSs to monitor the prisoners' email traffic, such as Oscar's love poems, which Ford and his mates would access whenever they wanted a bit of a laugh.

The warder had noticed a recent increase in the volume of incoming and outgoing traffic in Holmin's mailbox. The contents were sometimes illogical and the warder suspected information or instructions were being transmitted in code of some sort. One of the outgoing messages referred to the 'music lists'. Attachments were not allowed so Holmin's 'lists' were included in the body of the email.

The first list was headed 'Normal' and comprised four pop song titles. There were another three in the second, headed 'Extra'. A third, much longer, untitled list featured sixty-two songs, including the seven tracks named in the first two. There was no obvious sequence in the lists. Tracks were not numbered and not in alphabetical order.

To test the water, Ford had said to Holmin, 'we're working on the code, Maurice. We think we've cracked it.'

'What the hell are you talking about?'

'At the moment it's just me and a friend. I can't decide whether or not to let the Governor in on it.'

'Fuck off.'

'"Normal" and "Extra". Not so subtle.'

The prisoner had paused before responding.

'Okay, Harry. I'll level with you. It's a business deal I'm organising and I don't want commercially sensitive information getting into the wrong hands.'

'Fair enough. Shall I tell the Governor that?'

'Tell you what. If I pay you a consultancy fee you can be part of the deal.'

'So what do the lists actually mean, Maurice?'

Holmin laughed. 'You bullshitter! You told me you'd cracked the code.'

'No, I said we're working on it.'

'Alright, let's stop buggering about, Harry. Here's what we'll do. You'll receive a cheque for five grand from a friend of mine who runs a legit business. You can tell anyone who wants to know that you helped me with the rules and regs setting up the new venture.'

'When do I get the dosh?'

'I'll let you know.'

'Okay, you're on.'

And that's where the matter had rested until the warder had decided to change the arrangement.

Now the prisoner turned back to his monitor. 'You'll get your money. Now clear off. And if you pull this stunt again I'll make sure you die a very painful and long drawn out death.'

Ford reached out to put a hand on the prisoner's shoulder, then thought wiser of it.

'Hey, that's no way to talk to a friend.'

Holmin turned his eyes on to the warder and the unspoken words got through. Ford stood up and returned the chair to the next console. A derisive cheer came from the football pitch. Either someone had scored a goal or someone had been thumped. Ford grinned at the other two men as he walked out of the room but they ignored him.

'Arseholes,' he muttered.

Maurice Holmin was still looking at the monitor but his mind was elsewhere. Perhaps he was thinking back to the moment soon after he was incarcerated when Ford and two other warders had brought him a glass of orange juice. The glass was half full, at least until Ford had unzipped his fly and urinated into it. The three warders, two holding kitchen knives and the other a potato peeler, had then invited the new inmate to quench his thirst.

Less than ten years. You'll get what you deserve sooner than you think. And so will I.

CHAPTER 2

'Meteor 808, turn left heading three zero zero, call established,' radioed Approach Control at East Midlands airport.

Captain Wilf Jagger thumbed his transmit button. 'Left three zero zero to establish, 808.'

Ed Park, Wilf's copilot, adjusted the autopilot controller and both men watched their instruments intently as the Merchantman freighter lumbered round onto the new heading.

Jagger, in the left-hand seat, reached down to the central pedestal to preselect Tower frequency on the radio. A tall, spindly man ('lean and wiry' in his own mind, 'gaunt' to others), he would soon arrive at his fifty-third birthday, a meeting he would be happy to put off as long as possible, if not forever. But there was no denying the march of time. It was true that his face was not heavily lined, but it was also true that his hairline had begun to recede. And at his last six-monthly medical check the doc had had a surprise for him. *Your near point's receding, Wilf. You'd better get yourself some specs for reading - you're going to need them soon.*

Yes, thought Jagger now, *I could do with them tonight. I can read the instruments okay, but it's a bit of a strain.* His grey eyes peered at the panel, monitoring the aircraft's flight path. There was nothing to see outside. The night was as black as the bottom of a coal mine. Jagger could hear the rain hosing past the windscreen. He hunched his bean-pole figure forward a little to adjust the weather radar. The screen was a mass of glowing colours.

'There's a lot of shit out there,' he muttered.

'Are we okay on this heading?' asked Park. The copilot was not as tall as Jagger, but whereas Jagger was definitely on the scrawny side, Park was stocky, ideally built for the rugby he played in his spare time. With wavy fair hair and mischievous blue eyes, he was a magnet for anyone of the opposite sex. Naturally his wife, Elaine, was afraid that one day temptation might be too strong for Ed to resist. Even her best friends flirted with her husband. In reality she had no cause to worry. Ed had kept himself on the straight and narrow and was content with his domestic life. He was still in love with Elaine and he doted on his two young children. Only the week before he had found himself propositioned by an attractive neighbour he happened to bump into at the shops. *Mike's away for two weeks, Ed. If you want to pop in for a coffee sometime you'd be welcome.*

You mean, with Elaine and the kids? Ed had said, deliberately teasing.

Now, you know that's not what I meant, the neighbour had replied, brushing her breast against his arm. *Don't forget, Ed, anytime at all.*

Park's family life might have been as he wanted it, but his working life was not, not just yet. Flying 'Zulu Charlie' (as the Merchantman was registered) for Meteor Air Express in the middle of the night earned enough to pay the mortgage and the bills, but Park had been doing it for two years now and the novelty had worn off. He was about to move further up the aviation ladder, having just landed a job with Central Airlines as a first officer on Boeing 777 jets. At last—daytime flying—well, mostly—more pay, modern equipment. He'd be sorry to leave Meteor. He enjoyed driving the old four-prop Merchantman. (Or 'Vickers Vibrator' as the vulgar soubriqet had it. Vickers was the name of the company that had orginally built the aircraft and the alliterative nickname derived from the shuddering power delivered by four Rolls Royce Tyne engines.)

And Park liked flying with blokes like Wilf Jagger and old Bernie Crowburn, Meteor's other captain.

'Localiser,' called Jagger.

'Check,' acknowledged the copilot as the autopilot banked Zulu Charlie towards final approach.

'Radar's still full of weather, Ed. No way to avoid it. At least there's no electrical activity.'

Electrical activity. Airmen's euphemism for lightning.

'808 established,' transmitted Jagger.

'Roger,' replied Approach, *'cleared ILS, call Tower, goodnight.'*

The Instrument Landing System comprised two radio beams, fanning out like the feathers of a dart, which would guide them to the runway.

Tonight the autopilot was behaving itself (it frequently didn't). Zulu Charlie rode out the turbulence well enough, the flight deck 'nodding' in the way peculiar to Merchantmen freighters. Converted from Vanguard passenger airliners in the early seventies, the Merchantmen had had their floors strengthened to withstand loading with cargo pallets, but a side effect was that the modified fuselage structure was more rigid. In rough air the floor bounced like a diving board.

'Glideslope.'

'Check,' responded Park. 'Gear down, approach flap. Final checks.'

Zulu Charlie intercepted the glideslope and both pilots heard the altitude lock disengage.

'Land flap,' called the copilot.

Jagger moved the lever, watching the gauge. It was slightly blurred. *Must go to the optician tomorrow.*

'Land flap you have,' he said. 'Checks complete.'

They were less than two minutes from touchdown.

'808, four miles,' transmitted the captain.

'Meteor 808, cleared to land,' replied Tower, *'wind two three zero, twenty.'*

Park opened the throttles a little to maintain speed. 'Touch of crosswind there, Wilf.'

'A mere breeze. Beautiful weather.'

Decision height was 200 feet. Descending through 500 they were still in thick black bumpy cloud. The rain streamed past.

'We may have to go around,' said Park, meaning that if they couldn't make visual contact he would abandon the approach.

'I hope not.' A diversion to another airport would cost Meteor a lot of money.

At 400 feet there was nothing.

At 300 feet there was still nothing.

'One hundred above,' called the captain. If the approach lights were not in sight at 200 feet Park would have to open up the engines to full power and climb away again.

Jagger watched his altimeter passing 250 feet. Park's eyes flicked from instruments to windscreen.

'Decision,' called Jagger.

'Contact,' replied Park. 'I've got the lights.'

The captain also looked up. Through the waterfall of rain and ragged wisps of dark cloud could be seen the approach lights streaking past underneath.

Park knocked out the autopilot and skilfully fought the aircraft down to the runway, ruddering it straight and sticking the mainwheels firmly onto the wet surface.

'Ground idle, please, Wilf.'

Jagger pulled the props into fine pitch. The flattened blades were now airbrakes and Zulu Charlie shuddered as it decelerated.

'Lock in.'

Jagger engaged the lever and took the wheel from Park to wrestle the elevators and ailerons into their gust locks to immobilise them.

'Nice landing, boy,' he said in a mock Texan drawl.

'Did you expect anything else?' acknowledged Park with a wink.

Tower cleared them to taxi to the freight apron.

When an airliner parks and shuts down its engines, it is immediately engulfed in a fussy swarm of activity. Mobile steps, catering vehicles and fuel trucks home in like wasps to a jam jar. Personnel arrive to chock the wheels, plug in electrical power units, supervise passenger disembarkation and so on. Trains of baggage trolleys nestle up to the belly holds so that loaders can hurl suitcases onto them. 'Honey wagons' drain the contents of the toilets. All this bustle goes on simultaneously, because the idea is to turn the aircraft round as quickly as possible and get it flying again. Airline accountants do not like aircraft sitting idly on the ground, expending money rather than earning it and passengers do not like hanging around, waiting for their bags.

Charter freighting is not the same. Cargo does not complain if it is late. When Ed Park cut Zulu Charlie's engines, there to meet them was a solitary airport worker who dragged a set of mobile steps to the Merchantman's crew door on the right side of the freighter and then slouched off without bothering to make contact with the crew. As the props gradually ran down and Park finished the shut-down checklist, Jagger released his harness and disappeared aft. At the forward end of the hold he swung the heavy crew door onto its catch and peered out at the black, wet night. In its passenger service days, the aircraft had had an identical door on the opposite side of the fuselage. After shut-down, a set of mobile stairs would have positioned up to the door for the occupants to disembark. Zulu Charlie had no passenger door. In its place was a huge cargo door which could be opened and closed using the aircraft's hydraulic system.

Between them, the two pilots switched everything off, inserted the landing gear locking bars and chocked the wheels. The cargo, a light load of computer parts, would be taken off when the loaders turned up in the morning. Ed Park dragged the mobile steps back to the edge of the apron to comply with the security regulations that demanded removing all means of access to unoccupied aircraft.

The two pilots made there way back to the Meteor office. It was as they were splashing through the puddles, carrying their flight bags, that they noticed a light on in the office.

At this time of night? thought Jagger. *I'll have to have a word with Caroline about switching lights off when she goes home. We're not so flush that we can afford to waste electricity.*

East Midlands Airport forms the southern tip of a triangle whose other points are the cities of Derby and Nottingham. Like every airport in the world it is continuously growing, trying to match the ever increasing demand for air travel. One of the main air mail parcel distrubution hubs in Europe, the airport was at night host to a stream of arriving and departing freighters. Sometimes the big boys such as UPS or Fedex ran out of capacity or serviceable aircraft and Meteor would pick up a lucrative ad hoc sub-charter.

The main passenger operator at East Midlands was Central Airlines, soon to be Ed Park's new employer, a company expanding as quickly as the airport. The airline's recently completed administration block matched its grandiose plans for the future, soaring even higher than the new passenger terminal standing in its shadow.

To the west of the passenger terminal was the cargo area, tucked into a corner of which could be found Meteor Air Express. The operations headquarters was styled 'Meteor House', a rather grand appellation for a Portacabin structure sandwiched between a large Customs shed and a hangar owned by DHL.

Meteor was a one horse outfit. Its sole serviceable flying machine was Zulu Charlie. Other assets included another Merchantman, Echo Victor, whose certificate of airworthiness had expired but which was useful for spares, and two extra Tyne engines. Echo Victor would never fly again. Its final resting place was an oil-soaked patch of bedraggled weeds between the hangars, out of public view. Few outside eyes ever caught sight of the faded, peeling paintwork, deflated tyres and empty engine nacelles. Nevertheless the wreck was an irritation to the airport management who had begun to send letters and emails to Jagger to the effect that either he got rid of it or they would start charging parking fees. So far the owner of Meteor Air Express had managed to keep this problem at bay by promising to consider plans for disposal 'in the near future'.

It wasn't totally correct to say that Echo Victor would never fly again. Bits of it were still in service. Its rudder now kept Zulu Charlie heading straight and it had also donated its left wing flap to its canniballistic sister ship.

The Portacabin was also owned by Meteor as was the Hydromatic loader, which lifted the freight pallets up to Zulu Charlie's cargo door, and sundry miscellaneous items of equipment, some of which were in working order.

Sole proprietor of Meteor Air Express was Captain Wilf Jagger. The other hats he wore were managing director, chief salesman, chief engineer, chief training captain, chief pilot and chief accountant. There were four others on the payroll, including three pilots.

Bernie Crowburn, recently retired from British Airways, was the other captain. The two First Officers were Ed Park and Nathan 'Bish' Bishop. Although Park would be deserting to Central in a few weeks, Jagger could take comfort in the knowledge that Bishop would never leave Meteor, not with his history.

The company's only female employee was Caroline Moore, but that would soon be changing. Caroline was Jagger's secretary, personal assistant and confidante. She also kept the office tidy and organised Meteor's catering requirements. This meant supplying sandwiches and coffee for the pilots when needed.

There were a few part-time workers who were called in as necessary when cargo had to be loaded or unloaded or sundry other jobs needed attending to. Jagger paid cash for their services and kept no record of their employment details. He had not taken the trouble to verify that the arrangement was legal, but it was difficult enough trying to run the business without getting involved in the complexities of employment legislation.

Jagger owned Meteor Air Express. That is to say, he owned about 40 percent of its assets. The remainder belonged to the Hong Kong General Bank, who owned two and a half of Zulu Charlie's engines and one of the spares and leased them to Meteor. The Merchantman's airframe was worth not much more than its scrap value. The outfit (Jagger always considered it presumptuous to refer to his business as an airline) was reconstructed from the wreckage of the pilot's life three years previously.

Jagger had been a captain with an airline which had suddenly and unexpectedly bitten the dust, leaving no funds for redundancy payments. *The directors express their deep sympathy to all employees.* With a masterly sense of timing his wife Phoebe chose the same moment to walk out on him, taking their young son with her. *I'm sorry it has to be this way, Wilf, but you do see my point of view, don't you?* An all-out family war was only averted because their daughter kept the peace. Jane, at twenty-two, was less volatile than her mother and better at coping with human shortcomings than her parents.

After a period of wallowing in self-pity and alcohol, ignoring his daughter's pleas to stop wasting his life, Jagger eventually pulled himself together. Good flying jobs for old pilots were virtually non-existent unless he was prepared to go abroad or swallow his pride and accept work as a copilot. But Jagger could not stomach the idea of playing second fiddle to captains younger than himself and with only a fraction of his experience. The only alternative was to start his own airline.

And thus, Jagger Aviation Services was conceived and painfully born on borrowed money, one serviceable plane and vast reservoirs of hope. After a year the fledgling company was even deeper in debt and the bank was getting restless. Jagger changed his brainchild's name in the desperate hope that it would bring better luck. A friend suggested Phoenix, *rising from the ashes, Wilf,* but the name was too similar to his ex-wife's and he finally settled on Meteor Air Express.

After two more years Meteor had paid off its extra debts and was beginning to trade profitably. As the only remaining airworthy Merchantman in the world the old freighter was much in demand at air displays and fees thus earned added to the revenue from freighting and boosted the company's publicity. Jagger found he could meet his overheads and his lease payments on Zulu Charlie and pay his staff a decent wage. There was nothing left in the kitty for himself. Not until Bernie Crowburn stepped in.

Crowburn was generous to a fault. After a long and contented career with British Airways he had eventually retired with a comfortable pension. Many of his colleagues in the same position had either signed on with other airlines or else given up flying altogether to follow other pursuits. But Crowburn wanted peace and contentment and 'old fashioned aviating'. With his wife's approval he answered Jagger's advertisement for a Merchantman captain, sold his house in Camberley and bought a modest bungalow on the outskirts of Derby. The transaction was completed by divesting himself of the resulting profits in favour of a Developing World charity.

Caroline had let it slip in conversation that Jagger was paying himself nothing. *I don't know how he manages, Bernie, unless he lives on bread and water. His wife took everything. He lives in that pokey flat in Nottingham. It's such a shame.* Crowburn had approached Jagger and suggested that his salary be deferred until Meteor was in better financial shape. Jagger was touched by this offer but refused to go along with the idea. *You work for me, Bernie, you get paid for it.* Crowburn tried again. He would pay his salary into a new account at the Hong Kong General. It would be called the Meteor Special Fund, to be used at Jagger's discretion for any purpose he wanted without needing to consult anyone about it. *That's very kind, Bernie, but it's your money, not Meteor's and not mine.* Jagger had in fact borrowed from the Special Fund once or twice when things were a bit tight but always paid back what he took as soon as he could.

God knows the bills are heavy enough thought Jagger now, *without leaving lights on in an empty office.*

But the office wasn't empty. As the two pilots stood dripping in the doorway a middle aged, slightly overweight man of Asian complexion got up from the secretary's chair. A thick moustache matched his grey hair. Standing at his side was a tall man about thirty, good looks spoiled by the hint of a superior smirk, dressed in the sharp clothes of a city slicker.

'Captain Jagger?' asked the older man.

'Yes,' answered the pilot. 'Who are you? How did you get into my office?'

The stranger showed an ID card. 'Inspector Sahay. Nottingham CID.' The accent was thick Black Country. 'My colleague here is Detective Sergeant Turner.'

As Jagger examined the card his mind ran through his recent past, looking for a possible reason for a visit from the police. Give or take the odd parking offence he was a law abiding citizen. He glanced at his copilot for inspiration but Park just raised a quizzical eyebrow.

Mollified, and berating himself for the nervous frisson that even innocents feel when confronted by the law, Jagger handed back the ID. 'What can I do for you?' he asked.

'Forgive me for disturbing you at such a late hour, Captain.' The Brummie *you* rhymed with *cow*. 'The security guard let us in. I'm trying to contact one of your employees, a Mr Bishop. I've phoned his number several times and got no reply. I've been round to his house twice but he never seems to be in.'

'Probably staying at his girlfriend's house,' offered Jagger, wondering if he was giving away a confidence.

'We thought of that, sir, but we don't know where she lives. Maybe you can help us. Have you got his mobile number?'

'I don't know anything about the girlfriend, I'm afraid,' said the pilot. 'I can give you his mobile number though if you need it. What's the problem?'

'I need to ask Mr Bishop some questions, sir.'

Park took off his wet leather jacket (Meteor's finances did not stretch to uniforms for its pilots) and filled the kettle at the sink in the corner.

'Will you have a drink with us, chaps?' asked Jagger. 'Please sit down again. Our standard post-flight tipple is coffee reinforced with this.' The pilot picked up a half empty brandy bottle from the bookshelf.

'Just coffee, thank you, sir. No reinforcements.' He glanced at his colleague, who nodded concurrence.

Jagger motioned to the chair and he and the two police officers sat down. 'Is this a personal matter, Inspector, or is it something I might be able to help you with?'

Sahay considered for a moment and then reached inside his coat. He took out a photograph and handed it to the pilot. 'Do you make anything of that?'

There were three faces. The picture had been taken in a pub or club. The faces belonged to three men slumped into low chairs round a table sprouting a forest of glasses. Bishop's face was the one in the middle. He was dressed like a seventies glam rocker, open-necked psychedelic wide lapelled shirt, gold medallion round the neck. No other airline would tolerate shoulder length hair, but then no other airline would employ Bishop anyway. Jagger had taken him on because he had a Merchantman rating on his licence and he was a competent pilot, whatever his past misdemeanours. And in Meteor no-one, least of all Jagger, was bothered about length of hair.

The other two men in the photo were unknown to Jagger. The man to the left of Bishop was about the same age, early thirties, more conventionally dressed. His swept back dark hair accentuated his high forehead. The one on the right was much older, about fifty, slim built with mournful eyes and thinning grey hair. The hollow cheeks were slightly skeletal. Jagger tapped the picture.

'Who are these other blokes?'

'The younger one is Michael Shepherd. He's a dispatcher here at the airport. Works for Central.'

Jagger nodded. The job of dispatchers was to ensure that flights departed on schedule. They coordinated passenger boarding, aircraft fuelling and loading of baggage and dealt with the masses of paperwork necessary to get any aircraft off the ground. It was a responsible job and Central paid its dispatchers commensurately. At Meteor Air Express the task was done by the pilots themselves. No dispatcher with any self-respect would come anywhere near the ancient freighter and Jagger certainly couldn't afford one on the payroll.

The pilot looked at the photo again. Park handed mugs of coffee to the policemen and brought one to his employer. He peered over Jagger's shoulder. 'Who's the old guy?'

Sahay took a sip of his coffee as Park poured a generous slug of brandy into his own mug and Jagger's. The police officer indicated to his side-kick that he should explain.

'His name is Winslade. He's bad news, I'm afraid, right little villain. Been giving us a lot of bother.' Turner spoke with the glottal stops of fashionable Estuary English.

'What do you mean? Is he a criminal or something?'

The sergeant nodded. 'Drug dealer. Big time. Heroin, cocaine, crack, ecstacy, everything.'

Jagger knew that Bishop sometimes kept dubious company, but drug dealing? Surely Bish wasn't involved in all that nonsense.

'Is there some connection between Bish and the other two?' he asked eventually.

'That's what we want to find out,' said Turner. 'The picture is this. Winslade is a big operator. His normal patch is south London, where I work. He's with a firm who've got mob connections, supplying the local pushers with junk.'

'How come he's not in the slammer?' interrupted Park.

The sergeant smiled sardonically. 'They're pros, these people. We can never pin anything on them. The underlings actually do the dirty work, trading on the streets. They're the ones who get nicked. On the rare occasions the big boys end up in the dock their legal bods get them off the hook. Most frustrating, as you can imagine.'

The pilot picked up the photo. 'Was this taken in London?'

'No,' said Turner. 'That's the point. As a matter of course we keep tabs on Winslade, just to see what mischief he's up to. Not long ago one of our lads tailed Winslade when he drove up here. Winslade met Shepherd in the Arriba Club in Nottingham. That's where the pic was taken. My constable reported that Bishop joined them later in the evening, whether by coincidence or not he didn't know. All we've got is that Shepherd may have some connection with Winslade and Bishop may be a friend of Shepherd. At the moment there's no way of knowing if Shepherd or Bishop are involved in anything naughty'.

A thought swam into Jagger's mind. 'Did they know they were being photographed? Wouldn't that worry a criminal like whatever this bloke's name is?'

'Winslade,' said the sergeant. 'The constable was discreet. No flash. Low light concealed camera. We do it a lot.'

After a pause Jagger shook his head. 'Doesn't sound like Bish to get himself mixed up with people like that. I mean, I know he's a bit of a tearaway, but drugs . . .'

His voice tailed away. A paper lying on the desk took his attention, a printed memo from Caroline.

Bernie asked me to ask you about Sarah's training. She's made a start on her circuit work. Are you going to do the rest or do you want Bernie to? Also I've got an enquiry about a possible charter coming up soon. I told them we'd send them our tariff. Customers' name: Euro Traders (they're new to us).

The pilot read the memo with mixed feelings. He did not want to fly with Miss Sarah Amberley-hyphen-Kemp on account of the fact that he didn't particularly like her. On the other hand, as soon as her circuits were finished she'd be able to start her line training and it was important that she got her licence signed up before Ed Park went off to Central. Still, if Bernie was happy to complete her circuits and bumps that was fine as far as Jagger was concerned. He'd have to give Bernie a call in the morning to sort it out.

And a potential new customer, assuming that Meteor got the contract. Would it be a one-off or a series of flights? Either way, Jagger allowed himself a brief moment of optimism. It was a good sign that a customer had approached him directly. It meant that Meteor was beginning to make a name for itself. Usually Jagger relied on Jenny Trimble, his agent, to find contracts for him. Altogether business was picking up quite healthily of late. Could it be that one day he would actually make some money with his shoestring airline?

'I think you're right, Captain Jagger,' the corpulent Inspector was saying. 'Bishop has no form as far as we know, not in the drugs scene. Although . . .' he looked the pilot directly in the eye, '. . . I believe he has crossed paths with the law sometime in the past.'

It was a question as much as a statement. Irritation welled up in Jagger. 'That was nothing to do with this sort of thing. A totally different matter.'

'Yes, sir,' said Inspector Sahay. 'I believe that's correct. That's why I want to ask him a question or two. To establish his innocence.'

Park came over. 'Inspector, just supposing Bish was involved in something . . . irregular.' The copilot ignored the black look from Jagger. 'If you start interrogating him won't he tip off the others?'

'It's a chance I'll take,' said Sahay. 'Look, we strongly suspect that Winslade is cooking something up, maybe with Michael Shepherd. Even if Bishop's got nothing to do with it he might have some info about Shepherd that would be useful to us.'

There was silence as Sahay drained the last of his coffee. He stood up and offered a card to Jagger. 'Well, we won't keep you any longer, Captain. In case I can't get hold of Mr Bishop please give this to him and ask him to call me. My number's here.'

Jagger took the card. 'Okay. I'll give it to him the next time I see him.'

The police officers took their leave. It was nearly midnight and Jagger felt very tired. He opened his flight bag to complete the documentation for the trip they had just completed, unable to stifle a yawn as he extracted the papers.

'Another slug, boss?' Park held up the brandy bottle.

'No thanks. It'll send me to sleep.'

'Can I give you a hand with the bumpf?'

'Thanks, mate, but it won't take me long. You slope off.'

Park shrugged. 'Okay.' He finished his coffee and donned his still damp jacket. At the door he turned to his employer.

'What do you reckon about Bish, Wilf?'

The pilot stared back blankly. 'Don't know. It's difficult to imagine him in a drugs ring. I'm surprised the Old Bill brought up Bish's spot of bother in the past. Just shows you, doesn't it, Ed? You can't pick your nose these days without someone watching you, writing it all down.'

'Yeah, let's hope Bish is in the clear.'

Jagger nodded. 'He's got to be. Where can I get another copilot if he's out of circulation?'

Park laughed. 'There's Sarah thingummy-whatsit.'

The other grimaced. 'I'll need her anyway when you run out on me, Ed.'

'Maybe she's got a sister who's into flying.'

'God forbid.'

CHAPTER 3

The cold front that had soaked the British Isles had been flung across northern Europe by a great anticyclone centred over the Adriatic Sea. The southernmost arc of this giant carousel wheeled into the Sahara, gathering heat and dust, and then curved away again to bathe the western Mediterranean in an unseasonably warm zephyr. Even though February was only a few days old the temperature in the Majorcan city of Palma had climbed to eighteen degrees by midday. Global warming or not, hoteliers smiled at the golden sun, hoping it would herald an early start to the tourist invasion.

Thirteen kilometres to the west of Palma as the gull flies the town of Calvia was dozing on the flank of the Font mountain. The *casas* bounced the solar rays between their white walls, pushing the thermometer a degree higher, despite the altitude.

A traveller leaving Calvia by the steeply graded road dropping towards the coast would first pass the church of San Juan and then, two hundred metres further south, a walled residence whose opulence sometimes drew resentment from those local *habitantes* condemned to meaner accommodation.

Besides its several bedrooms and bathrooms, the house cosseted itself in several hectares of cultivated *jardin*, into one corner of which a concrete helicopter pad intruded. From the main reception room sliding glass doors gave onto a generous terrace which in turn enclosed a large, deep swimming pool.

It was by the pool that the owner of the house now sat, going through business papers. Luis Dominguez was a swarthy man in his early forties. He was powerfully built, but carried a few kilos more than his doctor would like, the penalty of an indulgent lifestyle. With classic Latin looks and dark brown eyes, he had no difficulty finding attractive women to share these indulgences, some of them less than half his age. *You're not going to make it to seventy* the doctor had admonished him on his last check-up *unless you live your life at a slower pace. There's a murmur on your ECG, mi amigo.*

So what thought Dominguez. *If I can drink and smoke and make love until I'm sixty and then drop dead, that sounds like a good deal to me.*

On this beautiful spring day he had his usual props to hand on the poolside table. A mobile phone and a chilled Grolsch next to a packet of Cartier cigarettes, one of which the Mallorcan had just lit, drawing the tar laden smoke deep into his lungs.

Stretched out on a lounger alongside was the sinuous body of Kelda, a Scandinavian ex-model who had not yet left her teens. Nature had not endowed Kelda with a powerful intellect but She had more than compensated with physical attributes. Taller than Dominguez but only two thirds his weight, she would have aroused most men, particularly as she was dressed now. Or rather undressed. Under the towel draped across her back the only scrap of clothing was a tiny lime green bikini bottom. Had she been lying on her back, without the towel, it would have been impossible not to notice her firm conical breasts and huge nipples which covered almost half their area and which swelled to the size of grapes when excited.

Kelda turned her head from the magazine she was reading.

'I think I'll go inside for a shower, *cariño.*' She had been living on the island for less than a year and her Mallorquin was still accented.

Dominguez nodded. 'Okay.'

The girl reached out and stroked his leg with her long fingers. 'Do you want to shower with me?'

Her lover looked down at her and felt the familiar stirring. He was half tempted. But a shower with Kelda would take thirty minutes and he would be exhausted by the time they had finished. His face split into a grin.

'Now, my angel, don't tempt me. Remember my poor old heart.'

Kelda pouted. 'It's not your heart I'm interested in.'

Dominguez smiled again. 'What you need is cooling down.' He suddenly leapt to his feet, picked up the girl around her midriff and hurled her into the pool. Her squeals of protest were drowned by the splash.

When Kelda surfaced, spluttering a stream of expletives, Dominguez was still laughing. The girl launched into a brisk crawl, burning up her chagrin and frustration in physical activity.

Dominguez turned back to his papers again. Of immediate concern was his accountant's report on the previous month's business. A frown pushed the smile off his face. Profits from drugs were down again. The problem was the ever-falling street price, the result of more abundant supplies filtering into the island despite the activities of the Aduana and Policia. Or perhaps because of them. The corrupt officials were clearly allowing more merchandise in. A simple case of greed. And the bribes they demanded increased even as the value of the drugs went down.

It was never like this in the old days thought Dominguez as he crushed out his cigarette. He let his mind drift back to the past. As a youth he had had a less than brilliant school career, although he did win the admiration of his classmates, not to mention a few bets, by successfully seducing the wife of the head teacher in a field in broad daylight, for which triumph he was summarily expelled.

After a variety of menial tasks Dominguez managed to find a job as a waiter in the prestigious Gran Vida hotel in Palma. He had been there less than a week when an American guest had asked him if he could get him some cocaine. The Mallorcan youth knew about the drug but had never tried it himself although he had met people who said they had. The white powder was expensive and to buy it you had to deal with some dubious people. When two other hotel guests made the same request a few days later Dominguez decided to make some enquiries. He borrowed some cash and bought a few grams to experiment with. Now he understood its temptations. But what excited him even more was the discovery that he could sell the stuff to hotel guests for three times what he paid for it. He was in business. Soon he quit the waiter's job to devote all his energies to dealing, moving into marijuana and heroin as dictated by demand. He would sell the *extranjeros* or anyone else for that matter anything they wanted if the price was right.

The enterprise expanded. By ruthless elimination of opposition from the law or from rivals Dominguez had clawed his way up to being one of the main dealers in the island. Most of his stock came by sea and some by air, always disguised as part of a legitimate freight shipment. Human couriers were too unreliable and could not carry large quantities.

After a while Dominguez had decided to begin investing his profits in legal operations. He diversified into property development, building hotels for the tourists and *casitas* by the sea for those who wanted to buy their own places in the sun.

The Mallorcan brought himself back to the present. *The golden days are over* he thought to himself at least as far as drugs are concerned. He was making less and less money and getting more and more hassle. Greedy customs and police officers. Undercutting by other operators of whom there were now too many to wipe out. Some of the upstarts were brazenly moving into his own territory, unthinkable a few years previously unless they wanted to end up feeding the fishes in Palma bay.

Dominguez picked up the accounts he had been looking over. No doubt about it. He was making more profit on his property deals and boutiques. Perhaps it was time to get out of drugs. Life would be safer. No more attempts by the opposition to eradicate him. He fingered the old scar on his left forearm where a bullet had gone straight through the flesh, evidence of a bungled attempt to kill him. No more paying off cops. He would miss the excitement, of course, but perhaps it was time to settle down to a quiet life. His doctor would be pleased, anyhow.

'Perdone, señor'. Carlos, his burly manservant and bodyguard had approached unseen. Now he stood at his master's table, white jacket dazzling in the sunlight.

Dominguez looked up. 'Qué quieres, Carlos?'

'Señor Rabal is here, Señor. He wants to see you.'

'Okay, Carlos, bring him through.'

Until recently, Dominguez would have trusted Paco Rabal with his life. Rabal was doing well under his patronage and was now the main supplier on the north coast. Rabal also ran a thriving brothel in Puerto de Soller and owned several bars and restaurants in Soller and Pollensa. His only fault so far as Dominguez was concerned was that his ambition was just a bit too keen. *Take it easy* Dominguez had said to him more than once. *If you try to run too fast you're more likely to trip over.* And now Rabal had crossed the line of propriety.

'Hola, Luis. Cómo estás?' Rabal was nearly ten years younger than Dominguez, a dark Madrilenian whose looks were spoiled by an oversized broken nose and equally large protruding ears. *El elefante*, people called him. Although not to his face.

Dominguez waved a hand in greeting and ordered Carlos to bring two more Grolsch. He noticed Rabal's eyes. *He's flying. Why didn't he realise the idea was to sell the junk to the suckers, not use it yourself.* He motioned Rabal to sit down.

'Paco, I've been thinking about our little disagreement.' The argument had been about who supplied the pushers in the town of Andraitx on the western tip of the island. Dominguez had been sharing business fifty-fifty with Rabal but now the younger man wanted to increase his percentage. Dominguez took a swig of beer and continued. 'I'm prepared to discuss it further. I'm sure we can come to a mutually acceptable arrangement.'

Rabal shook his head. 'Not good enough, Luis. Andraitx is my patch, not yours. I should decide the cut.'

Dominguez began to protest but the other silenced him. 'There's another problem you've got to face, Luis.'

The Mallorcan sat up, surprised. What on earth had got into the man? Lately he was coming on like a bloody American gangster. Was it the muck he was pumping into his veins?

'Do go on,' Dominguez said, his voice edged with sarcasm.

Rabal took a long pull at his beer. 'Javier has told me he's increasing the licence fee.' The 'licence fee' was a euphemism for bribes paid to corrupt police officers to turn a blind eye to criminal activities. Javier was a senior officer in Andraitx and it was under his protection that the drug dealers did their business.

It was a while before Dominguez responded. A more sober mind than Rabal's would have sensed the danger from the look in his eyes. Eventually a muted 'I see,' escaped his lips. He looked at his watch. Willi Prosch would be arriving soon. He turned to Rabal.

'These are serious matters, Paco. I think we'll have to arrange a meeting with all interested parties. Maybe work in a game of golf.'

Rabal stood up. 'Okay, but you'll have to see it my way. I'll be waiting to hear from you. *Hasta la próxima.*' He drained off his glass and walked out, leaving the other in deep thought. A few moments later Dominguez heard the sound of Rabal's car starting up. *If you haven't got a chauffeur with you I hope you're not too stoned to drive safely,* he muttered to himself. But then a new thought hit him. *Although if you do kill yourself it'll save me the job.*

Kelda, who had been languidly drifting up and down the pool throughout the exchange now climbed out and splashed over to her lounger to pick up the towel. 'He gives me the creeps, that man.'

'Never mind Paco, my dear. There are other things to think about. Willi will be here soon. Is lunch being prepared?'

'Of course, my sweet.'

'Good. You'd better go and get changed. I know Willi prefers boys to girls but his minders might get over-excited if they see you swanning around like that.'

The girl clucked her tongue disapprovingly and slouched off indoors. Dominguez pondered for a short while and then picked up the mobile. It only took a few minutes for the necessary arrangements to be made.

Just as Dominguez was switching off the phone the tranquillity of his hacienda was disturbed by the chatter of a helicopter. The EC155 Dauphin approached rapidly and alighted on the helipad fifty metres from the pool, sending up swirls of leaves and dust.

Three men got out, crouching low to keep their heads well away from the spinning guillotine of the rotor. As soon as they were clear, the pilot took off again and the aircraft vanished as quickly as it had appeared, restoring the garden to peace.

Dominguez moved forward to welcome his visitors. Two of them were heavily built, menacing in dark glasses. The third was dwarfed by his cohorts, a short, spindly man whose wrinkled skin added a decade to his forty years. Pale watery eyes squinted against the Mediterranean sun through the tinted corrective lenses of his specs. All three men wore grey business suits and ties. Dominguez felt himself somewhat casually attired in comparison, with his open neck shirt, shorts and flip-flops. He grinned and offered his hand to the smallest man.

'Willi, welcome, good to see you again. Was the helicopter waiting for you?' The German had arrived at Palma airport in his private jet.

Now Prosch bowed slightly. 'Yes, everything was as planned, thank you.' His Spanish was almost perfect. 'Your usual efficiency, Luis.' A grimace crossed his lips, which Dominguez took to be a smile.

'Good, good. Now, Willi, lunch first, then we'll get on with business.'

They went indoors where Kelda, now in a cool Dior frock, was waiting to receive them. Carlos appeared to take their orders for aperitifs. After a little small talk, Prosch's henchmen took themselves to the pool table in the next room and Kelda returned to the kitchen to assist the cook. Dominguez and Prosch sat down and picked up their conversation.

'You know, Willi, I'm beginning to look forward to the day when I can retire. Everything's so complicated now. Every day brings more problems. Just this morning I found out I'm being crossed by a man who I trusted, who used to be my friend.' Dominguez told his guest about Paco Rabal.

'You mean, he's lying to you about this police officer in Andraitx?'

'Exactly, Willi. I myself fixed a deal with Javier only last week. Everything was agreed, So, you see, Paco is trying it on. He's not an asset to me any more, he's a burden.' There was a pause. 'He's got to go.'

A glimmer of interest flickered in the German's lifeless eyes. 'Can I be of help, Luis?' He pointed to the next room. 'Johann and Kurt are very good at . . . punishment. Shall I tell you what they did to the last man who cheated me? It was exquisite. I watched them do it. They're artists, those two. First of all . . .'

Dominguez held up his hand. Although there was a smile on his face he shivered inwardly. God knew what miseries had been inflicted on Willi's victim. It was one thing to kill a man who had to be got rid of. These things had to be done from time to time. It was a different matter entirely to enjoy doing it, the way Prosch obviously did.

'No,' Dominguez said. 'I'm dealing with it myself.'

Prosch licked his lips. 'May I ask how?'

The Mallorcan sighed. 'There's an American warship anchored outside the harbour. That means there'll be lots of sailors on shore leave, some making a nuisance of themselves as they always do. Paco will be stabbed to death and then dropped by helicopter into the bay during the hours of darkness. On his body there will be evidence linking him to the *gringos*. A bundle of dollar bills and a note written in English, perhaps. The harbour police will find his body floating in the water and deduce that he was murdered by an American sailor for some reason.'

'It might cause some discomfort for the United States Navy,' observed the German.

'My heart bleeds,' said Dominguez wryly.

'Clever, Luis.'

Kelda swept into the room. 'Why is Luis clever, Herr Prosch?'

'Kelda, please call me Willi. Luis is clever because he has found such a charming lady to share his life.'

'Don't flatter her too much, Willi,' laughed Dominguez. 'It'll go to her head.' He turned to the girl. 'Is lunch ready?'

'That's what I came to tell you. Carlos has set the table on the patio.'

'Excellent,' said Prosch. He clapped his hands smartly and called to the pool room. 'Johann . . . Kurt . . . *das Mittagessen wird geservieren.*'

After a meal of lobster *ibicena* and rice Dominguez suggested that they all repair to the swimming pool. As a concession to the warmth the two German bodyguards took off their jackets and unfastened their ties and sat in the shade sipping beer. Prosch himself took up Dominguez's offer of a loan of shorts and now the two sat at a poolside table under a parasol. Kelda, wearing both halves of her bikini under a bathrobe, had stretched out on the lounger to soak up more solar radiation.

Dominguez spoke to the German in a low voice. Kelda was out of earshot and the minders did not understand Spanish, but the Mallorcan's instinctive caution took over.

'Okay, Willi, can you expand on what we talked about on the phone?'

Prosch nodded. 'We're just sorting out the final details now. What are you paying at the moment?'

Dominguez considered for a moment. There was no point in floating a fictitious figure in the hope of getting a better deal. Prosch probably knew the going rate and would not take kindly to being tricked. He quoted a price accordingly.

'Yes,' said the German. 'That's about right'

Dominguez congratulated himself on his shrewdness. 'What are you offering, Willi?'

'Half of that, give or take, if the sale is big enough. More expensive for smaller quantities.'

Dominguez whistled. 'How much would I have to take? If it's too much I won't be able to get rid of it.'

Only a short time was needed to agree the terms.

'You've got a good deal there, Luis. You'll be able to undercut your competitors and re-establish yourself.'

Dominguez nodded. He had been thinking the same thing himself. 'Where's the stuff coming from? What's the quality?'

Prosch looked round. None of the others could overhear him. There was no reason why he shouldn't tell Dominguez. The two men had done business together many times over many years and each trusted the other. Sharing sensitive information was proof of trust and would ease the way for future deals.

'It will be shipped out of England, to Düsseldorf initially. It will be first class merchandise.'

Dominguez raised his eyebrows. 'That's not a normal supply route.'

'That's why we chose it.'

'How will the stuff get to England in the first place?'

The German smiled. 'It's already there. Awaiting collection. Let me explain . . .'

The sun had been sinking for three hours and was now plodding homewards. There was not even a breath of wind to stir the air. Warmth and full stomachs had drugged Kelda and the two German stooges into sleep. Above the chirruping of the birds the murmur of Prosch's voice was barely audible except to his intent one-man audience.

'That's amazing,' was Dominguez's opinion when the German had finished.

'You must agree, it's highly original.'

'If it works, it's brilliant. Now, let me have details of delivery dates and so on . . .'

The two men discussed their plans for a few minutes more and then Dominguez picked up the phone to summon the helicopter that would take Prosch and his cohorts back to their jet at Palma airport.

'Now, are you sure you don't want me to deal with your troublesome friend before I fly home?' shouted the German above the whistle of the Dauphin's turbines as it flared for landing.

'It won't be necessary, Willi. The arrangements have already been made.'

'Pity. Never mind.'

The three men ducked under the whirring rotor and climbed into the cabin. As soon as the door was closed the pilot eased up his collective lever and lifted the aircraft off the ground into a dancing hover. Then he dipped the nose and the helicopter accelerated away, soaring into the cloudless afternoon sky. Soon it was just a black speck and then it was gone.

Dominguez strolled back to the pool and stood at the edge, watching the clear blue ripples on the water surface. He felt good. The new supplies from Prosch would give him back the initiative in the ceaseless fight to come out on top. He could postpone his decision to quit dealing—for a while anyway.

'You look pleased with yourself, *cariño*.' Kelda had materialised beside him. She had divested herself of her clothes. 'I've sent Carlos off to do some shopping. He's taken Pilar home.' Pilar was the cook. 'We don't need her tonight.'

Dominguez turned to her. Thoughts of wheeling and dealing were instantly pushed from his mind by a more basic instinct. 'Shall we have that shower now?' he suggested, his voice thickening.

Kelda pouted at him. 'First things first, my love.' She suddenly gave him a hefty shove. He twisted, trying to keep his balance, but it was no use. He toppled over the edge and crashed into the water in an exposion of spray. He floundered to the surface and turned to face the girl, treading water. She laughed quickly and then dived in herself.

Kelda glided up to him. 'Darling, why are you swimming with your clothes on? Don't you think you should take them off?'

She slid under the water and Dominguez could feel her nimble fingers unzipping his shorts and pulling them down. She surfaced again and wrapped her arms round his neck. 'There, isn't that better?'

Dominguez nodded. Kelda squeezed herself tightly against him. The geometry was perfect as she entwined her legs around his.

Well doc, if my heart can take this it can take anything.

CHAPTER 4

The day was not going well for Wilf Jagger. To start with, he discovered that the last two slices of bread in his kitchen cupboard had gone mouldy and there was none in the freezer. As he had already run out of cereal it meant that for breakfast he was reduced to a shortcake biscuit and a cup of coffee.

This sumptuous repast had been interrupted twice by the phone. The first call was from Bernie Crowburn.

'Good morning, Wilf. How is the Chief Pilot today?'

'Don't ask,' grunted Jagger.

Crowburn laughed. 'Hangover, is it?'

'Impossible. I can't afford to get drunk these days.'

Another laugh. 'I thought I'd update you on Sarah's progress. You're going to finish her off today, aren't you?'

'That's what she needs, finishing off,' Jagger muttered before admonishing himself for his bad humour. It wasn't her fault that she was young, attractive and wealthy where he was old, repulsive and hovering slightly below the poverty level.

'Don't be unkind, Wilf,' said the voice on the phone. 'She's a nice lass and a bloody good operator. She can already drive the Merch better than me.'

Jagger made an effort to raise himself to greater equanimity. 'Okay, Bernie. Just fill me in on what there is still outstanding.'

'I've finished all the four-engine work. We made a start yesterday on engine-out stuff. Let me look at my notes . . .' Jagger could hear paper rustling. 'Yes, we did a shut-down at height . . . some three-engine general handling and a relight.'

'No circuit work?'

'No. I briefed her on the EFTO, ready for the next detail.' Crowburn was referring to a simulated engine failure during take-off.

'Right, thanks, Bernie. What time did you ask her to report today?'

'Eleven, I said, knowing how terrible you are at getting up.' A chuckle.

'Bernie, you're fired for insulting the Chief Pilot.'

'I want full redundancy payment.'

'In that case you're reinstated, but you must go to the bottom of the captain's seniority list.'

'Unacceptable. I demand to be Deputy Chief Pilot.'

'Granted. By the way, which one of us is doing the Rotterdam on Friday? Do you want to?' Meteor held a contract to fly in sixteen tons of dairy and horticultural products.

'Suits me. Shall we use it for Sarah's line training?' asked Crowburn.

'That's what I was thinking. We've got to get her checked out before Ed leaves us.'

'Okay. Will you sort it out?'

'Yes, I'll be off to the airport in a few minutes,' said Jagger. 'I'll tell Caro what we've arranged. How are you going to spend the next two days of leisure?'

'Oh, the usual,' laughed Crowburn. 'Pottering around in the garden. Bit of writing. MTAs.' The acronym stood for Multiple Trivial Activities.

'How's the book coming along?' The older pilot was writing a history of British steam locomotives between the wars.

'Getting there. I'm doing the chapter on Midland compounds.'

'Sounds fascinating.'

'Don't be cheeky.'

The two pilots swapped a few more pleasantries and then rung off, Jagger thinking to himself that he would quite like a garden to potter around in.

Fat chance. The flat he rented was the upper storey of a dismal semi mired amongst a hundred others in an equally dismal corner of peripheral Nottingham. The rooms were adequate in size for an occupancy of one, although yellowing ceilings and faded wallpaper indicated that the landlord was in no hurry to redecorate his property.

Certainly Jagger was no do-it-yourselfer. The paintbrush was a hated object as far as he was concerned. Of course in the old days when he had a commodious house and a reasonable income the idea was to pay someone else to attend to such mundanities. In the old days there was a garden to relax in, a spacious lawn where one could sink into a deck chair on a summer's evening with a glass of chilled lager and watch the rooks circling the tops of the elm trees.

There was no garden now. Well, there was a straggling patch of dirty grass behind the house but even that was out of his domain. The occupants of the lower flat had the dubious privelege of access to the weed-infested scrap of land. They were a pair of college students who devoted as much time to keeping the garden neat as Jagger did to smartening up his rooms.

When he first moved in the pilot promised himself that the arrangement was temporary. As soon as he was back in financial shape he would find himself somewhere more salubrious to live, something less dissimilar to what he was used to. There were still occasional bright moments of optimism when it seemed he might be able to honour his promise but they were convincingly outnumbered by those of bitter realisation that he might be stuck in his dingy prison for ever. Served him right for transferring ownership of his share of their house to his wife when he got into debt and she baled him out. It was the sad outcome of a failed aviation business venture which had been brought down by an incompetent and dishonest partner.

As Jagger skulked in his kitchen the phone rang again. It was Phoebe, telling him that she was moving. To Washington.

'America?' Jagger was incredulous.

'Still an ace at geography, I see,' observed his ex-wife.

'Why Washington? I suppose the ape man is going there to work.'

'Don't be so rude or I'll hang up. Yes, Osmond's new job is in the States so of course we're going with him.'

'Including Dan?'

'Including Dan.'

'For heaven's sake, Phoebe. How will I get to see him?'

'Simple. You get on an plane and you fly to America. Or I suppose you could fly yourself in your old Marketstall freighter. Or is that in the Science Museum now?'

'It's a Merchantman,' replied Jagger through clenched teeth, unable to stop himself getting wound up. 'As well you know. But for Christ's sake I can't go to Washington every fortnight.'

'That, my dear, is your problem.' The phone could not hide the ice in her voice.

'Then Dan will have to come and stay with me for half the year.'

'In your tiny pigsty? Out of the question.'

Jagger could feel his temper going. 'Alright, he can stay with Jane. Is she aware you're clearing off to the other side of the universe?'

'She knows. She's perfectly happy about it. She even wished me good luck. Not that I expect anything like that from you.'

'Look, Phoebe—'

His ex-wife cut in. 'I'm prepared to let Dan come over from time to time and—yes—Jane says he can stay with her and her boyfriend. No doubt you'll get to see him then if Jane doesn't mind.'

'No, that's not good enough. I insist on my rights of access. I insist that—'

Again Phoebe interrupted him. 'My solicitor has informed me that I am perfectly within my rights to take my son with me to the States. He also says—'

Jagger blew a fuse. 'Fuck your solicitor!' he screamed, slamming the receiver down.

He paced up and down the sitting room like a caged animal, fuming. Damn the woman. Surely he was entitled to see his own child. What right had the bitch got to take him away? He would need to get onto his own solicitor to see if she could be stopped.

It took a good ten minutes for the pilot to find his composure, sipping at another coffee as he checked his emails on his laptop. The only message of significance was the one which Caroline had printed out a copy of the previous day about a possible charter. Jagger rinsed his coffee cup and inverted it on the drainer, after which he made a half-hearted effort to tidy his domicile. Phoebe was right. 'Pigsty' just about summed it up.

The flat did not boast a garage. Jagger had an informal arrangement with the landlord of the pub just across the road to use the car park there. It didn't cost much, although there was the drawback of no protection from the elements nor from vandals, both of which frequently attacked Jagger's elderly Vauxhall Cavalier.

Another overnight front had lashed the country with wind and rain and was now dragging a wintery northwesterly behind it. Today the chill dampness stole a few more volts from the Cavalier's doubtful battery. The starter could barely crank the engine through a few weary revolutions before the battery gave up the struggle. Further frantic twisting of the ignition key produced only momentary dimming of the warning lights.

'Sod you, you bastard!' shouted Jagger to the unhearing machinery. 'How am I supposed to get to the bloody airport?'

The car didn't answer.

Back in the flat, the pilot phoned the garage to get the Cavalier sorted out and then put through a call to Meteor.

'Caro, it's Wilf. My car's playing up and I'm not wasting money on a taxi. Can you be a dear and come and collect me? I'll pay you for the fuel.'

'Okay, I'll see you in twenty minutes.'

'Thanks, angel.'

A minute later the phone rang again. 'Wilf, it's Caroline again.'

'Problems?'

'No. Sarah's here. She's volunteered to pick you up. Then I can get on with office work.'

'All right. Will you give her directions? What sort of car should I be looking out for? A Roller, a Porsch? Coach and horses?'

'Don't, Wilf, it doesn't become you. Just a tick, I'll ask her.'

The pilot could hear muffled voices.

'It's a red Polo.'

'Oh.' Jagger was mildly disappointed. 'Okay, see you later.'

As he waited on the pavement, shivering in the chilly February wind, hands deep in his jacket pockets, the pilot let his thoughts turn to his newest employee. Sarah Amberley-hyphen-Kemp. Sarah. The name suited her. Stuck-up upper middle class snot-nose. Daddy some sort of company director. Huge house in hundreds of acres. Tons of money. No doubt servants to pander to their every whim.

Jagger was intelligent enough to realise that his dislike of the girl was rooted in pure envy. But her lah-di-dah public school voice didn't help, nor her condescending manner.

But you couldn't argue with economics. He needed a copilot to replace Ed and no-one suitable had answered his advertisements in the aviation media. Why should they when more respectable airlines were offering potential recruits twice what he could afford to pay? A few young hopefuls had shown an interest but only because the bigger airlines had turned them down as being too inexperienced. It looked as if Jagger would have to take the best of these. He would also have to pay the training costs himself, which would set him back several grand. It would mean borrowing from the Special Fund, which he hated to do.

Bish was the one who supplied the answer. One of his friends turned out to have a sister who was nuts about flying and who would finance her own training costs to get into airline flying. Bish had told her to write to Wilf and the Chief Pilot of Meteor recognised her proposition as an offer he couldn't refuse, as the old saying went. Sarah duly joined Meteor's payroll, but without pay. The contract stipulated that she would start drawing a salary the day she qualified as a fully trained Merchantman First Officer.

The red Polo eventually showed up and executed a nimble three-point turn. As it halted in front of him Jagger saw a tan leather-coated arm reach over to open the passenger door. He doubled up his lanky frame and squeezed himself into the little car.

'Thank you, Miss Kemp. It's very kind of you to help me out at short notice.' Jagger couldn't bring himself to use her first name or, for that matter, her full surname.

If the girl felt slighted she gave no sign of it, greeting the pilot with a grin. 'Think nothing of it. It wasn't far to come.'

Jagger had only met her once before, when she came for her job interview at Meteor. Her accent was enough to put Jagger off although he had managed to keep himself within the bounds of politeness as he made his offer of employment. Beggars can't be choosers. Apart from that they had communicated by phone or email. Up to that moment all her flying training had been Crowburn's province. Now as his nostrils picked up her expensive perfume Jagger was reminded of her beauty. It irritated him. Like him, she was too tall for the Polo, her long legs tucked up so that the thighs almost touched the steering wheel. Her green eyes were friendly and open and a bell of honey blonde hair cascaded around her face. Under her leather coat she was wearing red slacks and a pink mohair jumper. *Bet they didn't come from Marks and Spencer* thought Jagger.

They made small talk for a while, he doing his level best to keep resentment out of his voice. Jagger was mildly curious to see that the girl religiously observed all the speed limits as they drove to the airport while most other cars overtook impatiently. Finally he remarked on it.

'It's the law. Why break it?' came the response.

'How quaint,' he parried.

Clearly the girl was not immune to sarcasm. 'It may be quaint, but it's correct.'

'Don't you ever exceed the limit?'

'No, not unless there's a very good reason.'

The exchange over, they sat in silence, the atmosphere now cooler. Perversely Jagger took faint pleasure from having antagonised the girl but he was honest enough with himself to acknowledge this behaviour as a personality defect.

It was time for a peace offering. 'How did you get on with the engine-out work with Bernie?'

The girl responded in kind. 'Okay. I found the rudder loads quite heavy. Thank God for the power trim.'

Jagger nodded. 'Did Bernie tell you about his spot of bother at Milan a few decades back?'

'No.' The girl turned her questioning face towards him.

'Engine failure just as they got airborne. Bernie was the copilot. Runway three six. A real sod's law case. Filthy night, storms all over the Po valley. Aircraft loaded to max weight.'

'Sounds horrid.'

'Horrid is not the word, my dear. They lost number one. Turbine blew up. To make it worse the prop didn't auto-feather.' Jagger glanced across to watch the girl's reaction. Yes, she understood. Heavily laden plane trying to stagger into the air, barely controllable, heading straight for the Alps. 'What would you have done, Miss Kemp?'

The girl grimaced. 'Probably wet myself. The name is Sarah.'

Jagger laughed at her self deprecation. *She's not all bad.* 'Me too, I expect, but there was more to come. While Bernie was trying to manually feather the engine the captain went for the power trim and found it wasn't working.'

'Good grief,' muttered Sarah, changing down as they neared the airport approach road.

'There they were. As much rudder as the captain could hold, full aileron, but the aircraft still banking left. Bernie ordered the third pilot to wind on trim manually as fast as he could. They eventually got out of it somehow. The crew were commended afterwards if I remember right, but Bernie never talks about that bit.'

'They were lucky,' said Sarah.

'And skilful,' added Jagger.

32

The girl parked outside Meteor House and switched off. As she took the key out of the ignition she turned to Jagger.

'That Milan incident. What I meant was, the crew were lucky to have an extra pilot on that trip. He was the one that trimmed the aircraft when the other pilots couldn't spare a hand. He saved the day.'

'That was nothing unusual. British Airways always flew with three pilots. The taxpayer paid the salaries in those days.'

'If that incident had occurred to Zulu Charlie with only two pilots it would have . . .'

'. . . speared in,' supplied Jagger, resorting to military banter.

'And presumably that's why Bernie always checks the power trim before take-off, even though it's not in the check list.'

'Exactly.' Jagger aimed an exaggerated smile at his new protegee. 'Now, young lady, shall we go and do some flying?'

About an hour later the two of them were strapped into Zulu Charlie's flight deck, he in the left seat, she in the right. They had done the pre-flight inspection between them and were now ready for engine start. The vibrant thrumming of the ground power unit outside could be felt as much as heard. An umbilical snaked up from it into the Merchantman's nose, feeding the electric current vital to the plane's organs. The two pilots could see Mike Merriman, a part time dogsbody standing in front of the nose, grimy hands in grimy overall pockets.

'Pre-start checks complete,' announced Sarah, placing the checklist on top of the glare shield. She fidgeted with her seat controls and adjusted her headset.

'Call for start clearance,' ordered Jagger.

The girl pressed the transmit switch on her control wheel. 'Tower, Golf Charlie Alpha Zulu Charlie, start up.' It was the plane's full registration number spelt phonetically.

Zulu Charlie, cleared to start. Temperature eight. Altimeter one zero zero four.'

The pilot caught Merriman's attention and lifted his left hand to the windscreen with the four fingers spread apart and the thumb drawn in. Merriman repeated the gesture and with the index finger of his other hand drew a vertical circle in the air. These archaic signals meant, respectively, 'Is number four engine clear for start?' and 'Engine number four clear for start'. In most airlines communication between flight deck and ground crew was by headset, the latter plugging his own into the plane's socket provided for this service. Such luxuries were not to be found in Meteor Air Express's equipment inventory.

'Start four,' Jagger ordered his copilot.

The girl reached to the control panel over her head and depressed two switches.

'Master start on. Starting four.' The hum of the ground power unit dipped momentarily as it took the heavy load of the engine starter motor. The massive outboard propeller on the right wing began to rotate.

Sarah was watching the gauges, calling out the revolutions of the high pressure and low pressure turbines.

'HP turning . . . LP turning . . . three thousand . . .'

On the centre console Jagger opened the number four fuel cock. In the bowels of the engine a fountain of kerosene sprayed over sparking electrodes in the combustion chambers, firing an instant inferno. Jagger added his own call-outs to Sarah's litany.

'Fuel flow normal . . . light up . . .'

Sarah: 'Four thousand . . . starter cut-out . . .'

Jagger: 'Turbine temp normal . . . four stable.'

The engine was alive, self-sustaining, the individual prop blades just about visible as they sliced through the cold air.

The captain held up three fingers and Merriman acknowledged.

'Start three.'

Soon all four engines were running. Jagger signalled to Merriman to unplug the ground power unit and remove the wheel chocks. Then he flicked the fuel flow control levers forward. In response to their enriched diet the engines slowly built up to their normal idling speed as the props blurred into invisible discs. Outside, Mike Merriman had his hands covering his ears, protecting them from the ear-splitting whine.

It was much quiter on the flight deck.

'After start checks, please, Sarah.'

Soon they were ready to taxy to the runway holding point. The plane was unladen for this training flight, cargo hold cavernously empty, fuel tanks only half full, so that when Jagger edged the throttles open the Merchantman rolled briskly forward.

'Zulu Charlie, confirm your intentions. Are you staying in the circuit?'

Jagger pointed to himself to signify to Sarah that he personally would reply.

'Yes, that's the idea. Mainly three-engine work.'

'Roger, Zulu Charlie, call ready for departure.'

Now all the pre-take off checks were complete and Tower permitted them to line up on the runway.

Jagger gave his pupil her final briefing. 'Right, Sarah, once we're airborne I shall throttle back one of the outers and call "practice engine failure", okay?' He glanced across at his new copilot. A nervous frown tarnished her composure and Jagger chided himself for finding amusement in her discomfort. She looked so young and vulnerable and at that instant, not quite so self-assured. *Don't be cruel, give her a bit of encouragement.* 'Hey, cheer up, lass,' he said, adding a wink. 'Just do everything slowly and methodically and it'll work out fine.'

'I hope I don't cock it up,' she answered.

The unladylike language proved her apprehension, thought Jagger. At least it shows she's not bloody Miss Perfect all the time.

'Zulu Charlie, cleared take off, wind two nine zero degrees, fourteen knots. Call downwind.'

'Cleared take off, Zulu Charlie rolling,' replied Jagger.

The captain pushed the throttles fully forwards and, engines in crescendo, the plane leaped forward with alacrity.

'Power set . . .' called Jagger, '. . . speed building . . . eighty knots . . . rotate . . .'

Sarah pulled the wheel firmly back. Zulu Charlie lifted its nose and broke away from the ground. Jagger pulled back the throttle closest to him. 'Practice engine failure, number one.'

Robbed of half its left side thrust the freighter began to swing. Sarah pushed her right foot forward on its rudder pedal. The yaw slowed but was not arrested.

'Keep it straight,' prompted Jagger, 'more rudder . . . more rudder . . .'

The girl responded. It took all her strength.

'That's better. What next?'

'Gear up!'

Jagger raised the selector. The landing gear wheels would tuck up into the aircraft to reduce air resistance and help it fly.

Fighting with the control wheel, Sarah could just about manage to fumble for the electric rudder trim, giving it a three second burst. To her evident relief the rudder load all but vanished.

That was better. Now she was winning the battle. The big freighter was gaining height, under control, six knots in hand over the correct engine-out speed, gear retracted.

'Feather drill, number one,' she called.

'Well remembered.' The captain simulated the engine shut down.

Her confidence building, Sarah climbed to 400 feet and dropped the nose a little to pick up speed. 'Flaps up.'

'Selected. Flaps retracting.'

The struggle was over. 'Engine failure checklist, please.'

'Coming up, ma'am.'

As the Merchantman cruised over patchwork farms on the downwind leg Jagger turned to his copilot.

'A good effort for your first engine cut. We'll do a three-engine full stop landing now and taxy round for another take off, okay?'

The girl nodded, wiping her sweaty hands one at a time on her expensive red slacks.

'And remember, kill that yaw as soon as you see it. You've got to keep the bugger straight all the time.'

'Okay, I'll try.'

'Never mind try. Do it.' But the scold was not unfriendly.

Round and round the circuit they went, Sarah's youth and enthusiasm boosting her progress.

'You can do this better than me,' said Jagger eventually.

'I know that's not true, but thanks for saying so.'

After an hour's circuits they taxied in and shut down for a lunch break. Caroline had brought in some sandwiches and now master and pupil were washing these down with coffee as Jagger continued his debriefing in the office.

'Good progress, young lady,' he said through a mouthful of egg mayonnaise sandwich. 'We'll do another hour after lunch to consolidate and that will just leave the night work.'

'Tonight?'

Jagger shook his head. 'You'll need a good rest tonight. Anyway, the plane's doing a parcels run.' It was one of Meteor's ad hoc contracts to fly mail packages to Glasgow and Belfast, a tit-bit thrown to Jagger by one of the big boys. Lucrative but irregular. Jagger would have dearly liked to pick up a steady parcels deal for himself, but he would have needed another aircaft and another two or three crews. Some hope.

Anyway, I've got to do some shopping tonight. The cupboard is bare, remember. Jagger inwardly shuddered at the delightful prospect of pushing a trolley round the supermarket, battling with middle class housewives stocking up with middle class provisions.

The pilot realised that Sarah was talking to him.

'Sorry, miles away. What was that?'

'I asked you how Nathan was. I haven't seen him for a while.'

'He's fine. Or at any rate he was when I last saw him.' Jagger thought it best to leave unspoken the bit about the police. The episode had nearly caused a ruction between himself and Bishop. After several days of indecision Jagger had finally taken it upon himself to find out the story. It was not mere prying. Desperate as he was not to lose his pilots, he didn't need an outlaw flying his aircraft. Jagger still cringed when he remembered how the exchange had gone.

'There was someone here looking for you last week.'

'Uh-huh. Who would that be?'

'Inspector Sahay. CID.'

'Well, he found me.'

'Good.'

'Nothing to concern you.'

'He showed me a photo of you in a night club with some . . . doubtful characters.'

'Look. I'm a member of the Arriba club. I go there often and I meet people there. So what?'

'Sahay asked me if there was a link between you and the other men in the picture. He said one of them was a criminal.'

'Is that right? I wouldn't know.' Bishop was getting angry but Jagger pressed on.

'Do you know them?'

'With respect, that's not your business.'

'My apologies. Forget it.'

'If you must know, I went to the Arriba that night to meet a friend but he couldn't make it. I saw Micky Shepherd who I vaguely knew through Sarah's brother and went over to talk to him. The other guy I didn't know from Adam. That's all there was to it. Now, can we drop the subject?'

No further reference had been made to the matter although it took a while for the natural friendship and respect the two pilots had for each other to erase the last lingerings of bad feeling.

'Do you know Bish well?' Jagger asked Sarah now, reversing the questioning.

'He's a friend of my brother. I suppose I've known him a couple of years.'

Jagger grunted and attacked another sandwich. 'My hippie copilot. The only person I know who thinks we're still living in 1975 even though he was only a baby then.'

'He's a lovable rogue,' laughed Sarah.

A fair description concurred Jagger.

'And considerate, too,' added the girl.

'You mean, getting you fixed up with us?'

'I wasn't thinking of that,' Sarah said, 'although of course it was sweet of him to set that up. Particularly as the airport is close to home—I didn't want to have to move away as most of my friends are here and I haven't got my own place yet. And I'm sure the Merchantman will be far more interesting to fly than the twin-jets that rookies usually start on, even if Meteor is a bit . . .' She belatedly stopped herself but embarrassment flushed her face.

'"Downmarket" is the word you're looking for.'

'I'm sorry.' She attempted a smile. 'I didn't mean to be rude.'

'No offence taken.' *Well, only a little thought Jagger.* But she's only being honest. Maybe even 'downmarket' was too good for the shambles he called Meteor Air Express.

'No, I was thinking about Giles, my brother.'

Giles? Fancy inflicting a name like Giles Amberley-Kemp on anyone. Sounds like a contender for the Upper Class Twit of the Year Award.

'What's amusing?' asked Sarah, and Jagger realised he'd betrayed himself with a smile.

'Sorry, private thoughts. You were just telling me about Bish and your . . . Giles.'

Sarah turned away. She was silent for a moment. 'Giles went through a bad patch a while ago. He went off the rails. Mummy and Daddy had given him up as a bad lot. He got mixed up with the wrong people. Nathan saved him from calamity. It's as simple as that.'

Jagger waited for further enlightenment but it was not forthcoming. The snippet Sarah had confided added a few more stones to the mosaic of Bish's background. As his employer, Jagger was familiar with his professional history.

Bishop had earned enough money playing guitar as a session musician to pay for flight training. Newly qualified, he found work as a freighter copilot, which is where his Merchantman rating had come from. Then after a few years he had been hired by a big airline as a jet copilot. From then on his career seemed settled, advancing in step with his seniority number, with promotion to captain not too far away. Until the day he had reported for work 'in an unsuitable condition', as the official report had coined it. This euphemistic phrase meant 'pissed out of his brains'. The recent gory death in a motorbike accident of his best friend was a good reason to hit the bottle, conceded his Flight Manager, but not just before a trip. He was formally cautioned and suspended from duty. Not long after reinstatement a repeat performance sealed his fate. Not even Bish's seniority number could shield him from being thrown out on his ear.

Thereafter he had slid a long way down the slippery slope. He'd found work sporadically with sundry small air taxi companies until the day a passenger complained that he had no intention of flying anywhere with a drunk at the controls. The Civil Aviation Authority looked into this incident and deemed it necessary to relieve Bishop of his pilot's licence for two years. There was the additional bonus of a £4000 fine and a suspended prison sentence.

The shame was too much for his wife to bear. She released herself from the burdensome man who was a brake on her social and financial advancement. *I've put up with you for too long* she told him as she left. *I'm destined for better things.* Equanimous at their parting, he told her to drop dead.

Jagger had learned that much about his senior First Officer straight from the horse's mouth, and also how Bish had eventually got himself sorted out. He gave up drinking, picked up his guitar again to build up some capital and, when he had won back his licence, offered himself again to the world of professional aviation. There were no takers. No one wanted a convicted drunk anywhere near their aircraft. That is, until he'd walked into Jagger's office one day, tossed his licence on the desk and announced, 'I'm a Merchantman-rated commercial pilot. I am also an ex-alcoholic. Do you have a vacancy?' Jagger empathised immediately with the man who had rebuilt a shattered, drink-sodden life, almost parallelling his own miserable history. He signed Bish on.

Meteor's Chief Pilot finished off his coffee and stole a glance at Bish's friend's sister. He caught his mind wandering into areas that had nothing to do with aviation. *No* he conceded, *it would never work out. Middle aged impoverished cynic and young, intelligent, attractive, aristocratic debutante. Even Hollywood wouldn't try that one.*

With a big effort Jagger purged the carnal thoughts from his mind. He was about to ask Sarah if she was ready to do battle with Zulu Charlie again, but the girl beat him to it.

'Oh, while I remember, Wilf. We're having a party soon. At home. Would you like to come?' She pulled out her diary to check the date.

'Thanks, I will if I'm free. Special occasion?'

'Bron's twenty-first. He's my younger brother.'

Jagger frowned. 'Bron?'

'Short for Auberon. Yes, I can read your thoughts. But you're wrong. Auberon is a nice name.'

Time to change the subject. 'Is Bish going?'

Sarah nodded. 'It's vital he's there,' she said mysteriously. 'Assuming you don't make him work that evening.'

Jagger consulted the wall planner. 'No. Nothing for Meteor that night. Not yet, anyway.'

'That's good. Ed and Elaine are planning to come if he's not required. I asked Bernie but he and his wife have a prior engagement. Perhaps it's for the best. Most of the guests will be Bron's age. The music will be very loud and modern.'

'I may be too old myself,' said Jagger wryly.

Sarah smiled. 'You may be at that, but why not take the gamble?' She touched his arm. 'You can always lie about your age. What about your daughter—Jane, isn't it?—would she like to come? She could bring a partner or friend if she wanted.'

'Thanks, I'll ask her,' he said. His unspoken words were *You'd make me feel young again. Or at least, certain parts of me.*

CHAPTER 5

The Foxhound was an inn just outside Banbury on the road to Oxford. The building dated back to the late eighteenth century when its beamed walls and thatched roof had been home to a wealthy wool merchant. Had he been alive to see it, the original owner would have recognised his property two centuries later, although latter day accoutrements might have puzzled him, especially the cars parked between the building and the road and the incongruous satellite dish stuck on the side wall.

A dark blue BMW 5 Series saloon heading north along the road pulled up, turned right into the car park and braked to a halt. Having switched off, the driver sat motionless for a while, watching. The sad grey eyes in the skull-like face flicked to and fro as they locked onto the cars tearing along the road just beyond the fence. Myron Winslade had chosen this venue on the recommendation of a business acquaintance. It was about the same travelling distance for himself and the man he was meeting and safer than a city location, where there was more likely to be police presence.

Satisfied that no-one was watching Winslade got out, locked the car and made his way quickly indoors. In the Cotswold bar he ordered himself a lime and soda and settled into a leather armchair by the window, his attention divided between the view from the window, messages on his mobile and the time on his watch. Like many older people, Winslade found the analogue presentation on his gold Rolex quicker to interpret than the digital read-out on his phone.

After twenty minutes his ears caught the growl of a motorbike engine, just audible through the double glazing. He watched the rider dismount and prop the machine on its stand. Black leathers bulked out the rider's frame and an astronaut helmet hid his face. He lifted it off his head, revealing a man in his thirties, high forehead, swept back black hair.

Having hung up his leathers in the hallway, Michael Shepherd entered the bar and caught sight of Winslade. A grin cracked his face and he winked. Winslade acknowledged with a pained half smile. In contrast to the business suit and tie the older man had chosen Shepherd was wearing a sweatshirt, jeans and trainers. He ordered a drink for himself and sat down in the adjacent chair.

'No problems, I hope,' said Winslade. What he meant was *why are you late?*

'Nope. Got a bit tied up with other things. Everything's okay.'

Winslade held his silence as the barman brought Shepherd's glass of lager.

'I have good news,' he said finally. 'Our German buyer has confirmed agreement to our terms.'

'Great. Everything is going well at my end. Are we cool on the payment to the American?'

'Yes, you can tell him we'll give him what he wants.'

'Will do.'

The skull head nodded, satisfied. 'The transport is organised and I've picked my men. We're now firm on the three date options. I take it the plane's schedule hasn't changed?'

'No, regular as clockwork. Every other weekend, as you'd expect. So option one is still looking good. But I think the third date could be a problem if we can't hack it on the first or second choices. Nights getting too short.'

'Quite. We're still hoping we can launch on the first option. We need to discuss the precise wording on the recordings. I've made a rough draft. You need to check the wording about the airliner stuff.'

A waitress came to take their lunch order. Scampi and salad for Winslade. Shepherd chose cheeseburger and chips.

The discussion about the recordings continued as the food disappeared from their plates. When they had finished eating the waitress appeared with the dessert menu but Winslade waved her away. As soon as she was out of earshot he carried on.

'You're sure the onward transport arrangements will work out? It's a bit . . . uncertain. There is concern about the company you've chosen. They sound a bit . . . Micky Mouse. Just remind me why we're not using a big airline.'

Shepherd sighed. 'Myron, we've been through this.'

'Just humour me.'

'They can't guarantee the stuff goes out on a specific date, not unless we charter one of their planes for our own use. Which would look suspicious, particularly since the load will be so light for a big plane. Plus, they'd probably want to do their own security screening, which is no good to us.'

'Alright. It had better work. There's big money and big people tied in with this.'

'It'll work. It's foolproof, Myron.'

'Okay, and just recap about the pre-warn message.'

'It'll go out a few days before the operation. The Met have got a hotline for anonymous tip-offs about suspected terrorist activity. We'll need someone to call the number and say the date and time, but with duff gen obviously.' Shepherd was referring to the Metropolitan Police, based in New Scotland Yard, London.

'They've got to alert the Home Office and the military authorities, remember,' said Winslade. 'That way we'll get a quick response when the operation starts.'

'Correct. We'll say that an IED will go off—'

'IED?'

'Improvised explosive device . . . it'll go off at an unspecified military establishment. That should get them on their toes.'

'Alright. I'll get one of my lot to make the call from a public phonebox somewhere well away from the action.' Winslade smiled at his fellow conspirator. 'I'll get word to Maurice that everything's working out.'

'That's affirm,' said Shepherd in aviation-speak.

'Okay,' said the older man. 'In that case I think we're done for today.'

'Okay, Myron . . . listen, I'm curious about something.'

'Go on.'

'Where did the funny name come from?'

'Funny name?'

'Yeah . . . Dammmer . . . Damo . . . '

The older man smiled patronisingly. 'Damocles,' he provided. 'What do you about Roman mythology, Michael?'

'Bugger all, mate.'

Winslade took a breath. 'About 300 years BC the city of Syracuse in Sicily was ruled by King Dionysius. The story is that Damocles, one of the court hangers-on, irritated Dionysius with comments about how opulent the king's life-style was. So the king invited him to a grand banquet so he could experience it for himself. He allowed Damocles to sit on his throne, the centre of attention, surrounded by luxury.'

'What good would that do?' asked Shepherd. 'It would prove he was right to criticise the king.'

'During the meal, Dionysius pointed to the ceiling above Damocles' head, where there was a sword hanging over him suspended by a single horsehair.'

'Signifying . . . '

'It's obvious, Micky. Life might seem to be going well for you but you never know how precarious things might really be.'

Gradually a smile curled Shepherd's lips. 'I get your drift, Myron. Danger hovering overhead. Yes, how appropriate. Very clever.'

CHAPTER 6

At the helm of the 35-foot yacht *Louie Louie* Mitchell Fradini brought the bow a few degrees to port and told the Puerto Rican girl in the cockpit to wind in the mainsheet a little. From the transom a creamy wake bubbled away at six knots, glistening in the Caribbean sun. The boat's sails were comfortably filled by the northeast trade with a mere hint of turbulent airflow fluttering the jib leech. On the horizon St Lucia's inland mountains were pushing up against the sky and now *Louie Louie* was heading for the bay between the Gros Piton and Petit Piton hills guarding the beach. It would be not too difficult to sail right into the anchorage but Fradini was feeling lazy and pressed the starter button for the Volvo diesel.

In his mid-thirties, Fradini had the tanned healthy glow of a Californian playboy, sun-bleached blond hair ruffling in the wind, eyes hidden by wrap-round Versace shades. He wasn't short of a dollar or two and the yacht was his own property, as was the scarlet Corvette parked in the Royal Marina in Miami Beach, from where he had set sail a month previously. Not to mention the turboprop Piper Malibu at Fort Lauderdale airport.

The girl drumming her fingers on the varnished side decking was about fifteen years younger, an attractive college student Fradini had picked up during a stopover in San Juan. She provided him with the usual services and in turn the American was teaching her the fundamentals of sailing. The plan was that they would spend a few days in St Lucia and then head back to her homeland, hopefully before she missed too much of her spring trimester. He would then sail on to Florida, perhaps looking in on Nassau on the way home.

'You haven't heard my phone ring, have you?' he asked now. 'I'm expecting an important call.' The American's mobile, lying on a table in the cabin, could receive calls relayed through the SeaView satellite TV antenna, one of *Louie Louie's* creature comforts.

The girl laughed. 'Yeah, you told me a hundred times. No, I haven't heard it. Now, forget about your goddam phone.'

No doubt about it, Mitchell Fradini had done well for himself, considering his chequered background. Smart rather than intellectually gifted, the teenager had struggled to break away from the austere honest drudgery to which his parents had sacrificed themselves. The boy wanted more from life than the forty-five hours a week in a processed foods factory and the clapboard house in a low rent district of Jackson, Mississippi which seemed to satisfy his father.

But the younger Fradini's short cuts to making money took him off the straight and narrow. His parents despaired of their son's perfidy and dreaded the inevitable day when he would end up in trouble with the law. Salvation seemed to come when Mitchell agreed with his father's suggestion that he apply to join the army. The military were apparently less critical of his dubious personal qualities. They signed him up and taught him to fly helicopters.

The young pilot soon proved himself above average in ability and his commanders liked his fearlessness and the ruthless streak he would deploy to get his own way. They would not have been so pleased if they had uncovered his supplementary activities, such as selling military ordnance to outsiders who needed it for their own dark purposes. Patriotism was not allowed to cloud the issue. No qualms ruffled his conscience when he managed to sell three anti-tank rockets to an Arab intermediary.

Eventually alarm bells began to ring and the army told Fradini they didn't need his talents any more. There was not enough evidence to mount a court martial and so his discharge was honorable, at least on paper. The new civilian picked up the contacts he had dealt with before and was soon on his way again. By now he had formulated his Grand Design for the rest of his life. Crime was lucrative. He'd proved that. The big trick was avoiding the twin perils of punishment by the law and a harsher revenge from his competitors.

The army veteran came up with the concept of 'occasional forays', an expression he remembered from history lessons at school.

'Fradini, describe the fighting between the Sioux Indians and the white settlers.'

'Well, sir, it was a hit-and-run sort of thing. Attack them and then get the hell out before the settlers knew what was going on.'

'A delightful turn of phrase you have, boy. Personally I would have used the expression "occasional forays".'

Call it what you will, it was the pattern Fradini had adopted. Law-abiding respectability with just the occasional foray over to the other side when the payoff was worth the risk. He had enjoyed flying in the army and he had gotten himself trained for civil airline work, finding a job with Meridian Airlines as copilot on the Galleon fleet, based in Charleston. After a while he was promoted to captain on the twin-jet.

His pa was delighted. 'Good to see you settling down, son. You've done well for yourself.'

Even his mother was mollified. 'I'm glad you appreciate the benefit of making honest money. That's the only kind worth having.'

Dead wrong, ma! But Fradini was smart enough to keep his less salubrious exploits out of his parents' knowledge. He had discovered the rewards of stock market crime such as insider dealing and mis-selling mortgages and insurance, always working through front men to insulate himself from the dirty work.

Other contacts had drawn Fradini into the drugs market. He judged that the higher risks were justified by the higher rewards. At that time, pilots prepared to fly cocaine from Latin America to Florida were making very big dough. Fradini had done one trip himself before realising it was sucker country. The Drug Enforcement Administration was getting hotter at intercepting drug-running aircraft and ships and the business was turning very nasty. Look at that Cessna that was approached by another plane over the Gulf. The intruder was not a law agent but a rival dealer. A machine gun had stuck its snout out of the open door and blasted the Cessna to pieces. That was how the papers had reported it but no-one knew for sure what happened because the only evidence was scattered debris, including several bags of cocaine powder. No doubt sharks had dealt with the human remains.

No, get some other sucker to fly the stuff. Controlling the supply was where the action was, and the big money. And all the while I'm a respectable airline pilot, my father's pride and joy.

Fradini's well honed intuition about when to quit had served him well and the last 'occasional foray' was safely over, had been for some time. He was doing okay. His airline pay was a joke but he enjoyed the flying and the job furnished his shield of respectability. Legal investments were pulling in more than his salary from Meridian, and he had learned how to keep the Inland Revenue Service vultures at bay.

And then a short while ago an old contact had approached him about a job in England. Flying, outside the law, maybe dangerous. Fradini's first reaction was, forget it. The contact had left a phone number and as a parting shot mentioned a tempting amount of money. Fradini skirted round the bait warily. What about it? Time for one last 'occasional foray'? Good money. More importantly, big kicks. He could get high doing a really big job, fooling the cops. Spice up his life a bit. He called the number. The job sounded good. Tricky though. He'd kill himself if he screwed up. *Double the bucks and you've got yourself a deal.*

As the *Louie Louie* approached the coastline the Pitons reared up above them. Several boats were anchored in the bay and one or two larger motor vessels were tied up to the quay at the southern headland, next to the helipad. Sitting on the forested hillside above the long stretch of sand could be made out the stucco-walled Plantation Hotel, a palatial colonial residence built two hundred years previously to house the original self-indulgent English owner of the acres of inland sugar cane and banana holdings. Scattered about the main building were individual chalets for any guests willing to pay $400 a night to stay in them.

Fradini handed the helm over to his companion so he could roller-reef the jib and lower the mainsail, the boat dawdling at barely two knots under the languid power of the idling Volvo. Then he dialled a number on his mobile.

'Hi, we're on our way in right now. Can you send out a tender in say ten minutes. Save us getting our dinghy wet. Twenty minutes . . . okay . . . that's great . . . thanks.'

They tied up to a mooring, covered the mainsail and tidied everything away. As the sun went down the wind eased and the American and his friend sat in the cockpit, sipping chilled Michelobs from the icebox. The girl had brought out the portable TV attached by cable to the satellite antenna and found a channel showing a rock concert.

'Here they come,' said Fradini, indicating a small launch leaving the quay and swinging round to point at them.

The girl picked up the remote to switch the TV off but hit the channel change button by mistake. A newscaster filled the screen.

' . . . and finally, the Majorca affair,' the announcer was saying. 'There seems to be an impasse in the case of the Spaniard found drowned in Palma bay. The Majorcan authorities are insisting there is definite proof that he was murdered by an American serviceman. The dead man was known to the local police as a criminal. They say they have evidence proving that he was procuring girls for personnel in the the US Navy, an accusation vehemently denied by the Navy. It appears that cruiser Nebraska, currently stationed in Palma as part of the Sixth Fleet, may be ordered to leave Spanish waters along with other support vessels unless the difficulty is resolved . . .'

The hotel tender bumped alongside and this time the girl hit the right button. She put the TV back in the cabin and Fradini closed and locked the hatch. The big Caribbean boatman put their suitcases in the launch and soon they were heading for the quay. The boatman grinned at his passengers.

'Welcome to Saint Lucia, boys and girls. You gonna have a good time here.'

'Yeah, I guess we are,' grinned back the American.

In their chalet Fradini lay on his back on the bed, toying with his phone, eyes half closed.

The Puerto Rican came and stood at the side of the bed.

'You gonna have a good time here,' she said, mimicking the boatman. 'I'll make sure of that. Here, give me that.' She took the phone off him and put it on the bedside table. Then she slipped out of her summer dress to reveal her lithe naked body and suddenly Fradini realised that he didn't feel tired at all.

The phone rang. 'Oh, damn,' he muttered.

'Leave it, sugar,' cooed the girl. 'You lie there like a good boy because I'm gonna make you feel real good.'

'I gotta answer it. I've told you I'm expecting an important call.'

'Well, make it snappy,' said the pouted lips.

Fradini picked up the phone. 'Yeah, it's me . . . are we in business? . .'

The girl started to unbutton his shirt as he spoke. '. . . yeah, we were going to agree the money . . . hey, wait a minute, baby! . . no, not you, buddy . . .'

It was difficult to concentrate as his pants and boxers were removed and the tongue roamed over his legs. '. . . yeah, that's what I'm asking for . . .' The raven-haired head was moving higher. '. . . alright, you've got yourself a deal . . . I'll call—'

The girl took the phone out of his hand and purred into it. 'He'll call you some other time, honey, he's busy right now.'

Yeah, she knows how to turn me on, thought Fradini as the tongue found its goal, shooting a delicious shudder of anticipation through him. *But the best aphrodisiac is money. Two million dollars . . . for a bit of flying . . . two million little beauties!*

CHAPTER 7

Within a few years of joining Brycewood Electrics as a graduate management trainee in the mid seventies it looked as if Hugh Amberley-Kemp might have made a bad move. Brycewood had done well in the post-war boom but since then, along with most of British manufacturing industry, the company had been gradually slipping behind what was happening in the rest of the world. It was the classic blight of under-investment, amateur management and out-of-control unions, with inefficiency masked by state subsidies. A change of government in the late seventies meant that the flow of taxpayers' money was abruptly shut off and the old dinosaur came close to death.

In the ensuing catharsis many of Brycewood's higher flyers took off for pastures new. A sense of loyalty, not to mention canny foresight, kept Amberley-Kemp and a handful of equally astute senior managers in the coop. They persuaded the directors to start dealing pragmatically with the unions and to look for foreign investment to compensate for lack of domestic funding. Gradually the medicine worked and the company stepped back from the brink.

Today the lifeblood of the Brycewood Corporation was American and Chinese money, but the company was going from strength to strength and was now one of the major employers in the city of Derby. Amberley-Kemp had clawed his way up the greasy pole all the way to the top, finally reaching the lofty pinnacle of Chief Executive Officer, his status underlined with a knighthood from a grateful government for performance in the export market, not to mention contributions to party coffers.

This morning Sir Hugh was at his desk in his spacious office, thumbing through a report. The intercom buzzed, interrupting his work and bringing a frown to his brow.

'Yes, Fiona?'

Electronically distorted, his secretary's voice came back to him. 'I have an Inspector Sahay on the line. Wants to talk to you. Will you take the call?'

Sir Hugh was perplexed. Rapidly he scanned his memory, looking for possible reasons for an overture from the police. There was nothing. Unless . . .

'I'll take it. Put him through.'

A click of connection on the speaker phone. 'Hello, is that Sir Hugh Amberley-Kemp?' Black country nasal.

'Yes, can I help you?'

'I hope you can, sir. I'm Detective Inspector Sahay, Nottingham CID. I'm calling to ask you a favour.'

'Of course,' replied Sir Hugh with the over-sincerity people use when they mean *I hope it's nothing awkward.*

'In a way it concerns your son Giles. Or rather, people he knows.'

Just as he had feared. The CEO's heart sank. *Not that again, I thought all that was finished.* 'Is there any trouble?' he found himself asking.

The pause on the line did nothing to reassure him, nor the non-committal response that followed. 'I understand there's going to be a social function of some sort at Orchard Lea Grange one day soon.'

'Do you mean my younger son's birthday party? How does that concern you, Inspector? How do you know about it anyway?' Sir Hugh tried to keep the chagrin out of his tone.

'Forgive me, sir, I know it seems an invasion of privacy. It's a favour I'm asking you, not a demand.'

Pacified a little, Sir Hugh asked the police officer to elaborate. As the rounded vowels filtered into his ears his eyes strayed to the family portrait on his desk top, only recently taken. For a studio photo it wasn't bad, not too stilted. Lady Elizabeth beautifully made up. The picture took ten years off her. The two boys. Well, young men now. Giles. Sir Hugh had always had a special affection for his elder boy who was somehow more vulnerable than Bron. Perhaps the generous open smile did it. But Giles had given him and his mother some headaches over the years. A clever boy at school, he had gone up to Oxford to read history and got himself mixed up with a bad lot, mainly through through his disreputable girlfriend. *You can't possibly dream of getting engaged, Giles, she's a damned addict.* And the horror of his answer. *So what, so am I.* The court case. A suspended sentence for possession and a hefty fine. Almost ended up inside. Thank God their barrister friend Toby Ingram defended so well in court. But the boy was sent down from college in disgrace. After that he had drifted awhile, out of work, still mixing with the wrong types. On the road to ruin until that pilot chappie had befriended him. Nathan Bishop. Looked like a hippie but was basically sound, even if he had been an alcoholic. Nathan was now accepted as a family friend, as well as Giles's guardian angel. The elder Brycewood boy was now gainfully employed in a graphic design company and his rehab was complete . . . wasn't it?

If only Giles had turned out like his sibling. Bron was a credit to the family. Not as intellectual as Giles, but a worker. And astute too, training for accountancy. Knowledge of money matters was vital these days and Bron was making good use of his talents in commodity broking. Earning a good living too. Large house in green belt Surrey, his weekend retreat from the City. Two cars, half share in a yatch. And why shouldn't the boy enjoy the fruits of his labour? From the photo the boys grinned at him. Bron was the better looking of the two. And yet somehow he lacked his brother's charm.

And Sarah. Middle child and only daughter. She'd inherited her mother's quiet beauty. In the photo a wistful smile played on her lips and her clear green eyes flecked with grey seemed to look inside you. Science graduate, all set for a career in biochemical research, until this silly flying bug hit her. And now Nathan had got her fixed up with that freight company at East Midlands. And she was loving every minute of it. *The Chief Pilot's a real character, Dad. Bullies me at times but he makes me learn. Funny chap, bit of a chip on his shoulder. Divorced, lives in Nottingham. A bit mean and moody at times but he's okay.* Sounded like a social misfit to Sir Hugh, but perhaps that was a bit unfair as he had never met the man. He only hoped that the Chief Pilot was taking good care of his darling Sarah. Charter air freighting sounded a bit seedy. Bron had been dismissive. *Big sister's working for a kerbside flying outfit, probably go bust any day now.* Not for the first time Sir Hugh found himself wondering why his daughter couldn't just get all this flying nonsense out of her system. Find an eligible chap and settle down. There was no shortage of suitors, but she had only allowed one of them to get close to her. He had seemed okay to Sir Hugh but for some reason Sarah broke off their relationship.

'. . . as to how I know about the party,' the Inspector was saying, 'one of my officers has infiltrated a gang of pushers. From the info he provided we worked out what they were probably referring to.'

'You say Giles is not under suspicion, Inspector.'

'Not at the moment, sir. I'll admit we've looked at him closely because of his . . . background . . .' Sir Hugh was grateful that instead of 'criminal record' Sahay had chosen a euphemism. 'But he's in the clear up to now, anyway.'

The CEO of the Brycewood Corporation sighed in relief. 'So what is the favour you're asking of me?'

'As I said, sir, it's not Giles himself we're interested in. What does bother us is that there's a chance some drug dealing may be done by other people at the party. If that happens, we need to be there to get evidence.'

Sir Hugh was nonplussed. 'In my house? Surely guests wouldn't . . .'

'You'd be surprised what people get up to in other people's houses.' Sahay sounded resigned. 'Remember, my info is from as inside man.'

'In that case I'll vet all the guests, and anyone whose background we don't know will be barred.'

'I'd rather you didn't sir.' The police officer's voice was weary now.

'But, Inspector, I can't have those sort of people in my home . . . it's unthinkable.'

'Well, I'm asking you to think the unthinkable, sir. That's the favour. We want you to allow us to plant an officer at the party.'

'You mean your undercover man?'

'Er . . . no, sir . . . he's . . . on leave.' Not strictly true. Sahay's man was doing a month's porridge to enhance his credibility amongst the pushers, for which duty he would be paid a special allowance.

'So it would be a different man?'

'It would be a woman, sir. A WPS.'

'WPS?'

'Woman police sergeant. She would be at the party as a guest of yours. She could keep an eye on our villains.'

'I see . . .'

'Tell you what, sir. You probably need some time to consider it. You can turn me down if you want. I can't force you into anything. But it would be a big, big help if you went along with this. I'll call you back later to see if you've decided.'

CHAPTER 8

It had been a good game. The visting Crystal Palace team had been thrashed 4-0 and Lichfield, the hosts, were now five points clear at the top of the Championship table. No-one would have bet on them missing out on promotion to the Premier League at the end of the season. Hardly surprising, considering the amount of money the club's owner had spent on new players.

Dmitry Chegolev was no robber baron. The source of his vast wealth was the Siberian copper mining industry he owned, which he had acquired mostly legally, relying on his business skills rather than the chicanery that had enriched other Russian oligarchs after the collapse of the USSR. Further revenue came from Chegolev's share in the the rapidly expanding tourist industry, with newly wealthy Russians eager to travel the world.

As usual on Saturdays after a home match, Chegolev went to thank his players for their efforts, followed by a chat with their manager. From the new 60,000 seat stadium the Russian would normally be driven to his hotel in Lichfield to spend the night. Sundays would take care of any other football business and Chegolev's private Boeing 767 airliner would then take off from East Midlands airport on Sunday evening for the overnight flight to San Francisco, where he was usually domiciled.

It was a two-week cycle. Most alternate Fridays the big jet would fly in to East Midlands, sit on the ground on match day and return on the Sunday. Any maintenance work required during the stopover was entrusted to Britair Engineering, who also serviced the planes of Central Airlines and the various freight and parcels carriers based at the airport.

An observer would note the contrast between the opulent flying apartment owned by the Russian, with its communications centre, bar, luxurious lounge and individual cabins, each with shower, WC and satellite TV, and Meteor Air Express's ancient propeller-driven freighter parked half a mile away. There was no bar in Zulu Charlie and its toilet could best be described as basic, an unenclosed chemical WC at the nose end of the freight hold.

The same observer might find a similar contrast between Wilf Jagger's scruffy Nottingham flat and the grandeur of Orchard Lea Grange, to which the pilot was now driving.

Among the illustrious previous owners and occupiers of the Grange were an Admiral of the Fleet whose father had fought alongside Nelson at Trafalgar, a courtesan of Edward VII and a proprietor of the London and North Western Railway. Sir Hugh Amberley-Kemp had acquired the property in the same year that the Brycewood Corporation had elevated him to the position of CEO.

The large three-storey house was built of Portland stone and reigned over an expanse of wooded grounds whose flank reached to the bank of the meandering river Trent. When the wind was from the south a person enjoying the serenity of the large ornamental gardens in front of the house or the lake behind it would sometimes be able to catch the distant buzz of racing cars at the Donington Racing Circuit two miles away or the muffled roar of airliners taking off from East Midlands airport.

Convenient for Sarah to live so near to work thought Wilf Jagger as the tyres of his old Cavalier crunched the gravel surface of the long curving driveway leading to the portico. Jagger estimated that it would take less than fifteen minutes by car from the massive oaken front doors to Meteor's scruffy headquarters at the airport. No wonder she didn't want to move away. Who wouldn't want to live in a pad like this?

It had been diplomatic of Sarah to invite him to her brother's party but now his misgivings arose when he saw the assorted cars parked around the drive. He couldn't help cringing as he trundled past the glittering Porsches, Mercedes and Rollers in his well-past-its-prime wreck. He tried to outstare the equally glittering young partygoers lounging against their cars, some of whom did not bother to hide their amusement at the apparition rattling past them. Voices drifted in through his open window.

'Jeremy, can you believe that.'

'Supercool. I must get one of those.'

'That's so sexy. I could let myself go in that.'

Jagger clenched his teeth but managed to control his temper. 'Brats,' he muttered to himself as he drew up in a vacant space. He took some childish revenge by backing the old Vauxhall to within an inch of an unoccupied lurid red Lamborghini. *Get out of that, shithead.*

The front doors were open and Jagger walked through into the hallway, feigning nonchalance. He took in the polished floor, the grand staircase sweeping to the upper floor and the long mahogany table from which sprouted a pair of silver candlesticks. On the walls were oil paintings of race horses, some darkening with age. Different world. His entire flat would fit into this vestibule.

A growing sense of unease brought his feet to a halt. This was not his place. Some of the party guests were drifting past him as he stood rooted to the spot—faces alive, disdainful, bored. The bad vibes multiplied, unsettling him. He hadn't seen anyone he recognised and the strange attire and language of the weirdos he had already encountered, not to mention their youth, compounded his alienation. It crossed his mind to turn on his heel and escape to the sanity of his local. A pint and a game of darts would be a hell of a lot more fun.

'Wilf, my man.'

It was Bish. At last, a normal person. Well nearly.

'I thought I was in a nut house,' confided Jagger.

'Yeah, there's a few oddballs around. They're friends of Bron. Some of them are okay. It's called the generation gap. You were probably the same twenty-five years ago.'

'Thanks for reminding me how old I am. But you're not so far behind.'

'Age is nothing to do with years, mate.' He tapped his flowing locks. 'It's how you think.'

'What I think is I've landed on another planet.'

Bish laughed. 'There you go.' He turned to the girl at his side. 'Wilf, can I introduce Miranda, the belle of the ball.'

Nothing wrong with his copilot's taste in women. Miranda was a stunning blonde whose stature soared to within an inch of Jagger's own. He took the proffered hand. 'Pleased to meet you.'

'My pleasure.' Glossy lips, sparkling teeth. 'Nathan has told me a lot about you.'

'If it's good it's true. If it's bad, it's probably true.'

'I only told her the bad bits, Wilf. Had to protect your image.'

'Oh, there you are, Wilf.' Jagger turned round to see Sarah smiling at him. He nearly melted. In her black cocktail dress and pearls she was a picture of sophisticated beauty. She had two oldsters in tow, or rather an oldster and a middle ager. Had to be Daddy and Mummy.

The introductions were made and then Bish and Miranda went off to join the crowd in the anteroom, leaving Jagger with his hosts. Out of the corner of his eye he spotted Ed Park being served a beer by a blue jacketed waiter.

'Busy night for the servants,' observed Jagger.

Sir Hugh either missed the nuance of sarcasm or else feigned to. His daughter shot a warning glance to the pilot.

'They're hired caterers, Captain Jagger,' said Lady Elizabeth brightly.

Jagger waved a self-deprecating hand. 'The name is Wilf.' He brought himself to civility. 'Surely you need people to help you run this place?'

'There's a butler, a maid and a cook,' said Sir Hugh. 'They've got the night off.'

'We don't consider them as servants,' added Sarah, her voice cold. 'They're employees and they like it here. They're free to leave us any time they want.'

The girl's mother intervened again to defuse the situation. 'Sarah, I'm sure . . . Wilfred . . . would like some refreshment.' She smiled graciously at the pilot. 'Please forgive us, Wilfred. We're taking the evening off ourselves. Off to see some friends. We'll leave you youngsters to it.'

'Oh, mummy,' said Sarah, 'he's nearly as old as you.'

Touché thought Jagger.

'Well, you look young to me, dear,' said Lady Elizabeth, patting his arm.

'How's the girl doing at her job, Wilf?' Sir Hugh's tone was that of a parent asking his child's teacher for a progress report.

'Daddy, do you mind?' Sarah was miffed again.

'She's doing fine,' responded Jagger, sensitive enough to feel Sarah's embarrassment.

The father's eyes turned serious. 'Take care of her, Wilf. She is my only daughter.'

'Oh, for heaven's sake, Daddy . . .'

Jagger interrupted. 'She'll sink or swim on her own merit. As far as I'm concerned she's a pilot just like any other. If she doesn't come up to scratch, I'll fire her.'

His words torpedoed the conversation. Even Sarah's mother was taken aback. Strangely, Sarah herself seemed mollified.

'And that's exactly how it should be,' she said. 'I don't want any favours.'

'Yes, I'm sure you're right,' said Lady Elizabeth, but not with conviction.

Sir Hugh was silent for a long moment. Then he took his wife's arm. 'We'd better be getting along, dear, or we'll be late. Nice to have met you, Wilf.' His courteous dignity had not diminished. 'Perhaps we'll see you again soon.'

'I shall look forward to it.'

As soon as her parents had gone Sarah flashed hostile eyes at Jagger.

'Look, I don't mind you insulting me if you feel you have to, but I can't take you being rude to Mummy and Daddy. There's no disgrace in being wealthy, you know.'

Jagger nodded. 'Yes, I'm sorry. Pure envy, I'm afraid. One of my many character defects.'

Sarah pursed her lips. 'Sometimes I wonder about you. You may be a great pilot but you're not such a brilliant human being.'

'I get by. I behave better when I've had a drink or two.'

'Okay, truce. Let's go and get a drink. And cheer yourself up. This is supposed to be a party.'

As if to underline the point a heavy disco beat started up in a room farther away. Sarah accompanied Jagger to the bar in the anteroom and went off to circulate. The pilot propped himself against the wall and sipped at his pint while he surveyed the assembled company. Not many over the age of thirty. Only himself and Bish and that other bloke—where had he seen him before? High forehead, swept back hair. Yes, he was in that photo that police chappie had shown him. Jagger watched him curiously. He was in deep conversation with a group of people, including two men whom Sarah had already pointed out as her brothers. Near them, apparently alone, was a woman of who looked older than most of the other guests. She seemed out of place, not involved in the conversation, but vaguely attached to the group. None of the people nearby paid her any attention as she stood by herself, occasionally lifting a wine glass to her lips.

'Hi, boss.' Ed Park and his wife had come over to talk to him.

'Enjoying the party, Wilf?' asked Elaine. 'You look a bit lost.'

Jagger shrugged. 'I'm okay. Just watching the younger generation at play. Very interesting.'

Elaine took his arm. 'Come on, you boring old fart, come and have a dance.'

Park shot him a don't-blame-me look as he was dragged away.

The alcohol in his blood and the heavy second and fourth beat stomp combined to liven Jagger up and he threw his limbs about in a vague imitation of what was going on around him. From time to time Elaine shouted a comment but her dancing partner, unable to hear above the noise, simply smiled back. How could anyone converse when their ears were under assault from threshold-of-pain rock music? Elaine said something about 'Bish playing later' but Jagger might have misheard. 'Maybe,' he shouted back, hoping it was the right response.

The pilot's stamina gave out after ten minutes and he pleaded for a rest. He took Elaine back to the anteroom but Bish showed up and immediately whisked her off for more musical calisthenics. There were a few chairs and sofas dotted around and Jagger slumped into one of these, followed almost immediately by Sarah and the unaccompanied woman he had seen earlier. Before the hostess had a chance to introduce them to each other she in turn was taken off to the dance room by Ed Park.

Jagger pointed to himself. 'Wilf. Can I get you a drink?'

The dark haired woman smiled back. Jagger noted a curvaceous outline, friendly eyes and an open, freckled face.

'Hilary. White wine and soda, please.'

'Friend of the family?' asked Jagger.

'Sort of.'

'Me too, sort of.'

The two chatted for a while, neither giving anything away, until Sarah returned.

'Oh, I see you're getting on okay. You haven't arrested him yet, then, Hilary?'

'Not yet.'

'What are you on about?' said the pilot.

Sarah lowered her voice. 'Hilary is a policewoman, sent here by her boss because he thinks Giles is mixed up with international criminals.' It was a loose paraphrase of her father's explanation and her scorn was not masked by her flippancy.

Hilary looked embarrassed. 'Routine surveillance, that's all,' she said. Jagger remembered her earlier apparent interest in Sarah's brothers and their cronies. Fascinating.

'Do you work for Inspector . . . what's his name? . . .'

'Sahay. Do you know him?'

'He came to see me a while back. He wanted me to identify some people in a photograph. In fact—' He cut himself off, undecided whether or not to elaborate.

'I've seen the photo,' said Hilary. 'Nathan Bishop, Myron Winslade and Michael Shepherd. Two of them are here tonight, as you can see for yourself. I'm just keeping an eye on things.'

Jagger steeled himself. 'Is Bish in trouble?'

Hilary smiled. 'Not that I know of. We don't think he's involved in anything illegal.'

'Just as well,' muttered Jagger. 'How can I run my business with one of my two First Officers in jail?'

The policewoman was perplexed. 'I beg your pardon?'

'He's got his own airline,' explained Sarah. 'Meteor Air Express at East Midlands.' She turned to Jagger. 'You've got three First Officers, Wilf, or don't I count?'

Jagger grinned. 'You're right. How could I ever forget?'

'Your own airline,' said Hilary. 'I'm impressed.'

'Don't be. My so-called airline consists of one worthless fifty-year-old aircraft, a few engines and miscellaneous aeronautical junk. There are five pilots, including myself . . . and Sarah . . . four if you arrest Bish.'

'I'm not planning to arrest anyone,' laughed Hilary. 'Though I'd like to say a few home truths to the idiot who parked his car right on top of mine out in the drive.'

'Hilary's got a super car,' said Sarah. 'Lamborghini.'

'Fancy,' was Jagger's only comment, wondering if he could discretely move his wreck without Hilary realising who owned it.

'About time you got yourself a new car, Wilf,' continued Sarah. 'Then I wouldn't have to run you into work. You'll just have to get rid of that decrepit old Cav—'

'Ladies and Gentlemen,' boomed the disco PA, saving Jagger in the nick of time. 'The moment you've been waiting for. Here to play live for the birthday boy and his guests, I give you . . . Cataclysm . . .'

Jagger heard a crash of drums and a mighty guitar chord, pursued by the introductory bars of an old rock 'n' roll number. The partgoers in the anteroom began to drift towards the magnet of sound.

'C'mon, let's go and watch,' said Sarah, pulling Jagger and Hilary.

'Sounds just fine from here,' said the pilot.

'What, don't you want to see your senior First Officer laying down the beat?'

'What do you mean?'

'Nathan . . . Wilf, didn't you know? Nathan's playing tonight.'

'Isn't he a bit old to be a rock star? I though he gave all that stuff up years ago.'

Jagger allowed himself to be coerced into the other room to see the performance. The music was tight and very, very loud. Cataclysm had five members, including Bish, who was now in Jimi Hendrix mode, cavorting suggestively with his guitar. Jagger had never heard him play before and was suitably impressed, even if rock music wasn't really his cup of tea. Bish was clearly a man of many talents.

After a while the relentless throbbing of the music soured into a headache and the surrounding throng of hot twitching bodies became oppressive. Jagger eased himself out of the room and made for the front door. A walk in the fresh air outside would do him good.

The moonless night was dark and refreshingly cool, a last vestige of the winter. Formless blobs of grey-back cloud cruised through the starry skies on a light wind. Despite the music, audible even out here, a mantle of peace settled around Jagger as he strolled slowly over the lawn past a row of budding magnolias.

He turned and looked at the mansion, an ancient haven of solid security in an unsettled world. What was life like when those massive stone walls were rising from the ground? What would he have been if he had been living in those times? A merchant? A lord? A peasant? Jagger's own family were nothing special. Lower middle class, the sociologists would probably say. Several rungs below the Amberley-Kemps, no doubt about that. Even a grammar school education couldn't close that gap.

The pilot resumed his stroll, intending to walk right round the house and back to the driveway to move his car out of the Lamborghini's territory. His feet led him back to the pathway, just visible in the gloom, and towards the next corner of the building. Suddenly a sound stopped him in his tracks. Muted voices. Jagger edged closer to the corner, ears pricked. The voices were clearer now although the talkers were still out of sight. Suppressing the feeling that he was violating someone's privacy, Jagger listened.

'. . . a hundred kilos each according to my source.'

'Nice. That should make us a quid or two.'

'Assuming the Yank does the business.'

'Christ, we're paying him enough.'

A laugh. 'We'll get our investment back many times over.'

'What about the recordings?'

'Sorted.'

'Do you really think it's going to work?'

'My honest opinion? I'd say the chances are about eighty percent.'

'Suppose they shot the guy down?'

'Unlikely. Too risky. Anyway, if it all comes to grief we're both in the clear. Now, how's about we rejoin the party. It's getting a bit cold out here.'

'You still reckon that dark-haired woman is fuzz?'

'Maybe. Really can't tell. I can usually smell cops a mile off. Her I'm not so sure about but I can't take any risks. Maybe she's just a friend of Sarah's. Anyway, she can't hear us out here. Come on, let's go back in . . .'

Jagger thought quickly. He took a few brisk paces back the way he had come, then spun round and walked towards the corner again, thinking that if the men turned the corner on their way back they would assume he was walking towards them and therefore had not heard them talking. But the men did not appear, so Jagger continued to the corner and went round it, expecting to see them walking away from him, taking the long way back round the building to its entrance.

No sign of them! They can't have just disappeared! Perhaps they had gone in through one of the doors. Jagger tried them but they were all locked. Then he realised what had happened. He looked up and noticed that the rooms on the first floor each had a balcony. The men must have been standing on the balcony nearest the corner and must have re-entered the house from there.

The pilot walked back to the entrance and went straight to the dance room. The sweating bodies quickly warmed him up again as he wormed his way towards Hilary and touched her arm.

'I've got to talk to you,' he shouted, just managing to best the strident decibels of a Bish guitar solo.

'God, your hand's freezing. Where have you been?' Hilary shouted back.

Jagger led the policewoman away into the anteroom where there were a few fellow refugees from the music. He passed on what he'd heard to Hilary as accurately as he could. As he spoke her face took a grim set and she got out a notebook from her handbag.

'A shame you didn't see them, Wilf. That would have been really helpful. I was trying to listen in earlier but no-one was saying anything. Perhaps they'd sussed me already. Or else they were just being careful.'

'Do you know what's it's about, what I heard?'

'Not much.' Hilary looked around but no-one could hear them. 'Confidentially, Inspector Sahay thinks there's a big operation planned for the near future. A drugs deal. Overseas connections.'

'The men I overheard—who do you reckon they were?'

The police woman shook her head and swept her hand round the room. 'Could be anyone here.'

'Not Bish, though,' said Jagger. 'He's still murdering that guitar.'

Hilary smiled. 'Not Bish.'

'And who is going to be shot?'

'No idea.' The policewoman looked at her watch. 'I think I'll clear off now. Write up a report so I can hand it in first thing tomorrow. Will you make my excuses to Sarah?'

Jagger nodded. 'Okay. Are you sure you don't want a drink before you go? Or a coffee? The perc's on over there.'

'No, I'd better be off now.'

'In that case, I'd better come with you.'

'Why?'

'To let you out. I'm the idiot who parked his car by yours.'

Having helped Hilary extricate her car, Jagger waved goodbye as the red sports car growled off. How come a policewoman could afford a Lamborghini? Another spoiled brat with stinking rich parents, like the Amberley-Kemps? *Well, who cares?*

CHAPTER 9

United Airlines Flight 404 landed at Heathrow only twenty minutes late just before eleven o'clock in the morning. The plane had been full but Mitchell Fradini had spent some of his advance payment on a Business Class ticket and was thus spared the misery of trying to sleep in the slave-trader accommodation in Economy. As the passengers disembarked Fradini regarded his red-eyed fellow travellers with contempt. *Suckers! If you gotta go, go in style.*

It was several years since he had been in England but the teeming airport soon reminded him of the claustrophobia he had felt before in this overcrowded little island, when he had come to visit a friend, the same friend who would confirm his cover story if the police wanted to see him after the operation. *Yes, officer, I know what you're looking for, but I've been travelling around England in a camper van and then staying with my buddy.*

After the usual hassle of immigration Fradini picked up the camper from the car hire company and before too long was driving through the tunnel towards the outside world. *What a dumb way to access an airport. Through a hole in the ground, for Chrissakes!*

His journey was not as easy as he had imagined from checking the map. *Sure it's highway all the way, but why do these guys drive on the wrong side of the road! And what the hell is this* he fumed as he ran into a two-mile long four lane traffic snarl up on the M25.

Well, may as well use my time constructively.

Fradini switched on the stereo and lifted a CD from the passenger seat. The music on the radio cut out as he pushed the disc in. After a few seconds an American voice drawled from the speakers.

' . . . Trans-State Airlines . . . Boeing 767 Pilot Training Course, Lesson 6 . . . The Hydraulic System . . . The 767 has three hydraulic systems, designated left, center and right . . .' As the traffic at last began to move Fradini relaxed in his seat and listened carefully. The Boeing aircraft was similar in its characteristics to the Chinavia Galleons he was used to, but the technical differences were not insignificant and Fradini needed to revise the basics to top

up what he had learned from data downloaded from the internet, including You Tube videos.

But surely, officer, you're looking for a 767 pilot. I'm only qualified on the 737 and the Galleon. Never flown a 767.

It was nearly three o'clock when the pilot finally pulled off the motorway and followed the road signs to Nottingham City Centre. What a relief to get away from the insane driving of the English. *Okay, everyone busts the speed limit but these guys are suicidal.*

The road jumped over a railway and then snaked round a hill on top of which Fradini saw a castle. *Maybe that's where Robin Hood lived.* He knew his knowledge of English history was even patchier than that of his own country.

The American drove through the City Centre looking at hotels and finally chose the Holiday Inn near the castle.

'Good afternoon, sir, may I help you?'

'Yeah, I want a room for a night, maybe two.'

'Do you have a reservation?'

'No. I want a double.'

The receptionist tapped at her keyboard. 'I'll see what we've got.'

Why don't Americans ever say 'please' or 'thank you'?

The girl gave him a registration card to fill in.

'Have the porter bring my bags up,' said the American as he wrote.

'Yes, Mr Mason,' replied the receptionist, reading the card. 'Enjoy your stay.' Her tone belied the sentiment.

Fradini grinned at her. 'I will, honey, you can bet on it.'

In his room the American took a beer out of the minibar and stretched out on the bed. He let his mind mull over recent developments. The time frame for the operation had turned out to be tighter than he had originally supposed. He'd had to abandon the leisurely sail back to Florida in *Louie Louie.* The boat was now tied up in a marina in San Juan, where he had dropped off the lovely Rosita before flying home. When the operation was over and the hubbub had died down he would make his way back to Puerto Rico to pick up the boat and sail it home. Maybe he would be able to find Rosita again and take her along for the ride . . . *literally!*

A knock on the door was the porter with his bag. The old man stared at his ten dollar tip without comprehension.

'Take it, Gramps, it'll buy you a drink or two.'

As soon as the porter had gone Fradini took out his mobile and dialled.

'Hi, it's your buddy from over the water. I'm in Nottingham.' He pronounced it 'Notting Ham'.

'Okay,' said the receiver. 'We'll need to meet to discuss details. Where are you staying?'

'No deal,' answered Fradini. 'I'll tell you how it'll be. Number one. Have you paid the next installment into my bank account?'

'Yes, $250,000, as agreed.'

'I'll check that. Second. I want my directions in writing. Stick them in an envelope and leave it at the Parkway Hotel, in Reception.'

'Is that where you are?'

'No comment.'

A pause. 'Right. Is there anything else you need at the moment?'

'Nothing I can't get for myself.'

There was a pause at the other end of the line. 'It might be a good idea to use an English accent from now on. For your own protection as much as the operation.'

'Yeah, I've been practising.'

'Good, call me again in two days and I'll update you on the arrangements.'

'You got it, baby, *ciao*.'

Fradini rang off and picked up the hotel phone.

'I need to call the Hauptstadt Bank in Zurich. Can you get them for me? . . .'

CHAPTER 10

In the Britannia Concert Hall the last climactic bars of Ravel's Bolero crashed through the auditorium and the first half of the concert was over. As usual after this work the clapping quickened when the percussionist took an extra bow, the audience acknowledging the magnitude of his task, rapping out the staccato tempo on the snare drum non-stop for fifteen minutes.

Jagger joined the tide of patrons making their way to the bar for refreshment and managed to get served without too much waiting. Nursing his glass of red wine he fought his way to a reasonably quiet corner. He was on his own, which was perhaps to be expected even if not what he wanted.

Over the past weeks his relationship with Sarah had improved somewhat, he careful not to antagonise her, she responding with guarded warmth and good humour. Her training on Zulu Charlie was proceeding apace. She had shown herself above average in aptitude and had tamed the lumbering freighter with dogged determination and so there had been little for Jagger to find fault with. During their last trip they had talked about the party at Orchard Lea, and Bish's playing with Cataclysm, and from there they had wandered into classical music. Sarah mentioned that her favourite composer was Beethoven and Jagger had lied that his was too. In truth he was a Tchaikovsky fan. The Russian's occasional descent into despair mirrored his own perfectly. But it was the right moment to take a chance. Jagger had been half intending to go to this concert and he had asked Sarah if she would join him. The girl thanked him for his invitation but turned him down on the grounds of a prior engagement. Of course, he had no way of knowing if the excuse was genuine.

Never mind. Jagger had come to his senses and realised that the most natural relationship between himself and his new First Officer was one of warmish neutrality, and that any efforts to make something more of it would most likely have the opposite effect. What he would have to guard against was that the uncomfortable amalgam of resentment, envy and desire did not twist his behaviour towards her into boorishness. *Keep your sarcastic mouth in check, my son, you need her for your crummy airline.*

As he sipped his wine, Jagger mused that at last things were looking up for his shaky enterprise. He had just offered positions to two young and inexperienced pilots looking for work. Kids, but sound enough. The deal Jagger had offered was—*I'll meet the cost of training you onto the Merchantman if you promise to work for me for at least three years.* And they had both accepted. It meant that if he promoted Bish to captain, which he fully intended, he would have three complete crews even allowing for the loss of Ed Park. And with the current upturn in the air freight market Zulu Charlie would be in the air more, earning its keep.

'Hello.'

Jagger turned. It took him a second to recognise the face because of the change in appearance. Casual clothes had given way to a Prussian blue evening gown and diamond necklace. The chestnut hair had piled itself into ringlets and there was a touch more make-up round the eyes. Only the freckles were as he remembered them. It was the policewoman at the party.

The pilot smiled. 'Good evening.' *Wish I could remember her bloody name.*

The woman saved him from further embarrassment. 'Hilary,' she said, returning his smile.

'Wilf,' he said to remind her. 'Fancy seeing you here.' There didn't seem to be a companion. 'On your own?'

'No, Adam's here with me. He's my son.' As if on cue, a tall, slender youth moved over to them carrying drinks. Hilary made the introductions.

They talked about the concert for a while and then Jagger turned to other matters.

'Any progress on that drug business . . .' He stopped himself short, wondering if he'd been indiscreet in front of the youth, but Hilary did not seem concerned.

'Not much more, I'm afraid. We know something's on but we're still stuck on where and when. The naughties have kept it very tight. No gen has leaked out yet. We're still watching Shepherd and Winslade and their acquaintances.'

'Why don't you question your suspects?'

'It's the old story, Wilf. If we pull them in they'll probably close down the whole operation. Then we've got nothing apart from potential crooks who haven't as yet broken the law. So we'll have to let them get on with it in the hope that we can nab them when they're on the job, so to speak.'

They all sipped at their drinks and then Hilary asked: 'Are you by yourself?'

Jagger nodded. 'The person I invited turned me down.'

A whimsical smile settled on the woman's lips. 'Unrequited love, was it?'

Unrequited lust, thought Jagger. 'Something like that.'

The first bell sounded for end of intermission.

'There are some empty seats next to us,' said Hilary. 'Why don't you join us?'

'Thanks, I think I will.' On the spur of the moment he added: 'I was considering going for a coffee after the concert. Do you and Adam fancy joining me?'

The police officer turned to her son. 'What do you think?'

'You go if you want, mum, but I'd better get back home straight away. I've got my audition tomorrow. I want to be in good shape for it.'

'Oh, yes, I'd forgotten that. I think we'll have to turn you down, Wilf. Adam hasn't got his driving licence yet. So I'll have to take him home.'

'No, you go, mum,' said Adam. 'I'll get the bus home.'

'Don't let me muck up your transport arrangements,' chipped in Jagger. 'Maybe some other time.'

Hilary pursed her lips, thinking. 'Well, it would be a nice end to the evening. Are you sure it's safe taking the bus, son? I'm just concerned about the nutcases you get on buses in the evening.'

'Don't worry, mum. I'll be okay. I can look after myself. I'm nearly seventeen years old, remember.'

The second bell rang. 'Okay,' said Hilary, 'I accept your gallant offer, Wilf.'

The woman took one arm of each male and the trio returned to the auditorium.

*****

In the Petit Caprice bar the pilot smiled at the waiter who brought them their cappuccinos. The topic of conversation was the people at the party.

'Sarah and Bish both work for you, didn't you say?', asked Hilary.

'They will be my entire copilot strength when Ed leaves for better things. Until I've got my new boys trained up.'

'Is it difficult, running a business like that?'

'I would have used the word impossible.'

Hilary smiled at him. 'Tell me how you got involved with flying.'

Jagger was amazed. 'Do you really want to know? It's incredibly boring.'

'I'll risk it.'

'You may regret this.' The pilot launched into a potted history. It hit him that no-one apart from Phoebe had ever asked him before. No-one had shown that much interest in his past. Humble origins. Nearly made it to university. Eight years in the Air Force. Then trading military excitement for civilian money in the airlines. The financial collapse of his employer and the emotional collapse of himself. The struggle to get going again. Gratified by the unfamiliar sensation of talking about himself he warmed to his task, hoping that he was not crossing Hilary's boredom threshold. But she seemed attentive enough. After a while she touched his hand.

'Excuse me, Wilf, I've just got to make a phone call. Back in a mo.'

Fair enough. Time to change the subject anyway. Who is she phoning? Presumably her husband. I was getting so carried away I never even gave him a thought.

'I feel happier now I've phoned home,' were Hilary's words as she slid into her seat again.

Jagger tried some gentle prying. 'Your hubby's letting you stay out late, is he?'

The policewoman smiled ruefully and dropped her eyes. 'He doesn't have much say. He's been dead for quite some time.'

'My apologies.' *Put your foot in it, haven't you?*

'You weren't to know. No, I was calling to check that Adam had arrived safely. I wasn't really happy about him travelling on the bus alone. There's some funny people on buses at this time of night.'

'Modern life,' was the only comment Jagger could think of.

The thread broken, the two of them were silent for a while. Hilary's mood had darkened a little since the mention of her late husband and Jagger didn't know how best to guide her back to levity.

Eventually he plumped for: 'Have you got any other offspring?'

'No. Just Adam. Giving birth to him mangled up my insides, I'm sorry to say. So the family is just him and me.'

'I see.' *So much for trying to find something brighter to talk about.*

But now Hilary had a go. 'What about you, Wilf. How many kids have you got?'

Jagger restarted on his history, chapter two. Phoebe, Jane and Daniel. The split up. The Ape Man.

Hilary laughed. 'The who?'

'He calls himself Osmond. He is just about to take my wife and my son to America. For good.'

'I'm sorry, I shouldn't have laughed. It's not a funny subject. You must be devastated.'

'It wasn't the best thing that happened to me.'

Another pause as the waiter came over to ask if they needed refills.

'I'm enjoying this, Wilf. I don't get out so much these days.'

Jagger's curiosity overcame his sense of tact.

'Do you have a . . . partner now?'

Hilary didn't reply straight away and the pilot wondered whether he'd overstepped the mark.

'Well . . . that's a difficult one. There is someone, sort of . . .'

'Forgive me, I had no right to pry.'

The woman smiled. 'It's alright. I don't mind talking about it. The picture is that I've been seeing someone for quite some time. There were even vague plans about marriage. But . . . I don't know if it's going to work out.'

'Oh dear.'

'He can't make up his mind. The truth is I suspect he's thinking about trading me in for a newer model. I think he's found someone else and he hasn't got round to telling me about it yet.'

'That's familiar territory to me.'

'Well, that's life. Everything balances out. I lost my husband but I've got my son.'

'What did he do? As a job, I mean?'

'Copper, same as me.'

Jagger was tempted to ask about his demise but this time he held himself in check. He went off in a new direction instead.

'What about Adam? Is he interested in joining the Force?'

Hilary shook her head. 'Music is his main interest. He's auditioning for the Midland Youth Orchestra tomorrow. That's why he didn't want to get home too late tonight. It's important to him to do well.'

'What does he play?'

'He's good on the clarinet and saxaphone, but I think he likes the cello best of all.'

'A future Rostropovitch.'

Hilary smiled. 'Maybe. He's in two minds. He really wants to play serious music but he's tempted by the fame and fortune of rock. He plays sax in a semi-pro band now. They're reckoned to be pretty good.'

'Talking of which, I was amazed about Bish,' said Jagger. 'I had no idea he had such a following.'

'It seems your copilot is pretty famous in music circles around here. Adam was mortified that I didn't get him into the Orchard Lea party to hear Cataclysm. He didn't believe me when I told him I knew nothing about Bish's musical prowess.'

Jagger grinned at his companion. 'Well, if Adam changes his mind about his career, tell him to learn to fly and come and work for me. I'm always short of pilots.'

'I'll pass that on, but I think that if he didn't make the grade in music the Force would be his next priority, despite what happened to his father.'

From her choice of words Jagger judged that Hilary might not mind if he followed up.

'What did happen?'

The policewoman looked at her companion. 'He was stabbed at a football match. There was a riot after the game, which Simon and other officers tried to break up. Simon was attacked. He bled to death before anyone could help him.'

'He was on duty, then?'

'Yes, in uniform. That's why he was attacked.'

'Did they get the culprit?'

Hilary shook her head sadly. 'Culprits. Conspiracy of silence. It was a gang of thugs that set about him and they all closed ranks after Simon died. "No-one saw nothing" was the statement the ringleader made in court.'

'When did it happen?'

'Seven years ago. Seventeenth of February, five minutes past five. That's what the evidence said.'

The waiter chose that moment to bring them the bill and Jagger took out his wallet.

'Thanks,' said Hilary.

They fell silent for a while. Jagger did some thinking. Hilary's revelations forced him to face a few home truths. He'd always considered that fate had dealt harshly with him and he had a right to view life through cynical eyes. A man with more money than brains had stolen his wife and son. He himself lived in a hovel and was always stuck for cash. He spent most of his waking hours trying to keep his fly-blown airline out of the bankruptcy court. And yet here was Hilary, whose husband had been murdered by mindless hooligans and who would never bear another child no matter how much she wanted too. The cold workings of fate hadn't dented her cheery disposition. *You should count your blessings, Wilf.*

'Did you get compensation for your husband's death?'

She nodded. 'I can't complain there. Compensation is generous for those who are killed on duty. And we had life insurance too. Adam and I bought a better house and a few creature comforts.'

'Like the Lamborghini?'

Hilary smiled. 'Exactly. I know it's wrong, a middle-aged woman driving around in a ridiculous toy like that. Resisting temptation is not something I'm good at.'

'My car is also ridiculous, but not quite in the same way.'

'And you the managing director of an airline.'

'That's not exactly how I'd put it.'

Hilary looked at him. 'Would you say that flying was more dangerous than police work?'

'You see before you the world's most devout coward. I wouldn't go anywhere near an aeroplane if I thought there was any danger. The old cliché is absolutely true. The most hazardous part of any pilot's job is the drive to the airport.'

'Haven't you ever had any emergencies?'

'I've had my moments,' said Jagger. 'But it's not like the movies, you know. If a problem crops up, you think carefully, discuss it with your copilot and then sort it out. That's why he's there. Or she. A pilot could easily fly an airliner on his own, but the idea is that two brains are better than one. Each pilot watches what the other one's up to. I always tell new copilots that their main job is to stop the captain being a wally.'

'I've flown as a passenger, of course, but I've never seen the flight deck of an airliner.'

The notion came to Jagger straight away. 'Why don't you come on one of my flights, Hilary? You can sit behind us in the cockpit and watch us plying our trade. My freighter isn't exactly the last word in aerial technology but you might find it amusing.'

'Wilf, I'd love to.' Hilary was obviously delighted at his offer.

'Well, I'll check the programme and find a suitable trip. I dare say you'd prefer a day flight rather than a graveyard shift. I should be able to find something suitable. I've got a Budapest coming up soon, that might be okay. And I'm in the middle of negotiating a contract to bring some stuff back from Banjul.'

'Where's that?'

'Gambia. It would be a two or three day job. A long flog, though. I'd have to stop en route to refuel. We're talking about ten hours' flying each way. I think that would bore you to tears.'

'Not at all, Wilf. Any flight would be lovely, long or short. I'd just need sufficient advance notice to arrange my roster at work.'

'Good, that's agreed, then.'

'On one condition.'

'Name it.'

'You must let me invite you to dinner at my place. Repay the compliment, so to speak.'

'I accept.'

CHAPTER 11

Mitchell Fradini strolled into Reception at the Parkway Hotel and casually looked round to make sure that there were no prying eyes. He walked to the desk and spoke to the girl on duty, doing his best with his English accent. She went into the office and came back with an envelope which she handed to him. They exchanged false smiles and then Fradini left, his glance again sweeping round like a lighthouse beam, but there was nothing to worry about.

*****

The lock-up was part of a semi-derelict Victorian warehouse on the bank of the murky canal bypassing Beeston on the industrial outskirts of Nottingham. When Shepherd arrived on his motorbike he took off his helmet and looked around but he didn't see anyone. He unlocked the rusting double doors and pulled them open against squeals of protest from the ancient hinges. The day was unseasonably warm and Shepherd pulled off his leathers and draped them over the bike. He wandered through the weeds to the canal bank and sat on the edge, smoking a cigarette and idly wondering if there were any fish alive in the oily rubbish-strewn water.

One or two strollers passed by on the tow path but without paying attention to the man at the water's edge.

And then disturbing the vernal tranquillity could be heard the rattle of a truck engine. The ten tonner lurched up to the warehouse and stopped with a sigh of brakes. The legend on its flank was 'Quality Clothes from Casu-Wear'.

Shepherd got up to meet the man climbing down from the cab. He was looking around at his surroundings with disdain.

'I had trouble finding this place,' he grumbled. 'No-one around here seems to have heard of Euro Traders.'

'Yeah, this is just temporary. We store things here when our main warehouse is full. Bit of a dump, isn't it?' He pointed to the back of the truck. 'I'll give you a hand getting the stuff out.'

Inside the vehicle there were seventy large boxes of sturdy cardboard, each with the Casu-Wear logo. The labels attached to the boxes stated '100 Pairs High Quality Vaquero Denim Jeans'. Shepherd took a penknife from his pocket and slit the sealing tape on the carton nearest him. When he lifted the flaps he could see that the contents were as the labels indicated. He nodded to the other man.

'They seem okay. Let's start unloading them.'

It took about twenty minutes for the two men to transfer the truck's cargo on to the four wooden pallets in the lock-up. Even with the help of a fork lift both men were sweating freely from physical exertion in the close spring air by the time the task was complete. They sat down on the vehicle's floor for a rest, dangling their feet over the back, smoking cigarettes. Then Shepherd gave the delivery man a tenner for his trouble and sent him on his way. He checked that all the boxes were sitting securely on the pallets, eighteen on three of the pallets and sixteen on the other, double stacked. He covered the boxes with plastic sheeting and, satisfied all was in order, closed and locked the doors.

A quarter of an hour later he turned his bike off the main road and headed for his cottage in the little village of Hillgate. He knew that Charlotte would be at work, which suited him fine. There were things to be done that couldn't be done with her hovering around. His girlfriend had put the morning's mail delivery unopened on the cake tray reserved for this purpose in the breakfast room. Shepherd riffled through the envelopes and found the one he wanted. It contained only an untitled CD-R.

He powered up his laptop and opened his mailbox. Yes, there it was.

The mouse hovered over the message he had received two days previously. Shepherd clicked on it to open it for re-reading.

A copy of the communication we discussed has been dispatched to you by first class surface mail. Please confirm safe arrival as soon as you receive it. The unlock code is the name of the operation. Let me know if you want to make any changes. You must ensure that no-one else has access to this communication.

Shepherd inserted the disc into his laptop. On the screen popped up a dialogue box consisting of eight smaller boxes. There was no other information or instructions. The dispatcher's fingers tapped out the sequence on the keyboard . . . D . . . A . . . M . . . O . . . C . . . L . . . E . . . S . . . The screen blanked and a voice sounded.

'This message is addressed to the British Government and must be relayed to them immediately. The ministers concerned must give their authority for the following instructions to be carried out exactly as detailed in this communication. Please note the time limit available for compliance with this directive and please note the penalty that will be incurred if total compliance is not forthcoming . . .'

As the sombre voice echoed round his kitchen, Shepherd let out a whoop of delight.

'Brilliant! Absolutely bloody brilliant!' he yelled.

CHAPTER 12

Myron Winslade had spent a lot of money on the forgeries, but it had been worth it. The results were as perfect as modern graphics and printing technology could make them.

Firstly, the new passport for Maurice Holmin. The photograph was genuine although the name of the bearer was given as Cyril Smith. The year of issue had been chosen as 2006 so that the forgers would not have to embody the microchip featured in later examples. A human observer would not have been able to detect any flaws in the document although an inspector armed with a tape measure might have picked up that the spacing of the passport number digits on the title page were spaced very slightly too far apart. The error was only three millimetres over the whole sequence. The document would have passed muster at any immigration checkpoint not equipped with the code reader for scanning the photo page. Which meant that 'Cyril Smith' would have plenty of choices for his new domicile, especially where immigration procedures were not as robust as in Europe or Australasia or the USA.

The documents for the cargo were more straightforward. Central Airlines frequently carried cargo on its passenger flights so the data was available in house. Since the origin and destination were both within the European Union there were no formal customs regulations. The only complication was the security requirements. The carrier they were planning to use was not a Registered Shipper as far as the Department of Transport was concerned, which meant that the cargo would have to be screened by an accredited forwarding agent before it could be loaded onto an aircraft. Shepherd decided to use Midland Freight Forwarding, one of the larger local companies, as cover. 'Euro Traders' would approach MFF to arrange handling of their cargo. Of course the cargo which actually arrived at East Midlands would not have been processed by the forwarding agent. However it would be accompanied by MFF Airway Bill documentation, which would appear genuine under all but the most detailed examination. Shepherd had acquired original MFF examples and posted them to Winslade so that the forgers could scan them and make copies. Winslade had also arranged the set up of a false Euro Traders website in case anyone happened to want to check up on them. Immediately after the operation the website would be deleted. There might be an electronic trail left behind but it would not lead directly to any of the Damocles people.

The East Midlands Airport ID was not too difficult to manufacture. Shepherd had lent the forgers his own card for copying. The photograph on the forgery was of Mitchell Fradini, although the holder's name had become 'William Mason'. Job Title was now 'Engineer' rather than 'Dispatcher'. Likewise the card's header had metamorphosed from EAST MIDLANDS into LONDON GATWICK. Again, to the human eye, the ID looked genuine. A chemical analysis of the plastic base would have revealed a different composition from the original. Unlikely to be a problem for the purpose the Damocles group intended it for. Like Holmin's new passport, the only complication with 'William Mason's' ID was that it was impossible to incorporate the magnetic data strip, which meant the security swipe scanners would reject it. Which is why the card bore the Gatwick heading. The regulations would be met by a security officer checking the photo against the physical appearance of the person presenting it and noting the ID card number on the log held at the checkpoint. The number on the forgery was false, of course, but it was assumed that no-one would think to verify it until after Damocles was over.

Winslade, Shepherd and Fradini had decided to test the efficacy of the ID card they had produced. The test would serve the dual purpose of firstly checking it was fit for purpose and secondly allowing the American to try a dry run of the opening phase of the Damocles operation. If it turned out that the card was detected as fraudulent when it was presented at the security checkpoint they could postpone and rearrange the operation. Of course, there was the consequent possibility of Fradini's arrest. *But we're paying you two mil, to take the risk, Mitchell, don't forget. And, as you know, our lawyers have already worked out a cover story for you along the lines of you, as a pilot, wanting to check how good British security procedures are.*

There had been some discussion in the group about how the Extra Pack should be carried through Security.

'The holdall will have to go through the scanner.'

'Yes, but the EP won't show up as anything suspicious. There'll be clothes on top to make it less obvious if there's a physical bag check. They'll be the clothes I would have changed into when I took the overalls off so Security won't be suspicious.'

'And if you wear the EP, it might look a little bulky under the overalls.'

'No, the type I've chosen is very slim. But the metal components might trigger the alarm when I go through the body scanner, which means a body search.'

'Yeah, that's no good.'

'So it's got to be the bag.'

'What about the metal bits?'

'I've removed the biggest part. Don't need it. The other bits are quite small. They'll look like the buckles you get on clothes.'

'Okay.'

*****

The runway at East Midlands Airport is a tarmac strip almost 3000 metres long, running east-west. Almost all the airport buildings and facilities lie in the area to the south of the runway. At the western end is the vast Cargo Area, a small corner of which was home to Meteor Air Express. Next comes the Western Maintenance Area, then the Main Apron (for passenger aircraft) and the General Aviation Apron (for business jets). At the eastern end of the strip lies the Eastern Maintenance Area, home to Britair Engineering. The terminal and control tower are situated just to the south of the Main Apron.

The airport layout was convenient for the Damocles plotters. The Central Airlines Admin block, including the office in which the dispatchers worked, lay between the Main Apron and the GA Apron, giving them a good view of both areas. Additionally, security checkpoint Delta was sited between the GA Apron and Britair's base and so was in frequent use by the maintenance company's staff.

The dry run worked as hoped, but with an unexpected wrinkle. Two weeks before Damocles Day Fradini had driven the car supplied by Michael Shepherd to the airport and left it in a car park.   Carrying a small holdall and wearing the slightly grubby Britair overalls and yellow hi-viz jacket the dispatcher had acquired for him he presented himself at checkpoint Delta.

'It's a Gatwick ID,' he said, handing over the card and dropping the holdall onto the bag scanner track. 'Won't work in your swiper.' Fradini's English accent had been copied from watching TV programmes and he had learned to turn his 'T's into glottal stops.

'What's a southern boy doing up here?' asked the security officer.

'They're a bit short apparently. Understaffed.'

A chuckle. 'Yeah, like everywhere these days.'

'That's right.'

The security officer started the scanner belt and Fradini's bag rumbled into the machine. Then he scrutinised Fradini's ID card and turned to tap at a computer keyboard. The American held his breath, alarmed. Shepherd had told him the officer would manually record the ID card number in a log book. Perhaps the computer was merely doing the same thing. But if it was accessing a data base covering all British airports the American was done for. If there was trouble he would either have to act as if he couldn't understand why the card wasn't recognised, with an 'it was OK last week' type of response or else resort to the 'testing security' cover story. A third option, more drastic, would be to do a runner back through the entrance door and hope to get away before anyone could catch him.

But the officer didn't seem concerned as he finished typing. Obviously the computer was not flagging up any alarms. Fradini began breathing again. Maybe he should see if he could find out a bit more about the new system. It might be relevant for Damocles Day.

'Last time I was here they wrote the ID number in a book.'

The security officer waved at his monitor. 'Brand new last week. Complete waste of money. The old way was easier.'

'So the system doesn't check all the other airports when you input the card ID number, then?'

'I think that's the plan eventually. At the moment we just use it instead of the old log. There you go.' He handed Fradini his ID back and motioned him through the body scanner. Simultaneously the holdall emerged unchallenged from the bag scanner and the American pilot picked it up and walked out.

Once airside Fradini walked left towards the GA Apron, noting the layout of the buildings and control tower. There were CCTV cameras here and there which the American was careful not to stare directly at. *Mustn't look like I'm casing the joint.* Then he reversed direction and headed for the Britair area, nodding and smiling at a couple of engineers walking in the opposite direction. Reaching the end of the maintenance apron he turned into the Britair building and sat down in the rest area with the newspaper he'd been carrying in the holdall. The room was quiet and, apart from small talk with another man at the coffee machine when he decided to take refreshment, no-one spoke to him. Fradini looked at his watch. Give it half an hour and then out again. *Yes, it'll work as long as we're not fucked up by that computer in security.*

Afterwards there had been a discussion about the new computer. Shepherd did some checking and discovered that the countrywide data base would not be operational for several months.

Damocles was on!

CHAPTER 13

For a propeller-driven aircraft the Merchantman was quite a mover. Its four Rolls Royce Tyne turboprop engines dragged the sixty ton freighter through the air at three hundred and thirty-five knots, almost four hundred miles per hour. At full blast each engine turned its propeller with the power of five thousand horses. Even when throttled back in the cruise the huge props spun fast enough for the blade tips to nudge the speed of sound.

In the time it took for Sarah to say, 'There goes Santiago. Next track is two two zero', the aircraft had put another half mile behind it.

Jagger grunted his concurrence. He reached forward and adjusted the autopilot and Zulu Charlie swung round onto the new heading. Then he sank back in his seat again and allowed his thoughts to wander. Hilary was supposed to have been travelling on the flight with them and he had been looking forward to showing her the ropes. But at the last minute she had had to cry off.

I'm sorry, Wilf, I've got to go to court to give evidence. One of my villains is up before the beak and the arrangements can't be changed. I'm really annoyed about it. I really wanted to come with you. Can we try some other day?'

Jagger drew some comfort from Hilary's obvious disappointment. He'd been half afraid she was just patronising him. He couldn't deny that her friendship filled a space in his life that had been empty for a long time. Apart from the occasional physical interlude with a divorcee who lived nearby his life had been devoid of involvement with women. But she had started to claim more from him than he was prepared to give, which was nothing more than mutual carnal satisfaction, and he had taken flight. Self-imposed celibacy was not as intolerable as the divorcee's cloying embrace.

He had met Hilary two or three times since the concert. Their last date was the promised dinner at her house. It had gone well. Good food, good wine, good music, good company. And how convenient that Adam, Hilary's son, was staying away overnight with a school friend. Had Adam arranged that, or his mother? After dinner Jagger and his hostess had repaired to the settee for more intimate contact. But he never got to find out if Hilary would have succumbed to his advances because at that moment her son arrived home. As the adults separated themselves, trying unsuccessfully to mask their embarrassment, Adam explained that his friend had been taken ill and so he thought it best to come home.

Would it have been a night to remember? Since then Hilary had been filtering into his thoughts quite a lot. If she had been able to come with him to Banjul, would she have shared his bed? And what did the future hold for them?

He turned to his young copilot. 'Can you drive for a bit, Sarah? I'm going to take a break. We'll have lunch soon.'

'Okay, sire, I've got her.'

Jagger flicked the compass switch to the right. The autopilot was now under her control. He took off his headset, picked up the newspaper, slid his seat back as far as it would go and settled down to read. There was one more thing. With a sideways glance at Sarah he reached into his flight bag and pulled out the case holding his new spectacles. He was still unfamiliar enough with them to feel awkward as he settled the half moon frame onto his nose.

'Most becoming. You look quite scholarly.'

'You fly the plane, lady, and leave me in peace.'

'Yessir.'

There wasn't much to hold his interest in the paper and soon his mind was floating off again. It was satisfying to bask in the knowledge that Meteor was at last making headway. Bernie and he had found the two new copilots quick to learn, endowed as they were with the enthusiasm that went with their tender years and Jagger had enjoyed informing Bish that he could now start his training for command. The response 'Hey, that's cool,' Jagger took to be an intimation of pleasure.

And the work was picking up all the time. New customers, repeat business from old ones. Lately the 'in' commodity to shift by air seemed to be clothes. The flight he and Sarah were doing now was to bring back clobber from Banjul, exotic apparel knocked out by cheap Gambian labour for sale to English women at fifty times the cost of production. The concept of exploitation of the workers never got within miles of Jagger's conscience. It was just a job, a good one, and it would trickle some more geld into Meteor's coffers. And when Zulu Charlie returned from the Gambia the day after tomorrow it would be off to Düsseldorf very early the next morning with clothes made in England. The customer wanted to export a load of denims to Germany. There had been uncertainty about the date until the last minute, which was unusual. The customer had mentioned three possible Sundays, a fortnight apart. Confirmation had arrived only a few days previously. It was to be the first of the three options. The charter looked like a one-off rather than a series but anything was grist to Meteor's mill if he could turn a profit. If people wanted to shift clothes then he would shift clothes for them. Jagger smiled inwardly. Maybe he should rename his company 'Ragwing'. Overtones of dowdy romanticism, how suitable. Again, Jagger did not let his mind wander along the road of querying the apparently illogical economics of importing clothes into England and then exporting other clothes out again. The obvious question: why didn't the German customer get his denims made in the Gambia and fly them direct? never troubled his thought processes.

The soporific droning of the Tynes and lack of mental activity weighed Jagger's eyelids down and he didn't even notice that the newspaper had dropped from his hands. His last thought before Morpheus switched off his brain was to wonder how Bish would get on in the left hand seat on the Düsseldorf flight . . .

At first the sight of the captain slumped in his seat, mouth agape, oblivious to the world, didn't trouble Sarah at all. He was evidently tired after their early start and it was only natural that he should fall asleep. Sarah reached over and retrieved the paper and folded it up, careful not to disturb him. She looked at him more closely. The glasses gave him the careworn air of an overworked schoolmaster.

There was no doubt that Jagger was more personable of late. The turning point seemed to have been the party. Maybe he realised he had insulted her parents and was making an effort to be more civilised to people in future. Certainly there had been fewer snide wisecracks from his sardonic mouth. He seemed less distrustful of his fellow man, altogether softer. Suddenly a thought hit her. Could it possibly be . . . a woman?

Well, why not? He wasn't unattractive when he wasn't trying to shock the world. In some ways he had the same endearing naivity that had messed up the life of her older brother. But where Jagger's cynicism was his shield against the harsher punches of life Giles had no protection.

Giles. Brainier than his younger brother but not half as smart, Sarah had to admit she loved him more. Perhaps it was the maternal instinct. She felt the blows fate dealt him almost as much as he did himself. People were too quick to judge him as the product of a spoiled childhood, but they didn't know the truth. They didn't understand how vulnerable he was.

Anger stirred inside her as she recalled the latest developments. Why were the police watching him again? Why couldn't they leave him alone? They suspected he'd lapsed into his old ways but she knew him better than they did. Sarah just knew her brother had left the drug scene for good. He had a good job, a nice girlfriend and—

'Meteor 115, maintain level 220 and contact Lisboa on 128 point 9'.

The call from the Madrid Radar Controller snapped Sarah back into the freighter's flight deck. With his headset off Jagger slept unhearing through the interruption.

Sarah changed frequencies and checked in with Lisbon control.

And now there was a problem for her to face. For no apparent reason the data panel on the satellite navigation receiver mounted on the instrument panel flickered twice and then went blank. The girl checked the input leads and switched the receiver off and on several times but its empty face proved the futility of her efforts. To compound her misery, the signals from the Santiago radio beacon were fading and, starved of bearing information, the course indicators on the pilots' instruments were wavering drunkenly. In a few more minutes the signals would be out of range entirely and there would be nothing to guide Zulu Charlie on its way to Tenerife, where they planned to land for refuelling.

A twinge of panic touched Sarah and she almost succumbed to the temptation to wake Jagger up to ask him for help. *Look at him, sitting there snoring, not a care in the world, while I'm left on my own in this flying tramp steamer over the middle of the ocean with nothing to steer by.*

No, she would sort it out herself, by dead reckoning. She picked up the weather charts they had printed out at East Midlands and turned to the forecast wind diagrams. Hmm, in this region the prediction was northwest, twenty knots. That meant about four degrees of left drift. Sarah tweaked her heading bug and Zulu Charlie momentarily dipped its wing in response.

Ten minutes slipped by, then another ten. Sarah was happier now, even though the Merchantman was bereft of any navigational guidance. She was quite certain she was playing it right. As her confidence flourished her mind opened itself to other sensations. Like hunger. The lunch box was behind and between the two pilots' seats. Inside Sarah found some cheese and cucumber sandwiches *à la Caroline* and two flasks of coffee.

As she ate the absurdity of the situation struck her. Here she was, in total charge of a large aircraft with which she was not yet completely familiar. Whose captain was the sleeping beauty in the left hand seat, grunting and twitching in his dreams. In skies in which she had never flown before. Munching cheese and cucumber sandwiches. What would her friends think?

Zulu Charlie droned on without concern, looking after itself. Sarah slid her own seat back a notch and scanned the world outside. Not much to command attention. An infinity of slow, grey-green ocean, oily surface scored by the wake of an occasional crawling ship. Hazy featureless empty atmosphere. Even the blue of the higher heavens seemed to leak away at the bleached horizon. Luckily the sun was so high that only a few of its searing rays could penetrate the flight deck windows.

She stole another glance at the pilot-in-command. He was well away, dead to the world. Sarah's face softened as she watched him. He wasn't so bad really. Maybe if he was a few years younger . . . But a secret corner of her mind whispered to her. *It's not Wilf who has got hold of you . . . .*

'Huh.' Jagger grunted again, loudly enough to propel himself into consciousness. He sat up and yawned.

'How long was I out?'

Sarah grinned. 'Hours. I overflew Tenerife. We'll be landing in Banjul soon.'

Jagger sighed. 'If only.' His professional eyes swept round the flight deck, absorbing the information the quivering instruments confided to him.

'What happened to the GPS?'

'It's sulking. I've tried cycling the power input but it's not playing. I'm dead reckoning.'

There was a pause. The captain took off his specs and gazed outside for a minute or two. Then he turned to his copilot, speaking through another yawn.

'We're south of track.'

Sarah was non-plussed. 'How do you know?'

The captain winked at her. 'Turn right ten degrees. That should do it.'

Sarah tried to keep the irritation out of her voice. 'Why? I've calculated the drift angle. I reckon we're bang on track.'

'Ten right, Sarah.'

The girl hesitated, her face reddening. 'Very well. You're in charge.'

In the old days Jagger would have followed up with a cutting comment. Sarah was half expecting it. Instead he was silent for a short time. When he spoke again his voice was friendly.

'A bet, my dear. If we are more than three degrees off track when we pick up Porto Santo, I'll buy you dinner with champagne tonight. How's that?'

'Okay. Deal.'

They half smiled at each other and the tricky moment was over. Sarah offered control of the aircraft back to Jagger but he made a dismissive gesture.

'No, you keep it while I'm having a bite to eat.'

Zulu Charlie inched its way across the vastness of the Atlantic, Sarah minding the shop while Jagger finished his sandwiches and attacked the crossword in the paper. Another attempt to resuscitate the GPS proved fruitless. The girl had given up arguing with Jagger about the heading they should be on. She was convinced they were now well to the north of the planned route. It was fair enough to assume he knew what he was doing but she wished he wasn't so damn certain about it. Eventually he began to take more interest in their progress. He checked his watch and made some measurements on his chart, using his pen as a scale.

'Well,' he pronounced, 'I reckon we'll pick up Porto Santo within five minutes.'

'Let's see if you're right,' answered Sarah, hoping perversely for the opposite. She started the stopwatch on her panel.

For two minutes the sweeping hand of the clock mesmerised both of them. On both course indicators a little reg flag saying 'OFF' mocked the captain. Only radio signals from the Porto Santo beacon would pull the flags down. Sarah listened for the identification code but there was nothing. Dead as a dodo.

'Aha!' The second hand was ticking towards the expiry of the fifth minute but first one, then the other, of the warning flags twitched, flickered in and out of view and cleared. At the same time a weak but decipherable dit-dit-dit dah-dit dah filtered into the pilots' headphones. Morse code for S . . . N . . . T. Porto Santo. A few moments later the distance readouts sprang into life.

'Lucky,' said Sarah. 'Ten seconds to spare.' It wasn't the accuracy of Jagger's timing that annoyed her so much as the accuracy of his navigation. The bearings and distances were spot on. Zulu Charlie was exactly on track.

Sarah looked across and saw Jagger grinning. He winked at her mischievously. 'Who's a clever clogs, then?'

The girl smiled back at him. 'Okay. How did you do it?'

'Dead easy. FTJ navigation.'

'Never heard of it. FTJ? What's that supposed to mean? Nothing rude I hope.'

Jagger feigned shock. 'Rude? Me? Perish the thought.' He pointed up through the windscreen. 'There.'

Fifteen thousand feet above them a jet streaked through the sky in the opposite direction trailing dazzling white streamers of exhaust.

Realisation dawned on the girl.

'You've been watching for other aircraft and following their vapour trails.'

'Precisely. FTJ. Follow the jets. Never fails.'

'Suppose the one you're following is going a different way?'

Jagger didn't answer. He had in fact done precisely that once in the past, an embarrassment he would rather forget.

The airway led past the island of Madeira, a dark smudge on the horizon to the right, then turned further south to Tenerife. The two pilots were silent for a while, Jagger studying the approach charts for Reina Sofia airport and Sarah hynotised by an irregularity on the horizon ahead that imperceptibly grew into a white capped mountain.

'Mount Teide,' said the captain. 'Over twelve thousand feet high.'

'Yes, it looks like a volcano, with snow instead of lava.'

'It is a volcano. All the Canary islands are volcanoes sticking out of the sea.'

'I presume they're dormant?'

'That's what people say.'

As they edged closer Sarah could make out the other islands scattered around the horizon. Zulu Charlie pressed on towards them as if drawn magnetically to the slumbering peaks. Now the pilots could see surf breaking on the rocky northern coast of Tenerife. At Jagger's prompting Sarah got clearance from Canaries air traffic control to begin descent.

The arrival route swept past tattered rags of cloud cloaking Teide's foothills and then followed the western coast. The soaring mountain pivoted and climbed above their left wing tip as Zulu Charlie dropped lower, an insignificant speck against its vast flank.

Reine Sofia was busy but control managed to fit them into the sequence of arriving aircraft. They followed an Airbus down the approach and when it had turned off the runway Tower cleared Zulu Charlie to land. Jagger brushed the freighter's main wheels onto the runway almost exactly six hours after they had left the ground at East Midlands.

A yellow follow-me car led them to the cargo apron where a set of steps and a Hydromatic loader was waiting for them. Although the main purpose of the flight was the Banjul charter, Jenny Trimble had found Jagger a miscellaneous cargo for the sector from England to Tenerife which would avoid taking an empty aircraft southbound and hence improve the economics of the whole arrangement. Jagger supervised the unloading of the pallets while an engineer from Iberia helped Sarah to refuel the aircraft. Zulu Charlie thirstily drank several thousand gallons of kerosene for the onward sector to Banjul. Jagger paid for the handling services and the fuel with a credit card and promised the agent an extra cash handout if he could get the empty pallets back on board within the half hour.

It was just after two o'clock when the Merchantman eased itself off the runway again and swung its blunt nose south to point at the western bulge of Africa far beyond the horizon. Sarah was now at the controls, indulging herself by flying manually, laughing at Jagger's supercilious remarks about ripping the autopilot out of the aircraft if no-one was going to use it. The GPS had inexplicably resurrected itself and was once again leading them on their way.

Twenty minutes wrestling with the aircraft was enough to tire her. She engaged the autopilot and relaxed in her seat, content to watch the unfeeling machinery do the work but miffed that its clinical accuracy was so much better than her best.

'Good idea,' offered Jagger. 'You'll get muscles like an Russian shot putter if you try to drive this bugger yourself.'

'I could do with a curvier figure.'

'The shape you are now is fine.'

Sarah reddened slightly and changed the subject.

'What's the plan of action again, Wilf? Have we got the day off tomorrow?'

'You have. I'll need to go to the airport to sort out the loading. It'll be too late to do it tonight. Anyway we'll be too tired.'

'Don't you want me to help you tomorrow?'

'Thanks, but no need. It's only a matter of watching the natives stick the cargo on the pallets and getting them on board.'

'Have they got a Hydromatic loader?'

'Maybe. There must be other freight airlines operating there.'

'If not, how will they lift the pallets up to the cargo door?'

'We'll think of something.'

'And then we set off early the next day.'

'Very early. I'm planning to get back home by five o'clock on Saturday afternoon.'

There was a pause. 'Do you know much about Gambia?' asked Sarah finally.

Jagger shook his head. 'Only been to Banjul once before. That was ten years ago, in an MD11.'

'Did you stay long?'

'An hour. Enough time to disembark three hundred passengers and embark three hundred more.'

'Were you a captain then?'

'I was.'

Sarah opened her mouth to speak but changed her mind.

'No need to say it, dear. I know what you're thinking. Yes, I have slipped a few rungs down the ladder since then.'

'No, it was the opposite. You've been dealt some bad cards but you haven't thrown your hand in. You've made the best of it.'

'Leave off, Sarah. you'll have me in tears in a minute.'

The girl turned to him. 'You shouldn't be so hard on yourself. Other people respect you. You should respect yourself a bit more.'

'Thank you, Sigmund Freud. I'll manage.'

This acerbic response killed the exchange and both pilots found other things to do to mask their discomfort, Sarah refolding her airways chart and Jagger inscribing the readings on the engine gauges into Zulu Charlie's technical log.

'Land ahoy.' It was some time since either had spoken and the captain's words were an intrusion against the steady hum of the engines.

The waste of sea had come up against a vague shoreline on the aircraft's left. As they edged closer the brown mass of the Sahara pushed the Atlantic to one side. The pilots stared down but there was nothing to catch the eye.

'Incredible,' said Sarah, leaning over for a better view. The wilderness was unscarred by the workings of mankind. 'You wouldn't think anyone lived here at all. Could be another planet. Look at those beaches. Completely deserted.'

'Yeah, a bit different from downtown Nottingham,' said Jagger. 'Mind you, your dad's grounds are nearly as big as this, aren't they?'

Sarah quickly looked at him but there was no acid in the remark. He was smiling at her.

'Are you ready for a journey back in time?'

'What do you mean?'

'It's a well know fact,' said Jagger. 'The further south you go in Africa the more primitive the facilities. Look at the chart. Not many radio beacons round here, are there? And we'll probably find that most of those aren't working. Aerial navigation in these parts is like it was in Europe before the last war. Strictly do-it-yourself.'

Sarah looked concerned. 'I hope the GPS doesn't die on us again. There aren't even any other aircraft to follow.' The radio had been completely silent apart from their own position reports.

'No problem. We'll use FTC.'

Sarah worked it out and grinned. 'Follow the coast?'

'You're learning fast.'

After a while the monotony of the view anaesthetised their senses and they both slumped in their seats as the freighter crawled onwards. Jagger made another half-hearted attack on the crossword while his copilot gazed into space, nibbling peanuts from a packet she had found in the lunch box. Without realising it she nodded off to sleep. Jagger saw her head drop and flicked the compass switch to his side. He stared at Sarah, taking guilty advantage of her unconsciousness to let his eyes absorb her beauty. Through the open neck of her blouse could be seen a hint of bra strap. Atavistic desires stirred inside him. But the shame of his voyeurism finally squeezed his mind back into more gentlemanly confines. With a sigh he picked up the paper again.

The girl eventually woke up again just as Zulu Charlie trundled over the city of Dakar. She yawned and stretched and gazed down at the speckles of white buildings scattered across the promontory of Cap Vert.

'Nearly there,' said Jagger.

Yundum airport had cloaked itself in the Saharan haze of late afternoon and the Merchantman was almost on top of it before Jagger's eyes could separate the black runway from the featureless khaki mass of the encircling promontory at the mouth of the river Gambia.

'Can you see it, Sarah?'

The girl flew Zulu Charlie overhead and swung into a right hand pattern, dropping down to circuit height on the downwind leg. Without any prompting from her mentor she turned onto final approach at just the right point and eased down for a perfect landing.

'Not bad. There's hope for you yet.'

Apart from a weary-looking 727 and a motley collection of smaller aircraft of varying vintage the apron was empty when Jagger cut the engines. He opened his sliding window and a blast of tropical heat burst into the flight deck. The incongruous splendour of the dazzling new terminal and control tower emphasised the surrounding drabness of the older, crumbling buildings dating from the 1930s that he remembered from his previous visit. Other than a handful of bored ebony-skinned labourers sitting on baggage trolleys and disused oil cans there was little sign of human activity. Yundum International Airport.

A new Mercedes saloon drove up and Jagger watched the driver get out. He was an Asian, about fifty, smartly dressed in crisp white shirt and tie. His air of authority was confirmed as he barked out orders to the lounging labourers. Two of the men roused themselves and went off to drag a set of aircraft steps up to Zulu Charlie.

Jagger went to open the crew door while Sarah finished the shut down checks and switched off the battery. The Asian mounted the steps and held out his hand, grinning profusely.

'Captain Jagger? Welcome to Gambia. My name is Gulu Patani.'

The pilot recognised the name from the correspondence dealing with the charter. Patani owned the factory which was turning out the merchandise Meteor was contracted to fly to England.

Jagger began to talk about the loading arrangements but the Indian cut him short.

'Relax, Captain. I have organised everything. When we have secured the plane I will take you and your copilot to the Oceanic Hotel. I wanted very much to join you for dinner but sadly there are other things I have to attend to this evening. But there are many other British guests at the Oceanic. I am sure you will enjoy their company. On the way to the hotel we can discuss . . .'

Sarah had just appeared. She offered her hand to the Indian. He bowed deeply.

'How enchanting,' said Patani, talking like a character from an Agatha Christie novel. 'Captain, you are lucky to have such a beautiful copilot.'

'I know,' said Jagger, 'I never stop thinking about it.'

Patani seemed to miss both the irreverence in Jagger's voice and the stop-taking-the-mickey glance from Sarah.

Having completed immigration formalities, Patani had the pilots' bags loaded into the boot of the Mercedes and invited them to get in. Thankfully the car was blessed with a functioning air conditioning system and soon after the engine was started a soothing mantle of cool air caressed their sweating skins.

The road left the airport and swung northwards through dusty, nondescript vegetation, its surface testing the car's suspension as it steadily deteriorated in smoothness and integrity. After a while a sprinkling of decrepit shacks showed they were approaching a settlement. Sarah looked out from the rear seat and was immediately transported to Tobago, where she had spent a holiday with her parents as a teenager. The same pathetic hovels strung along the road side, the same dingy shops made out of corroded corrugated metal sheeting, the same flaking hand-painted adverts for Coca Cola and Marlboro cigarettes. And the same disturbing mien of the local inhabitants. Proud, resigned, arrogant. The dark eyes that watched the Mercedes sweep past were not friendly. Bitter residue of a repressed colonial past? Sarah knew little about Gambia. Was this what the British left behind or was it self-inflicted decay? Even the gathering dusk could not dissolve the miasma of stifling poverty.

Jagger paid scant attention to the dismal scenery passing by. He and Patani were sorting out the next day's business.

'I'm afraid the Hydromatic is not working, Captain, but I have got a small crane. I suggest we lift the goods straight into the plane.'

'Yes,' concurred Jagger. 'I think that's best. Leave the pallets on board and secure the cargo onto them. What time do you want me there?'

'The trucks will arrive about ten or eleven o'clock.' Patani grinned, revealing gold-capped teeth. 'I'll send a car to pick you up at the Oceanic, but I can't say exactly when. Time is a variable quantity in this country, Captain. The local people have a saying. Translated, it means "things never happen before the Gods allow."'

'Most civilised,' said the pilot. 'What about fuel?'

'I have contacted the Shell agent. The bowser will come out whenever we want. We can refuel at the same time as loading.'

'Perfect.'

The Indian turned to flash his grin at Sarah.

'Will you be coming to the airport, Madam?'

'If Wilf wants me to.'

'No need,' interjected Jagger. 'I've told Sarah she can take the day off, Gulu. Perhaps she can get out and see the sights.'

Patani frowned. 'It might not be easy. It would be most unwise for her to travel on her own. There are tours arranged for the hotel guests but I don't think there are any going tomorrow. I would be delighted to be Madam's guide myself but I have much business to attend to. Maybe one of my employees . . .'

'Please,' put in Sarah. 'I don't want anyone to go to any trouble for me. If I'm not needed at the airport I'll be happy swanning around the swimming pool at the hotel.'

The pot-holed road had escaped from the meagre dwellings and now turned towards a mangrove swamp, its direction parallelling the coast. Behind the car a palisade of trees was silhouetted against the evening light. Jagger remarked that the ride was better, less torture for the shock absorbers.

'Of course,' said their chauffeur as the car rumbled over a wide creek, 'This is the Banjul-Serekunda Highway. Serekunda was the town we passed earlier.'

The captain raised his eyebrows. 'Highway' and 'town' were stretching nomenclature into the realms of hyperbole.

Patani accelerated the Mercedes past an ancient truck, transportation for about thirty locals, their black bodies swaying with each axle-shaking bump in the road. This time Jagger noticed the contemptuous stares.

'They look happy,' he observed.

Patani turned to him. 'They have escaped the shackles of imperialism but not those of poverty which are a hundred times heavier.'

'How do you get on with them yourself, Gulu?'

The Indian shrugged. 'I provide work and I pay them for it. And don't forget I am a victim of racialism, too. The people know that.'

'What do you mean?'

'I had the misfortune to be born in Uganda. In 1972 my father's properties were confiscated and my family and I were expelled.'

Jagger thought back to his childhood. 'That was when Idi Amin was running amok.'

'Precisely, Captain. I suppose we were lucky to escape with our lives. Some of my countrymen did not.'

'Are your family here with you?'

'My wife, yes. My two daughters have—what is the expression—flown the nest. One is a student in New Delhi and the other lives in the United States. She is married to a physician.'

Patani started to ask Jagger about his own family but the pilot was dismissive.

'Divorced. Two kids. That sums it up.'

Undeterred, the Indian spoke over his shoulder to Sarah.

'Is Madam married?'

'Please, call me Sarah. No, I've escaped that fate so far.'

'She's waiting for the right chap,' added Jagger.

'He will be very lucky,' said Patani as the Mercedes rumbled over a rusting girder bridge.

Yes, he will thought Jagger, but he left his opinion unspoken.

They reached the Oceanic Hotel a few minutes later. It was fairly new, a two storey building with white stucco walls surrounded by palm trees, through which could be seen the dark sea beyond. Patani went with them to Reception to verify that the rooms were available and then took his leave, telling Jagger that he would phone in the morning to advise him when the car would arrive.

A porter with insolent eyes conducted them to their rooms, which were adjacent. It was agreed that they would meet in the bar for pre-dinner drinks in an hour's time. Jagger was relieved to find a serviceable air conditioner and an intact mosquito screen.

Satisfied, he undressed himself and made for the shower, allowing the hot water to sluice away his fatigue and then gradually turning down the temperature until it was just below blood heat. That was better. He felt almost civilised.

The bar was pretty full when Jagger went in. Mainly Brits, as far as he could judge. A few loud, pompous English voices punctuating the low murmur of a hundred conversations. Sarah showed up a minute later, stunning in a fresh blouse, skirt and sandals, unavoidably reminding Jagger of her cool femininity. He ordered a Gordon's and tonic for his companion and a lager for himself and they took their drinks to a table in the corner.

'Gulu was saying there are some good places to eat round here, but I'd be happy to have dinner in the hotel tonight,' said Jagger.

Sarah smiled. 'Suits me fine. It's been a long day. I'll be ready to hit the sack as soon as I've eaten. Perhaps we can go out tomorrow night.'

A waiter brought them two menus and they studied them silently.

'Good God! Sarah! What are you doing here?'

Jagger and the girl glanced up. There were four people looking at them. Two men and two girls, all in their twenties, judged Jagger. The voice belonged to a handsome bloke with blond hair and a wide grin on his face.

Sarah smiled at him. 'Hello, Spence. Fancy meeting you here.'

The man turned to his party. 'Chaps, allow me to introduce Sarah Amberley-Kemp, the most beautiful biochemist in the universe. And the cleverest.'

'How many others do you know?' asked Sarah.

'Enough.' He turned to Jagger. 'Excuse me, I don't think I've had the pleasure. You can't be Sarah's father—I've met him.'

The pilot was lost for an answer. Sarah filled the gap. 'This is Captain Wilf Jagger, my employer.'

The subject of the exchange found his voice. 'Shall we shorten it to plain "Wilf"?'

The foursome joined the twosome and names and fragments of information were passed around. It turned out that the one called Spence had been a fellow student of Sarah's at university. He was in Gambia on holiday with his fiancee, Marguerita, the petite brunette at his side. The other couple, Marcus and Joanne, were friends accompanying them. Jagger relapsed temporarily into the old envy. *Twerps with more money than sense.* But with an effort of will he dragged himself back to equanimity and set about the task of behaving sociably. Further conversation revealed that Sarah and Spence had once been intimate friends. The ex-boyfriend was surprised at the twist Sarah's life had taken.

'Flying? As a career? Are you serious, Sarah?'

'Deadly serious. Wilf is training me to be an airline pilot.'

The waiter returned to discover their intentions. Spence and his gang were going out to a local French restaurant and invited Jagger and Sarah to join them.

'You go if you want to,' said Jagger. 'I'll be asleep soon.'

'I'll eat here with Wilf,' said the girl.

'Hey, what are you two doing tomorrow? We're going out to the Abuko reserve. See the local fauna and flora, all that stuff. Do you want to come?'

Jagger spoke first. 'Thanks, but I'll have to dip out. I've got things to do.'

'I'd like to go, if Wilf doesn't mind.'

'You're off duty till Thursday morning,' said Jagger. 'You can do exactly as you please.'

The arrangements were made and Spence and his friends went off.

Over dinner, Sarah filled in a few more details about her erstwhile lover.

'We were going steady for over two years. It looked like we were heading for marriage and the happy-ever-after scene. Mummy and Daddy approved of him. Everything was hunky-dory.'

'What happened, or shouldn't I ask?' He remembered what she'd said to Patani about marriage. *I've escaped that fate so far.*

The girl paused for a moment. 'I realised there was something not quite right. Something . . . missing . . .'

Jagger held his silence, unsure what to say, whether to pry further.

'I loved him,' continued Sarah. 'But something inside told me it wouldn't last. When push came to shove I was too scared to go through with it. I broke it off.'

Despite tiredness dulling his mind, Jagger's own fondness for the girl drove him on. Sarah was allowing him a glimpse of her innermost self. The occasion might never arrive again.

'What about now? Have you . . ?' He stopped, stuck for the right words.

Sarah smiled. 'If you're asking me if there's a steady boyfriend, the answer is no. But if you're asking me . . .'

A waitress chose that moment to appear with coffee and the spell was broken. Jagger could sense the shutters closing in Sarah's mind. She would never finish her last sentence.

'Wilf, forgive me boring you with my dreary past.'

'Not at all. I just hope that your present is not too dreary for you.'

The girl briefly rested her hand on his arm. 'I'm happy enough. I've got most of the things I want . . . for now.'

They went up to their rooms together, Sarah's arm through his. At her door she brushed his cheek with her lips and whispered goodnight.

Alone in his own bed, it took Jagger a long time to get to sleep.

CHAPTER 14

Caroline Moore poured two cups of coffee and handed one to Gerry Chalmers, sprawled in an easy chair in the middle of the office. The other she took to her desk where she had been checking emails on the computer. She sat down and kicked off her shoes.

With Wilf Jagger away in Banjul, Caroline was guarding the fort. The task was not onerous. In effect she was fulfilling the role of human voicemail. There were a few clerical chores to occupy her but no earth-shattering decisions to make while her boss was away. Caroline didn't mind. She wasn't there for cerebral stimulation. Not that she didn't enjoy helping Jagger with his problems. The Chief Pilot had got into the habit of mulling things over with her and she was happy to join in when asked. Her work hours were flexible and she could usually take a day off when she wanted to. And it was not beneath her dignity to make lunchboxes for the pilots or to chauffeur her employer to and from work when his heap of a car was misbehaving. All in all Caroline was content with her job.

And so was Gerry Chalmers. As a casual labourer he too had plenty of free time. Meteor paid him by the hour and Jagger's money and various state benefits were adequate for his modest lifestyle. There was enough to pay for the basics of life, including beer and smokes and the miniscule rent on his little room. His widowed landlady took the balance of her dues in companionship.

Today Chalmers was doing some tidying up in the hangar in which Meteor rented space and had just come in for a break. Now he ran a work-blackened hand through his thinning frizzy ginger hair and cleared his throat.

'So Mr Bishop's going to be a Captain, then.' His voice was a high-pitched country burr.

'Looks like it, Gerry. We'll have three complete crews when the new boys have finished their training.'

'That plane'll be flying more. More work for the likes of you and me.'

'Don't you want more work? You'll get more pay.'

'I've got enough work and I've got enough pay. Mr Jagger'll have to get another man.'

Caroline sipped her coffee. 'Mike might be happy to earn more.' Mike Merriman was Meteor's other dogsbody, of course.

'So he might, love. But I don't think so. He's older than me, you know. Hasn't got my stamina.'

The secretary suppressed a smile. The words 'Gerry Chalmers' and 'stamina' were a contradiction in terms. Jagger had once told her that watching him at work was like watching a film running at half speed.

'Talking of which,' Caroline said now, 'are you available tomorrow night to help Mike? If not I'll book an airport loader.'

'I'll do it,' said the workman. 'He needs someone to keep an eye on him.'

The door opened and the airport postman came in.

'Morning, all. Any spare?'

Meteor was his last port of call and he usually tried to scrounge a cup of coffee.

'There's hot water in the kettle, Jack,' said Caroline. 'Help yourself.'

The postman tossed a few envelopes on the desk as he passed. The secretary idly picked them up and flicked through them. Mostly from officialdom as far as she could make out. As the two men mumbled platitudes at each other between gulps of coffee Caroline set to work with her paper knife. One of the missives brought a sigh. It was from the airport management, demanding again that Meteor dispose of Echo Victor, the partly-dismembered Merchantman that furnished spares for their serviceable plane. Wilf Jagger had remarked before that the wreck wasn't in anyone's way and wasn't doing any harm. 'Bloody image merchants don't want an old aircraft spoiling their pretty little airport,' he had scowled. But now the management were threatening legal action. Well, it would have to wait until Wilf got back from Banjul.

Caroline switched her attention back to the computer. She clicked the mouse on a new message from Euro Traders, the company who had booked Zulu Charlie for the following night. They were delivering a cargo of clothing manufactures for export to Düsseldorf.

There were one or two odd things about this charter. To start with, the company had initially approached Meteor directly, rather than through an agent. Wilf Jagger had been flattered. *Shows we're getting better known, Caro. Our reputation for cheerful and efficient service is spreading.*

Maybe. More puzzling was the veil of intrigue that Euro Traders had wrapped round the transaction. They had not confirmed the date of the flight until shortly beforehand. And they were adamant that the cargo should be flown out as soon as it was delivered. For something time-sensitive like perishable foodstuffs or livestock their concern would be understandable. But for clothes?

Now Caroline read the latest correspondence from their mysterious customer, closing her ears to the mindless banter of the two men in her office.

'. . . *we can now confirm the final arrangements for the charter to Düsseldorf. The merchandise will be delivered to East Midlands airport by Midland Freight Forwarding at 0300 hours or soon afterwards on Sunday morning.*

We understand that Meteor will organise reception of the cargo and its transfer onto aircraft pallets. As the cargo will already be loaded and secured onto Euro Traders pallets in accordance with the regulations notified to us by MFF the process will consist merely of transfer of these onto the Meteor pallets. Security clearance has already been arranged by MFF and all the necessary export documentation will accompany the cargo so that loading should proceed without delay. Two representatives of Euro Traders will be present while the merchandise is being transferred to verify that all arrangements are carried out as planned. Take off must be as soon as possible after delivery. Failure to adhere to these terms may invalidate the contract . . .'

Weird. Okay, Euro Traders were the customers and they had the right to dictate the terms of carriage. But they were behaving as if it were a military operation. A shiver of unease pulsed through Meteor's secretary. She scrolled to the bottom of the message and found a link to the company, which she clicked on.

Well, the website looked normal, advising anyone who cared to look that they were a dynamic new import-export company based in Nottingham. There was a link to the email address and a contact number. Hmmm.

On impulse she phoned MFF and was a little disappointed to discover that the contract seemed to be completely normal. They were expecting delivery of the cargo on the specified day for onward shipment.

Caroline shook her head. It still seemed an awful lot of fuss over a few clothes.

CHAPTER 15

'So, tell me about it.'

Jagger and Sarah were halfway through dinner at Le Fou, 'the best French restaurant in Africa' according to the sign outside.

'Some bits were more enjoyable than others.'

'Where did you get to?'

Sarah sampled her wine. 'We went to Banjul city first. Had a look round the market. From the parts I saw it's not an inspiring place. Ugly concrete buildings mostly. We were told that it started off as a military base built to try to stop the slave traders in the early 1800s.' She lowered her voice. 'It smelt like a toilet.'

'I didn't miss much then.'

'You would have enjoyed the nature reserve, Wilf. It's delightful. The pathways weave through these huge trees. You have to go on foot—they don't let cars in. It's a bird watchers' paradise. You've never seen such colourful plumage. There were some enclosed animals, lions and hyenas and what have you. I don't like to see living creatures trapped like that. But most of the animals are free to come and go. Antelopes, monkeys, crocodiles. The biggest lizard I've ever seen. We all thought it was spectacular, well worth the visit.'

'Didn't your friends want to join us for a meal tonight?'

Sarah hesitated. There were a few details about her day which were best kept from Jagger. Mainly the fact that Spence had paid her rather more attention than either she or his fiancee considered healthy. Meaningful glances, the occasional surreptitious squeeze from his hand or 'accidental' touching of thighs in the jeep. Sarah was acutely aware of Marguerita's disapproval even if the philanderer was not. Sarah managed to control the situation by the expedient of keeping her distance as much as possible, hoping that her efforts were appreciated by Marguerita. But by the time they arrived back at the Oceanic everyone in the party sensed a tension in the air and they got out of the jeep in silence. Spence had briefly attempted to restore harmony, suggesting with forced cheerfulness that they all dined together but the damage had been done. Marguerita coldly informed him that she had a headache and wanted an early night. Marcus and Joanne muttered that they would eat in the hotel restaurant. Sarah made her escape as soon as she decently could and went off to shower and change before meeting Jagger in the bar.

'Marguerita felt a bit tired and the other couple didn't want to come out,' said Sarah, answering Jagger's question with a half truth. She tilted her head coyly. 'My company not stimulating enough for you?'

'You'll do.'

Sarah hit a different chord. 'Are you sorry Hilary couldn't make it?'

'Yes, I think she would have enjoyed it. Maybe she can come on another trip sometime.'

The girl pressed on, emboldened by the wine. She decided to test her earlier hunch. 'Are you going out with her?'

Jagger was silent for a moment. 'We have been meeting socially, if that's what you mean.'

When no further elaboration was forthcoming Sarah tried again. 'Do you like her, Wilf?'

Another pause. 'Yes, I do.'

Sarah took another sip of wine. 'A lot?'

'What is this? The third degree? Listen, young lady—'

But his words died as the restaurant plunged into gloom. A power failure. A not infrequent occurrence in Gambia, as they had already discovered. But eyes quickly adapted to the golden light from the candles on the tables and the momentary silence was immediately invaded by a renewed buzz of conversation as the diners took up where they had left off. Leon, the self-styled 'mad Frenchman' who owned the restaurant, flitted from table to table like a bat, reassuring his customers.

'How can you cook when the power's off?' Jagger asked him, intrigued by the technicalities of the situation.

'No problem, monsieur. I 'ave another cooker. She uses gas from a bottle. You know, propane.'

The distraction had broken Sarah's train of thought. Her frown told Jagger that she was trying unsuccessfully to find the thread. She looked at him.

'Why are you smiling?'

'I'm showing my delight at sharing a candlelit dinner with a beautiful woman.'

'Don't be flippant.'

'I wasn't.'

Sarah's memory came back. 'Do you like her more than me?'

'How much do you like her?'

'You know that's not what I mean.' The alcohol in her bloodstream was sapping her powers of intellect. 'What I mean is . . . what do I mean?'

Jagger kept his silence and topped up his glass.

'I'll have some more, please,' said Sarah, pointing to her own glass.

It was practicality rather than chivalry that stopped him from complying. They had an early start the next morning. The last thing he needed was a hungover copilot. But by a sleight of hand he swapped the wine and water carafes on the table and filled her glass with the less dangerous liquid. As he had hoped, his companion was oblivious to the subterfuge.

Sarah was doggedly pursuing her theme. 'What I mean is . . . how can you like someone who is persecuting an innocent man?'

Jagger blinked. 'No, you've lost me.'

'Hilary . . . spying on Giles.'

Understanding dawned. 'Oh, that. She wasn't spying, Sarah, just observing what was going on at the party. She was only carrying out her duty.'

'I call it spying. The police have no reason to suspect Giles. Okay, he made a mistake in the past, but that was a long time ago. I tell you, my brother is as honest as the day is long.'

Jagger paused. 'Are you sure?' He remembered the snippet of conversation he had overheard at the party. Something suspicious was apparently being planned. Was Giles part of it?

Sarah's eyes darkened with anger. 'Yes, I'm sure. Why shouldn't I be?'

Jagger said nothing. No point in upsetting her further.

Sarah was in full flood. 'Wilf, they're wrong about Giles. Absolutely wrong. How can you have anything to do with that bloody policewoman? She's trying to destroy my brother, just like the rest of them . . .'

The girl fell silent and Jagger saw that she was now crying, her anger suddenly melted into sorrow.

The girl took a handkerchief out of her bag and dabbed her eyes. 'Take me back, please, Wilf,' she said quietly.

'Don't you want dessert?'

'I want to go back to the hotel. I'm sorry I've ruined your dinner.'

As if to obliterate the last remnants of their rapport the power chose that moment to surge back and the lights burst into life.

Lover's tiff, thought Leon as his two grim faced customers left the restaurant. *Quel domage, they looked to be getting on so well, even if he was too old for her.*

In the ramshackle taxi the two passengers were silent, Sarah's tearful sniffs gradually petering out as they approached the Oceanic.

'Do you want a coffee before you turn in?' Jagger asked as they walked into the hotel. 'I'm going to have one.'

Sarah tilted her head and bravely smiled. 'Yes, but here in the lobby. I couldn't stand facing Spence and the others in the bar if they're there.'

'Agreed.'

The coffee arrived.

'Wilf, I apologise for my outburst. Perhaps I had too much to drink. I shouldn't have insulted Hilary like that. I know she's only doing her job.'

Jagger was glad the girl was thinking positively. He pushed her along this track a bit more.

'Could be you're right about Giles and the police are wrong,' he said, wondering if his words might actually be true.

The girl nodded but didn't reply. Only a tinge of red round the eyes betrayed that she had been crying not long before.

Coffee finished, they walked to their rooms, not touching. But at her door Sarah reached for Jagger's arm. He turned to face her. Never before had she looked so beautiful to him, wistful smile, eyes now sparkling.

'You're a great person,' she said.

Jagger's voice was thick. 'It takes one to know one.'

And as he spoke the lights went out again. In the velvet darkness the two reached for each other and kissed, gently at first but soon with more urgency. The primaeval passion that couldn't be denied swept around and over and through them.

Sarah held his face in her two hands and forced him to break away.

'This won't do,' she said breathlessly.

Jagger caressed her hair. 'Do you want to make love?'

Still holding his face, the girl kissed the tip of his nose.

'Yes, I do. But I'm not going to.'

'Why not?'

'It would . . . spoil things. For both of us.'

Jagger sighed and slackened his embrace a little.

'You don't want to exceed the speed limit, is that it?'

'We mustn't even start the car.'

Their vision was now accommodating to the lack of light. Sarah looked deep into Jagger's eyes. 'We're not destined for each other, Wilf. I know I could fall for you if I let myself. Perhaps I'm a bit in love with you but that's not the way things are meant to be.'

'How are they meant to be?'

'I don't know.'

They kissed again, less hungrily this time, and parted with whispered goodnights.

For the second night running a troubled Wilf Jagger tossed and turned in his bed for a long time before sleep finally claimed him.

CHAPTER 16

Dmitry Chegolev's luxurious Boeing 767 had arrived the previous evening, as it usually did when the Russian's football team were playing at home. It was standard practice for any maintenance work required to be carried out by Britair Engineering on the Saturday while the big jet sat on the ground at East Midlands Airport. Sometimes the aircraft needed only basic turn-round servicing and refuelling. Chegolev's pilot would ask for the tanks to be filled, giving the 767 the range to return to San Francisco with more than adequate reserves. Sunday's preparations were therefore usually little more than uploading fresh catering for the tycoon, his staff and the plane's crew. Central Airlines dispatcher Michael Shepherd was well aware of the routine and had been closely monitoring it for several months. This particular Saturday he could easily see what was happening on the bizjet apron by looking out of the window in the Operations Room where he worked. It was the same picture—of the same aircraft—that had originally sowed in his mind the seeds of what Myron Winslade now called the Damocles Plan.

Yes, here we go! Shepherd saw a set of stairs being positioned towards the forward left passenger door of the Russian's plane. The handler driving the stairs extended the stabilisers and then jumped out of the cab. Shepherd watched him climb the stairs and remove the anti-tamper tell-tale tape that Security had stuck over the door operating handle. Within a few seconds the door was retracted up into the fuselage, leaving the entrance open. Shepherd was tempted to reach for the Ops Room binoculars to get a better view but then changed his mind. Mustn't do anything that might arouse suspicion!

'Wake up, Michael!'

The dispatcher jumped, suddenly realising Senior Controller Greg Barfield was standing beside his desk.

'Sorry Greg, what was it you asked me to do?' The dispatcher tried to keep the nervousness out of his voice.

'LMCs on the Heraklion. Captain's crapping himself with worry, silly old woman. Apparently you said you were going to send the revised load sheet ten minutes ago.'

'Yeah, sorry Greg. I did the amendments but must have forgot to transmit it. I'll do it now.'

'Good boy. Don't want a whingey pilot sending a non-compliance report to our glorious managers, do we?'

Quickly the dispatcher ran his eyes over the document on the screen in front of him. It showed the load disposition on the Heraklion flight scheduled to push back in less than a quarter of an hour. Four late reporting passengers had showed up and needed to be added as Last Minute Changes. Shepherd had made the alterations but had forgotten to send the new load sheet to the aircraft's ACARS communications system. He clicked on 'TRANSMIT' and a few seconds later was rewarded with a 'LOAD SHEET RECEIVED' message.

Barfield wandered off and the dispatcher was again alone, with nothing to do workwise for ten minutes or so. He got himself a coffee from the dispenser and resat himself at his desk. For the sake of appearances he picked up a newspaper but his eyes went outside again to the apron where the business jets were parked.

There were one or two people working on and around the 767. A fuel servicing truck was pumping tons of kerosene into the fuelling point under the left wing's leading edge through hoses connected to the underground distribution system port. From Sheperd's vantage point the scene was as he would have expected. He looked at his watch. He'd sent a coded text message to Fradini's mobile to advise him that it was time to start Damocles.

But out of the dispatcher's sight, on the other side of the aircraft, things were not exactly as normal. The large jet engine had its cowlings propped open to expose its innards, a maze of pipes and electrical cables. After a previous flight the engineers had noticed tiny metal fragments in the magnetic chip detector which had been traced to a failing bearing in the accessory gearbox. The gearbox had been changed but maintenance procedures required monitoring of the detector to prove the problem had been solved. Now engineer Andy Forsythe was pleased to note that the detector he held in his hand was clear of any contaminants. He quickly swapped the detector for the temporary plug in the engine, screwing it into the casing with only a few drops of oil lost. He tightened the detector as much as he could by hand and then remembered that a colleague had borrowed his torque wrench. He went off to find it, noting with a glance at his watch that he was already nearly half an hour past the end of his shift. By good fortune he bumped into another Britair engineer, Tim Harkness.

'Can you do me a favour, Tim? I'm supposed to be home and I'm already late.'

'What's the prob?'

'MCD check on the right engine. It's clean and I've put it back but it needs torquing and signing off.'

'Can do. You owe me one.'

'Thanks, mate.'

It is a well known fact that even though human beings have devised procedures to counter the effects of their naturally erratic behaviour the safeguards don't always work. Engineer Harkness had understood his colleague's request but hadn't attended to the matter straight away as he was busy on another job. When the 767's detector resurfaced in his 'things to be done' list his memory omitted the 'torquing' requirement, in other words tightening the detector in its housing to the degree specified in the aircraft's maintenance manual using a calibrated torque wrench.

Now, having verified that the detector was in its correct position, Harkness automatically tried to unscrew it by hand to check it was tight. By misfortune, the anti-clockwise twist he gave the detector was not as strong as the clockwise twist Forsythe had used. *Seems okay to me.* Satisfied that it was secure, he closed the engine cowlings and fastened the clips.

Andy Forsythe was a consciencious engineer. In the paperwork associated with the detector check he had taken the trouble to annotate the entry in the 767's technical log with the procedure's reference number. So the Maintenance Required section of the page read: *Right engine MCD removed IAW 45-19-2 for contamination check.* 'IAW' was engineer speak for 'in accordance with'. Back in the office Harkness opened the tech log and reread Forsythe's entry. *Good, won't have to look up the ref, Andy's already done it.* It was a pity that Harkness did not check the manual because the procedure instructions would have reminded him to check the torque setting. On such minor details significant events sometimes hinge.

So, in the Action Taken section of the page, Harkness wrote: *'Right engine MCD clear of contamination. Refitted IAW 45-19-2.'* As required by the rules he validated the entry with his official stamp and added his signature. *Job done.*

CHAPTER 17

At checkpoint Delta Security Officer Sally White took the proffered ID card and turned to the swipe scanner.

'It's a Gatwick ID,' said Fradini. 'I don't think your scanner can read it.'

'Okay,' smiled Sally, noting that engineer's overalls could do with a run through the washer. 'Plonk your bag on the belt, would you?'

Sally tapped the ID number into her keyboard while Dan Goodland, her seated colleague, watched the screen as the holdall passed through.

'Can I take a quick shufti?' he asked.

The American forced a grin. 'Of course.' *Will I have to run for it or bluff my way out of trouble with the cover story?*

Goodland unzipped the bag and lifted the top layer of clothes, a jacket and trousers, to check underneath. He reached down and took out a small wind-up torch, which he examined. Beneath these items were a clean shirt and change of underwear and beneath them . . . the fabric cover of the EP.

'Thank you,' said Goodland, dropping the torch back in the bag and refastening it. Simultaneously Sally handed back his ID card and took that of the next employee waiting to pass through, the leader of a team of chattering aircraft cleaners.

Fradini's smile was now genuine. 'Cheers, mate,' he responded, wondering how authentic his English accent sounded.

He let out a sigh of relief as the exit door closed behind him. *So far so good.*

Without pausing the American turned right and walked towards the Russian 767. There were steps at the left side forward passenger entrance, which was open. One of the fuellers was just closing the fuel station panel under the left wing, standing atop the ladder attached to the rear of the fuel servicing truck. His colleague was retracting the hoses into the vehicle.

Fradini went under the 767's tail and then turned to walk along the aircraft's right side, passing under the wing just outboard of the engine nacelle. Both the aft and forward cargo doors were closed. He continued forward, walked past the nose. A casual glance down to note the size the chock in front of the left nosewheel. *Standard size, shouldn't be a prob.* Fradini turned towards the steps to complete the circuit.

A voice called out. 'Can you sign for the fuel, boss? Save me taking the paperwork over to the office.'

Fradini walked as nonchalantly as he could over to the truck.

'Yeah, sure. How much went in?' It was a normal pilot response and the American immediately wondered whether the question might arouse suspicion. However, engineers also needed to know fuel uplift when writing up details in the tech log, so maybe it wasn't a bad mistake after all.

'You probably drained the airport dry, mate. Sixty-one three-twenty.' It was the litreage of kerosene which had been pumped into the aircraft's tanks. Almost fifty tonnes, plus whatever was in the tanks before refuelling. 'Get to Oz and back on that.'

Fradini smiled. 'Has the Russian got a footie team there, too?' He signed the docket with an illegible sprawl.

'Probably,' chuckled the fueller as he handed back the top copy. He waved goodbye and climbed into the cab where his colleague was already sitting behind the steering wheel.

The truck pulled away with a growl of diesel. Tucking the fuel docket into a pocket, Fradini walked back to the steps and went up to the passenger entrance. This was a tricky moment. He might bump into other engineers or personnel servicing the 767. He would just have to smile at them and hope they didn't challenge him. Hopefully his Britair overalls and hi-viz jacket would be adequate disguise. There were also CCTVs covering the area, but with luck anyone monitoring the screens would not pay particular attention to a Britair engineer working on the aircraft.

Having entered the passenger door Fradini turned right and slowly walked through the cabin, which seemed to be empty.

Wow! Talk about luxury! Instead of the two to three hundred seats usually to be found in a Boeing 767 the forward cabin had leather covered fully reclining sleeper seats for about twenty passengers, each with its own entertainment system, computer station, bag storage area and wardrobe. The seats could be individually curtained off for privacy. There were four commodious toilets. Aft of this cabin was a well appointed cocktail bar and further aft again two separate conference rooms, equipped with the sort of communications equipment and high tech facilities you would expect in a modern office. *Now where . . . ah, there they are.* Fradini noted the location of the overwing emergency exits in the forward conference room area, two each side.

There was a spacious galley for meal preparation and then came the individual cabins. There seemed to be eight of these, accessed from a corridor on the left side. Each cabin had a bed, wardrobe, writing desk and chair, armchair, large TV, computer station and shower.

Decision time. *Do I check out the rest of the plane and the flight deck now or stay in one of these cabins until Security close the plane up again? If I carry on wandering around I might come across other people, engineers or whatever. Best to stay here for now.*

Fradini chose one of the individual cabins, dropped his holdall on the floor and flopped onto the bed. Very comfy. He took his mobile out of his pocket and tapped a coded message to Shepherd.

Good. All I have to do now is wait.

CHAPTER 18

'Ah, dear old Blighty.'

Jagger had been fiddling with the weather radar. A luminous green blur pulsated at the top of the screen. He tapped it with his finger. 'Land's End.'

It was eight hours since they had left Banjul laden with exotic ladies' wear. The flight plan had initially taken them to Casablanca for a refuelling stop. Jagger anticipated that half an hour should see them airborne again. It was not to be. When Sarah called for engine start the Tower advised them in heavily accented English of 'indefinite delay.' Jagger took over the radio, trying to keep the irritation out of his voice.

'This is Meteor 116, please explain the reason for the delay.'

This transmission was ignored, as was the identical, more emphatic, follow-up.

'Either they don't understand or they're being bloody minded,' scowled Jagger.

Sarah had a go, speaking fluent French. Her reward was a friendly reply in the same tongue. She was amused at Jagger's twitching eyebrows. He obviously couldn't decide whether to be angry at the Moroccans for ignoring him, angry with Sarah for succeeding where he failed, jealously dismissive of her linguistic skills, or pleased that they were getting through at last.

'There's a problem with French Air Traffic,' the girl translated. 'They've cut the flow rate through their airspace. We're stuck here until we get a slot, I suppose.'

Jagger shook his head. 'Oh, no, we're not. Look, tell them we'll refile our flight plan. We'll route towards Santiago then out to the west of the Bay of Biscay. That'll keep us out of French airspace.'

Sarah was troubled. Vague shadows formed in her mind. 'Can we do that legally? We've got no nav capability if the GPS fails again and we've got no HF.' She meant that they had no alternative means of navigating over the sea and no High Frequency radio to report their progress to Oceanic Air Traffic Control. At least on the flight to Tenerife they had been operating within the law—just.

The captain turned to her. 'They don't know that, do they? We'll be alright down at twenty-one thousand. There'll be no-one else to collide with. All the other stuff'll be well above us. We'll pretend our HF went duff after we took off and get other aircraft to relay our position reports on VHF.'

Jagger's words did little to ease her disquiet. She knew that what he intended was probably safe enough. Any doubts on that score and she would have got off the aircraft there and then. It came to a simple choice. Either wait for God knows how long for a legal passage through French skies or else bend the rules more than a little and route over the Atlantic. In the end her sense of pragmatism overpowered her sense of propriety and she went along with his suggestion.

Fortunately the ruse worked as planned. This time there were no jets to follow but in response to their prayers the GPS kept on going and led them accurately over the grey waste of water.

The early start to their day had weakened the pilots' resistance to drowsiness and there were no mental stimuli to fight it off. Jagger succumbed first. Sarah let him have half an hour but by then her own eyelids were losing the battle against gravity. She woke the captain up in case she dropped off herself. Jagger, relatively refreshed, allowed her to doze undisturbed. When she came to, he was peering at the weather radar, watching the tip of Britanny sliding down the side of the scope. Sarah was relieved. It at least proved they weren't lost over the middle of the Atlantic.

Even when they were both awake few words passed between the pilots. But it was a comfortable silence. When they had met at breakfast Jagger was clearly on edge, not knowing what to say. Sarah had put her hand on his and told him how much she had enjoyed the previous evening.

'Even the last bit?'

'Even the last bit.'

'Does that mean . . ?'

'It means we're friends, Wilf. Nothing more.'

The best I can hope for, conceded Jagger to himself.

Now their two heads drew closer to examine the radar scope. The green blur expanded towards them and a scattering of fragments speckled the screen at closer range.

'Scilly Isles,' explained Jagger. 'Nearly home.'

Soon their navigation radios picked up the beacon at Land's End.

'Plain sailing from here on in,' said the captain.

They checked in with London Control. Inexplicably the reassuring radio contact was an anti-climax for Sarah. As the rocky promontory of England's foot reached out to them she realised that her little African adventure was over. In less than an hour Zulu Charlie would touch its tyres onto the runway at East Midlands.

Sarah couldn't prolong the flight but she could maybe hang on to her companion for a while longer.

'Wilf, what are you doing when we get back?'

The captain grunted. *Check Bernie and Bish are okay for the Düsseldorf tonight. Check emails. Collect reams of paperwork from the office, take it home. Shove dirty clothes in washing machine. Clear mouldy food out of fridge. Nip out for a pizza. Sink a pint at the local. Crash out.*

'Light domestic duties,' he summarised.

'Why not come back and have dinner with me at home?'

Jagger looked at her. In the old days it would have been impossible to resist a jibe about making things difficult for Cook and the butler. Now he paused before responding.

'That's very kind. Are you sure it's convenient?'

'Of course. Mummy and Daddy will be there, possibly Bron too. Giles is going out to dinner somewhere with his girlfriend, a charity do or something. I'm sure my parents would like to get to know you. You didn't really meet them properly at the party, did you?'

'Do both your brothers live at the Grange?'

Sarah shook her head. 'Giles is a permanent resident at the moment until he's sorted out something for himself. Now his . . . troubles . . . are behind him and he's got regular work I expect he'll want his independence again soon.'

Jagger wasn't so sure about Giles's troubles being over but he said nothing except: 'And the other one?'

Sarah chided him with a laugh. 'You can say the name "Bron", you know. Your tongue won't fall off. No, he's only staying for a while. A working holiday, he told me. He's got a place of his own down in Surrey. Tennis court, swimmimg pool, stables, acres of ground, the lot.'

Probably a Lombard. Jagger remembered the derisive acronym from a TV programme he had seen. *Loads Of Money But A Real Dickhead.* He would not be disappointed if he did not meet this pair, the druggie and the city slicker. But Sarah's company was something he could put up with.

'How about I take you out for dinner instead?'

'No, you come to the Grange. Betty won't mind an extra place at the table.'

'Betty?'

'The cook.'

'Of course.'

The girl looked at him, ready to tell him off, but his smile was mischievous rather than cynical.

'Okay, that's settled.'

*****

Jagger landed Zulu Charlie not long after five o'clock. The freighter hit the runway firmly and bounced.

'Ouch!' commented Jagger as he wrestled the aircraft back to the ground. The second touchdown was less shattering to the Merchantman's structure and to the captain's ego.

'Hopeless,' he muttered as Sarah pulled the props into fine pitch. 'What did I do wrong, do you reckon?'

Zulu Charlie slowed to taxying speed and the copilot engaged the control locks. 'Late flare?' she ventured, realising Jagger was converting his embarrassment into a training point.

'Correct, and I probably called for idle power too soon.'

'I did wonder . . . but you know best!'

Jagger laughed. 'Well, you won today's landing competition. A greaser at Casablanca.'

Sarah smiled impishly. 'I've got a good instructor.'

'And so you have. Okay, after landing checks, please.'

'Yessir!'

They taxied in and shut down and a few minutes later walked into the Meteor portacabin. Caroline, the secretary, did not normally work on Saturdays and the only other person in the room was Nathan Bishop, absorbed in the documents and charts covering the table in front of him. He looked up briefly, muttered 'Hi, children,' then bent to his task again.

Meteor's Chief Pilot picked up the bundle of envelopes Caroline had opened and left on the desk top. *Mainly bills by the look of it.* He flicked through the addresses to see who his new creditors were. With a grunt of disapproval he dropped the offending missives back onto the desk and sauntered over to check what his senior-copilot-soon-to-be-most-junior-captain was up to.

'When's take off, Bish?'

'Not till the wee hours.'

'Well, I've heard of enthusiasm but coming in to work this early is overdoing it a bit, isn't it?'

'I'm a pro, man,' said Bishop without raising his eyes. 'This is unfamiliar territory for me. It's a while since I've been to Düsseldorf.' He tapped the charts on the table. 'I'm doing all this planning stuff now. Then I'll go home and get some shut-eye before the trip.'

Jagger decided a bit of encouragement was called for. 'First go in the left hand seat, eh? Our new fledgling Captain stretches his wings for the first time. Anyway, you'll have Bernie keeping his beady eye on you. I hope it goes well for you.'

Now Bishop looked up. 'Thanks, boss. It'll be cool.'

'Yes, good luck, Nathan.' This from Sarah, who had been sitting at the other table finishing off the paperwork for the trip they'd just completed.

Jagger noticed the way she looked at Bishop, the sparkle in her eyes speaking volumes. *So that's it. That's how the land lies. How come I never noticed before? Deluding myself she might fancy me when all the time it's Bish she's fallen for. Talk about chalk and cheese.* Jagger looked for a signal from Bishop, a reciprocation. But he just smiled at her and threw a casual half wave.

The three were silent for a few minutes, each engrossed in clerical chores. Sarah was the first to speak again.

'That's the Banjul paperwork done, Wilf.' She was sliding the documents into one of the large brown envelopes purchased for precisely this purpose. The records of each and every flight Zulu Charlie did were stored in individual envelopes and stacked in a cupboard. Navigation logs, fuel calculations, cargo manifests, aircraft weight computations, weather reports, administrative records. It was not that the Chief Pilot was graced with a sense of history or nostalgia. It was the law. After the statutory six month period had elapsed the contents of the envelopes were unceremoniously dumped into the recycling bin for disposal. Ever alert to the possibilities of frugality, Jagger had instructed Caroline to re-use the envelopes until they were too tatty to be of further service.

'Okay, Sarah, thanks. You push off now. I'll follow in a while.'

'I'll tell Betty you're eating with us. You're sure you can remember the way to the Grange?'

'No problem, assuming my car starts.'

Again Bishop looked up from his work. 'Hey, dinner at Orchard Lea. You're moving in high society now, Wilf.'

'I'm planning to shower and change when I get home,' said Sarah to Jagger. 'You can do the same when you arrive, if you want, Wilf. I'm sure I'll be able to find one of my brothers' shirts for you to wear.'

Jagger could feel the grime of a long day's work clinging like a film to his body. 'Yes, I might take you up on that.'

At the door Sarah turned to Bishop. 'Best of luck tonight,' she repeated. Again her eyes gave her away and this time Jagger noticed the wistful smile and wink she received in return. *He's got the message alright.*

With Sarah's departure silence descended once more. Jagger went through the letters on Caroline's desk with closer scrutiny, sorting them into those which could be safely ignored for a short while and those which could be ignored for longer. He switched on his laptop and accessed his emails. His brow furrowed.

'Strange,' he muttered, reading one of the messages.

Evidently deciding that no response was called for Bishop kept his attention on his work.

'Euro Traders,' continued Jagger, 'what do we know about them?'

This time Bishop made a contribution. 'They're the charterers for this trip tonight.'

'Yes, I know. I take it the stuff hasn't arrived yet, then?'

The younger pilot shook his head. 'Coming later apparently.'

'Yeah, that's what it says here. "Arriving at 0300 or soon afterwards. Take-off must be as soon as possible after delivery",' Jagger paraphrased. A light flashed on in his memory. 'Now I remember. They're the people who paid my asking price without argument. With a fifty percent advance.'

'That is weird,' commented Bishop.

'How much cargo?'

Bishop pointed to the partially completed freight manifest document on his own laptop screen.

'Just under five tonnes, give or take. Seventy boxes at sixty-six kilos each, plus the weight of the pallets.'

'Clothes, it says here. That's all we seem to carry these days.'

'Yeah.'

'How are you going to load them, Bish?'

'Well, according to the instructions in the attachment each of their pallets will have eighteen boxes in two stacks of nine. Their pallets are smaller than our our metal ones so we can load them straight onto ours. Eighteen boxes on each pallet. So . . . four pallets we'll need.'

'CG?'

'I'll put the load over the wings and go for an aft CG to reduce trim drag for max fuel economy.' Bishop was referring to the aircraft's centre of gravity, which would be affected by the disposition of the cargo. 'If we put the load in stations four to seven we'll get about 28 percent chord.' The pilot was saying that the aircraft's centre of gavity would be between a quarter and a third of a wing width back from the leading edge. There would be empty spaces in front of and behind the line of four pallets. It was standard practice to concentrate partial loads in the overwing area of the fuselage to reduce stresses on the nose and tail sections.

'What's the aft limit?' Jagger was testing Bishop's knowledge of the limitations.

'Thirty-one point two at this weight.'

'Sounds good.' Jagger came over to view Bishop's screen. 'Five tonnes. Not much for our bird.' The Merchantman could lift more than three times this weight. 'I'm surprised they didn't find a smaller aircraft. Save their money.'

'We're probably the cheapest.'

'But price didn't seem important to them.'

The younger pilot shrugged. 'Are we bothered, Wilf? It's an easy job and they've paid a big chunk in advance. He who pays the piper calls the tune and all that crap . . .'

'Yes, you're right. I'm worrying too much. The date and time they choose to deliver the freight isn't our business. Nor is the weight unless it's too heavy for our ship.'

'Look on the bright side, Wilf. If they like our style we might get repeat orders.'

'Yeah,' agreed Jagger. 'And the rates they're happy to pay would help to keep the wolves from the door.' He switched off his computer, stacked the letters into Caroline's in tray and stretched, fending off the anaesthesis of fatigue. 'Right, that's it for today. I'm off.'

'Give my regards to Giles if you see him.'

Jagger looked at his employee. 'I don't think he'll be at home. He's going out somewhere tonight apparently.' After a moment's contemplation he said: 'Forgive my asking, Bish, but are you a close friend of the family?'

The younger pilot tapped his pen against his chin, delaying the answer.

'Yeah, you could say that. I've known Giles for ages.'

Treading carefully through the minefield Jagger lobbed the next question.

'What about Sarah?'

'What about her?'

'I get the impression she's keen on you.'

'Uh-huh.'

Bishop's tone discouraged Jagger from pursuing the matter. 'Yep, I understand. It's none of my business.'

Bishop gave him a disconcertingly direct stare. 'You may be right, Wilf. If she fancies me as much as I do her it could be the romance of the century.'

'I thought you were spoken for already.'

'Miranda, you mean? She can't make up her mind. There's a bloke with a big wallet after her and I think she might go for it.'

'Doesn't it bother you?'

Bishop paused before replying. 'Doesn't do much for my pride, I guess. Otherwise, no great loss. We've had our moments.'

Jagger found himself blurting out: 'Don't hurt Sarah.'

Bishop raised his eyebrows. 'Wilf, my friend, are you saying . . ?'

The Chief Pilot hid his emotion in a growl. 'I'm not saying anything.'

'I know how it is, mate. Sarah's special. I could go stupid over that girl.'

'It's just a shame about her brother, though,' said Jagger.

'What do you mean?'

The older man spoke cautiously, measuring his words.

'Bish, is Giles on the level?'

'Explain.'

'I hope I'm not causing offence. You say he's a close friend of yours.'

'So?'

Jagger sighed. 'It's just that the police think he may be involved with drugs people again.'

Bishop's face darkened. 'Total crap. He's as straight as you are. Okay, he's got a dodgy past. But that was ages ago. No, man, you're way off the beam there.'

'Look, Bish, I have to tell you this. I overheard a suspicious conversation when we were at Bron's party. The police think there's some sort of deal being done. They think that Central dispatcher is part of it and maybe Giles too.'

The other pilot didn't try to hide his anger.

'Whatever you heard, chum, you're wrong about Giles.' Bishop started to rise from his seat but suddenly he checked himself and seemed to calm down. 'Micky Shepherd may be a bad lot. I don't know him that well. Giles is a good bloke. Believe me.'

'So you're not a friend of Shepherd yourself?'

'Do me a favour.'

'But the police think Giles may be in it, linked to Shepherd.'

'Then they're wrong.'

There didn't seem to be anything more to say. Jagger was surprised at such a vehement defence from Bishop for his friend. Was there something amiss about that? *Methinks he doth protest too much . . .* A dark shadow formed in the Chief Pilot's mind. *Surely Bish himself isn't wrapped up in all this? He was in that damned photo, after all.*

Unsettled, Jagger put on his coat to leave. He made an effort to restore harmony by adding his own good wishes for the Düsseldorf trip.

The response was a cool 'Yeah.'

Jagger could think of nothing else to say to repair the damage. He shrugged, picked up his bag and walked out of the door.

CHAPTER 19

On the A14 near Bury St Edmunds the late afternoon Saturday traffic was not heavy. The eastbound eighteen wheeler articulated truck cruised comfortably at fifty, driver Chas Lummick accompanied by two other men in the cab.

'How far now?' asked Lester McAndrew, sitting on the left side.

'The Tom-Tom says nine miles,' said Ron Maynard pointing at the satnav screen attached to the dashboard. 'We hit the turn-off for the A1101 in a couple of miles.'

'Are you sure you put the right numbers in?'

'Yes, I'm sure.'

All three men were petty criminals of one sort or another and all were currently on the payroll of Myron Winslade, who had also paid the rental on the truck they were now driving to the rendezvous. In the truck trailer were four large wooden pallets holding the Casu-Wear cardboard boxes. The label attached to each box stated '*100 Pairs High Quality Vaquero Denim Jeans*' but the contents of some of the boxes no longer matched what the label said. Two days previously Michael Shepherd and Ron Maynard had met at the Beeston lock-up. Inside the building they had removed the protective sheeting the dispatcher had previously draped over the boxes. Shepherd cut the sealing tape on the boxes in the top layers, Maynard opening each box in turn and throwing out 20 odd pairs of jeans.

More intricate surgery was required on four of the boxes. Some of their sides and bases were cut away and the remaining sections taped together, making a large cardboard container two boxes high and two in length. The tape joining the sections was positioned inside the construction so that from the outside it had the appearance of four individual boxes. On the top surface of the construction Shepherd cut a flap in the cardboard and bent it so that it could cover or reveal a square aperture approximately five centimetres across.

The final part of the task had been to wind pallet wrap tightly round each pallet to halfway up the top layer of boxes. The plastic wrapping would secure the boxes during onward transit. Later on during the operation the pallet wrapping would be extended to fully cover the boxes.

Now the four pallets sat in the trailer of the truck cruising along the A14. Despite removal of some of the box contents, each pallet weighed over a tonne. Fortunately Myron Winslade had paid the extra and hired a truck whose trailer incorporated rollers in the floor, so that it was not too difficult for the three men to manoeuvre them into position.

'Here we are,' said Chas, dropping through the gears as he slowed to turn left on to the narrower A1101.

*****

When Prison Officer Harry Ford had boasted to prisoner Maurice Holmin that he had decoded the cryptic email Holmin had sent out he was bluffing. He had mulled over the strange lists of pop songs but could make nothing of them. In frustration he had passed the printout to a friend who was an ace at pub quiz questions. The friend took less than ten minutes to find the solution.

'Lat and long, Harry.'

'What?'

'Latitude and longitude. "Normal" means "north" and "Extra" means "east". They're geographical coordinates.'

'So it refers to a location?'

'Correct. Look at the "Normal" list. Four songs. Now find where they are in the main list of sixty-two songs. I've added sequence numbers to the list so you can work it out.'

Ford perused the list. 'Right, the songs are numbers 52, 18, 41 and 2. Which means . . .'

'52 degrees, 18 minutes, 41 point 2 seconds North.'

'Amazing. But that won't work on the "Extra" list. There are only three songs.'

'Well, I reckon that's because the first number is zero. So the longitude is zero degrees, 37 minutes, 15 point 9 seconds East.'

'Where the hell is that?'

'About 30 miles north of here. If you look on Google Earth it's a spot on the A1101, a lay-by about six miles north-west of Bury St Edmunds.'

'Okay. I wonder what the significance of that is.'

'Can't say, Harry. If the decode is correct it's in the middle of nowhere.'

Ford wasn't sure what to do with the new information. One day he drove to the spot himself, parked in the lay-by and took a look around. Nothing. Just a litter-strewn stretch of crumbling concrete on a nondescript curve of road. If he passed his knowledge to the authorities, what could they do? Keep an eye out for suspicious activity? If Holmin's outside contacts saw the police sniffing round they would report back to the prisoner, which meant Ford might not get his payment and might also be 'punished' for his betrayal. *Remember the poor sod Maurice dragged along behind his car until there wasn't much left of him. So, sit tight and wait for the dosh. Always assuming, of course, that the decode was correct in the first place. But it must be right. Otherwise Maurice would not have agreed to pay me, even if he suspected I might not have worked out the code. He couldn't take the chance.*

Ford's pub quiz friend had indeed hit upon the right answer. The numbers he had worked out were the same numbers that Ron Maynard had inputted into the artic's satnav and which now brought the vehicle to the same spot that Ford had reconnoitred. Chas Lummick manoeuvred the truck onto the lay-by and switched off the engine. He and his two chums knew they had a few hours to wait. Lester McAndrew put a Shania Twain disc into the CD player and Chas produced a pack of cards.

CHAPTER 20

Jagger knew he was out of his place. His jitters started when he drove up the gravel driveway in his wreck of a Cavalier. It was a rerun of the time he had come to the Grange for Sarah's brother's party. This time the huge oak door was opened to him by a character out of an old black and white Ealing film. Ancient, wrinkled, myopic and apparently hard of hearing, he was formally attired in a dark suit which was at least one size too big. The pilot scanned his memory banks. He had met Sarah's father briefly at the party. This superannuated creature wasn't him.

'Follow me, Mr Jackson. Miss Sarah asked me to show you to the drawing room. I believe she is completing her toilet.'

'Excuse me. Jagger, not Jackson.'

'As you say, sir.'

The butler, as Jagger supposed him to be, offered him a sherry and asked him to make himself comfortable. Alone in the cavernous room, the pilot shuffled uneasily around the furniture, his scruffy shoes sinking deep into the pile of an acre of Chinese rug. Try as he might, he couldn't stop himself comparing the opulence of his surroundings against the dingy hovel he called home. Either side of the stone hearth bookshelves stretched from floor to ceiling and from corner to corner. A grand piano lived at one end of the room. At the other end the heavy curtains had not yet been drawn over the windows which in daylight looked onto the lake. Now the panes were black against the white framework. The soft light from two chandeliers made the room less unwelcoming to its uneasy guest.

A short while later Sir Hugh and Lady Elizabeth Amberley-Kemp appeared and reintroduced themselves, apologising for the absence of their sons, who were both apparently out with separate groups of friends. Sarah's parents were followed by their daughter, fresh and vibrant in a cream blouse and beige skirt, reminding Jagger that he could do with a clean-up and change himself.

Evidently Sarah read his thoughts. 'When you've finished your drink, Wilf, you can use the shower if you want. I'll look out some bits and pieces from Giles' wardrobe that should fit you.' She took a sip from her wine glass and then left the room.

The affability of his employee's parents put Jagger more at ease and he opened up a bit. The conversation swung towards business, Jagger suggesting that Meteor's problems were tiny compared to the headaches of running a major corporation.

'Well, Brycewood has had its difficulties over the years, that's for sure,' said Sir Hugh. 'Fortunately at the moment things are chugging along smoothly. Plus I've got some good people helping me to run the show. It must be harder for you, doing all the management tasks yourself.'

'I get by okay,' replied Jagger. 'Like you, I've got good people working for me.'

'Including Sarah?'

'Including Sarah.'

'I'm pleased to hear that,' said Sir Hugh. 'I remember when we last met that you told me you wouldn't hesitate to sack her if she was . . . unsuitable.'

Jagger winced inwardly, unable to avoid remembering his rudeness when he had previously met Sarah's parents. 'I'm sometimes short on diplomacy, Sir Hugh. I apologise. Your daughter has taught me lessons in courtesy that I shouldn't really have forgotten.'

'Don't mention it,' came the reply. 'I would rather deal with someone who spoke his mind than a sychophant who told me only what he thought I wanted to hear. I've come across quite a few of those in my time, I can assure you.'

Lady Elizabeth put her hand on Jagger's arm. 'Wilf, would it be possible for me to see the plane that Sarah flies? I still can't quite visualise my little girl at the controls of a big plane. I wouldn't have thought she would be physically strong enough to do it.'

'Well, that's an interesting technical point, Lady Elizabeth—'

Sarah's mother interrupted him. 'Just Liz, please Wilf.' She turned and smiled at her husband. 'And Hugh for the old man.'

'The controls will be hydraulically powered, I take it,' said Sir Hugh.

'No, that's the clever thing,' explained Jagger. 'Only the landing gear and flaps are driven hydraulically. The flight controls are moved by tabs. You see, when you move the control wheel or rudder, you're just moving small tabs hinged to the trailing edges of the main surfaces. It's the airflow past the tabs that moves the main controls. Very old-fashioned, but it works.'

'Fascinating,' murmured Lady Elizabeth, not understanding a word.

'But yes, I'd be delighted to show you our big bird,' continued the pilot. 'You could come on a flight with Sarah, if you wanted, with either myself or Bernie as Captain.'

'Oh Wilf, that would be lovely,' said Lady Elizabeth, smiling again.

'And you too . . . Hugh . . . you'd be welcome.'

The Chairman of the Brycewood orporation nodded. 'Yes, I might take you up on that, old boy.'

'I'll have my secretary give you a call to make arrangements. When would be a good time for her to—'

Jagger stopped in mid-sentence because Sarah had just swept into the room, a frown on her face and a sheet of paper in her hand, which she waved at the others.

'I've just found this in one of Giles' drawers. I don't know what to make of it.' Sarah looked flustered.

Her employer took it from her and ran his eyes over the text, puzzlement shaping his face. 'What the hell is this about?'

SCHEDULE SUMMARY (PHASE 8) FOR H5

Date: 19/03 H5 will meet B2 at F2 to confirm final arrangements.

Date: 20/03 A1 will make the go/no-go decision and advise all parties in Appendix 2 accordingly. Q3 will arrange to take the 767 from EMA at 2000 hours. It is expected that Objective One will be achieved by 2300 20/03 and Objective Two by 0300 21/03. Timing is not critical as long as the mission is not compromised.

Date: 21/03 H5 will contact C5 to arrange meeting for completion of financial transactions. C3 will initiate Phases 9 and 10 and notify H5 accordingly.

NOTE: Only those persons listed in Appendix 1 have the authority to abort the mission. Other persons encountering difficulties must contact one of the listed persons for instructions.

Sarah's concern had communicated itself to her father. 'What's the matter, darling?' he asked.

'I don't know,' said Sarah. 'It's crazy. EMA is East Midlands Airport. What can it mean? Q3 will take the 767 at 2000 hours. 'Take' as in catch a flight as a passenger or . . . '

Jagger began to marshal his thoughts. 'Either it's a wind-up or else it's something dodgy going on. Look at this date—it's tonight. I think we should tell the police, let them check it out.'

'No!' said Sarah, so vehemently that the others turned to her. 'Not the police—not yet. I know Giles is out at a do of some sort tonight. That's probably got nothing to do with this. I'm not having the police harrassing him for no good reason. I suggest we find out about it ourselves.'

Jagger's features hardened. 'Look, Sarah, if this is for real then the police must be informed. Just because Giles is your brother, it doesn't mean he should be protected if he's doing something wrong.'

'Giles?' said Sir Hugh. 'What's he been up to this time?' His wife's smile had vanished and she suddenly looked ten years older.

'Nothing, Daddy, I'm sure. There's probably an innocent explanation for this information and why it was in his room. It might just be a heap of nonsense, a joke of some sort. The police won't thank us if we send them off on a wild goose chase. Some people are too suspicious for their own good,' she hissed at Jagger.

'Okay, okay,' conceded her employer. 'Forget the police for the moment. But I'm going to the airport to see for myself. I'll phone Security on the way. They can check it out. They might decide to call the police.'

'Fair enough. But please leave Giles out of it.'

'Okay. I promise I won't mention Giles. How's that?'

Sarah considered for a moment. 'Alright, Wilf, I trust you. Giles has had a difficult time recently and he deserves to be left in peace.'

Jagger nodded, but said nothing. *A difficult time of his own making. Well, I'll shop him if necessary, even if it means breaking my promise to Sarah.*

There was a polite cough from the open doors. It was Sharples, the butler. 'Dinner will be served in two minutes, if you are ready, Madam.'

Lady Elizabeth looked at he others, searching for guidance.

'Well, Wilf?' asked Sir Hugh.

'I'm sorry,' he said, waving the paper. 'I've got to sort this out.'

The head of the household addressed his servant. 'It'll just be Lady Elizabeth and myself and Sarah, then, Robert. Apologies to Betty.'

'Very good, sir.'

The mood of bonhomie well and truly shattered, Jagger took his leave of his hosts and got into his car.

'Sod it,' he cursed when it refused to start. He walked back to the large oak front doors and rang the bell.

It was Sarah who answered.

'Bloody car won't start.'

'We'll take mine,' said the girl. 'I'll tell Daddy what's happened. Let me get a jacket. Have you got your ID?'

The red VW Polo was soon driving along the road leading back to the airport. After a minute's strained silence, Jagger spoke.

'We'd better call Security . . . oh damn, my mobile's in my car. Have you got yours with you?'

'No, it's at home.'

Jagger gave her a sideways look.

'Are you suggesting I'm lying?' asked the girl with an edge in her tone.

'Look, Sarah, brother or no brother, we call Security as soon as we get there.'

The girl responded through clenched teeth. 'Okay.'

They parked in front of Meteor House to find the office dark and deserted. Jagger let himself and the girl in, switched on the light and immediately picked up the phone. He punched in a sequence of numbers and then let out an exasperated sigh.

'I don't believe it. The number's engaged.'

'I'll check the departure page. See what's leaving at 8 o'clock.' Sarah switched on the monitor on Jagger's desk and clicked on the menu to access the Airport Operations Departures page. The layout was similar to those displayed throughout the airport terminal but with extra data included, such as aircraft type and registration, expected load and estimated delays. The girl ran her finger down the screen.

'Central have a 767 leaving at 1940 for Warsaw—' she looked at her watch '—about now . . . then the next 767 is an Albion flight to Perpignan at 2055. The only stuff going around 20 hundred is a Trans Ocean MD11 to New York and a Fedex A330 to Miami.'

Jagger came and stood behind her, looking over her shoulder. 'What else is going out tonight?'

Sarah scrolled down the screen with the mouse. There was nothing that tied in with the slip of paper found in Giles' room. Near the bottom of the screen was MTR 231, aircraft type VC9F, departure time estimated 0400, destination DUS. It was Meteor's Merchantman Zulu Charlie, bound for Düsseldorf. Bish and Bernie, pilots for the flight, would both be at home at that moment to get some sleep prior to reporting for duty.

Jagger grunted and redialled Security. 'Shit, why can't you get hold of these people when you need them?' He looked at Sarah. 'I'll take a look airside anyway. Do you want to go home or wait here? I'm a bit stuffed without a car.'

'Now I'm here I may as well stick with you.'

'Okay. I'll tell Security what we're doing when we go through.'

'Wilf, can I give Giles a call on his mobile? He might be able to explain all this.'

Jagger was silent, evidently deciding what his response should be. He knew he should refuse, in case Giles warned off his fellow conspirators, if that's what this was all about. He looked at Sarah's pleading eyes.

'Okay.'

The girl took the office phone from Jagger and punched the buttons. 'Damn,' she said tersely, 'he's got it switched off. It's his voicemail message.' She paused, obviously waiting for the record tone.

'Darling, it's Sarah. Please give me a call as soon as you get this message. It's important. I'll be at home later this evening. Bye.' She hung up.

'Right, let's get going,' said Jagger, his face grim. He handed Sarah a Meteor hi-viz jacket and donned one himself.

They walked briskly to Security checkpoint Alpha, the nearest to Meteor's base. The officer swiped their IDs and watched them walk through the scanner. Jagger knew him quite well.

'Dave, is everything normal this evening?'

'Yes, as far as I know, Wilf. Why do you ask?'

Jagger took out the folded paper Sarah had found in her brother's room and showed him. The guard rubbed his chin.

'Where did you get this?' he asked.

Jagger looked at Sarah. 'It was found . . . by accident. It might be a hoax of some sort.'

'Let me call Sandra. She's the Chief tonight.'

The guard dialled and then frowned and looked at his phone. 'Engaged.'

'Yes, it was a few minutes ago when I tried,' said the pilot. 'Look, we're going to take a look around. We'll come back and tell you if we see anything.'

'Alright. I'll try phoning the Chief again in a few minutes. She can decide what she wants to do about it.'

The two pilots exited airside and walked onto the Cargo Apron. It was a bustling scene. Two freighters were being prepared for service and one was closed up, anti-collision strobes flashing, about to start its engines.

*****

It would take a good five minutes to walk to the other end of the airport. Jagger's eyes swept the area as the two pilots followed the marked out pedestrian pathway at the edge of the aprons. Plenty of activity, but nothing obviously abnormal.

Sarah was thinking out loud. 'The paper said Q3 or whoever would "take" the 767. Could it be a hijack? Maybe it's a flight that's already departed, in which case there's not much we can do.'

'I suppose if Dave has managed to contact the Security Chief they may be able to double-check passengers on tonight's remaining departures,' offered Jagger.

'Suppose it means "take" as in "steal"', suggested the girl. 'What's to stop someone getting in a plane, starting it up and taking it off?'

'Difficult without accomplices,' answered Jagger. But it was true that if you had the know-how and you could get inside an airliner's flight deck you would be able to start the engines. There were no immobilisers, even on modern aircraft, and no ignition keys necessary. 'I mean, you'd need someone to detach the jetty and someone else to operate the push-back tug. Anyway, surely you'd be seen by other people. How could you taxy to the runway without the Tower spotting you?'

'Suppose it was parked remotely, away from the terminal,' persisted Sarah. 'No-one could see what you were up to if all your lights were off. And you wouldn't need a push-back tug.'

As they approached the General Aviation Apron they could see that it was quieter than the rest of the airport. Business jets don't usually fly at night. The largest aircraft parked there was Dmitry Chegolev's luxurious Boeing. There was no sign of any sort of activity near it as it sat unattended on the apron, its left side illuminated by the floodlights.

'Well it's a 767, isn't it?' said Jagger. 'Let's take a look.'

CHAPTER 21

The Security HQ was in the admin block on the east side of the Main Apron. Besides the usual office equipment there was a bank of TV monitors on one wall linked to the CCTV cameras positioned around the airport. Two of the three officers in the room were watching the screens. The third, Security Chief Sandra Beckridge, a slightly overweight woman of about fifty, stood on the other side of the room. A frown had settled on her normally cheerful face. Hands on hips, she was looking down at the communications technician who was crouched by an open metal cabinet by the wall, screwdriver in hand. Coils of multicoloured cable tumbled out of the cabinet onto the floor.

'Do you think you'll be able to sort it?' she asked. 'The phones have been out for nearly half an hour now.'

The technician grinned up at her. 'It's a problem with one of the the synchro multipliers. But I reckon you'll be up and running soon. I've put a new one in. Just got to test it.'

'Quick as you can, please.'

'Of course.'

*****

Luis Dominguez looked at his watch. Twenty forty-five. That would be nineteen forty-five in England.

He was sitting in his salon, listening to the rain pattering against the patio window. He took a drag of his cigarette. His other hand held the email printout which Carlos had brought him a few moments previously.

Pilar, the cook, was also in the house with Dominguez and his manservant and delicious smells from the kitchen reminded her employer that he was hungry. It was about time Kelda got back from her shopping expedition to Palma where she had gone with a friend to fritter money away on expensive clothes. *Spend what you like, querida!* Plenty more where that came from, now that the deal was going through.

Things were looking good for the Mallorcan. Life had been easier since Paco Rabal had gone for his swim to eternity. Besides removing a nasty thorn from his side the demise of el elefante had warned other would-be upstarts that crossing Luis Dominguez was not good for their health. Once again he basked in the respect radiating towards him from lesser men, just like the old days.

And now this. He brought the paper into his line of vision and read the typed words again.

I have been told by my friends in England that the baby has been born. If he is healthy he will be brought to me early tomorrow morning. I will contact you to confirm his arrival. When I have received your present I will send you the photographs.

Tu amigo, Wilhelm

Once again Dominguez decoded the message in his mind. The Damocles plan had been activated. If everything worked out as it should Prosch would receive the merchandise in the morning. As soon as Dominguez had transferred his down payment he would get his cut of the haul.

*****

Another message with disguised meaning had just been sent to Mitchell Fradini's mobile from Michael Shepherd. The American had been lying on the bed in one of the 767's private cabins reading the novel he had brought with him to while away the hours. The aircraft's electrical system was dead, of course, so he was reading by the light of his wind-up torch. He had pulled the window shade down so that there was no chance of any stray rays of light from the cabin reaching the outside.

As he hoped, he had seen no-one since he had first entered the aircraft. All the doors were now closed and no doubt Security had sealed them with tell-tale tape before taking the stairs away so all would appear as it should to an outside observer. In the last fading light before total darkness fell the American had started his exploration of his new surroundings. In the galley he had found some chocolate bars and crisps to keep his hunger at bay and bottled water to drink if he needed it later. Again he checked the placards giving the instructions for opening the overwing emergency exits.

He waited until night had fallen and then made his way forward, carrying the Extra Pack. He carefully entered the flight deck, looking through the windows to make sure there was no-one who could see him from outside. The apron floodlights illuminated the left side of the aircraft so Fradini dropped the EP onto the jump seat and then slid himself into the right hand seat, where the shade would hide him. There was enough light to show the general layout although not enough to reveal detail. No matter. He knew the arrangement from the manuals he had studied previously and the systems indicators would be visible once he powered up the electrics.

Yes, there was a steering tiller beside his right knee so he could taxi and fly from this seat. Awesome. He wouldn't have to risk moving to the left seat where the apron lights and CCTVs might pick him out. Next to the tiller wheel was a recess in the sidewall in which a metal box was fixed, about the size of a shoe box, although slightly wider. Stencilled on the side were words in Cyrillic characters. There was a spring clip securing the hinged top. Fradini unfastened the clip and reached inside. A gun!

It was a 9mm pistol, a bit like a Walther PP. The trigger and safety catch looked similar to the German design, as did the magazine release, which revealed the gun to be fully loaded with eight rounds. Fradini looked across to the captain's seat. Another box with the same Russian annotation, presumably another gun. Obviously Dmitry Chegolev had a thing about potential hijacking.

The Damocles plan had been evolved on the basis that Fradini would not need a gun, primarily because it would have been impossible to get it through Security. If the plan went wrong, the escape options therefore came down to either making a dash for it if challenged or, if arrested, trying the 'pilot-testing-airport-security' story concocted for him by the group. It was flimsy but it was the best they could come up with.

Well, now he had a third option . . . a gun to shoot his way out of trouble with. Hopefully he would not need to use it, but you never knew . . .

One more thing to check. There were four or five other business jets parked on the GA Apron. Was there enough room to taxy out without colliding with any of them? The only problem could be that Cessna Citation in the next bay. Its tail looked higher than the 767s wing tip. But if Fradini did a little jink to the right as he moved off he should be clear, even if his wing had to pass over the Cessna's.

Having satisfied himself that he had checked everything that he could have checked, Fradini had repaired to the cabin where he was now stretched out on the bed with the novel. The torch light was dimming so the pilot put the book down and started pumping the handle to recharge the battery. The chime of his mobile made him jump.

See you at the pub at 8. Steve.

Fradini grinned and punched the air. *'Yesss!'*

I'll be there he texted back.

He went forward to the first conference room and across to the emergency exits on the right side. By the light of the torch he located a small square cover in the side panelling adjacent to the aft exit hatch. 'ESCAPE SLIDE ACTIVATOR' was stencilled on it.

He opened the cover to reveal a red painted T-handle. It was orientated with the handle aligned with a red mark annotated 'ARMED'. Fradini twisted it through ninety degrees into the 'DISARMED' position. Then he took hold of the handles on the hatch and lifted it out of its housing. Had he not disarmed it, the activator would have deployed and inflated the overwing escape slide designed for passengers evacuating the aircraft in an emergency to safely drop to ground level.

Fradini brought the hatch into the cabin and placed it on the floor. Then he moved forward again.

Time to go!

*****

Michael Shepherd checked his phone.

We're off! He looked out of the window. The 767 still looked dead but the dispatcher knew that Mitchell Fradini would very soon be bringing it to life. The area around it was clear. There was a Cessna in the next bay but the American should be able to get past it okay. Shepherd checked his watch. Two minutes before eight. So far so good. He looked out of the window again and his brow furrowed. *What was that?*

Two people were walking towards the big jet, a tallish man and a woman a little shorter. They were wearing hi-viz jackets but they were too far away and the light wasn't bright enough for the dispatcher to see the logos on the jackets.

Horrified, Shepherd watched as the two figures approached the 767 and then stopped, looking up at it. *What's going on?*

No time to think about consequences. He would have to act without delay. He called across the office to Senior Controller Tomislav Kalmeta, who had taken over from Greg Barfield after his shift finished.

'Tommy! Got to dash. Can you spare me for a few mins?'

'What is it, Mike?'

'Got to sort something out. Pronto. Tell you when I get back.'

'Okay . . . but we'll be busy soon.'

Shepherd had grabbed his hi-viz jacket and reached the door.

'Cheers, mate. Back ASAP.'

CHAPTER 22

'Well, there's nothing happening here. It's all secure. The tapes haven't been tampered with. We're back at square one.'

Jagger nodded. 'Looks that way. Let's take a wander round, see if there's anything.'

'Do you accept that Giles is innocent of any wrongdoing?'

'Yes. I'm sorry.'

The two strolled round the big jet. It was darker on the right side but there was still enough light to pick out the aircaft's features.

'Hey, look at that!'

Sarah's eyes followed Jagger's pointing hand. 'That's not normal, is it?'

'Well, they may have been doing maintenance work on the emergency exit hatch but surely they wouldn't leave the plane like that. If it rains it could mess up the electrics.'

'At least no-one can get in through it. It's too high up.'

'Unless you climbed on the engine and got on to the wing that way.'

'Yes, that's possible.'

'Alright, let's go back and inform Security. We'll drop in at Britair Engineering on the way, tell them about it. Maybe one of their bods forgot to replace the hatch.'

'Okay.'

*****

Mitchell Fradini adjusted the seat controls on the copilot seat to make himself comfortable. The fore-and-aft position was further back that usual because the American had the EP strapped to his back. He reached forward to check that he could easily operate the control wheel and rudder pedals. Satisfied, he fastened his straps.

Right, let's switch on the battery and start the APU.

As Fradini reached up to the overhead panel his mobile rang. It was Shepherd's number. *What the hell! They were supposed to communicate only in coded text. Is he aborting the mission?*

The American touched the *'Accept call'* option.

'What?'

'Big problems.'

'Go ahead.'

'There are two people snooping round the plane.'

'Security?'

'Don't think so.'

'What are we gonna do?'

'I'm on my way down. I'll challenge them, find out who they are.'

'Shit! Do we abort?'

'Not yet.'

'I've got a gun. Does that help?'

'A gun! How—'

'Never mind. Can you—'

'Brilliant! Yeah, when you see me, drop the gun from the copilot sliding window. Gives me a few more options.'

'Right. Don't fuck it up. I'm opening the window now. If you're not here in one minute I'm outa here!'

'How—'

'Through the overwing! Get on with it!'

*****

Shepherd ran down the stairs but as soon as he reached Security checkpoint Charlie he forced himself to slow to normal speed. He smiled at the officer who swiped his ID and ambled through the exit door. Once outside he paced more briskly but he was aware that the CCTVs could see him so a mad dash across the apron was definitely not on. As he approached the Russian 767 he could see the legs of the two intruders on the other side. They were aft of the wing. Good. With luck he would be able to reach the nose without them spotting him.

The sliding window was open. In the darkness, Shepherd could make out the shadowy form of Fradini's face. An arm extended from the window, holding an object. Shepherd raised a thumb and caught the gun as it dropped.

No words were exchanged.

The dispatcher was familiar with the more common hand guns. This one looked similar to the ones he'd used, if slightly bigger. Without pausing he walked past the right engine to where the Meteor pilots were standing talking.

'Who are you? What are you doing here?'

The pilots stared at the dispatcher.

'And who are you?' said Jagger, overcoming his surprise.

'Shut up! I've got a gun here and I'll blow your fucking brains out unless you do what I say. Put your hands behind your head.'

The two pilots looked at each other, bewildered and shocked.

'Now, you arseholes!'

Jagger and the girl did as bidden.

'Walk forward to the front of the engine.'

Gun in his right hand, Shepherd hit the redial button on his mobile.

The pilots listened to the one-sided conversation, both wondering what was happening and what they could do about it.

'Plan B, power up the cargo door circuits . . . yeah, battery power . . . I can operate the controls from here . . . a couple of minutes . . . yeah . . . yeah, I'll stay on the line . . .'

Shepherd looked at the pilots and waved them forward until the three of them were by the forward cargo door.

'Stop!'

'Now look,' started Jagger.

'Hey,' said Shepherd, looking at Sarah. 'You're Giles's sister, aren't you?'

'Yes. Who are you?'

Shepherd raised the run and shot Sarah through the left shoulder. The girl screamed in pain.

'I'll kill you both if I have to. Shut up and do what you're told.'

Sarah's face was wracked with pain. She instinctively moved her hand to the wound to stop the flow of blood.

'Hands behind your head,' hissed Shepherd, 'or you'll get another one.'

Beside the large forward cargo door there was a hinged panel, which Shepherd opened. Still pointing the gun at the pilots he moved one of the switches under the panel and held it in position. With a whirring of electrics the door locks disengaged and the door itself opened outwards and upwards. When it was half raised the dispatcher released the switch and the electrics cut out. The door oscillated to a stop.

The dispatcher reached up into the pitch black void of the hold. The door sill was about seven feet above ground level. He pulled a short aluminium ladder from its stowage and held it towards Jagger.

'Clip it on to those recesses where the red marks are.'

The ladder rails hinged at the top so that it could be fastened securely to the door sill. Having done what he was told, Jagger moved back towards Sarah, who was clutching her wounded shoulder with one hand. Blood trickled through her fingers.

'Get in.'

'What!'

'You heard! Get in. Put her in then get in yourself.'

'You can't—'

'You've got one second. Then I'll start shooting again . . . wait! Get under the wing! Move!'

Shepherd had seen an approaching aircraft taxying towards the runway for take-off. Although it was darker on this side of the GA

Apron he didn't want to risk being spotted. Damocles was not quite going to plan but maybe it could be salvaged. *Think of the money!*

The dispatcher and his captives crouched under the 767's wing close to the fuselage. Their six eyes watched a Fedex A330 freighter taxy past, its engine noise deafening them. As it moved away the smell of burnt kerosene wafted across the apron towards them.

'Okay, back we go.'

Jagger helped Sarah up the ladder into the hold and turned towards Shepherd.

'Isn't there some way we can—'

'Get in.'

Jagger climbed into the blackness of the hold.

'Move back!'

Shepherd unclipped the ladder and threw it into the hold. Then he closed the door, listening for the locks to engage. He released the switch and secured the panel covering the controls. He breathed a sigh of relief. He might have to work out a cover story for his dash out of the office but for the moment they could carry on with the plan.

He walked to the nose and looked up. Fradini moved his face towards the window and with some cockpit lights now on Shepherd could just about make out the querying eyebrows. He grinned and raised both his thumbs.

'Go, baby, go!' he called up.

Fradini nodded and withdrew his face. Shepherd watched him wind the sliding window closed. *What about the gun? Got to get rid of it!* The dispatcher looked around for inspiration. No good just throwing it away somewhere where it could be found again. It would have his fingerprints and DNA all over it. Yeah, that'll do! He walked back under the wing root and threw the pistol into the main landing gear bay through the gap where the bracing strut protruded. *Now . . . what shall I tell Tommy?*

CHAPTER 23

Security officer Derek Ridyard was watching the monitor covering the GA Apron and was mildly surprised to see two figures walking across. The camera resolution wasn't brilliant but it was good enough to show a man and a woman approaching the Rich Russian's plane. They didn't seem to be hurrying or acting furtively and they were both wearing regulation hi-viz jackets.

'Sandra,' he called out to his boss, 'anything going out from GA this evening?'

The Chief looked across from where she was hovering beside the metal cabinet housing the communications cabling, sipping a coffee. 'Check the Departures page, you lazy sod!.'

'Can't, till we get the system up again.'

Sandra Beckridge shook her head. 'Sorry, Derek, wasn't thinking.'

'You'll be reconnected to the outside world in a mo,' said the technician repairing the fault. 'Just got to run a test.'

When Ridyard looked at the screen again the two figures were no longer visible. He decided that if the Departures page wasn't available within five minutes he's get someone from checkpoint Delta to go and have a mosey around.

The phone rang. 'Hooray,' cried Sandra, 'at last.'

She picked up the receiver and heard a pre-recorded test message. She nodded at the technician. 'It's good. Thanks very much.'

'Don't mention it. Might take a few minutes to get your data systems on line but everything checks out here.' He refastened the clips on the cabinet.

What now? thought Derek Ridyard. Another man seemed to be walking across the GA Apron. The Security officer watched on the monitor as the solitary figure moved towards the nose of the 767 and then disappeared behind it. Ridyard tapped some keys on his computer. 'Unable to display Airport Movements Program,' said the screen. *Bugger!*

At least the phones were working again. 'I'm calling Delta,' he said over his shoulder to the Security Chief. 'Ask them to check out the GA Apron. There's a few people wandering around there we need to take a look at.'

'Thanks,' said Sandra. 'Keep me posted.'

*****

In the 767 flight deck Mitchell Fradini pilot reached above his head and rotated the auxiliary power unit switch to the 'START' position. The various flight deck warning lights dimmed as the battery diverted its energy into the electric starter motor. *Hopefully, using battery power to open and close the cargo door didn't discharge it too much, otherwise no APU start. And no APU start means no engine start.*

As the APU turbine accelerated, the fuel feed automatically tripped in and the igniter plug sparked into life. The starter disengaged itself and the turbine spun up to its operating speed. The generator automatically came on line and powered up the aircraft's electrics. The blank display screens on the panel in front of Fradini flickered, then lit up. The American took the copilot headset hanging on its hook by the window and put it on. Then he reached down to the centre console and verified the VHF was tuned to East Midlands Tower frequency. Once they realised what he was up to all hell would break loose and he needed to know when the moment happened.

Ten past eight. *This is it. Should have started ten minutes ago. Those jerks, snooping around. They won't be having much fun, locked up in the hold. Tough shit!*

On the outcome of the next few minutes hung the success or otherwise of Damocles. This was the critical time. If it worked out okay a lot of people would soon be a lot richer. If it didn't . . .

Nothing much happening on the VHF. After a last glance to check that the coast was still clear outside Fradini reached up to the overhead panel again and switched on the left engine starter. High pressure air from the APU surged into the engine under the wing, spinning it into action. On the console to his left he opened the fuel lever. The engine quickly lit up and stabilised.

No time to start the right now. I'll do it as I head for the runway.

Fradini opened the left throttle and the engine responded with noise and thrust. Initially the nosewheel chock prevented forward movement. But chocks are designed merely to stop an aircraft moving if their parking brakes have failed. They cannot stop a determined effort to override them with a burst of engine thrust. As Fradini pushed the left throttle forward the engine responded with a crescendo of power and suddenly the 767's nosewheel jumped over the chock and thumped back onto the ground. The pilot allowed the asymmetric thrust to pull the aircraft over a little as it rolled forward to make sure he cleared the Cessna's tail and then eased back on the power. It was not too difficult to find the taxyway guidance markings even though his landing lights were off. The apron floodlights illuminated the paved area adequately. *Good enough for the moment!*

The question now was, how far would he get before someone realised what was going on.

*****

Derek Ridyard was on the phone to Sally White in checkpoint Delta. 'We saw a few people wandering around on the GA, Sal. Can you or Dan check it out if you're not too busy.'

'I'll send Dan out.'

'Great. If you . . . hang on a tick. Sally, the Russian 767 is moving. I didn't know it was leaving tonight. Why isn't it showing any lights? What's it doing?' Ridyard stared at the monitor, trying to make sense of what he saw.

'Do you want Dan to go out?'

'No, stay put. I'll call the Tower. Find out what's happening.'

Ridyard rang off and immediately dialled the Control Tower. 'The Russian plane's taxying out, Sandra,' he called over to his boss as he waited for a response. 'Is the Departures page on line yet?'

'Yes, it's up and running. Let's see . . . nope . . . no mention of the Russian plane.'

*****

There were three Air Traffic Control Officers on duty in East Midlands Tower, one of whom was Russell Bruce, whose job it was to supervise aircraft manoeuvring on the ground. The console at which the two men and one woman sat was encircled by expansive windows, affording the occupants an uninterrupted panorama of the airport's manoeuvring area.

Bruce was transmitting at the same moment as Angela Whitby, who occupied the seat alongside his own, their two voices melding into a soft murmur of indistinguishable words. Angela was the Tower Controller, with responsibility for traffic in the airspace immediately surrounding the airport and on the runway itself.

Their simultaneous transmissions were not indicative of a busy spell. On the contrary, there was nothing much going on and the controllers' workload was light. At that moment there was only one aircraft waiting for take-off clearance, a Trans Ocean MD11 freighter. It was not often so. At busy times the queue could extend to ten aircraft or more. A Central Airbus A321 was on the approach, its shimmering landing lights piercing the black night with their brilliance. With nothing else to draw their attention the two controllers and their senior colleague, Watch Supervisor Oliver Beaumont, stared at the approaching aircraft. It sank steadily towards the runway, wings dipping and rising slightly as its pilot reacted to an eddy of turbulence in the approach path. The pattern of its lights changed as it landed and lowered its nose to the ground. A few seconds later a rumble of reverse thrust shook the control tower windows.

Angela keyed her mike. 'Central 398 landed time one two, vacate next left and contact ground, one two one decimal nine two.'

She turned to Bruce. 'He's all yours.' The Ground Controller would allocate Flight 398 his parking gate.

While Bruce was instructing the newly arrived flight Angela sighed and stretched. As soon as the Trans Ocean was away she would have little to do for a while. She would cover for her colleague and send him for a cup of the revolting brown liquid that came out of the drinks dispenser pretending to be coffee.

'Trans Ocean Three Zero,' she transmitted now. 'Confirm ready for departure.'

A voice sounded in her earphones. 'Trans Ocean Thirty, affirm.'

'Trans Ocean Three Zero line up runway two seven, cleared for take-off,' she replied.

Four eyes watched the big jet charging along the runway. Two happened to catch a shadow moving in the opposite direction, approaching the runway.

'What's that?' asked Beaumont. 'Something on the taxiway.'

The other two looked to where the Supervisor was pointing. Bruce reached for the binoculars on the console top in front of him. One of the phones on the console started to ring but no-one paid any attention.

'It's a 767, I think. Why isn't it showing any lights? Can't make out the colours. What's it doing?'

'See if it's on the frequency,' ordered Beaumont. A flutter of worry stirred his stomach.

'Aircraft taxying to runway two seven, say your callsign,' transmitted Bruce.

No answer.

'You try, Angie,' said Beaumont.

'Aircraft taxying, this is East Midlands Tower. Hold your position. Do you read me?'

Nothing.

The two junior controllers turned quizzical faces to Beaumont. He took the binoculars from Bruce and pointed them at the cause of their unease. The 767 was either not listening or else it had ignored the challenges. It was still moving towards the runway. Bruce picked up the ringing phone and uttered a terse 'Standby' to the caller. Then he put the handset down on the console, which meant that he did not hear Security Officer Derek Ridyard alerting him to a possible unlawful incident about to be perpetrated at the airport.

A buzzer sounded in Angela's left earphone. It was the radar controller reminding her to hand over the departing Trans Ocean flight to his jurisdiction.

'Sorry. We've got a problem up here,' she replied into her headset mike. She got rid of the MD11 and switched her attention back to the unfolding drama.

'How can we stop him?' asked Bruce.

'Like this,' said Beaumont, leaning towards the red alarm button on the console.

*****

'Aircraft taxying, this is East Midlands Tower. Hold your position. Do you read me?'

Yeah, I read you, honey, but I ain't answering. The American reached above him and initiated the start-up sequence for the right engine. Ahead of him the green taxiway lights led him towards the runway, the 767's nosewheel thudding over each one until Fradini eased over a little to run the wheel on smooth tarmac.

*****

'Ouch!'

'Sorry, I didn't realise you were there.'

It was pitch black in the 767's hold and Fradini's steering adjustment made Jagger fall over from the sitting position he had been in, colliding with Sarah in the process. It was difficult to stay upright with no visual reference.

'How's the shoulder?'

'Bloody painful. Literally. Maybe it's just as well I can't see the wound.'

'I don't like this much,' said Jagger. 'It sounds like both the engines are running. Maybe he's going to take off.' He paused for a second. 'Who was that bloke who locked us in here? I'm sure I've seen him somewhere.'

'I've just remembered. He was at our party at Orchard Lea.'

'Yes, that's it. A friend of Giles, according to Hilary.'

'Please stop going on about Giles. I'm sick of it.'

'Anyway, there are more important things to think about. How are we going to get out of here?'

The hold seemed to be as wide as the aircaft, with the lower walls sloping inwards to match the aircraft's body shape, but not quite high enough to be able to stand up. In the few minutes since their ordeal started Jagger had explored the limits of their prison, crawling on hands and knees and now and then colliding with the girl in the total darkness. The hold was less well insulated than the cabin, which meant that now the engines were running they had to raise their voices to make conversation.

The search had revealed very little. The main cargo door seemed to have no internal controls for opening it. In the ceiling he had found what felt like the lens covers of lights intended to illuminate the hold interior but no switches to turn them on. The forward end was separated from the rest of the area by netting but Jagger could not find a release mechanism.

'Looks like we're stuck here until we land somewhere else,' he deduced. 'Sorry there's nothing I can do about your injury.'

'It's not quite so painful now,' said Sarah. 'But I wish I knew how much it was bleeding. Why would someone steal an empty airliner? I hope it's not—'

'Suicide jihadists,' supplied Jagger. 'I doubt it. Considering what's happened to us it's more likely to be something criminal rather than something terrorist.'

The girl said, 'I still can't believe Giles has got anything to do with this.'

Jagger was about to contradict but held his tongue. He had other things on his mind. If the pilot climbed up to normal cruise level, how cold would their prison become? Although he knew his way round a Vickers Merchantman freighter that knowledge was no use to him here. To start with, the 767 probably cruised at about twice the height of the Vibrator. He cast his mind back to the time he flew passenger MD11s, recalling that occasionally they had carried livestock in their holds, dogs and cats and so on, which meant that heating of some kind had to be provided. Did the MD11 have controls for adjusting hold temperature? He couldn't remember. Of course, he and Sarah could always cuddle up together if necessary . . .

The girl was obviously following a similar train of thought. 'Wilf, are these cargo holds pressurised? If not we're not going to have enough oxygen to breathe.'

'Must be,' he answered, adding his thoughts about carriage of animals.

Sarah said something else but he voice was drowned out by the whine from the engines.

'Pardon?'

'I said, I'm scared.'

'So am I,' he said, unable to think of a better answer. The four arms instinctively reached out for each other like the tentacles of an octopus and the two captives huddled together. Incongruously, Jagger found himself regretting that there had been no time to take a shower before Sarah had found the incriminating note at home. Now he could feel her head resting against his chest. Maybe he didn't smell too bad after all.

*****

When the klaxon sounded, Chief Fire Officer Douglas Symonds was in the crew room with the rest of the shift, watching a comedy show on the television.

A groan went up round the room. One or two of the firefighters muttered curses. It was a fact of their working lives that over ninety percent of callouts were a waste of time and effort. Some of the alarms were triggered by the airport managers just to test readiness for action. Nearly all the genuine emergency callouts ended without action required by the RFF, the Rescue and Fire Facilities. Typically, the captain of an incoming flight would request the RFF if there was any chance they might be needed, even if the chance was remote. It was a not infrequent occurrence. On Symond's previous shift, for example, an aircraft had reported partial hydraulic failure, which left it with degraded landing performance. The pilot had had to make his approach with his flaps not fully extended, which meant a higher landing speed, which meant more distance to slow down after touchdown, which meant harsher use of brakes than normal, which meant the possibility of brake fire, which meant the possibility of an emergency evacuation of the passengers and crew on the runway. Symonds and his men had dutifully waited by the runway, lights flashing, foam pumps pressurised. The airliner touched down and the fire trucks raced after it. Symonds saw wisps of smoke escaping from its brakes but nothing worse. The aircraft stopped well within the confines of the runway and the fire trucks followed it to its parking stand like scarlet ducklings trailing after their mother. The passengers disembarked normally, probably not fully aware of the fuss going on round them (the captain would have informed them that the presence of the emergency services was merely precautionary) and the vehicles trundled back to their depots. For aircrew and RFF crew it was all in a day's work.

Now the firefighters were donning their protective clothing and helmets. Symonds picked up the red phone that was permanently connected to the control tower. He recognised Oliver Beaumont's voice in the earphone.

'Got some business for you, Doug. It's a funny one. Looks like someone's pinched a 767. It's taxying towards two seven and we can't stop it.'

'That's a new one,' said Symonds. 'What did you have in mind?' He glanced through the crew room window to the garage area alongside. The segmented steel doors were already folding back and he could hear the muffled roar of the fire truck engines starting up.

'Get the trucks onto the runway. He can't get airborne with you lot blocking his path.'

'Got you. We're on our way. Which bit of the runway?'

'Just get the trucks rolling, Doug. I'll direct you on the radio when you're out there. For Christ's sake hurry. He's nearly there.'

*****

Mitchell Fradini was turning the 767 onto the runway when he noticed the flashing blue lights streaming from the fire station halfway across the airport like a swarm of angry glow-worms. He immediately guessed what they were up to. Confirmation came in his earphones.

'Aircraft entering runway two seven. You are not cleared for take off. Return to the apron and shut down your engines. The airfield is closed and the runway is blocked. I repeat, you are not cleared for take off. Acknowledge.'

The leading fire truck was heading for the midpoint of the runway as far as Fradini could tell. Suddenly all the runway lights went out and the 767 was marooned in a sea of pitch.

Good try, guys, but not good enough. The American reached up to the overhead panel and switched on the aircraft's landing lights. From the wing roots two shafts of dazzling light lanced into the blackness, illuminating the ground markings and mocking the controller's desperate attempt to deprive him of visual guidance.

Adrenalin shot through Fradini's arteries as he pushed the throttles forward and the engines wound up in response. On the glareshield he pressed the autothrottle engage switch and now the levers moved themselves forward to take-off power. With no load apart from full fuel tanks the 767 leapt forward keenly. A mile in front of him the first fire truck had stopped on the runway and another was drawing up alongside.

Now it was a game of chicken.

*****

'He's started to roll, Doug,' called Beaumont on the radio. 'What's the situation with you?'

'We've got two trucks on the runway and a third about to join us. I'm in the second one, right on the centre line. The others are either side.'

'Great, that should stop him in his tracks. Surely he can see you.'

'We've got all our beacons and searchlights on and headlights on main beam. A blind man couldn't miss that lot.'

'Okay, when he stops, get your trucks in close so he can't move away again.'

Symonds was squinting his eyes against the two spears of light skewering them. There were getting brighter. Moving apart. That meant closer. He tried to keep his voice calm as he keyed his mike.

'Is he slowing down?'

A pause.

'Doug, we can't tell. Maybe . . .' Now Beaumont's voice rose and cracked under the tension. 'Get ready to vacate the runway, Doug. He seems to be accelerating . . .'

*****

One hundred knots! At one fifty this baby will fly! Outa my way, suckers!

Ironically the extravaganza of luminous energy bursting from the fire trucks was helping Fradini rather than hindering him. Although the 767's landing lights were bright enough to mark out the white centre line stripe the dazzling display was an easier target to aim at. Little blips on the rudder pedals kept the aircraft running true.

C'mon, get out of the way!

For the first time a shadow of doubt flickered through the American's mind. Quickly he assessed his speed, acceleration and distance remaining to the wall of light.

Not enough real estate! I'm gonna hit them!

*****

'Get off the runway, Doug, get off the fucking runway! He's coming right at you!'

The radio screamed at Symonds but he had already barked the same order to his driver and the other two fire trucks. Agonising seconds dragged past as the lumbering vehicles bucked and shuddered in response to panicky hands and feet on their controls. Now Symonds tasted fear as the two dragon's eyes hurtled suicidally at him. The screaming crescendo of jet engines was its deadly breath. Symonds winced and tensed himself for the explosion that would pulverise him into oblivion, not even aware that his bowels had emptied.

*****

Fly, you bastard, fly!

In desperation Fradini hauled the control wheel into his stomach and jammed the throttles forward as far as they would go. The engines roared in protest against such abuse as the fiery gases inside them tried to melt the spinning turbine blades.

The 767 lifted its nose reluctantly, warning the pilot that it wasn't ready to take to the air. The scattering fire trucks loomed large, scared faces lit ghostly white in the aircraft's landing light beams.

Might just make it! The airliner was trying to fly, wings clawing at the air at a speed much too slow for safety. In short succession three things happened. A shudder in the floor told the pilot that the aircraft's tail had hit the runway during the premature lifting of the nose. In his right hand the control wheel suddenly began to vibrate. The 767's sensors were telling Fradini what he already knew. It was flying—just—but its wings were hovering at the edge of a stall, the tortured airflow trying to break away and steal their lift. But before he could respond a massive thump rocked the airliner and an unseen giant hand snatched at it, wrenching it off course. Frantically the American kicked rudder against the shuddering yaw.

And then the awful sight was behind him and he knew he had won. Lights streaking past on the ground confirmed he was gaining height. Fradini very slowly eased the wheel forward and gratefully watched the airspeed creep towards safety. Sensing a healthier angle of attack for the wings the vibrating stall-warning system deactivated itself. That was better. Now Fradini could afford to pull the throttles back a little from their wide open position. As the engines relaxed so did the pilot, letting out a long held breath. The 767 climbed more confidently into the velvet night, its flight path smooth except for a tremble of vibration.

Must have hit one of those fire trucks reasoned the pilot as his heart beart slowed towards normality. He checked the readings on the panels in front of him. The engines seemed okay despite the punishment he had inflicted on them. *Ah, that could be the problem!* Above the landing gear lever glowed two green lights. They told him that the nose wheel and right mainwheel were still down and locked. The left mainwheel light was out.

Which means what? Did it hit one of those stupid trucks? Shall I bring the gear up? What extra damage will the left wheel do if I try that? Suppose it punctures the fuel tank? Could leave the gear down, but that'll increase fuel consumption because of drag and I have to make it last as long as possible. I'll take a chance on retraction.

Fradini reached over and raised the lever. After a few seconds a thud from underneath the floor him told him the nose wheel was up and locked. Its green indicator light extinguished to confirm it, followed by that for the right wheel.

The pilot let go of the control wheel for a few moments to check the aircraft's trim. *Yep, the ship wanted to turn left.* So the left side landing gear, or what was left of it, was probably dangling in the airflow. He felt for the control on the centre pedestal and fed in some right rudder trim. *That's more like it.* The offset rudder compensated for the drag of the damaged gear and the 767 straightened up. Fradini engaged the autopilot and sat back. So far so good.

'Aircraft climbing from East Midlands, confirm callsign November 3249 Alpha and squawk seven seven zero zero. State your intentions.'

My intentions are to get very very rich, baby! Obviously they had now identified the stolen aircraft. Although owned by the Russian Dmitry Chegolev it carried an American registration, N3249A. The 7700 code from the 767's transponder equipment would mark it out on air traffic control radar screens as an aircraft in an emergency.

Fradini made no reply to the radio call although he did switch on the transponder and dial up the code. It was important that the bozos on the ground knew where he was, if only to keep other suckers out of his way. A mid-air collision did not feature in the plan. Some more lights would be a good idea now that he had got off okay. He switched on the navigation lights and strobes. Revealing his location would hopefully convince the authorities that they were not contending with a 9/11 type scenario. He didn't want to have to use the Extra Pack before he was ready to.

'Aircraft squawking seven seven zero zero, say your intentions.'

I'm going to London! The pilot turned his heading selector and the autopilot swung the nose into a turn towards the southeast.

'Aircraft squawking—'

The transmission was cut short as Fradini changed the radio frequency selector to London Area Control. It was only a matter of time before he could expect a challenge on the new frequency.

A draught of cold air trickling in through the open flight deck door took his thoughts back to the cabin. With the gaping hole over the wing where he had removed the emergency exit hatch it was impossible to pressurise the cabin because the warm air from the engine feeds went straight through the hole. Fradini turned the air conditioning controls to full heat. It might help a bit.

The altimeter wound up to eight thousand feet and the autopilot eased the 767's nose down to level off as programmed by the American. The throttles automatically slid back to hold the speed at 340 knots. A high speed for low level flight but he needed to arrive overhead London as quickly as possible. The next job was to set up the routing. For the next few minutes the pilot huddled over the computer, tapping its keyboard with data from the navigation display. Occasionally his eyes flicked round the flight deck to check that all was well.

There, all done. Now the autopilot would take its instructions from the computer, following the route programmed into it. Fradini leant forward and peered through the windscreen. The clusters of amber street lights sprinkled over the ground below were occulted by skeins of black cloud drifting past. Above the horizon billions of scintillating stars speckled the night sky. Fradini was not impressed. He'd seen it thousands of times before. The main difference between this night flight and all the others he'd endured over the years was that tonight there was no copilot to mind the shop if he wanted a little shuteye.

The ship seems okay after its little tussle with the fire trucks. Apart from the landing gear, which I don't need anyway, it's in good shape.

Had the American been able to see inside the right engine cowling his complacency would have taken a knock. The magnetic chip detector which engineer Tim Harkness had neglected to tighten was mischievously easing off. A warm drip of amber engine oil under the detector swelled until its weight overcame its surface tension and then it detached itself and fell into the cowling. Already another pelican's beak of oil was expanding under the detector.

*****

A few feet ahead and to the left of the bleeding engine, in the blackness the forward hold, Wilf Jagger and Sarah Amberley-Kemp were still holding on to each other, their initial panic now abated somewhat. At least they were still alive. They had realised from the crescendo of engine noise that the aircraft was starting its take-off run, confirmation coming soon afterwards as they felt the floor tilt under them, sending them tumbling to the rear bulkhead. But before they could untangle themselves the left mainwheels had smashed into Doug Symonds' fire truck, the sickening lurch sending them flying again.

'Christ!' shouted Jagger above the howl of the engines. 'We've hit something! We're in trouble!'

'Are we going to crash?' cried Sarah, her arms grabbing tighter hold of him.

For terrifying moments they waited for the end, minds racing incoherently, hearts pounding, powerless to avert their fate. Ten agonising seconds went by, then another ten. A minute. They were still airborne and the aircraft seemed steady. They heard the engines ease back a little and a little while later the whine of hydraulic pumps, presumably retracting the landing gear and flaps.

'So where are we going?' asked Sarah, breathing more slowly now. She had relaxed her hold on Jagger.

'God knows,' came the reply. 'I'm not enjoying this very much. I wish I could find the switch for the lights. I'll have a feel around.'

'My shoulder hurts.'

Jagger disentangled himself from the girl and crawled carefully towards the door, thankful that at last he had something to do.

CHAPTER 24

'Oak Trees Hotel' was a rather pretentious name for a dingy bed-and-breakfast house in a Victorian terrace drowsing in the northern outskirts of Leeds. It had its good points—an outlook over Hyde Park, proximity to Headingley cricket ground and half a dozen pubs within spitting distance. But its rooms hadn't had a sniff of a paintbrush for many years and the plumbing was as old as the crumbling walls.

In his room Eric Watson was stretched out on the musty duvet and staring at the discoloured ceiling. The clock on the mantlepiece said ten to eight but Watson knew it was five minutes slow. From another part of the house the irritating muffled noise of a radio on too loudly seeped into the room.

Watson hauled himself from his supine position and ran his fingers through his tousled hair to straighten it. He was not one of nature's heroes. Although blissfully unware of it, he was one of the very few people whose IQ was exactly 100. He could never have been a nuclear physicist but on the other hand he was smart enough to be trusted to carry out duties that would have been beyond the mental capablities of many of his brethren in the criminal world.

On the chipped dressing table Watson's mobile started ringing. He stood up and wandered over, looking out of the window as he answered the call. On the horizon the castellated skyline of the University buildings melted into the backdrop of night.

'Everything okay?'

'Yes.'

'Has your courier been yet?.'

Watson checked his watch. 'Any minute now.'

'Good. Remember, leave your position as soon as the package has gone.'

'My bag's already packed and the bills are paid.'

'Right. Unless you hear otherwise, our next meeting will be on Tuesday, as arranged. You'll get your money then.'

The line went dead.

*****

Constable Clarke rubbed his eyes with his hand. It had been a long day and he should have been home an hour ago. But with the mortgage rate going up again he needed all the overtime he could get. Now he sighed and lifted up the object from the counter. He spoke to the man in bike leathers who had just brought it into the station.

'Can you say all that again, please?'

The courier spoke his piece while the police officer examined the delivery, a brown envelope bearing the legend 'URGENT' in large black letters. Another officer sauntered over.

'Problems, Matt?'

'What do you make of this?'

The other policeman examined it. 'Should we open it?'

'Do you mind if I go now?' asked the courier.

Clarke looked at him. 'Can I ask you to wait for a moment, please, sir? I want Sergeant Tucker to see this. Pete, go and get the sarge, will you?'

When Tucker opened the envelope a folded note fluttered to the ground. It said in writing what the courier had been told to say to the police officer on duty at the station, an instruction to the effect that the enclosed CD should be heard by the senior officer in the station immediately. Looking at the object suspiciously, Tucker inserted it into the nearest computer.

As the monotone voice delivered its message the policemen's faces went from puzzled to concerned to astonished.

'My God!' muttered Tucker. 'Matt, try to get hold of the Chief Constable. Tell him what we've just heard. I've got to phone the Met.' He grabbed the desk phone and dialled the emergency hotline number that would connect him to New Scotland Yard, Headquarters of the Metropolitan Police, whose SO15 unit dealt with terrorism threats.

Unbeknownst to Sergeant Tucker, seven other of his colleagues in the force had just had the same fright. It should have been nine others, but one courier was late, having got lost trying to find the main police station in Cardiff whilst another had collided with a car on the outskirts of Newcastle and been instantly killed.

CHAPTER 25

'This message is addressed to the British Government and must be relayed to them immediately. The ministers concerned must give their authority for the execution of the instructions that follow. Please note the time limit available for compliance with this directive and please note the penalty that will be incurred if total compliance is not forthcoming.

The responsible minister must immediately authorise release of Maurice Allan Holmin, prisoner number B62567013Q, from Stensfield Prison. An unmarked empty white Transit-type van with a full fuel tank must be made available outside the prison. Holmin will be allocated a standard police Glock pistol, fully loaded, with a spare clip of ammunition. The release of the prisoner must, repeat must, be completed by 2300 local time. If Holmin requires a hostage to guarantee safe passage this too must be authorised by the responsible minister.

No attempt must be made to follow the escape vehicle and all forms of surveillance are prohibited. No reporting to the media is permitted. If any of these instructions are ignored or if any tracking device is found in or attached to the vehicle the penalty will be invoked.

As you will be able to verify for yourselves, there is at the moment or shortly will be an airliner circling over the city of London. It is under our control and contains a large quantity of high explosive. If our instructions are not followed exactly the plane will be brought down somewhere in the city, with obvious consequences. Any attempt to interfere with the plane or to observe it from close quarters will bring the same result.

If, however, our instructions are obeyed, the plane will be made to leave British airspace and will be brought down over the sea. Clearly there is no time for vacillation. Bear in mind that the plane can keep flying only until it runs out of fuel. So long as you keep to the time limits just mentioned we guarantee that there will be sufficient fuel remaining to fly the plane out to sea.

End of message.'

For a moment there was silence apart from a sigh from Paul Grumbridge. He was a slightly overweight balding man of about fifty-five, dressed in a dinner jacket. It was scarcely twenty minutes since he and his wife had been dramatically summoned from their box at the Covent Garden Opera House by a Special Branch officer, halfway through the first act of La Boheme. In her high heels Beryl Grumbridge was as tall as her husband but of delicate build. Her grey hair revealed her age as about the same as his. She was wearing a black taffeta evening gown, her favourite dress for her favourite opera. Her normally twinkling blue eyes were now clouded and lips which had been a smile savouring the evening's entertainment had tightened into concern. The Right Honourable Mrs Beryl Grumbridge, MP, was the British Home Secretary.

As the police patrol car whisked them back to Westminster, weaving with lights flashing and sirens wailing through the muddle of London's theatreland traffic, Beryl had had a hurried phone consultation with Deputy Commissioner Sir David Jenkins, chief of the SO15 Anti-Terrorist Unit. Between them they decided to set up an incident room at the headquarters of Transec, the security arm of the Department of Transport.

The Grumbridges and Sir David had arrived within two minutes of each other, let in to the building by a guard. Jenkins was the liaison officer between SO15 and Transec, who had also been notified of the situation by Air Traffic Control managers. He had powered up one of the computers and played the message stored on the memory stick he had brought with him. Now they had recovered from the initial shock of what they heard they were beginning to formulate plans about how to deal with it.

'Margot Madeling will be here soon,' said the Deputy Commissioner to the Home Secretary. Margot was Transec's Duty Assessor and her job was to advise the Home Office and SO15 on how do respond to threats against aviation security.

'Do want me to stay?' asked Paul Grumbridge now. 'I'm happy to help if I can.'

His wife turned to Sir David. 'Is that okay, David? Paul only has basic CRB clearance.' The Home Secretary was referring to the Criminal Record Bureau check that many UK citizens in various jobs had to undergo. Her husband had not been vetted by Special Branch.

'I don't have a problem with that, Beryl.'

'You're in the team, then, Paul,' she told her husband with a wry smile.

'Delighted, my dear.'

Beryl turned to the police officer. 'Is this related to the warning we received the other day? Is that why you needed to know my whereabouts this evening?'

Sir David nodded. 'We think so. Although the warning they gave us talked about an IED at a military base. Nothing like that has been found so far. We now suspect they did it so we'd be ready when the real threat came.' He pointed at the computer which had just played the message emailed to the Met by the police stations who had received the CDs. 'Do you want to hear it again?'

The Home Secretary shook her head and looked at her watch. Quarter past nine. She bit her lip. A pity the Prime Minister was out of the country, in Singapore. Middle of the night there. Special Branch was trying to contact him but until they succeeded she would have to face this one on her own. Less than two hours to go. Surely no-one would think of such a despicable thing. To deliberately crash a plane loaded with explosives into the centre of a city. What sort of warped mind dreamt that up?

'Is it genuine?'

'Yes. It's just been confirmed there's a plane circling over the city now. Air Traffic Control are monitoring it.'

'Do we know who's behind it?'

'It's probably not Al-Qaeda, not political. Hopefully not another 9/11. Looks like it's a criminal gang, connected to the prisoner. Security at East Midlands Airport are processing ID data to see who had access to airside this evening.'

'How are they controlling the plane?'

'We're checking on that. I've got Boeing on a video conference line, waiting to speak to you. Shall we hook them up?'

Again Beryl shook her head. 'First things first. What are your recommendations, David? I'm inclined to authorise the release anyway. There's nothing to be gained by delaying it. If the bad boys get what they want they might keep their promise to remove the threat.'

'It hurts me to say so, but I agree. He's a nasty piece of work, Maurice Holmin. Inside for a pretty gruesome murder plus drug offences. He's killed other people as well, but we couldn't get enough evidence to get another conviction.'

'Okay, set it up, will you? Use any resources you think are necessary. I'll take responsibility. What about the military?'

'We're talking to the Air Force right now. They launched a couple of interceptors when they detected the threat but James had them brought back after we heard the message.' James Healey was Secretary of State for Defence. 'He's at home, waiting to talk to you.'

'Shall we use Babel?'

'Probably best.'

'Okay. Set up the prisoner release, would you? I'll try to get hold of James.'

The Babel system was installed on any phones the authorities might use for passing on sensitive information. Cabinet ministers' mobiles were similarly configured. Babel was a sophisticated digital form of scrambler. Signals were encrypted in the speaker's phone and decrypted at the other end of the line.

'Have you heard?' were the Defence Secretary's opening words. The Babel circuits distorted his voice slightly.

'I can't believe it.'

'You've heard their demands? We think it's the same bunch who warned about a possible IED this evening.'

'That's what SO15 think too.'

'The Air Traffic Controllers at Swanwick say there's an airliner circling over London. It isn't responding to instructions and it's totally screwing up flights into Heathrow. Aircraft are having to divert to Stansted and Gatwick. The military boys sent up a pair of Tornadoes from Wattisham to have a look, but I've told them to return and wait till I'd spoken to you and the PM. Have you talked to him?'

'Not yet. It's you and me at the moment. We'll have to go along with it, James. David's here with me, sorting out the prisoner release.' Beryl smiled across the room at the Deputy Commissioner, busy issuing instructions on his mobile.

'What about the PM's policy on terrorism and such like? He won't be too keen.'

'I know. He hates appeasement. I don't know how he'd handle this. But I suppose this is my burden in his absence. With hindsight it may be the wrong decision, but that's what I've decided.'

A pause confirmed the Defence Secretary's uncertainty. *'Okay, I'll back you up on that. Let's hope it's not the end of two promising political careers.'*

'Quite. Let's talk again in fifteen minutes. We might have more info then.'

'I could come over if you want.'

'Yes, good idea. Easier to sort things out if you're here.'

The Home Secretary noticed her husband subsiding into a sofa. He was undoing his bowtie and loosening his collar. *Damn and damn again!* She had been looking forward to tonight for a long time. She chastised herself for such irresponsible thoughts. How could she worry about missing an opera when a bunch of lunatics were threatening to blow up the capital? A terrifying image burst into her mind. A screaming airliner exploding into the Opera House, obliterating cast, audience, orchestra, everything. Some of her friends were there tonight . . .

'I was just thinking,' Paul Grumbridge said from the sofa, stretching his arms. 'If this is real then it's cost someone a lot of money to set up. And obviously there must be accomplices on the outside. Why is it worthwhile springing this Holmin fellow from jail?'

'We think he's got assets stashed away somewhere,' said Sir David, having finished his phone calls. 'Foreign bank accounts, maybe hidden arms or drugs that can be sold on. Enough to pay for a jail break and a life of luxury afterwards. One thing,' he continued, 'I told them to set everything up but not to actually release the prisoner until you give a final authorisation, Beryl. You never know, we might be able to successfully deal with it without letting that scum out of the nick.'

'Good point,' said the Home Secretary. 'That's fine. Talking about dealing with it, is there any way we can get rid of the threat? Can we get control of the plane somehow?'

'Do you want to talk to the Boeing people about it?'

'Yes.'

It took a minute or so to set up the video conference connection.

'Hi, this is Sam,' said the African-American face on the laptop screen. 'You got a problem with a hijack?'

'Yes,' said Beryl, sitting down to face the webcam. 'Sorry to keep you waiting.'

'No problem. Do we need to tell the CIA?'

'Already done,' said Sir David, loudly enough for the Boeing expert to hear over the conference link. 'And the Department of Homeland Security. But at the moment there doesn't seem to be any threat to the US.'

'Okay,' said Sam. 'They're orbitting a 767 over London?'

'Yes. They say they'll crash it into the city unless we do what they say. If we do as asked, they'll fly it away.'

'That's bad. What can we do?'

'We'd like to know how they're flying it. Could it be remote control? Can it be flown without pilots? You know, like a drone?'

'Not for take-off,' said Sam. 'They'd need a pilot to do that. But once the autopilot is in it doesn't need human input. The autopilot will follow whatever's in the FMC.'

'FMC?'

'Sorry,' smiled Sam. 'Flight Management Computer. It controls the vertical and lateral flight path.'

'So if it took off with a pilot he or she would still be on board?'

'Unless they baled out somewhere.'

Beryl's eyebrows lifted in surprise. 'Can you jump out of an airliner? I didn't think that was possible.'

'It's been done before. As long as the plane is depressurised you can get out through a cockpit sliding window or overwing emergency exit. Difficult, and dangerous, but not impossible.'

'So there may or may not be anyone at the controls?'

The face on the laptop screen smiled. 'My guess is they are still on board.'

'What makes you say that?'

'It would make more sense that way. The plane is obviously in a holding pattern. But you can't program the FMC to fly a certain number of orbits and then head off someplace else. It's not that sophisticated. So, assuming they don't want the repercussions of letting it run out of fuel while it's still in the holding pattern, they'll need a human pilot to vacate the hold and take up a new heading. Remote control is an impossibility, I would say.'

'I see. Well, thanks, Sam. Will you be available if we need more help from you?'

The laptop face grinned. 'At your service, ma'am. Good luck.'

'Thank you,' smiled back the Home Secretary.

The screen blanked. Beryl turned to Sir David. 'What about these explosives? Is that a bluff?'

'Probably. It would be impossible to get unauthorised material through Security.'

'They got an unauthorised pilot through . . . unless it's the normal crew flying it. Has anyone checked that?'

'They've been accounted for. They're staying in a hotel in Nottingham. They seem as surprised as we are. So is the Russian owner.'

The Home Secretary shook her head. 'What a mess!'

'My gut feeling is that there are no explosives on board,' said the Deputy Commissioner.

'I hope you're right, David.'

'There's fuel in its tanks, of course . . . '

Paul Grumbridge cleared his throat. 'What about evacuating the city, dear. Just in case everything went horribly wrong. Is that a good idea?'

Beryl deflected the question towards the Deputy Commissioner with her glance. 'What about it, David? Is it feasible in—' she looked at her watch—'ninety minutes?'

Sir David shook his head. 'Impossible. It would just create total chaos and the world's biggest traffic jam. Anyway, if the jet did crash, how do we know it would be in London? How much control do the bad guys have over it? Suppose we did evacuate London, which is beyond the bounds of possibility anyway. Suppose the jet came down in . . . I don't know . . . Maidenhead or somewhere.'

The Home Secretary's husband subsided again. 'It was just a thought. You have to hand it to these guys. They've got us over a barrel with their devilish little scheme. It's quite clever really. They should get some sort of prize for ingenuity,' he added with a smile.

'It's not amusing, dear,' said the Home Secretary. 'I'm sure David doesn't find it funny.'

But the Police Commissioner was smiling too. 'You've got a point, Paul. It's one in the eye for the good guys. Looks like the opposition have scored the first goal on this one. But the match isn't over yet.'

'Well, gentleman,' continued the Home Secretary. 'I just hope you're still smiling when that airliner runs out of fuel.'

CHAPTER 26

Yes, it's behaving itself nicely.

Mitchell Fradini had been watching the aircraft following an invisible race track in the night sky. He had programmed the navigation system to anchor the pattern over the centre of Britain's capital city. Below him the cloud was breaking up and the sprawling phosphorescent moss of the city's lights wheeled under his right wing as the autopilot uncomplainingly dragged the airliner round its monotonous flight path. He was still ignoring radio transmissions sent to him although he had left the transponder on the emergency squawk to make sure that they knew where he was. The idea was that they would eventually give up trying to plead with or threaten him.

Down in the 767's forward hold the occupants had made some progress. At least they were not cold. They could not know, of course, that Fradini had turned the air conditioning controls to maximum heating to compensate for the pressurisation air generated by the engines escaping through the open exit hatch. The same air source supplied both the passenger cabin and the cargo holds.

After a fruitless initial search feeling round the door frame area for the switch controlling the lights Jagger's fingers had eventually found it tucked away in a recess under a protective hinged panel.

'Eureka!' he shouted as the lights came on.

'Oh my God,' said Sarah, looking down at her front. Blood had oozed from the gunshot wound over her clothes. She was sitting in a pool of blood.

'Jesus!' said Jagger. 'Is it still bleeding?'

They had removed her jacket and blouse, Jagger temporarily unable to resist admiring her physique while Sarah winced in pain. It seemed blood was still leaking from the wound itself, but not in life-threatening torrents. Jagger folded the blouse into a pad for the girl to press against the source of bleeding.

'God, that hurts,' murmured the girl.

'Look, there's a panel,' said Jagger, pointing to an area on the forward bulkhead, ahead of the netting. 'Perhaps we can knock it out with this.' He was holding the aluminium ladder Shepherd had thrown in before closing the door.

'But wouldn't they hear us, the people flying the plane, if we start bashing away?'

'Good point. Okay, let's think of something else.'

He set to work to detach the netting at the forward end of the hold, enticed by the prospect of checking the contents of a grey box attached to the bulkhead in case it contained something useful. But their hopes were quickly dashed. Inside were tins of engine oil and hydraulic fluid, two empty Coca Cola cans and an ancient chocolate bar but no tools of any sort.

Disappointed, Jagger inspected the access panel. What was its purpose? Secured by six crosshead screws, it was easily big enough for a person to crawl through. But how could you unfasten it without a screwdriver or knife blade. Unless . . .

'Have you got a nail file on you?' he asked.

Sarah shook her head. 'My handbag's in the car, remember. Besides which I could never have got it through Security.'

'What about your earrings?'

The girl took one off and handed it to Jagger, who tried to rotate one of the screws with its clip but the flimsy piece of metal just broke off. The second one lasted no longer.

'Shit, there must be something we can do,' said Jagger. 'What about that placard?' The rectangular metal object attached the netting was a notice announcing in several languages that any bags behind the netting belonged to the crew and should not be removed by baggage handlers.

Jagger managed to bend the placard in half and then back on itself, again and again until the metal broke. He held the detached piece up triumphantly, like an actor winning as Oscar. He positioned a rounded edge into one of the hatch retaining screws and turned the makeshift tool but the metal twisted like cardboard and the screw stayed put.

'Bugger!' he muttered.

'Bugger,' she echoed. 'Well, it was a good idea anyway. Looks like we're stuck here till we land, Wilf.'

*****

Inspector Sahay looked at his watch. Just after ten. In all the hubbub dinner had eluded him and now his stomach was signalling demands for something for his gastric juices to work on. His eyes squinted against the dazzle of the television lights. This corner of the airport terminal main concourse looked more like a studio set. Beside him stood a stern-faced fireman, in uniform, and a thin callow youth in his teens. A production assistant was fussing around them. He pulled Sahay ten centimetres nearer the camera. Denise Watterham, the interviewer, looked up from her clipboard.

'Is everyone ready? Let's try a take.'

The assistant backed off, straightening the youth's jacket collar as he went. Denise started the item with a speech to camera.

'Drama at East Midlands Airport tonight. Just after eight o'clock an airliner took off without clearance, hitting a fire engine on the runway. The plane was a Boeing 767 belonging to Russian businessman Dmitry Chegolev. As far as anyone knows there are no passengers on board. With me here I have Inspector Sahay of the Nottingham police. Inspector, can you give us more details about this incident? What happened to the plane after it took off?'

Sahay took a breath, mentally reviewing how much he was going to disclose to the cyclops eye of the camera. He had agreed to the interview with some reluctance.

'Our information is that it headed towards the southeast, but we don't know its exact whereabouts at the moment.'

'Have you any ideas about who is flying it? Is it terrorists?'

'We have established that that is probably not the case.'

'So who could it be?'

'We have no information about that.'

'Have there been any demands of any sort?'

'Not to my knowledge.'

The interviewer turned to the firefighter.

'Fire officer Cartwright, can you tell us about what happened on the runway when the plane took off?'

'We got the alarm when it taxied out. Air Traffic Control told us to move our vehicles onto the runway in case it tried to take off.'

'Why didn't that ploy work?'

'It nearly did. I don't think any rational pilot would have tried to take off with only half the runway available. I think we're dealing with a nutcase here.'

'I understand one of the fire engines got hit by the plane. Was anyone hurt?'

'Yes, Chief Fire Officer Symonds and his driver were both injured.'

'How are they now?'

'The hospital says they're both stable. They're lucky to be alive. The Chief is still unconscious. The fire engine was totally destroyed.'

Denise turned to the camera again. 'One of the first people to realise something was amiss was plane spotter Gary Tomkin. Gary, where were you when the incident happened?'

The youth retreated slightly from the microphone thrust under his nose.

'I was on the observation platform. It didn't look like it was getting ready for departure in the normal way. It just suddenly taxied out and took off.'

'Can you tell us what you saw?'

'Well, it didn't have any lights on – navigation lights, I mean. There were some people walking round it before it went but I couldn't see who they were.'

'Crew members or engineers maybe?'

Tomkin shook his head. 'Like I say, I couldn't see.'

'Then what happened?'

'It taxied out and then it took off.'

'Still with no lights on?'

'It put its landing lights on for take-off.'

'Did you see the plane hit the fire engine, Gary?'

'Yes. It looked to me like the landing gear hit it. The fire engine was knocked over and tumbled over a few times.'

Cartwright chipped in. 'We can confirm that. We found debris on the runway. An assembly of four wheels.'

'From the plane?'

'Almost certainly.'

'Any other debris?'

'We're still looking, but we need daylight to search properly.'

'Is the runway closed now?'

'You'll need to check with Air Traffic Control about that. The latest information I have is that the runway is closed at the moment but they hope to open it again later. There's a backlog of flights waiting to go out.'

Denise brought the interview to a conclusion and the broadcast team began to pack up their gear, planning to take it up to the control tower to talk to the personnel on duty.

Inspector Sahay made straight for the cafeteria and bought himself a meat pie and a bar of chocolate. These he took out to his patrol car. He ordered his driver to take him back to the station in Nottingham. Sitting in the back seat, munching his way through his comestibles, he mentally reviewed the evening's denouement.

It had started with a call from the Leicestershire Constabulary, in whose jurisdiction the airport lay. Any serious criminal incident at East Midlands was automatically notified to the police Armed Response Unit in Nottingham as standard procedure, who in turn notified the CID. By chance, Sahay happened to be on duty. He was about to send a junior officer out to investigate when a second call came through, this time from the Met boys. They emailed him a transcript of the recording they had received. Sahay immediately conjectured that the incident might be connected to the big drugs deal they had been expecting. Confirmation came with another call from the Met, who told him the prisoner being sprung was an associate of Myron Winslade. The link between the criminal's demands and the incident at East Midlands Airport was therefore probably dispatcher Michael Shepherd of Central Airlines.

In a change of plan Sahay sent the junior officer round to the dispatcher's cottage in Hillgate and at the same time fixed himself up with a car and driver to get to the scene of the crime.

The first car drew a blank. Shepherd's girlfriend had no more idea than the police did as to his whereabouts. She had been expecting him home hours previously. The junior officer considered she was telling the truth. Sahay had got the report on his car radio as it neared the airport.

Nor was much joy forthcoming in the Central Airlines building. When Sahay arrived the place was swarming with police, looking busy and getting in each other's way. In the Ops room bemused Senior Controller Tomislav Kalmeta was fielding questions from a sergeant. Sahay dismissed the junior officer with a wave of his ID card and started on Kalmeta himself. He came straight to the point. Had Shepherd been at work that day? When did his duty end?

From Kalmeta, the Inspector learnt that his suspect had behaved perfectly normally until the moment he had dashed out of the office not long before the 767 took off.

'Was he behaving strangely after the incident?'

'Yes, but so were lots of other people. There was general panic. Micky came back to the office but seemed agitated. I thought maybe he was unnerved by what had happened, which was odd. He's not the sort of bloke who would go to pieces in an emergency.'

'So did he stay on duty?'

'Yes, until the end of his shift, I think. I vaguely remembering him asking me if it was okay to go home. We were in chaos, of course. The managers closed the airport and everyone was running around like blue-arsed flies, not knowing what to do. I never though to ask him why he had shot off just before the 767 was stolen.'

'I don't suppose you know where he is now?' asked the police officer.

'Well, at home, I guess.'

'No, he's not. When is he supposed to be coming to work again?'

Kalmeta found the staff roster. 'He's got three days off. He'll be in again next Wednesday.'

'I doubt it,' muttered Sahay to himself. He deflected a question from the Senior Controller about whether Shepherd was in trouble with the law and, deciding there was nothing else useful he could do at the airport, was about to make his way back to his office in Nottingham to see what new developments had come to light when he was intercepted by the TV news team.

Thus it was that Sahay had found himself under the lights stonewalling questions from an interviewer, denying all knowledge of the whereabouts of the stolen aircraft and of any demands or threats from the perpetrators of the crime. At the back of his mind was the sombre caution against interference he had read from the transcript. Spilling the beans on camera would not be a good idea.

And now his patrol car was speeding him back to Nottingham while he finished off his pie. Already he was cursing himself for not bringing in Shepherd earlier for questioning. The tubby detective sighed. Hindsight was always crystal clear.

*****

'There it is!'

Standing in the street outside the Transec building James Healey pointed up to the sky where the lights of a circling airliner flickered against torn shreds of cloud. Somehow the grace of its flight compounded its evil, an angel of death. Beryl shivered, not only from the cold. The previous aura of unreality about the whole crisis was instantly banished by the sinister flashing of the 767's strobe lights. The little group had been joined by Transec Duty Threat Assessor Margot Madeling, a black woman about ten years younger than the Grumbridges with friendly eyes and a ready smile.

It had been Paul Grumbridge's idea to verify the facts for themselves. Clutching at the proverbial straw, Beryl had revoiced her earlier suggestion that perhaps the whole thing was a hoax.

'Are you sure that's the rogue aircraft?' asked Beryl now.

'No other traffic around,' said Margot. 'Heathrow's open again but they're using the easterly runways. So the only plane round here is our friend up there.'

After a minute or two the evening chill overcame the mesmeric effect of the intruder in the night sky and the party trooped back inside to the warmth of the office. Now it was a waiting game. Sir David was on his mobile phone almost continuously, absorbing information, giving instructions. Meanwhile Beryl reviewed the developments of the past hour. There were a few crumbs of comfort. The Prime Minister had called from Singapore to tell them they were playing it right. He instructed Beryl to use her own judgement in any further decisions and keep him in the loop.

Next had come a debate on tactics. Beryl had again offered her husband the chance of retreating to his club for the rest of the evening but was inwardly glad when he opted to stay. His moral support was helping her to take the strain.

'Can't desert you in your hour of need, old thing. Might be able to chip in.'

Some of her husband's ideas were not too helpful, like the suggestion that they shoot the sod down. But occasionally he was able to offer points of view not immediately obvious to the others.

'Suppose we didn't go along with them.'

'Presumably they would carry out their threat.'

'But how? How do you crash an airliner? If it's not a suicide mission, what would happen to the pilot? Shall we try to get that Boeing man again? Ask what he thinks.'

Margot replied. 'I got hold of the Chief Pilot of Blue Planet Airlines. He's rated on the 767 and he's giving us technical advice.

He told me it would be easy to program the autopilot to start a gradual descent while it circled.'

'But what about the pilot?'

No-one had an answer. Beryl reprised the previous conversation about baling out. It didn't get them any further. Healey brought them all back to harsh reality with the blunt reiteration that they couldn't afford to take the chance of calling the bluff.

By this time the media were baying for the full story. They were already broadcasting the audacious theft of the airliner circling over London and now they demanded an update. From the beginning Sir David had recommended witholding further information. The last thing they wanted, he had explained, was swarms of helicopters full of reporters harrassing the intruder. Beryl considered this good advice and instigated a news blackout until the threat was over. At Margot's suggestion, she closed all airspace within ten miles of the city centre to all air traffic apart from commercial flights operating out of Heathrow.

Afterwards came the more practical business of organising the release of Maurice Holmin from Stensfield Prison. The Home Secretary had reminded the prison governor that he should get her permission before completing the procedure.

Now Beryl asked Sir David whether the police had worked out who the perpetrators of the crime might be.

'Well, we've got one or two ideas now more gen has come to light. Nottingham CID have been keeping tabs on a Central Airlines employee recently. A man named Michael Shepherd, suspected to be involved in drug dealing. I hear that this bloke has apparently just done a runner so he looks like a prime candidate. And the Met boys have a few villains in mind who might also be a part of it.'

Beryl turned to the Threat Assessor. 'How long did you say the plane's fuel would last, Margot?'

'According to the Blue Planet Chief Pilot its total endurance will be about twelve hours if it took off with full tanks. Say eight o'clock tomorrow morning. It'll be light by then of course. Not that that makes much difference to anything.'

'So how long could it keep circling over London?'

'The nearest areas of water are the Channel or the North Sea. Depending on speed it would take fifteen to twenty minutes to get to either.'

'And we're pretty well powerless until it leaves.'

'I'm afraid so, Beryl.'

CHAPTER 27

Prison Officer Harold Ford was doing a crossword in the Recreation Room when his pager beeped. The message told him to report immediately to the governor's office. None of the other three warders in the room had been called. His brow furrowed as he scanned his memory, searching for reasons for the summons. There was no way the old git could have found out about his little business supplying recreational materials, mainly booze, to the prisoners.

When he knocked on the door and walked in his jaw dropped. With the grim-faced governor were two uniformed police officers and prisoner Maurice Holmin, for some reason wearing civilian clothes. Alarmingly, the prisoner was not handcuffed or under any apparent restraint. More alarmingly, Holmin's mouth metamorphosed into a grin when he saw Ford, although his eyes conveyed a different message.

'Hello, Harry.'

Ford's eyes flickered from governor to prisoner and back again. *What was going on?*

'You sent for me, sir.' The statement was a question.

Governor Westgate sighed. His quiet evening at home had been ruined by the unexpected phone call. But as he had explained to his wife as he went for his coat, you don't argue with the Director General of the Prison Service and the Home Secretary.

'Harry, I'm sorry about this,' said Westgate, 'but a difficult situation has arisen. Prisoner Holmin is being released and he wants you to go with him. It seems—'

Maurice Holmin interrupted. 'It's true, Harry. You and I are going for a little journey. Needless to say, the governor doesn't really want to let me go, but he's got no choice. Let me explain.' He began a summary of the evening's events, the warder's face registering increasing incredulity as the story unfolded.

'Is this for real?' asked Ford, directing his question to the governor, who responded with a resigned nod of the head.

'Sir,' continued the warder. 'I can't agree. This man is a homicidal maniac. He'll kill me.'

The governor turned to address Holmin. 'Do you really need Harry to go with you?'

'Yes, I do,' came the reply. 'But I give you an absolute guarantee that he won't be harmed in any way. It's just that we need him for a while.' The prisoner spoke to the warder. 'Harry, you're just an insurance policy, that's all. When we've got what we want we'll let you go. There might even be a fee payable for your services. Come on, man, we've done business before, haven't we? This is just a bit more of the same.'

'What business is that, then?' asked the governor, looking none too pleased at this revelation. His gaze further discomforted the warder.

'I don't know what he's talking about, sir. He's just trying to blacken my name.'

'Don't panic, Harry,' said Holmin. He turned to the governor. 'It was all innocent stuff. When I wanted to trade shares in the stock market, Harry acted as my intermediary, that's all.'

'Is that true?' asked Westgate.

Ford relaxed a little. 'Yes, sir. Doing my bit to help rehabilitation. Nothing improper.'

'Is it on the Register?' Regulations to prevent corruption required full declaration of dealings between the imprisoned and their guards.

'I can't remember if I—'

'Okay, fellas,' interrupted Holmin with finality. 'The pow-wow is over. Time's a-wasting. We've got to get moving, Harry. That plane is burning fuel all the time.'

'You promise I won't be harmed,' asked Ford, his voice not entirely free of suspicion.

'I promise. Hey, you've three witnesses here.' Another grin, again with no warmth.

'Okay,' said the warder, seemingly not completely convinced. In his agitated state it did not occur to him to ask why Holmin had selected him and not another warder.

Outside the prison gates the white Transit van was parked alongside the police patrol car, whose lights were still flashing. One of the officers had driven the van in convoy with the car.

'Switch those lights off,' ordered Holmin. 'Where's the gun?'

There was a hesitation among the others, who looked at each other sheepishly.

'Gentlemen, this is not a game,' said Holmin with an edge in his voice. 'Who's got the gun?'

Governor Westgate nodded to the uniformed officers. One of them retrieved the silenced Glock 17 from the patrol car and handed it over together with a spare clip of ammunition, unable to disguise his revulsion.

With a wry grin Holmin released the safety and pointed the weapon at the officer at the officer who had given it to him. 'Do I need to test it?'

'It works fine,' said the policeman, trying to stay calm.

The newly released prisoner swung the barrel away from the assembled company and aimed at the front wheel of the patrol car. He squeezed the trigger and a muffled plop could be heard, followed immediately by the hiss of the deflating tyre.

'Good enough,' he said. 'Okay, Harry, this is where we say bye-bye to our friends. First of all, though, Governor Westgate, I'd like you to take Harry's cuffs and secure his hands behind his back.' He turned to the warder. 'Just precautionary, Harry. Remember I promised you you'll be returned in good shape.'

Having enjoyed the spectacle of the humiliated prison chief handcuffing one of his own men Holmin now ordered Harry Ford to get into the van on the passenger side. He looped the safety belt through cuffs several times and secured the end in its buckle, out of reach of Ford's fingers.

'No doubt you people have stuck a tracker somewhere on the vehicle,' said Holmin to the others. 'I expected nothing else. But remember, any interference and that plane comes down, okay? Now, who's going to give me their mobile as a little parting gift?'

The governor handed over his personal phone and watched Holmin dial a number.

'Hi, it's me. I'm setting off now. Is everything okay? . . . good . . . no, I've got a hostage . . . don't worry, he'll only be with us a short time . . . okay, see you soon.'

The prisoner got into the driver's seat and started the engine. The van swung round and disappeared into the night, but not before Governor Westgate caught a glimpse of a scared Harry Ford looking out of the window. Westgate felt a pang of remorse. Although Ford was not one of his star officers and there were a few question marks against his reputation, nevertheless he was one of his charges and therefore entitled to his protection. Now the governor found himself wondering if he would ever see Harry Ford again.

*****

Besides the artic there was another vehicle in the lay-by—a truck containing a small JCB mechanical digger. It had arrived earlier in the evening and its driver had handed it over to Ron Maynard as previously instructed by Myron Winslade. They drove the vehicle to Bury St Edmunds station for the driver to catch a train back to London and then Maynard took it back to the lay-by. The long wait resumed.

'Ah, this could be them now,' said Lester McAndrew, squinting against the approaching headlights. The white Transit pulled into the lay-by to face the artic. The three men in the cab jumped down to meet the newcomers.

Holmin got out of the van and approached them.

'No problems, then?' said Maynard with a grin.

'Like clockwork,' came the reply.

'Who's the guy with you?' asked Maynard, pointing to the passenger in the van. 'He doesn't look too happy.'

'A screw from the nick. I used him as a hostage but we don't need him anymore. Is everything okay in the lorry?'

'Yes, the stuff's loaded as instructed.'

'Good.' Holmin looked at his watch. 'Did you bring me a mobile? I had to throw the one they gave me away in case they were tracking it.'

Maynard handed the phone over.

'And the jerrycan?'

'Yeah, ten litres of petrol, like Myron said.'

'Okay, first things first. Get the JCB out.'

Winslade's men set about their task. There was little traffic going past on the road but the men were careful to watch for any sign that they were being observed.

The prisoner walked back to the van. He opened the passenger door and addressed Ford.

'Well, Harry, a puzzle for you.'

'What?'

'You tell me where we are and I'll let you go.'

The warder waited for a moment, obviously wondering how to answer.

'We're in the lay-by the coded emails referred to.'

'How do you know?'

'I drove here myself to check it out.'

Holmin nodded. 'I guessed you'd do that.'

'Are you going to let me go? I give you my word I won't say anything about this place.'

'I've just had a thought, Harry. When I arrived at the nick you gave me a special drink. Orange juice. Flavour was a bit odd but you made me drink it. Do you remember?'

'I'm really sorry.'

'I expect you are . . . now.' Holmin reached in his pocket and pulled out the Glock police pistol. 'Haven't fired one of these in ages. Maybe I could do with a little target practice.' He flipped off the safety catch and pointed the weapon at Ford's head.

'No, Maurice,' pleaded the prison officer. 'I'll do anything you say.'

Holmin laughed and lowered the gun. 'No, I won't waste a bullet on you. Tell you what, Harry, you're probably sick of the sight of me. So I'll get one of my chums to take you away. You won't want to see what we're doing here. Very boring.'

'So you're letting me go?'

'Not exactly.'

Chas Lummick was driving the JCB digger off the smaller truck's lowered loading platform onto the lay-by, watched by the other two. Holmin called Lester McAndrew over.

'My friend here likes being in this van so much he wants you to take him for another drive.'

'Sure thing.'

'Tiny problem, though.'

'Yeah?'

'The cops might have planted a tracker somewhere on the van, even though I told them not to.'

'You can't trust those bastards,' grinned McAndrew.

'You said it,' said Holmin. 'So it's probably best to take that can of petrol with you. Drive the van to somewhere in the middle of nowhere. Slosh the petrol around and then set light to it. That way the tracker will be destroyed. Then do a runner yourself.'

'What about me?' interjected Ford desperately.

Holmin ignored him. 'Any questions, Lester?'

'What about the . . . passenger?'

'Well, it's a bit cold this evening, isn't it. He may as well stay in the van when you go. The flames will keep him warm.'

'Okay. I'll go and get the petrol.'

'You can't just kill someone in cold blood,' pleaded Ford. 'Please let me go, Maurice. I'll do anything.'

'It won't be in cold blood, Harry. Hot blood maybe.'

Ignoring further pleas from the warder, Holmin watched McAndrew stow the petrol can inside the van and get into the driver's seat. He leaned in the window.

'Drive carefully, Lester. We don't want any accidents. Wouldn't want our passenger to get hurt, would we?'

'Best behaviour, boss,' grinned McAndrew. 'I'll drive like a little old lady on the way to church.'

'Off you go, then. Make your own way back to London. Myron will contact you about payment.'

'You got it.'

McAndrew started the engine.

'Please, Maurice, please . . .'

Holmin turned his back as the van drove off.

'Pathetic,' he muttered.

*****

Chas Lummick drove the JCB off the paved surface, through the gate in the border hedge and into the field the other side. Holmin and Maynard switched off all the lights on the artic and the smaller truck and then followed in the digger's tracks, supplementing its headlights with hand-held torches. Occasional glances backwards showed an empty road with just the odd vehicle hurrying by.

On the far side of the field were the trees of Loffley Wood. The small procession moved into the woods and after a minute or two stopped for Holmin to check their bearings. As he flashed his torch around the other two men noticed four red reflectors shining back at them from the tree trunks they were attached to. Holmin walked slowly into the centre of the area marked out by the reflectors, checking the angles with his torch. He nodded and summoned the JCB to where he stood. He pointed down.

'Here.'

It didn't take long for the digger to find the metal object buried half a metre below ground level.

'My little beauty,' said Holmin, leaning down and brushing away the dirt. 'Nice to meet you again. Sorry I had to leave you like that.'

Lummick used the JCB's shovel to clear the earth and vegetation away, the lights revealing a chest the size of a filing cabinet. The three men manoeuvred it so that it rested vertically in the shovel. From the cab they took ropes to tie the chest in position, after which Lummick raised it a metre or so off the ground. Satisfied that the load was secure the group retraced their tracks to the lay-by, the digger occasionally wobbling on the uneven ground under its increased weight.

Maynard reparked the smaller truck so that its rear faced the open doors of the artic trailer and then lowered its loading platform, onto which the three men manhandled the chest. Maynard operated the controls to lift the platform up to the level of the trailer floor. Pushing the chest into the trailer was again a three man job untill it reached the roller floor, after which it was easy to position it behind the row of pallets already there.

Five minutes later the artic was westbound back along the road it had come along earlier, Ron Maynard driving.

In the trailer Maurice Holmin and Chas Lummick set to work.

CHAPTER 28

Myron Winslade was at home in his Docklands penthouse, leaning back on the sofa in contemplation. He tapped his chin with his mobile, which for the moment was quiet. His partner, Jill, an elegant brunette, offered him a refill from the whisky bottle but he declined. There might be new problems to deal with. Got to keep his wits about him!

All in all the operation was running well. Phase One—Fradini boarding the Russian 767—had gone as planned. The first critical point was passed—the theft of the aircraft. The large wall TV was showing continuous coverage of the event, with live pictures of the aircraft circling over London from ground level cameras. It was good to note that there were no airborne shots, which proved that the authorities had heeded the warnings about surveillance. From his balcony, Winslade himself had seen the 767 circling above the broken cloud.

There had been glitches. They had hoped the element of surprise would enable Fradini to take off before anyone could stop him. It was brave of him to continue with fire trucks blocking the runway. The two million dollars they were paying him was obviously a powerful incentive, not to mention evading capture. From the TV reports it looked like the 767 had collided with one of the trucks and damaged its landing gear. Not a problem, as the aircraft would not be needing it again.

Michael Shepherd had had to revert to his back-up plan. After leaving the airport at the end of his shift he had phoned Winslade to appraise him of the unexpected appearance of two people, a man and a woman, on the GA Apron just before the start of Phase 2. He recognised the woman as the sister of Giles Amberley-Kemp. He didn't know what had triggered their interference as there wasn't time to question them. Luckily he had been able to incarcerate them in the 767's hold just before it left, so they couldn't compromise the operation.

The original plan was that as there would be no evidence to directly link him to Damocles, he would be able to continue to work at Central Airlines for a while, even if he subsequently came under suspicion. When the hubbub had died down he would then decide when to quit, his reputation untarnished any further. The payoff from Damocles would give him plenty of options if he wanted to start a new life elsewhere.

But, he told Winslade, it was obvious now that his cover was blown. The authorities would immediately link his irrational behaviour at work to the events of the evening. So that meant a bale out. He was at that moment staying in a hotel under an assumed name. He would have to leave the country as soon as the heat died down. The 'new life elsewhere' would have to be launched with the fake ID Winslade had provided for this eventuality.

Shepherd and Winslade had briefly discussed the two intruders, in case their turning up meant that changes needed to be made for the rest of the operation.

'So they definitely weren't security officers?'

'No. It was Giles's sister and an older man. I think she's a pilot. Him I don't know about.'

'Maybe it was random.'

'No. They must have found out something.'

'The Giles document?'

'Yes, that's what I was thinking. Perhaps they discovered it too soon. Sarah lives in the same house, remember.'

The document was the progeny of sibling hatred. Auberon Amberley-Kemp had always been jealous of his brother Giles, the apple of his parents' eye. Even his sister Sarah was not held in as high esteem as stupid, pathetic, druggie Giles.

Bron had first met Michael Shepherd at the Arriba Club, where they were both members. During a subsequent conversation it had become apparent to the dispatcher that there was no love lost between the two Amberly-Kemp brothers. Shepherd said he knew of Giles through a mutual acquaintance who had sold Giles drugs once or twice in the past. It soon became clear to Shepherd that Bron had few qualms about operating outside the law if the rewards were good enough. Thus it was, after careful vetting, that Bron joined the Damocles group, funding part of the operation for a guaranteed doubling of his investment if it came off. If they could implicate Giles in Damocles it would take the heat off the real perpetrators. Setting up the brother he loathed as the fall guy would be the icing on the cake.

In the aftermath everyone and everything remotely under suspicion would be investigated. When Giles came under scrutiny the police would search his domicile—Orchard Lea Grange. In his room, where Bron had hidden it in a clothes drawer, they would find a document giving details of the Damocles plan. Some of the data was clear and accurate, such as the 767 theft, some deliberately cryptic and some designed to confuse, such as meaningless coded identifications. When questioned about how the document had come into his possession, Giles would protest his innocence, of course, but the police would not be convinced. Poor Giles!

Well, thought Myron Winslade now, *they might have found the document earlier than planned but at least everything else is chugging along nicely.* Maurice Holmin had been sprung and, if the operation was running to time, he and the cargo would be heading back towards Nottingham and East Midlands airport at that very moment.

Not even Winslade knew the exact contents of the metal chest his men had just helped to dig up. He rightly suspected it was a drugs stash. He could not know that the original shipment was seven hundred kilos of heroin which had been smuggled into the UK by Holmin's men two years previously in a container on a freight train. Like most of the world's supply, the heroin had originated in the poppy fields of Afghanistan. More than half of the load had subsequently been sold on, making Holmin a very rich man. One of the dealers who had tried to cheat him over a consignment had ended up being tied to the towing hook of Holmin's car for a little drive in the countryside, for which misdemeanour Holmin had ended up being detained at Her Majesty's Pleasure.

Just over three hundred kilos of the drug haul had been secreted in a metal chest for hiding in Loffley Wood near Bury St Edmonds for future distribution. Of the highest purity, it had been packaged in plastic bags, each holding exactly two kilos. At current market prices the contents of the chest were worth around forty million euros. Even after paying for the Damocles operation there would be plenty of profit left for Maurice Holmin after the drugs had been sold on to Willi Prosch and other buyers abroad.

Getting the merchandise out of the country would not be easy. The police would be on high alert after Holmin's escape. The UK would be scoured high and low. The ports, airports and railway stations would be under intense surveillance, the authorities hoping to spot him if he tried to leave the country. Passengers and cargo alike would be under scrutiny. It was Michael Shepherd who suggested using the same airport from which the 767 had been stolen. *They'll spend their time questioning people who work there so they won't bother too much about freight transiting the airport, especially if it goes out the same night.*

Winslade had consulted with Holmin, who had agreed the plan. Originally it was proposed to pick up the drug haul in the Transit and take it to the Beeston lock-up near Nottingham, where the Casu-Wear boxes of clothes were stored. But Holmin was worried about the van being electronically tracked in contravention of their instructions so the plan was revised. The clothes boxes were taken to the drug stash instead. An artic driving back to Nottingham would be unlikely to be intercepted and the van, and any tracker attached to it, could be destroyed.

There was one problem which needed further attention. The plan was to take the cargo directly to the airport with the forged documents certifying security clearance by Midland Freight Forwarding. But supposing the airline contacted MFF for prior confirmation of the flight? A negative response might arouse suspicion. It was decided to approach MFF and arrange a normal contract, telling them the cargo would arrive on the day of the flight for immediate processing and onward transit. That would satisfy any query from the airline. Then Shepherd would call MFF and say the shipment was delayed by an hour or two, expecting them to notify the carrier in turn. To make sure the carrier didn't cancel the flight, Willi Prosch had arranged a genuine cargo to be flown by the same airline from Düsseldorf to Manchester the following day. By the time MFF had initiated the 'no-show' procedure the Damocles operation would be over.

*****

In the artic trailer Holmin's mobile rang. It was Ron Maynard calling from the cab.

'Just about to hit the motorway . . . er . . . boss. How's it going back there?'

'We're good,' replied Holmin, pleased that Maynard had remembered not to use names during phone calls. It was almost certain the cops or security people would be monitoring mobile networks.

They had spent the last hour and a half secreting the bags of heroin in the top layer of Casu-Wear boxes, inserting four or five bags under a few layers of jeans in each one and then resealing them with parcel tape. Three of the four pallets were now completely bound in transparent plastic pallet wrap sheeting, wound on with an applicator. The forged Midland Freight Forwarding documents were attached, certifying compliance with security screening requirements.

The first pallet had not yet been sealed. The top flaps of the enlarged construction of four combined boxes were open. Inside, at the bottom, Chas Lummick had positioned a low cushioned stool. Also in the enlarged box were a length of rubber tubing, taped to a broom handle at one end, and a backpack, containing a Stanley knife, a wind-up torch, a Kindle electronic book reader, a packet of biscuits and two litre bottles of drinking water. The gun was still in his jacket pocket.

'Well, here I go,' said Holmin now. 'Time to disappear.' He stepped inside the box and sat on the stool. 'It's not the Ritz,' he snorted, 'but I suppose it'll have to do for a while.'

'You'll be alright, Maurice,' grinned Lummick. 'It's only for a few hours, then you can stay in the best hotels in the world.'

'That's the idea,' said Holmin. 'Oh, nearly forgot. I'll need that empty plastic bottle too, Chas.'

'Yeah, what goes in must come out,' laughed Lummick, handing over the bottle.

Holmin made himself as comfortable as he could. Lummick passed in a block of foam rubber for Holmin to cushion his back against.

'Hey, back in my cell again,' said the escaped prisoner.

'But no screws to worry about. What was name of the one you brought with you?'

'Harry Ford. Harry Ford RIP, I should say. Let's try the breather, Chas.'

They closed the top flaps of the enlarged box. In one of them was the incision that had been cut by Michael Shepherd while the boxes were in the Beeston lock-up, three sides of a square about five centimetres in width. Holmin now pushed the broom handle up through the square, forcing it to hinge upwards. The plastic tube attached to it thereby gained access to outside air so that the occupant of the box could breathe. If required the contraption could be retracted so that an outside observer would not notice the modification.

'It's okay,' came the muffled voice from inside the box. 'Seal it up, Chas. Don't forget to attach the documents. I'll call Ron on my mobile to confirm everything's alright.'

Lummick used the applicator to wrap the boxes on the pallet which incorporated Holmin's hideaway. He cut an irregular gash just above the breathing flap so Holmin could push the tube through it when required. *There, job done!*

'Yeah, just coming up to the checkout, boss, five minutes to go,' said Ron Maynard in the cab, answering Holmin's call on his mobile. 'Checkout' was code for 'East Midlands Airport.'

CHAPTER 29

In the Meteor office Nathan Bishop picked up the satellite weather picture as soon as the printer had stopped. He added it the data sheets he had already retrieved from the computer and stapled them together. Then he sat down at a desk and perused the information, occasionally marking relevant passages with a red pen.

'Good evening, Commander.'

Bernie Crowburn had just come into the room. The allusion was to Bishop's new status as Captain-under-training. 'Your humble copilot reporting for duty.' He dropped his flight bag next to Bishop's and sat down beside him.

They were probably the only pilots at the airport not in uniform. Crowburn wore a navy blue blazer and tie, a sartorial contrast to Bishop's battered leather jacket with shiny metal studs spelling out SOD OFF on the back.

'Quite a little upset they had here earlier on, Bish. I saw it on the news before I left home. Anything new?'

'No. The 767's still swanning around over London. The official line is that the authorities are negotiating with the pilot, but that might be bullshit to stop people panicking, of course. No-one wants another 9/11. They've restricted the airspace round it but otherwise UK air traffic is operating normally as far as I know.'

'What about here?'

'Normalish. The airport's open but a lot of flights are still delayed.' Bishop tapped the computer monitor. 'Got an email from MFF. They tried to call us earlier but no-one was here of course.'

'What does it say?'

'Our cargo might be delayed by an hour or two.'

'Because of the upheaval here?'

'It doesn't say. I thought I'd finish the preps and then give them a call. See if they've got a new arrival time. I told Mike and Gerry to stay at home in case "an hour or two" turns out to be ten or twelve.'

'Suppose the cargo doesn't turn up. Do we scrub?'

'No, we'll still have to go, Bernie. Don't forget we're taking a load from Düsseldorf to Manch tomorrow.'

'What's tonight's cargo?'

'Clothes.'

'Shall I call MFF now, Nathan? See if they've got an update.'

The younger pilot thought for a second. 'Yeah, thanks Bernie.'

Crowburn went to pick up the office phone but it started ringing before he reached it.

'Yes . . . that's right . . . really? . . . excellent. Okay, you can start transferring it right away. Will you fix it with the Supervisor or do you want us to? . . . great . . . yes . . . don't know yet, depends on Air Traffic . . . that's right . . . thanks.'

Bishop raised his eyebows quizzically.

'Our cargo has just turned up,' said the older pilot. 'Reception are notifying the Loading Supervisor. Shall we bring in Gerry and Mike?'

Bishop shook his head. 'No, let's leave them in peace. We'll use airport loaders if they're available. Can you call ATC and tell them we'll now be ready for a departure on schedule? Find out if we can expect any delay.'

'Okay, Commander.'

The reply was optimistic. 'They've got most of the backlog cleared,' Crowburn advised his younger colleague, still holding the phone. 'Shouldn't be any probs for us.'

'Okay, in that case check with the Supervisor that loaders are available, Bernie.'

The reply was affirmative. Sunday rates of course.

'Well, I'm sure Wilf won't mind,' said Bishop. 'We got a good price for this charter.'

'Where is our Lord and Master this evening anyway?'

'He went to Sarah's for dinner. Maybe he's still there. Strange though. When I turned up for work the door was unlocked and the computer was on, and the lights.'

'That doesn't sound like our Wilf,' agreed Crowburn. 'He's neurotic about switching things off to save electricity.'

The two pilots went back to the routine of pre-flight preparations.

'Anyway,' said Bishop, 'here's the picture for tonight.' He summarised his flight planning to the older man. 'Weather's fine en route and at destination. Fuel's based on twenty tail, commercial alternate Cologne, fuel alternate Frankfurt, thirty minutes holding. Nothing significant on Notams.'

Looking at the charts printed out from the computer, Bishop had concurred with its estimate of a twenty knot tailwind. If they couldn't land at Düsseldorf for some reason they would divert to Cologne, the nearest alternate. But as an extra safety margin Bishop had based diversion fuel on Frankfurt, which was further away. The Notams, or Notices to Air Men, alerted crews to operational matters which might impinge on their flights.

A smile appeared on Crowburn's face as he cross-checked Bishop's work.

'Sarah thinks they should be called Notaps.'

Bishop thought for a second, then made the connection. 'Notices to Air Persons,' he said wryly. 'That's the feminist in her, I guess. The times we live in, eh?'

*****

The Cargo Area was even busier than normal as airport staff tried to clear the backlog of flights caused by the earlier closure. Although passenger traffic was very light in the middle of the night the airport buzzed with a constant stream of freighters and parcels aircraft arriving and departing.

Cargo Reception checked the documentation accompanying the four pallets of clothing and allocated Ron Maynard a parking bay in the vast Transfer Building, into which he now drove the artic. He and Chas Lummick watched the airport loaders lift the Euro Traders pallets onto a train of pallets belonging to Meteor Air Express. The loaders didn't notice the look of concern on Maynard's face when the Holmin pallet was dumped without finesse on to a Meteor pallet by an uncaring fork lift driver.

'Hey, careful,' he called out.

The fork lift operator shrugged. 'Keep your hair on, mate. It's only clothes.'

Maynard and Lummick watched the loaders secure each pallet with strong nylon netting. Then a tractor hauled the train out of the building through a security barrier. Winslade's henchmen smiled at each other. They had done their bit.

*****

The two Meteor pilots walked over to Zulu Charlie just as handlers were positioining a set of stairs by the forward right side door and plugging in a ground power unit. Another man was readying the Hydromatic loader on the left side of the aircraft. As Bishop climbed the stairs and opened the door Crowburn started his external check, flashing his torch into the Merchantman's nooks and crannies. A whine of hydraulics made him look up to see the younger pilot opening the large cargo door from inside the aircraft.

Before long the pallet train trundled alongside and the Hydromatic loader began the process of lifting them one at a time into the freighter. The cargo was quickly, if brusquely, manhandled into the aircraft and secured with large metal clips on the roller tracks in the floor in accordance with the disposition Bishop had notified.

Back inside the aircraft, Crowburn joined Bishop in checking that the cargo was secure and correctly loaded. Between they closed and locked the crew access door and the cargo door and then cross-checked each other's work.

Going forward to the flight deck Bishop momentarily moved towards the copilot's seat before remembering that tonight's seating arrangement was different. *Old habits die hard!* He smiled to himself and lowered himself into the captain's seat, taking a moment to take in the new perspective.

Crowburn slid into the copilot seat and looked across.

'Great, isn't it?' he smiled.

'I've waited a long time for this.'

'It's worth the wait, Nathan. Nothing's better that being in charge of your own aeroplane.'

Bishop nodded. 'First Officer Crowburn,' he said with a grin. 'Would you be so kind as to check in with ATC to see if our take-off slot is still valid.'

'Of course, Captain!'

*****

Meteor Flight 231 was one of the very few to depart East Midlands Airport ahead of schedule that night. Air Traffic Control allowed Nathan Bishop to start taxying at 0345, fifteen minutes early. In a temporary lull there were only two aircraft ahead of them in the departure queue.

'Meteor 231, cleared take-off, wind calm,' radioed Tower.

Crowburn acknowledged and Bishop pushed the four throttles forward to wind up the Tynes. The lightly laden Merchantman accelerated promptly along runway two seven and at 0359 Bishop rotated Zulu Charlie's nose up to the take-off attitude. As it had done so many times over the preceding half-century the old feighter hauled itself into the air.

Watching from the area where they had reparked the artic, Chas Lummick and Ron Maynard grinned at each other. Maynard dialled a number on his mobile.

'Phase Five complete,' he said.

*****

The radio call jolted Mitchell Fradini into alertness. Hours of nothing to do except watch the autopilot fly in circles had almost sent him to sleep. Occasional trips to the toilet or walks up and down the cabin had done little to relieve the tedium. There was no other food in the galley to supplement the biscuits he had already eaten.

London Control had given up trying to elicit a response from him although he had kept the left VHF tuned to their frequency. It was dead—all the other traffic in the vicinity had been allocated different frequencies to prevent intrusion. The right comms radio was tuned to a different frequency, pre-arranged with the Damocles planners, who had bought a portable transceiver from an aviation enthusiasts' store. They knew that the intelligence services would be sweeping the entire VHF spectrum, hoping to intercept any transmissions from the rogue aircraft. So Fradini could not take the chance of using the radio himself to check on progress. But he could receive inbound messages on the frequency, such as the one now audible in his headset.

'Lima five two,' heard the American. 'Lima five two.'

Anyone listening might try to decode the cryptic message but they would be wasting their time. It was chosen randomly to signify to Fradini that he should take the aircraft out of the holding pattern and away from London. It meant also that Damocles was still up and running. 'Alpha one zero' would have signified that they had failed. The plan called for Fradini to keep the 767 flying over London as long as practicable to give them the best chance of success and then dispatch it to oblivion. Even if Damocles didn't work out the American had told the group that he had no intention of sending the aircraft down into the heart of London. Not for any altruistic motive. *If the law catches up with me I don't want that rap laid on me.*

The prospect of imminent action drew adrenalin into Fradini's bloodstream. Now at last he could point the 767 onto its escape route and himself towards the balance of his two million dollars.

As the aircraft turned into yet another circuit Fradini switched the autopilot into heading select mode and dialled zero two zero into the counter. The aircraft dutifully took up its northeast heading and levelled its wings to fly straight. Its nose was now pointed at Stavanger on the south coast of Norway, several hundred miles distant. Fradini was not to know this, nor would he have cared. In a few minutes he would take his leave and the 767 would continue on its way unmanned. Apart from the two suckers in the hold, of course. There was about three or four hours' worth of fuel left in the tanks. After that time the aircraft would end up— where? Who cares? Eventually the engines would draw the last of the fuel from the tanks. Starved, they would falter and die. Without thrust to sustain it the aircraft's speed would decay and the wings would stall and lose their lift. The 767 would drop its nose and spin towards the ground—or sea. There could be only one outcome. The impact of delicate metal structure against ground or water would be like slamming into a wall of concrete.

The amorphous glow of London passed behind and now the dark mass of East Anglia drifted underneath the airliner, speckled here and there with the amber lights of smaller towns. The pilot scanned the view ahead with renewed concentration. Yes, this would do it.

Had Fradini been paying more attention to the data screens in front of him and less to the outside world he might have noticed that the oil quantity gauge on the right engine was decreasing, at first imperceptibly, now rather more quickly. Inside its cowling the loose magnetic chip detector had slackened off to the extent that the dribble of oil leaking away had swelled to a golden stream. The engine was pumping out its life blood into the cowling, where it oozed down into the drain orifice to be torn into a billion droplets by the rush of slipstream.

Now the oil quantity edged below the minimum allowed limit. An amber message appeared on the screen in the flight deck. 'RIGHT OIL QTY'. Fradini did not notice.

CHAPTER 30

'Yes, he's definitely heading away.'

Behind the Fighter Controller and his assistant sitting in front of the radar screen stood Air Vice Marshall Keith Humphrey, duty Air Defence Commander. The Air Surveillance and Control System Centre, which monitored all airspace activity over the UK and surrounding waters, was housed in a blast-proof semi-underground complex in a valley just north of High Wycombe.

The Controller took his eyes off the screen and turned to Humphrey.

'Launch the QRAs now, sir?'

The Air Vice Marshall pondered. He had sent two Quick Reaction Alert Tornadoes up from Wattisham to investigate when the bogey had first appeared over the capital, only to be warned off by the Defence Secretary. Now the situation was different. It looked like the bogey was making off. Quickly he came to a decision.

'Yes, get them airborne.' The fighter base at Wattisham was situated ten miles to the northwest of Ipswich. 'Vector them behind the bogey so they're outside his visual range. They mustn't be seen but they must be close enough to engage if necessary. They must follow the bogey until it's outside UK airspace or it comes down, then return to base.'

'Engagement code, sir?' asked the FC.

'Double amber.'

Humphrey turned to the FC's assistant. 'Tell NATOC and Swanwick what we're doing.' The NATO Coordinator would alert the Scandinavian defence forces in case the rogue aircraft entered their airspace. At the Swanwick Air Traffic Control Centre near Southampton the civilian controllers would also be watching the continuing drama on their own radars. In an emergency a direct land line connected Swanwick with High Wycombe to allow liaison between the military and the civilians. At the other end of the line this Saturday evening was Wing Commander Roland Atterell, Shanwick's Military Supervisor. Tonight the line was in continuous use.

'Suppose the bogey turns back towards London, sir?' said the Fighter Controller now.

'Destroy it immediately,' replied Keith Humphrey.

*****

The Air Vice Marshall also sent word to his political masters in Knightsbridge. Beryl Grumbridge sank into an easy chair, a sigh of relief escaping her lips. For a moment she just switched her brain off, allowing the tension to drain away. She was hardly aware of Deputy Commissioner Jenkins rattling off orders into his secure mobile.

'I want patrols to start looking for Holmin and the other suspects immediately,' came the command. 'There are no restrictions now.' He referred to the information that had been passed on to him from the Nottingham police, reading the notes on the piece of paper he was holding. 'That's Michael Shepherd and Myron Winslade. Also to be arrested and detained is Giles Amberley-Kemp. Send out descriptions and known addresses. This is top priority nationwide . . . what? . . . when? . . . okay, I didn't realise that. Anyway, get the girlfriend. She might know something.'

*****

The two Tornado GR4s streaked away from runway 23 at Wattisham with afterburners crackling and the Fighter Controller picked them up on radar. He identified himself to the interceptors as 'Grocer' and vectored them onto a heading to close with the 767.

'Green section, I'll be vectoring you behind the bogey.' Like Air Vice Marshall Humphrey the FC had ascribed to the airliner the term for a potential enemy intruder. Green Leader acknowledged his instructions but almost immediately reported trouble. His wings were jammed in forward sweep. He couldn't angle them back to cruise geometry.

'I can press on but I'll be manoeuvre limited.'

'Standby, Green Leader. We'll get back to you. Green Two, remain with the Leader while we sort this out.'

'Green Two, roger, holding formation.'

The reply came quickly.

'Green Leader, this is Grocer. Proceed to Whisky Tango Mike to hold, level zero eight zero. Green Two continue as briefed.'

The lead aircraft banked away to return to the airfield, its pilot muttering curses to his navigator to the effect that not only had he missed the Gulf War because he was too young, missed Iraq because he was doing a tour on Hawk trainers but now, just when the chance for some real action came along, they gave him a wreck that couldn't fly.

Green Two's crew watched their colleagues depart and then accelerated away.

'No need to gallop,' radioed Grocer, 'you're closing nicely with the bogey.' It meant keep the aircraft's speed below Mach 1. Going supersonic would waste fuel, not to mention shattering windows and nerves on the ground and the inevitable deluge of complaining letters that would follow.

It wasn't difficult for the pilot to pick out the 767's lights. He reported his sighting.

'Grocer, this is Green Two, I've got him in radar lock-on and visual tally. What range do you want?'

'Stay in his six, range three five zero.' The six o'clock position was directly aft of the airliner's tail. Green Two's navigator read off radar ranges to his pilot as the hunter closed to three hundred and fifty metres.

'Confirm you're monitoring one three five eight two five?' It was the London Control frequency on which Air Traffic Control had been trying unsuccessfully to communicate with the rogue aircraft.

'Affirm, Grocer. Nothing heard.'

'Okay, just a reminder. Do not transmit on the London frequency in case he's listening for interception.'

They soon found that their quarry was slowing down. The Tornado pilot throttled back and brought his wings forward again, increasing their lift to compensate for the reducing speed.

'What's he up to now?' wondered the navigator aloud.

*****

As the airspeed indicator dropped below 210 knots Fradini reached across to the flap lever and moved it into its first detent. With his engines at idle power the speed trickled back further and the American extended more flap to maintain lift. A warning horn sounded. The computer interpreted the deceleration as preparation for landing and the horn was to remind him to lower the landing gear. Instead, he reached behind to the rows of circuit breakers on the electrical panel and pulled one out. The horn stopped.

Now the autothrottle spooled up the engines to hold the speed Fradini had dialled into the autopilot control. With full flap down the 767 could safely fly at 130 knots, engines whining as they balanced the massive increase in wing drag.

The pilot got out of his seat and checked the straps of the Extra Pack, the lightweight glider pilot parachute he had been wearing since before starting engines. It was not too cumbersome and gave Fradini a chance to bale out through the flight deck sliding window had the military tried to shoot him down. Now he would use it for the purpose the Damocles group had intended.

Goggles would have been nice, but Security might have been a bit too curious. He would have to make do without. But he could take the torch. It wouldn't be bright enough to illuminate his landing spot until just before he hit but he might need it afterwards. The escape route over the flat and relatively unpopulated terrain of East Angla had been chosen to give the American the best chance of landing without snagging power lines or buildings.

Afterwards Fradini would dump the chute and make his way back to the camper van by some means or other to continue his innocent tourist activity before eventually returning to the States to spend the proceeds of the crime.

A final glance at the instrument panel to verify that the aircraft was in a stable flight path and then he opened the door and stepped into the cabin. Then a new thought struck him and he reentered the flight deck to retrieve the second gun from its stowage by the captain's seat. *You never know!*

Back towards the open emergency exit. As Fradini approached he could hear the roar of slipstream and feel the freezing swirls of outside air pulsing through the gap to ripple into the relative warmth of the cabin.

*****

It was Sarah who had the brainwave. The two captives had succumbed to fatigue and slept fitfully during their entrapment, leaning against each other for support. Now the girl roused herself from her semi-stupor and shook her companion awake.

'Wilf, the coke cans!'

Jagger yawned and stretched. 'What about them?'

'Get one of the ring pulls. See if we can undo the panel screws with it.'

'You're brilliant!'

The reinforced metal ring was thin enough to engage the screwheads and strong enough to turn the first one they tried.

The two pilots grinned at each other. *'Yesss!'*

But they hit a snag. Three of the screws were too tight, including the two central ones. After several minutes of cursing the resisting screws Jagger gave up. He could only bend back half of the panel, revealing a dark area behind. He stuck his head into the cavity. A few stray beams of light from the hold glinted dully on an array of narrow metal shelves with black boxes sitting on them. Gradually his eyes accustomed themselves to the dimness.

'I think it's the electrics bay,' he said, bringing his head back in. 'But I can't get into it unless I can get that bloody panel out of the way. Here, let me try and prise it off with the ladder.'

'Careful you don't make any noise. We don't want them to hear you.'

It proved impossible to lever the panel off no matter which position Jagger tried with the ladder. At one point he managed to smash it into the rack in the electrics bay with a metallic clang.

The two of them froze, waiting for a reaction.

After a minute, Jagger said: 'If it's dark in that bay then there must be a floor above it. Maybe that would muffle any noise.'

'If it's an electrics bay then there could be a hatch in the floor for engineering access.'

'Well, if there is, maybe we can get out through it.' He pointed at the bent back panel. 'Except that we can't get through this one.'

'Perhaps I can.'

It was difficult for Sarah to contort herself into the geometry needed to get through the opening. And painful.

'Ow!'

'Well, they would have heard that,' said Jagger grimly.

'Sorry, couldn't help it . . . damn, the wound is bleeding again.'

They waited a minute or two, Sarah holding the blood-soaked blouse against her shoulder. Then she started to feel for a light switch.

'That's more like it,' she said, finding what she was looking for. 'And yes, there's a hatch above me. With a handle. Shall I open it?'

'Be careful!'

CHAPTER 31

'Grocer, this is Green Two. Can I ease in a bit for a closer look? The bogey is down to 130 knots now. I'd like to check his flap and gear position. Maybe he's intending to land somewhere.'

'Affirm, Green Two. Use your own discretion. But stay out of his sight. Report back, please.'

The Tornado crept forward and dropped down a little until it dangled just below and behind the 767's tail. It was the closest the pilot had been to a civil airliner in flight. He edged a little right, careful to keep below the hot turbulent stream of its engine exhaust, and spent a moment staring at the tall graceful fin. The nav's voice came to him over the intercom.

'I reckon he's got his flaps full down, Joc.'

'Yeah, I'd go along with that. But his landing gear is still retracted. What's the bugger playing at?'

*****

The American gripped the edge of the exit for balance as he perched facing backwards, half in, half out of the aircraft, fighting the hurricane slipstream which tore at his left leg.

This was the moment of truth. Theoretically the downwash of air from the wing, further deflected by the camber of the extended flaps, would impel him downwards well below the tailplane which would otherwise have sliced him in half.

Here we go!

In one movement Fradini pushed himself out and dived towards the trailing edge of the wing. Twisting in the air he saw the 767 rise away from him. In apparent slow motion the aluminium slab of the tailplane flew over him with twenty feet of clearance. The theory was correct. Now Fradini reached for the plastic loop which would release the parachute and let it blossom into a voluminous white canopy which would float him safely to earth.

*****

'Jesus H Christ! What the fuck was that?'

The Tornado suddenly bucked and shuddered but before the pilot could react it was again flying smoothly. He tried out his controls and found them working perfectly. All the systems appeared okay. Only his heartbeat was in the amber sector, pounding in his ears.

'What did you do?' came the nav's accusing voice from the rear cockpit.

'Didn't touch it, mate. Something upset it, God knows what. Seems to be alright now. What do you think it was? Wake vortex from the bogey?'

'Behind the wingtips maybe, not in this position.' The Tornado crew scrutinised the airliner hovering beyond their nose but nothing had changed. Straight and level, 130 knots. A picture of innocence.

'Joe, look at our port wing.'

The pilot turned his eyes as bidden. Halfway along the leading edge an ugly deformation interrupted the streamlined profile. The light of the moon glinted on the periphery of a dent spoiling the aerodynamic perfection.

'Christ,' breathed the pilot. 'We must have hit something.'

*****

The Tornado crew were still speculating on what had damaged their wing when the nav saw something else more demanding of immediate attention.

'Joe, the bogey! His engine's on fire!'

A metallurgist would have found hours of intellectual stimulation mulling over the sequence of events leading to the pyrotechnic suicide of the 767's right engine. When the last of its oil finally escaped the machinery ran normally for a minute or two. In the flight deck an alarm chimed and a warning flashed up on the engine monitor screen. R ENG LOW OIL PRESSURE. There were no eyes to see it, no hands to shut down the engine before it was too late. Deprived of lubrication the bearings soon heated up, burning away any residual protective oil. Now metal came into contact with tortured metal. As friction slowed the turbines and fragmented the bearings the autothrottle fed more fuel into the suicidal engine to counter the loss of thrust. Slower, more fuel, hotter. The high pressure turbine blades glowed white, softened. Metal nucleii strained against the electron clouds holding them together. The atomic bonds stretched, yielded, broke. Centrifugal force tore the fatally weakened blades from their roots. More fuel. The contorted blades spewed from the exhaust duct like incandescent confetti. Unbalanced, the engine vibrated in its death throes. Thrust dropping. More fuel. Destruction.

The Tornado pilot saw the sudden spurt of flame from the bogey and instinctively pulled away, fearful of debris if the thing blew up. He transmitted what they had witnessed to Control.

'Roger, Green Two. Stay with him. Monitor his flight path. If it looks like he's out of control you are authorised to destroy the bogey. I repeat, you are authorised to destroy the bogey . . .'

*****

Using the metal shelves as footholds, Sarah raised herself a metre or so and, trying to ignore the pain in her shoulder, slowly pushed up the hatch so that her eyes were level with the floor. It was the first class cabin. There was no-one there. She pushed the hatch aside and continued her anxious scan. Still no-one. The flight deck door was partially open but she couldn't see into the flight deck. She lowered herself again and turned to speak to Jagger *sotto voce*.

'The forward cabin's empty as far as I tell. If you pass me that ladder I'll see if I can get out.'

Watching round carefully the girl climbed slowly out of the electrics bay, still unchallenged.

What next? Go forward to the flight deck? What would the response be? Should I . . . Suddenly through the windows Sarah saw the sullen orange glow flickering outside.

'God, we're on fire!'

Unable to marshall her thoughts coherently Sarah quickly moved forwards to the flight deck, now aware of a bell sounding. She pushed open the half-closed door.

Must be hallucinating. No pilots. Impossible.

It took a few seconds for Sarah to convince herself that the vista in front of her was no figment of the imagination. Questions crowded into her mind but she pushed them aside. Difficult to think with that bloody bell going all the time. Her eyes found the airspeed and altimeter indications. 115 knots. Awfully slow. Eight thousand feet, was that healthy? Where were they?

Priorities, Sarah. Put out the fire!

She dropped into the copilot's seat, desperately searching for the fuel levers. She found them behind the throttles. She pulled the right hand one to the cut-off position. Behind it the engine fire control handle was lit up red to identify the source of the conflagration. She pulled that too. But how to discharge the extinguishers? If this aircraft was like the Merchantman you twisted the fire control handles. Frantically Sarah rotated the handle, first clockwise then the other way. Apart from two captions illuminating to tell her EXTING DISCHARGED nothing else happened. The red R ENG FIRE message was still showing and the infernal bell continued its assault on her ears.

And now the aircraft was shuddering and the control wheel shaking in her hand. *Stall warning!* Horrified, Sarah saw that the speed had dropped to 105 knots. The autopilot computer, vainly trying to recover the situation, had pushed the left throttle to full power and wound the control wheel over to maximum deflection to fight the asymmetric thrust. It did not recognise that the violent buffetting was the sure harbinger of a fatal stall as the tormented airflow broke up into turbulent whirlpools over the wings.

Sarah knew! Galvanised by the stab of fear her human brain leapt into action. *Got to get some speed!* She grabbed the control wheel and pushed it brusquely away from her. The autopilot sounded a sulky tone to castigate her for overriding it and the aircraft tried to roll onto its back. *It's going to spin!* A panicky bootful of left rudder straightened the nose but the rolling motion reversed. *God help me, I'm losing control!*

A tiny voice from the furthest recess of her mind came to her rescue. Her instructor's words from her early days of flying when she was learning to subjugate the little Piper trainer and bend it to her will. *If it's getting away from you, let go of everything!* Sarah forced her hands to relinquish their fevered grip and her feet leapt off the rudder pedals. A blinding flash of intuition told her to cut back power on the good engine to neutralise the destabilising imbalance of thrust.

It worked. The aircraft was flying straightish but needed another pitch down to accelerate away from the incipient stall. The vertical speed indication silently informed her of a descent rate of three thousand feet per minute. Already she was down below four thousand on the altimeter. The ghastly arithmetic redoubled her determination.

Need more power! Need less drag! More composed now, Sarah gradually opened up the left throttle, carefully pushing on rudder to keep straight. The descent rate was halved. Much better. Now then, drag would be from landing gear or flaps. Where were they? She found the gear lever right in front of her and the indicator lights above. No green lights, so the gear was retracted. What about flaps? Luckily the control lever was in the same location as in the Merchantman. Fully down. No wonder the aircraft wanted to plummet earthwards.

Slowly, methodically, Sarah moved the flap lever up through its range, pausing at each detent to match increasing airspeed to reducing wing camber. *There, flaps are up. Speed's built up to just over 200 knots. Should be safe enough. And we're flying level, even climbing a smidge. And, heaven be praised, the fire warning bell has stopped!*

Having pulled herself back from the brink Sarah could afford to take a deep breath and assess her circumstances. The aircraft was under control, sort of. She was having to fly it manually, which was a bind. She didn't know how to re-engage the autopilot she had overridden during her panic. Ditto the autothrottle. She would have to judge for herself how much power she should draw from her healthy left engine but at least she was in vaguely familiar territory here. Her battles with Zulu Charlie when Wilf was simulating engine failures stood her in good stead. If only he could help her now. But she couldn't take the chance of leaving the controls to go back and talk to him.

Speed 216 knots, steady. That'll do. Zulu Charlie's minimum allowed flaps up speed is 200. Probably okay for the 767. Where are the pilots? Is this a nightmare after all? Assume it's real, Sarah. Altitude two thousand eight hundred. Is that safe? Are there mountains round here? Where am I, anyway? England? Europe? No clues on the nav display, must be on low range, don't know how to change it. Heading 280. What heading was it on before the upset? What about fuel? How much is there? How long will it last? One thing at a time, Sarah. Take a close look around, see what you can find out. Then start making some decisions. If only I didn't feel so tired. Maybe I've lost more blood than I realised.

*****

'I confirm the bogey is now heading west. It looked like it was about to go into a spin but it seems under control now. What is your advice?'

'Roger, Green Two. We consider that a shoot down is essential in case the bogey comes down in the Midlands conurbation. You are ordered to destroy the bogey. Use a Venom.'

Amongst the Tornado's armaments were two Venom radar-guided air-to-air missiles, either one of which could convert a Boeing 767 into so many tons of aluminium shrapnel. Now the pilot dropped back to put more airspace between himself and the bogey. He climbed a bit so that the debris from their victim would not hit them and add to their battle damage. The navigator went through the procedure to arm the first missile.

'Too easy, this,' said the pilot over the intercom. 'No evasive manoeuvring. No enemy radar jamming us.'

'You want him to fight back, Joe?' mocked the nav. He reverted to standard call-outs. 'Range two five zero. Lock-on confirmed. Arming complete.'

'Fire!'

The nav pressed the button, just as he had done hundreds of times before. Except this time it was for real, not a practice. This time the Venom would streak away, home in on its target and blast it to smithereens.

But it didn't. Instead of a fiery trail snaking away from the Tornado tipped with its deadly warhead of high explosive, a warning caption lit up on the nav's weapon status panel.

'Shit!' he exclaimed. 'Master warning. Guidance malfunction. Weapon has not released.'

The pilot followed the drill he too had practiced many times.

'Okay, disarm Venom 1, call weapon safe. Check status of Venom 2.'

'Confirming Venom 1 disarmed and safe. Status good on Venom 2.'

'Arm it. Call lock-on.'

'Range two six zero. Lock-on confirmed. Arming complete.'

'Okay, stand by to fire.'

*****

Of course, you silly girl! Why didn't you think of it before? Get your stupid brain in gear. The training mantra percolated into her mind. *Aviate, navigate, communicate. You're not on your own. Get someone on the radio!*

At her right shoulder hung a headset. Sarah lifted it from its hook and donned it, swinging the mike boom in front of her mouth. She listened. Silence. Were the radios switched on? Was the headset plugged in? *Try transmitting, girl, see what happens. Where's the transmit switch? Zulu Charlie's got it on the control wheel. Ah, this might be it!*

'Anyone on frequency, this is . . .' She scanned the instrument panel in front of her, trying to find the registration placard. There. '. . . November 3249 Alpha. Does anyone read this transmission?'

CHAPTER 32

At Swanwick it was as if a bolt of lightning had struck the London Area Controller. So unexpected was the message in his earphones that he jumped in his seat. The frequency had been cleared of all other traffic at the start of the emergency and he had long since given up trying to get a response from the rogue aircraft. But he was a clear headed man. He knew that the RAF were about to blast it from the sky and he leapt from his seat and immediately grabbed the land line phone from the grasp of a bemused Wing Commander Atterell to alert Air Vice Marshall Humphrey himself.

'He's talking to us. It's a woman,' he announced, unaware of the contradiction. He prayed that the Tornado crew had also heard the 767's transmission. He stared at the screen. If one of the pair of returns disappeared it would mean that . . .

The controller keyed his mike, keeping his voice as calm as his jitters would allow. 'November 3249 Alpha, this is London Control, reading you strength five. Please state your intentions.'

*****

Detective Inspector Jaipal Sahay looked at his watch. Half past four. Time to go home and give his weary brain a rest. He would quickly cast his eyes over the attachment that had just been emailed to him from the airport and then pack it in for the night.

It had been sent by Security Chief Sandra Beckridge, a list of all persons who had passed through the checkpoints in the last twenty-four hours, both those going airside and those returning. There were two sub-groups. The first set of data related to persons who were permanently based at East Midlands and whose IDs had been read by the swipe scanners. The second list concerned those with temporary passes and those based at different airports, such as visiting pilots and cabin crew. Their card numbers had been inputted manually by security officers.

One of the names on the first list was Michael Shepherd. Went airside just before the 767 was taken. Sahay had already informed the Met boys that the Central Airlines dispatcher might be linked to the crime through Myron Winslade, buddy of Maurice Holmin. It looked like Shepherd was on the run now, more proof of guilt as far as Sahay was concerned.

On the second list, three entries were highlighted in red font. As Sandra's message had informed the police officer, data mismatch errors such as these were usually the result of incorrect keyboard input of card numbers. *Further investigation required?* wondered the police officer. *Well, it could wait until tomorrow . . . or rather, later today.*

For a few seconds fatigue fought professionalism in Sahay's mind. *Sod it! Just a quick call to the airport and then home. Definitely!*

'The names in red,' he asked when he got through on the phone, 'why didn't the security officers deny access if there were queries against them?'

'Well,' replied Sandra Beckridge, 'under the new system they will. At the moment there's no direct link to other airport data bases so the errors don't show up unless we request a cross-check of ID data from them, which is how we identified the three rogue names on the list.'

'So were they genuine after all?'

'Two of them were,' said Sandra. 'When we checked we found that the wrong numbers had been typed in by security officers.'

'And the third name?'

'Still working on that, Jaipal. Drawn a blank so far, I'm afraid. Just remind me of the details. I haven't got the list in front of me at the moment.'

Sahay read from his monitor. 'William Mason, engineer, based at Gatwick.'

'Ah, yes. Well, when we checked we found that there's no engineer by that name at Gatwick. Or anywhere else in the UK, come to that.'

'What about the officers who let him through to airside. Would they remember him?'

'Possibly. But their shift finished at ten thirty. They'll be at home now. Do you want me to bring them in?'

The policeman thought for a moment. 'No, leave them in peace for now. I'll talk to them later.'

'Okay. Anything else I can help with?'

'No thanks, Sandra. I'm off home now.'

'Lucky you! I'm on duty till seven. And it's still pretty chaotic here after what happened.'

Sahay rang off and was about to hibernate his computer when another name on Sandra's list caught his eye. Sarah Amberley-Kemp. First Officer, Meteor Air Express, said the screen. Sister of Giles, who was an associate of Michael Shepherd and who his colleagues said was at that moment denying all knowledge of the crime. Another memory came into the policeman's tired brain. The photo at the Arriba night club. Shepherd, Winslade and . . . Nathan Bishop! Another Meteor pilot! And yes, on the list! Suddenly Sahay's weariness vanished and a new urgency hit him. Yet again he picked up the phone.

'Sorry, Sandra, another question.'

'Go ahead. As it happens, I was just going through the list again myself.'

'Meteor Air Express,' said Sahay. 'Have they got planes flying tonight?'

'Plane, Jaipal. They've only got the one. I think it took off a bit earlier.'

'So was it being flown by Nathan Bishop and Sarah Amberley-Kemp?'

'Er . . . no, that wouldn't be possible . . . look at the list. They're both copilots. The plane would need a captain . . . hang on a minute. Hmmm, interesting.'

'What?'

'Wilfred Jagger and Bernard Crowburn. Meteor captains. They both went through Security too.'

'So there are four Meteor pilots airside?'

'Yes. But look at the times. The Kemp girl and Jagger were timed at 1941, say twenty to eight. Bishop and Crowburn didn't go through until, oh, three thirty this morning.'

'So which of them are flying the plane?'

'Well, at least one of them has got to a captain.'

'Could all four of them be in the crew?'

'Don't know, Jaipal. Do you want me to try and find out?'

'Yes, that would be brilliant, Sandra.'

'I'll get back to you.'

'You'll get my voicemail message . . . no, I've got a better idea. Phone the Met. They're working on the problem with the Transec people at the moment.'

Sahay gave Sandra the number, then added: 'That's it, I've had enough. I'm going home for a sleep.'

'Sweet dreams!'

*****

'Green Two, this is Grocer. Do not attack. I repeat, do not attack. Engagement code Black. I repeat, engagement code Black. Acknowledge.'

'Acknowledged, Grocer, we heard the call from the bogey. All weapons confirmed passive.' The Tornado pilot transmitted compliance, relief in his voice. Unlike Green Leader he had fired weapons in anger. He had seen his laser guided bombs zero in on targets in Iraq. The elation of success had been shot through with regret, guilt even, that he personally had probably taken the lives of other humans, albeit enemies. Now he found himself immensely grateful that he had not had to kill someone again. Perhaps his days as a fighter pilot were numbered. The whole thing would take some thinking about once they were back on the ground and he had some time to himself to mull it over.

'Green Two, maintain station on the bogey. London Control is going to try and talk him down.'

'Roger,' replied the pilot. As he closed the gap between himself and the aircraft he had come within a whisker of obliterating he heard the nav chuckling over the intercom.

'What's so funny?'

'I was just thinking, Joe. Good thing the cold war's over. Imagine what the reds would have made of it. We launch two fighters. One goes sick as soon as it's in the air and the other can't fire its bloody hardware. What a joke!'

'Yeah, I wonder if the Russian Air Force is as shambolic as ours is. But what really worries me is, how are we going to explain that dent in the wing?'

'Simple, tell them the truth. You were flying too low and hit a telegraph pole.'

'Bugger off.'

*****

Sarah pressed her transmit button. 'London, this is 49 Alpha. I need some help. I don't know where I am and I'm not familiar with this aircraft. I don't know what happened to the pilots. They're not here.'

The London controller seemed to take this in his stride. 'Roger, 49 Alpha. Do you have any flying experience?'

'Affirm. I'm current on the Merchantman as a copilot.'

'On the what?'

'Merchantman. Vanguard freighter conversion.'

'Okay, that's fine. Is the aircraft under control?'

In a manner of speaking. 'Yes. I'm flying manually. I don't know how to engage the autopilot. And I'm on one engine. I had an engine fire and I shut it down.'

'Alright, 49 Alpha. You're in radar contact two zero miles north of Barkway. Can you climb to three thousand?'

Barkway! That's a beacon not far from Stansted! Knowledge of the aircraft's precise geographic location brought cheer to Sarah. Straightaway she felt less lost and lonely. She eased on a bit more power, rudder to match and raised the nose a trifle. The altimeter crept up.

'49 Alpha, London. We've got a 767 qualified pilot here to give you some guidance. Can you locate your fuel guages? They're in the overhead panel, in the middle.'

Also watching the radar screen intently was Judith Wilson, a senior Training Captain with British Airways, based at Gatwick.

She had been summoned from her bed in her Petersfield home to be a more immediate source of Boeing 767 expertise than the Chief Pilot of Blue Planet, who could only communicate by phone from his own home.

Sarah found the fuel gauges and relayed the figures to London Control.

'Good, you've got plenty of fuel.'

'Okay, but I want to get down soon. I've been injured and I don't feel too well, a bit faint. Can I route to Stansted for landing?'

'Negative, 49 Alpha. Stansted is closed for runway maintenance until 0600. I'll give you vectors to Heathrow. Turn left heading one nine zero.'

'What about Luton?'

There was a pause before Air Traffic replied and Sarah worried that she had lost radio contact. She repeated her suggestion and this time elicited a response.

'Er . . . 49 Alpha, Luton would not be suitable for you. You'll need plenty of runway for your single-engined landing. Luton might be a bit short. We think . . . er . . . it's possible you may have a landing gear problem.'

Before this sank in, London came up with another instruction.

'49 Alpha, look up at the fuel panel again. Look for the crossfeed valve and open it. This'll feed your good engine from all tanks to retain lateral balance.'

Sarah did as she was bidden. A new voice came on the air, a female.

'49 Alpha, can you tell me your name?'

Sarah thought the request uncalled for when there were more important things to worry about but the friendly authoritative tone softened her unease. Sheepishly she gave her full name over the radio.

'Right, Sarah. My name is Judith Wilson. I'm a 767 driver. This is the picture. We're going to position you onto the ILS at Heathrow. Radar positioning all the way. We'll do the navigating from down here, okay?'

'Okay.'

'Right. Here's how it is, Sarah. Fly the aircraft as if it's a Merchantman. I'll help you if you come across any major differences. Now, first of all, let's plug that autopilot in, shall we?'

Suddenly Sarah knew why the stranger's voice was so comforting. She sounded exactly like her history teacher at her old school.

'. . . You've got two problems to deal with. Landing on one engine. Dead easy. And your left landing gear is damaged . . .'

Sarah felt her insides churning. *God help me! I'll never manage that!*

'. . . Not quite so easy, but you can do it. We think an autoland might be your best option.'

In a few minutes 49 Alpha was sorted out, its autopilot and autothrottle flying it with greater precision than Sarah could ever hope for. Under Judith's tutelage she had programmed the computer to hold altitude, heading and airspeed. A touch of rudder trim balanced the asymmetric thrust and Sarah allowed her weary mind a crumb of relaxation. Of course it was impossible to close her mind to the looming battle of trying to bring the half-powered one-leg-missing aluminium cripple into contact with terra firma without smashing it, and its occupants, to bits. Thank God the autopilot would be able to do the actual landing.

How comforting was Judith's voice as she briefed her on the procedure for approach and landing.

'Let's just recap, Sarah. The autopilot's going to do the work, including the landing. You've got the APU running now so we should have full electrics even though the right generator will be dead. We'll get autoland capability confirmation once we're on the ILS and the radio altimeters kick in.'

'Okay.'

'Okay. But if the autoland is inop you'll have to land manually. Treat it just like the Merchantman. You'll get rad alt call outs. Flare height is thirty feet radio, got it?'

'49 Alpha, affirm.' The flare was the point at which the aircraft would have to raise its nose to flatten its descent path just before touchdown.

'Okay. For either autoland or manual landing close your good throttle during the flare. When the aircraft touches down chop the engine with the fuel control switch. The aircraft will swing left and probably come off the runway. Don't worry about that. Just try to keep it as straight as you can with the rudder while it slows down. As soon as it's stopped, open the sliding window beside you, throw out the escape strap and get the hell out. You remember where the strap is?'

'Affirm. Above the window. I press the red button to release it. In fact I could do that now, get it ready for deployment.'

'Good idea. Remember, the fire and rescue crews will be there to help you if you need it.'

'What about my friend?'

There was a pause. The 767 floated another half mile over the sodium yellow glow of central London. Inadvertently Sarah's eyes caught the various warning messages about the aircraft's failed systems on the status screen. Probably to do with the right engine being shut down. Too bad! She was too tired to bother with them.

'Sorry, 49 Alpha. We were discussing tactics here. What was your last transmission?'

'There's another person on board. He's trapped in the hold.'

'Okay, Sarah, I got that. Don't try to get him out yourself. The fire crews will rescue him. Let's try the gear now, see what we get.'

Sarah selected the landing gear lever down. She was vaguely aware of increased slipstream noise as beneath the flight deck the nosewheel lowered itself into the airflow. Above the lever two green captions lit up, NOSE GEAR and RIGHT GEAR, confirming those wheels down and locked.

A chime sounded four times and a new red warning caption lit up on the systems display screen. LEFT GEAR DISAGREE. Sarah passed the information to Judith.

'Okay, just as we expected . . . turn right now, heading two three zero. Arm the approach.'

Sarah pressed the buttons. 'Localiser and glideslope armed.'

The white localiser caption turned green and 49 Alpha banked itself to the right to lock onto the beam. When it straightened up Sarah could see, shimmering in the distance, the most beautiful sight she had ever beheld.

'Runway lights!' she almost shouted over the radio. 'I can see the lights!' At the same moment the glideslope caption went green. The autopilot altitude hold disengaged and 49 Alpha lowered its nose a trifle to settle onto the glideslope beam. The left throttle retarded itself correspondingly to prevent airspeed build up.

Her burden eased, Sarah slumped in her seat, suddenly fatigued. For a moment her vision blurred and she had to screw up her eyes to restore acuity.

'Looking good,' Judith was saying. 'Now we can get a bit more flap down. You're nearly home, Sarah.'

CHAPTER 33

The decision-making was a six way process, Home Secretary Beryl Grumbridge acting as chair. Still in the Transec office with her were Duty Threat Assessor Margot Madeling, Deputy Commissioner Sir David Jenkins and Defence Secretary James Healey. A video conference call hook up on the computer allowed the participation of Wing Commander Roland Atterell, Military Supervisor at Swanwick Air Traffic Control Centre, and Air Vice Marshall Keith Humphrey at RAF High Wycombe.

From East Midlands Airport, Security Chief Sandra Beckridge had relayed to the Met the answers to the queries raised by DI Jaipal Sahay before he went off duty. The police had in turn notified Sir David.

'So it looks like this William Mason is a fake,' he had told the meeting. 'And Sarah Whatsit is now flying the 767 and cooperating with Air Traffic Control. The big question, of course, is—was she part of the plot? And this other pilot, too. Wilfred Jagger. He passed through Security at the same time as her. Is he on the plane? Is he involved?'

'Didn't you say there were other links between Sarah and the others?' asked Margot Madeling.

'Yes. Via her brother Giles, Michael Shepherd and Myron Winslade. What we know so far is that Giles is under arrest, protesting innocence and Shepherd's done a runner, so he's obviously something to do with it.'

'Is this Winslade under arrest, too?' asked Beryl.

'As far as I know, he's helping us with our enquiries, as the old cliché goes. I'm waiting for an update on that.'

'So, what about the Meteor plane that East Midlands Security told us about? Who's flying that?'

'Presumably Bernard Crowburn and Nathan Bishop,' said Sir David. 'They both went through Security at the same time about half an hour before it took off. It might be significant that Bishop is apparently acquainted with Michael Shepherd, according to Nottingham CID.'

It was Margot Madeling who had suggested that, as the freighter hadn't landed yet, it should be ordered back to the UK, so that Nathan Bishop could be questioned if he was in the crew.

'Are we okay legally to do that?' said the Home Secretary, worried. 'We don't want to get sued if they say we're unlawfully interfering with a legitimate enterprise. There doesn't seem to be much evidence against this Bishop man. He just happens to know one of our suspects.'

'Correct,' said Margot. 'But Sarah Kemp is also employed by Meteor Airlines. And she's now flying the stolen plane. That's two links. Enough to warrant further investigation, I would say. Shall we get some legal advice?'

'No,' said Beryl. 'Let's just request that they turn back. If they're innocent they won't resist. If they refuse, we'll have the German authorities interrogate them on arrival. What do you think?'

The other parties agreed.

The Home Sectretary looked at the Threat Assessor quizzically. 'Which airport?'

'Usual procedure is to send rogue aircraft to Stansted,' said Margot, 'but it's night-closed for runway resurfacing. That leaves us with Heathrow, Gatwick and Luton.'

Sir David spoke up. 'We've got a major police presence at Heathrow because of the 767 arrival. Maybe we should send Meteor there too.'

Beryl nodded. 'Sounds okay. Anyone disagree?' She spoke to the webcam on the laptop. 'Set it up, would you, please, Wing Commander?'

*****

The trip was going well, but then Crowburn had not expected otherwise. The flight deck ambience was relaxed but professional and so far his protegé had encountered no trouble swapping from right seat to left. It was a not entirely new experience for Bishop. Crownburn and Jagger had both allowed him the privelege from time to time on past trips during cruise. Tonight though would see his first landing with left hand on control wheel and right hand on throttles rather than the other way around.

Zulu Charlie bored its way eastwards through the night. A few minutes previously it had penetrated the invisible boundary where British airspace butted against Belgian airspace half way across the Channel. Most of the housekeeping chores were completed, fuel checks, engine data recording, weather monitoring, landing weight calculation and a host of minutiae. Bishop had briefed Crowburn on the descent procedure for Düsseldorf in some detail since it was an infrequent destination for Meteor's freighter. Now the conversation strayed into non-aeronautical areas. The two pilots were discussing the results of a recent England rugby match when a call came over the radio from Maastricht Control.

'Meteor Two Thirty-One, Maastricht.' The English pronunciation was perfect, with just a hint of accent.

'Go ahead,' answered Crowburn.

'We have received a message from London about crew members on your plane.'

The two pilots stared at each other, puzzled.

'Go ahead with the message,' radioed Crowburn.

'Okay, sir, they want to know the names of the operating crew.'

Crowburn relayed the information requested.

'Thank you, Two Thirty-One. Is there also Wilfred Jagger on board?'

'No, just us two.'

'Okay, standby.'

'What the hell's all that about?' said Bishop. Crowburn shook his head. Zulu Charlie droned on, approaching the Belgian coast fifteen miles west of Ostend.

'Meteor Two Thirty-One, London ATC request that you return to base.'

Crowburn told Maastricht to stand by and waited for Bishop, as putative Captain, to make his response.

'Ask 'em if they know why before we commit ourselves.'

Crowburn did as bidden.

'We were not told the reason, except it is something important. I have no other information.'

'Roger, stand by,' transmitted Crowburn. To his colleague he said, 'What do you think, mate?'

'Jeez, that's a new one. Why won't they tell us the reason?'

'Well, they may be worried about other people listening in.' It was a well known fact that journalists continually monitored the control frequencies in the hope of getting an air incident scoop.

The set of Bishop's face showed he had made up his mind.

'Check our fuel state, Bernie. If we've got enough to get back with adequate reserves, then I'll turn round.'

'What do you mean by adequate reserves?' said Crowburn, putting on pressure to test his mettle.

The answer came straight back. 'Enough to get home, plus diversion to Birmingham plus normal holding reserves. Assume a turn round five minutes from now.'

'What wind component?'

'Thirty head should do it.'

'Okay, boss,' said Crowburn, reaching for the manual to make the calculation.

'Meantime, Bernie, I'll take the radio.'

'Okay.'

Bishop transmitted to Air Traffic Control: 'Maastricht, 231. We are assessing our fuel requirements. I suspect we might be a bit tight to make it back to East Midlands. My copilot is calculating it now.' The cheeky transposition of rank put a smile on Crowburn's lips.

'*Roger, 231. London have said you can land anywhere in the UK. They suggest you go to Heathrow.*'

'Meteor 231, roger. In that case we'll take a clearance back.'

'*Okay, turn left radar heading three zero zero towards Tebra. I can offer you a climb to level two zero zero or a descent to one six zero. One eight zero is not available due traffic. Your routing will be Golf Three Nine to Lambourne.*' Tebra was a waypoint just west of the airspace boundary. Turning round from east to west would mean a compulsory change of cruising altitude from their current 19,000 feet.

Bishop chose the lower level and read back the clearance over the radio to confirm it. He swung the freighter round on the autopilot, switched from altitude lock to speed lock and eased the four engines back on power. Zulu Charlie lowered its nose like an obedient cart horse and began to lose height, the slumbering drone of the engines now roused into a disturbed beating as the props momentarily went out of synch. Bishop turned to his older colleague.

'Okay, Bernie. You can put the manual away. We've got more than enough fuel to get to Heathrow. Get the descent charts out, will you? And take the radio. Ask Maastricht the landing runway at Heathrow.'

'Yes, O master,' said Crowburn. 'Right away.'

*****

'Shall we get her to switch to Heathrow Tower frequency?' asked the radar controller.

Judith Wilson in the assistant's seat alongside took a moment to answer. What a night it had turned out to be. At first she had thought that the phone call summoning her to Swanwick was a hoax, one of her pilot friends, no doubt inspired by the drama on the news bulletins, having a laugh at her expense. She wasn't so innocent herself. Once or twice in her younger days she had phoned mates up when they were on home standby and tried fictitious absurdly outrageous trips on them, pretending to be Crew Control. But none of her friends could imitate the Fleet Manager's voice that well. This was no joke. She had thrown on clothes and a coat and dashed out of the house and within the hour was ensconced with the controllers at the radar console. To start with she had hovered in the background, offering technical snippets when consulted but taking no active part in the weird episode.

And then the Sarah's plaintive voice had come over the air, lonely and afraid. Judith had swapped places with the assistant and had taken over the radio channel. She was Sarah's link with the safe haven of terra firma. The first bit was tricky, nurturing her confidence, getting her to tidy up the aircraft and engage the autopilot. Then the easy part, giving her headings towards Heathrow's ILS, the Instrument Landing System radio beam guidance. Now things were going to get difficult again. At some stage Sarah was going to have to get the thing onto the ground without wiping out the aircraft and half of the airport in the process. On one engine and two thirds of the landing gear. Well, she had gone over the important bits with her two or three times. The problem was that as Sarah got closer to the runway the radio signals between them would get cut out by terrestial obstructions and she wouldn't be able to hear Judith during the vital last moments. The obvious solution was to make Sarah switch her radio to Tower frequency so that a controller in the Heathrow control tower could keep in contact.

But was it a good idea to distract her now? Did she know the radio controls on 49 Alpha? Suppose she got it wrong and lost all contact. The Tower Controller wouldn't be much use to her anyway, even if he could see her. He wouldn't be able to tell her how to do the landing. She would be on her own for that.

Wing Commander Atterell solved the problem, using the Tornado shadowing the 767. He would arrange a relay on the London frequency via the fighter's avionics equipment so that Sarah could maintain good radio contact.

As soon as the link was set up Judith pressed her transmit key.

'Sarah, you're doing fine. Have you got a readout on the ASA yet?' The Autoland Status Annunciator would confirm the the aircraft was capable of landing iself.

'Er . . . yes . . . it says NO AUTOLAND.'

'What colour?'

'Amber.'

Damn! Judith had been expecting a green LAND 2 or LAND 3 caption, depending on the status of the various systems inputting to the autopilot computer. She thought for a second and then keyed her transmitter.

'Right, Sarah. We can do a go around if you like. Do some troubleshooting. See if we can restore autoland capability.'

'What's causing it?'

'Could be anything. Electrics, hydraulics, rad alts, ILS receivers. If you break off the approach we can go back to a hold and try to sort something out. It'll be dawn soon. You'll be able to see better.'

'No, I want to get down. I'm feeling not quite one hundred percent. I'll land it manually. You've told me the procedure. It might be better anyway. I can hold up the left wing with aileron to keep the damaged gear off the ground a bit longer.'

'Okay, that's fine Sarah. I'm sure you can hack it. A smart girl like you can cope with this without any more nagging from the likes of me. And remember, once you've landed I'll buy you a drink . . .'

CHAPTER 34

For once in his life Maurice Holmin was wracked by indecision. Something was wrong. He shone his torch onto his watch again. According to Micky Shepherd the flight time from East Midlands to Dusseldorf would be an hour and 30 minutes, give or take ten minutes for wind component. So why had the engines been cut back so early? Holmin had also sensed the change in floor angle. Why was the plane descending? Were they coming into land? If so, it obviously wasn't Düsseldorf. So where was it?

Did it mean the Damocles plan had been rumbled by the cops? Had someone grassed them up? He couldn't think of an obvious traitor. There could be other explanations. Maybe Micky had got the timing wrong or maybe the plane had a technical problem. The engines didn't sound as smooth as before. Should he investigate or stay put?

Up to then everything had been going according to plan. Okay, it wasn't much fun being cooped up in a cardboard box for two hours, breathing through a plastic tube. He wasn't too cold or too hot, just a bit stiff from lack of movement in the cramped surroundings. To pass the time he had been reading his Kindle by the light of his wind-up torch.

So, what to do? Sit tight and await developments? He still had the gun. He could shoot his way out of trouble if necessary after they landed. Or should he get out of his hiding place and ask the pilots what the fuck was going on? The gun would be useful in persuading them that he was the one calling the shots.

But hang on—now the engine sound was changing again, back to how it was before. And the front of the plane had lifted again. What did it mean? Were they not landing after all? *Damn, damn, damn! Make a decision, Maurice!*

With a sigh, Holmin took out his knife and sliced through the box top, the plastic pallet wrap and the netting. He pushed them aside and with creaking joints stood up and looked around. His box was in the middle of the freight hold, a long, wide, windowless tube. There was no-one else in the hold and the door leading to the front of the plane was closed. Without the insulating effect of the cardboard box he had been enclosed in the engine noise was louder. Holmin stepped out and glanced at the other boxes ahead and behind. Forty million smackers that lot was worth. But only if it got to Willi Prosch in Düsseldorf. Holmin sighed again. Time to go and have a quiet word with the drivers.

*****

'Heathrow Approach, this is Air Force 35, how do you read?'
The Fighter Controller at High Wycombe had arranged a handover so that Green Two could communicate directly with the civilians and had allocated him a different call sign in compliance with security regulations.
Air Force 35, you're loud and clear and we've got your squawk. Please state your intentions.
The Tornado pilot transmitted. 'We'll follow the bogey down the approach until he's landed then break off and return to base.'
Roger, 35. When you break off turn right radar heading zero six zero and climb flight level one one zero. We'll arrange your handover back to Alpha Delta.

*****

Both heads spun round when Maurice Holmin opened the flight deck door and stepped forward, sweeping the gun between both astounded faces.
'Who the hell are you?' asked Bishop. 'What do you think you're doing?'
'Shut it!' ordered the prisoner as he pointed the gun at him.
Both pilots were mesmerised by the intrusion, unable to keep their eyes off the weapon.
'Right, boys,' continued Holmin. 'First things first. You do exactly what I say when I say it. Exactly. Got it?'
'Don't let the gun go off,' said Crowburn. 'If a bullet goes through the aircraft skin the fuselage might explode. It's pressurised.'
'Is that right, Grandad? Okay, let me assure you I can fire it into your body in such a way that the bullet stays inside. So the plane will be fine and you will be screaming in pain. Do you want me to show you?'
'No.'
'Good. Right, first question. Where are we landing?'
Both pilots made the same assessment of the situation and came up with the same answer.
'Düsseldorf,' they both said simultaneously.
'Good. Why did the engines change just now? Why did we go down a bit?'
'Orders from Air Traffic Control,' said Bishop. 'There are several aircraft on this routing tonight.'

'Alright. Now, I want to hear what those guys on the ground are saying. How do I do that?'

'We're using these headsets,' said Bernie, pointing to his earphones.

'Okay, give me yours.'

When Crowburn hesitated Holmin pushed the gun into his cheek. 'Have you forgotten what I said, Grandad? You do what I say when I say it. Give me that thing.'

Pointing the gun at the older pilot Holmin fumbled with the headset with his free hand until it was in position on his head.

'I have to transmit position,' said Bishop. 'Is that okay?'

'Do it,' ordered Holmin.

'Maastricht, Meteor Zulu Charlie now established on Mike Nine Seven to Düsseldorf, flight level three six zero.'

While Holmin was distracted by this transmission Crowburn nonchalantly reached down and changed the code on the transponder.

'Why don't they reply?' asked Holmin.

'They will,' said Bishop. 'Maybe they're busy at the moment.'

*****

The Maastricht controller was puzzled. There was something very odd about this British freighter. First London had called them on the land line to ask that it be sent back, which the pilots agreed to, but now they were talking nonsense. Flying west but talking about Düsseldorf, the destination on the original flight plan. Giving their altitude as 36,000 feet, impossible for a turboprop freighter. And in any case, only military fighters could climb twenty thousand feet in a few minutes. Wrong callsign—they were using the aircraft's registration, not its flight number. Airway M97—no such thing! There was something about the pilot's voice, too. Definitely not right.

He had been about to transfer Meteor 231 to London Control and call them on the landline to warn them of a possible problem when the aircraft's data tag on his radarscope started flashing. It had changed its setting to the code for hijack. Hijack? On a freighter? Unlikely, but the transponder code and strange message said otherwise. Better tread carefully. The controller had practised hijack procedure many times and had once handled a real incident.

'Roger,' he transmitted now. 'Proceed as cleared. Standby for handover to East Sector.' He raised his hand to attract the attention of the Watch Supervisor.

CHAPTER 35

It was strange, almost like a dream. Why did she feel this way? Light-headed, detached, as if she was watching herself from a distance. The airliner was flying itself, its controls moving her hands and feet rather than the other way around. The lights shimmered closer, oh so slowly, but brighter, very bright now. And pretty. Dazzling white approach lights, green threshold lights, white and red glideslope indicators, mesmerising her. Was it a dream?

No, you silly cow! It's not a dream! Pull yourself together. Of course the thing's flying itself—the autopilot's coupled to the ILS. You feel woozy because you're probably suffering from loss of blood. Get a grip, girl. If you mess the landing up you're dead!

Sarah took a few deep breaths and forced her reluctant brain to think properly. She was aware of Judith's voice in her earphones but she couldn't summon up the effort to listen to what she was saying. What was the use? A still-functioning brain cell registered the altimeter dropping below a hundred feet and told her to switch out the autothrottle and autopilot for manual landing.

God, she felt tired. Memory was choreographing her hands and feet, sending the signals, but they felt so heavy, wouldn't obey the commands.

The radio altimeter call-outs jolted her out of her lethargy.

'Fifty . . . forty . . . thirty . . . '

Got to flare! Pull the wheel back! Pull it back! Lift the wing!

' . . . twenty . . . ten . . '

The right mainwheels hit the ground and the impact shook a few final grains of sense into her hazy mind. She wrenched the controls over to keep the damaged landing gear in the air as long as possible.

Hold the wing up, hold it up! It's dropping! Hold it up!

Inexorably the wheelless landing gear strut sank lower. It touched the tarmac in a shower of sparks, gouged a jagged tear and dug in. But 49 Alpha wasn't ready to stop its headlong rush. With a squeal of tortured metal the already injured strut tore itself out from its mounting in the wing root and the airliner collapsed onto its left engine, lurching off the runway. Another fiery plume of sparks, a suicidal cacophony of cowlings sundering themselves into shapeless pieces.

Sarah's hands gripped the controls harder but it was atavistic fear rather than reasoned logic that tightened the tendons as the striken airliner's shuddering pirouette buffetted her body. The engine scraped its delicate insides along the ground, shedding bits of itself. *Cut the engine, Sarah! Don't want another fire!*

With a last convulsion the 767 came to rest, facing the way it had come. The nosewheel and right mainwheel had survived the abuse and now 49 Alpha listed like a sinking ship. As the Tornado roared overhead and climbed away, its mission completed, a swarm of fire trucks screeched to a halt round the wreck, liberally coating it with a spray of foam.

Judging the crisis over, Sarah's overloaded brain tripped all its circuit breakers and switched itself off. Only unthinking consciousness was left, vague awareness that the chair she was sitting in was tilted at a peculiar angle and a chap with a funny helmet on was winding open the window at her side. She was powerless to help him, arms dangling uselessly, legs and feet dead. All she could manage was a brave attempt at a friendly smile as the window slid open.

'Alright lass,' said the chap in the helmet. 'We'll soon have you out of there.'

At the same moment the flight deck door swung fully open and the lanky form of Wilf Jagger propped itself against the angled frame, eyes wide in amazement.

'I managed to finally get out. What's happening?'

*****

At Swanwick they could hardly believe it when Maastricht offered them another hijacked aircraft. Although Rick Birch, the Lambourne Sector controller, had not dealt personally with the rogue 767 that had just landed at Heathrow after circling over London for hours and hours he was well aware of what was going on. 49 Alpha had flown through his airspace during the approach.

Just as the Swanwick people were congratulating themselves over the successful recovery of the 767 their Belgian counterparts had called them on the land line to advise them that the freighter that had been recalled was now squawking the code for 'unlawful interference', as the regulations put it. Maastrich told them that it appeared the hijacker was listening to the radio exchanges between the pilots and the controllers. It was clear that the pilots wanted to give the impression they were continuing to Düsseldorf.

Birch and his Supervisor discussed the best way of maintaining the subterfuge. If they used the normal frequency the danger was that other aircraft in the Lambourne Sector might refer to 'London

Control' during their radio transmissions, which the hijacker might hear. It was therefore decided to allocate the Meteor flight a discreet frequency used for emergencies or sensitive communications. If the hijacker was familiar with air traffic procedures he might be suspicious that there were no transmissions on the frequency from other aircraft, which would be highly unusual in airspace that was busy round the clock, but it was a chance they would have to take. The Supervisor suggested that one of the other controllers could throw in a few fake calls to increase the realism.

Now a voice spoke in Birch's earphones.

'Maastrich East, this is Meteor Zulu Charlie with you, level three six zero.'

Birch keyed his transmit button. 'Roger, Zulu Charlie, you are identified. Please advise if you wish to change level.' He tried to speak in the formal, stilted English that continental foreigners use. 'Landing runway at Düsseldorf is two seven left. You may route direct to centre fix.'

His words carried a bit of risk. Birch did not know the designations of the runways at Dusseldorf. If there was no runway 27 and the hijacker knew this fact he might be suspicious. The controller held his breath, waiting for possible trouble.

'Roger, Maastricht, Zulu Charlie proceeding direct to centre fix for two seven left.'

Rick Birch sighed with relief. That was alright, then. So far, so good. Hopefully the freighter crew would gather that he had just cleared them to Heathrow's runway of the same designation.

'Zulu Charlie, ready for descent.'

'Zulu Charlie cleared level nine zero.'

*****

In the Merchantman's flight deck Nathan Bishop acknowledged the descent clearance. The initial tension had receded a little and a sort of stoic cooperation had taken its place. The pilots had managed to convince Maurice Holmin that the lights of Margate they could see over on the left were those of Antwerp.

Bishop throttled back the Tynes and programmed the autopilot to start down. On the instrument panel the altimeters began to unwind.

'What happens after we land?' asked Bernie Crowburn.

'Nothing,' said Holmin. 'We just unload like you would do normally.'

'What happens to us?'

'I'm thinking about that right now.'

Now Bishop spoke. 'How did you get into the plane?'

Holmin lazily waved the gun at him. 'Magic.'

'What's in the boxes?'

'None of your business, sonny. You just fly the plane and let me do the thinking.'

*****

At Heathrow the Senior Operations Manager was reorganising his staff. The 767 problem was pretty well sorted out, which meant that he could turn his attention to the approaching hijacked freighter. The two people on the 767 had been detained for interrogation and medical checks. The fire trucks had returned to the base, which meant that the airport could be reopened when the authorities allowed, albeit with one runway still out of service. Two cranes were on the way to lift the wreckage of 49 Alpha clear of the runway it was blocking. Then an inspection would be required to see how much damage had been done to the surface and the necessary repairs carried out. With luck they would have 27 right back in use within 24 hours. It would be hell tomorrow—some flights would have to be cancelled or delayed with only one runway available for both departures and arrivals.

Now the problem was to disguise London Heathrow as Düsseldorf. It didn't help that the darkness was already fading as the dawn crept above the horizon. They had switched off the logo lights at the British Airways maintenance area and on the tail fins of some of their aircraft parked at the terminals to create a more balanced variety of airline colour schemes visible to any aircraft landing on 27 left. Even the lights illuminating the recovery of the 767 would be doused for the arrival of the Meteor freighter.

The plan was that it would taxy as normal to the cargo area on the southwest corner of the airport where the usual polyglot selection of aircraft were dispersed. Some of the police marksmen of the Armed Response Unit would be wearing their flak jackets under plain clothes and carrying their guns in their pockets. They would be out in the open, posing as airport workers. Others, armed with rifles, would be hiding behind items of ground equipment in full protective gear, including masks and helmets. The genuine workers had been bussed away to a safe area.

Commander Graham Bradley from the airport's Police Control Centre was organising the operation from a Peugeot saloon in Lufthansa colours now parked on the unloading area. He had seated himself in the front left seat in case the hijacker saw him as Zulu Charlie taxied in. Hopefully the steering wheel on the wrong side would be invisible. On the other seat was a megaphone and a gun. His glance swept round to check that the set-up was as he wanted it. Mounted on a rusting mobile maintenance gantry was a miniature surveillance camera set up to cover the area where the freighter would stop. The hidden marksmen could thereby see what was happening on the mini-monitors they carried in their pockets. An ambulance staffed with paramedics was standing by out of sight in one of the cargo sheds. Considering how little time they had had to sort something out he was satisfied that they were ready for anything even if bullets started flying. His radio crackled. It was his oppo in the control tower.

'India Four from Yankee Two. They'll be landing in three minutes.'

'Roger,' responded Bradley. 'All units stand by. Stay cool everyone. No shooters unless absolutely necessary.'

*****

At Swanwick controller Suzie Milligan had swapped places with Rick Birch and was pretending to be Düsseldorf Tower. Now Birch was handling the Lamborne Sector traffic at a different console. The Duty Tech Officer had hooked up a direct link to the Heathrow Tower transmitter to ensure two-way contact would be maintained to ground level. Suzie was known as an excellent mimic—one of her hobbies was amateur dramatics—and she toned her messages to the Meteor flight with Germanic inflections, hoping she was not overdoing it.

'Zulu Charlie,' she transmitted now. 'Vind two tree zero four knots, cleared to land runvay two seven left.'

*****

'Landing checks complete,' said Crowburn. 'Speed plus two, seven hundred down.'

Bishop, flying manually now, looked across the panel to check that the flaps were fully extended. Three green lights confirmed landing gear down.

Zulu Charlie, vind two tree zero four knots, cleared to land runvay two seven left.'

Bishop acknowledged the clearance and looked ahead. In the middle distance two miles of runway lights stretched out in front of them. Yes, they'd done a good job, he thought now. A pilot familiar with Heathrow would not be fooled, of course. Over on the right the M4 motorway paralleled the two main runways and the meandering black S cutting through the lit-up area beneath them was the River Thames.

'On speed, seven fifty down.' Crowburn was calling out deviations from target approach speed and rate of descent. Holmin was standing between them with the gun vaguely pointed at Bishop.

Hatton Cross might be a problem, Crowburn was thinking. If their uninvited guest saw the illuminated London Transport logo at the Tube station their deception would be rumbled.

'Plus one, six fifty.'

Fantastic, they've switched off the station logo lights. Well done, chaps!

Over on the right there appeared to be some sort of activity on the other runway but it was too dark to see clearly. Now they swept over the perimeter road and Bishop eased Zulu Charlie's mainwheels smoothly onto the runway. Crowburn was tempted to make a sarcastic comment but the circumstances were not right for levity. As Bishop braked to taxying speed Crowburn silently engaged the gust locks and retracted the flaps.

'Meteor Zulu Charlie take next exit to ze left, cleared to parking stand vun zero eight.'

The two pilots looked at each other. The female voice sounded like a Brit doing a crude impression of a German. Bishop turned further to look at the passenger's face but he showed no reaction apart from heightened tension, which the pilots now picked up themselves.

'No funny business, fellas,' said Holmin. 'When we stop you must do absolutely nothing unless I tell you. Got it?'

'Yes.'

The cargo area looked normal. It could have been any airport in the world. Stand 108 was next to an Air Zimbabwe Airbus A300. Apart from a worker or two slouching across the apron there was not much activity, but then it was half past five in the morning. Nearby was a Lufthansa car and a hydraulic hoist ready to unload Zulu Charlie. Two men were sitting on it with bored expressions.

'Cut engines,' ordered Bishop. 'Shut down checks.'

Holmin watched the pilots suspiciously as they ran through their procedures. 'What happens next?'

'We open the cargo door,' said Crowburn. 'Then they raise the hydraulic loader. We go down on it and go to the dispatch office to do the paperwork. While we're doing that the people here use the loader to get the freight off. When the plane's empty we shut everything down and go to our hotel.'

'Alright,' said Holmin. 'Do it. But remember—I'll be standing right by you with this gun aimed at your guts. I'll use it if I have to.'

The three men left the flight deck and Bishop and the prisoner watched Crowburn operate the cargo door controls. The massive door slowly hinged upwards, gradually revealing the left propellers slowing to a stop and the loader platform rising to the door sill, one man at its control panel, the other, hands in pockets, watching him.

Sergeant Tony Cattrow had been chosen for this duty because he could still remember a little schoolboy German. It was his hands on the loader's controls. His mate Ed McDougal, now feigning tedium, had been hurriedly coached in suitable brief responses in the same language.

Cattrow's inexperience showed itself when he took four attempts to get the loader level with Zulu Charlie's door sill. He also managed to thump the platform against the aircraft side hard enough for the pilots to wince. In other circumstances Bishop would have screamed at him to watch what he was doing. Now he just gritted his teeth as the Merchantman shuddered in protest.

The three men from the aircraft stepped onto the loader. Cattrow had no idea who were the pilots and who was the baddie. Chances were the older man was one of the crew as he had operated the cargo door controls. The photo ID info Cattrow had asked for hadn't come through on his portable data receiver. One of the three guys had his hand in his pocket, possibly holding a weapon. They all looked nervous. He smiled at them.

'Guten abend.'

'Hi,' replied the man with long hair.

'Is Willi Prosch here?' asked the other man.

'Was?' *What?* Cattrow remembered to sound his Ws as Vs.

'Never mind.'

Cattrow turned to McDougal. 'Im Winter ist das Wetter kalt, nicht wahr?' *In winter the weather is cold, isn't it?* It was a sentence from his schoolbook.

'Selbst verständlich,' muttered McDougal. *Of course.*

'Und die Bäume haben keine Blätter.' *And the trees have no leaves.*

'Ja.'

The long-haired man, the old man and the one possibly carrying a gun stepped onto the platform and Cattrow lowered them to the ground. A train of pallet trolleys was pulling up, apparently to take Zulu Charlie's cargo, its tug driver another of the Armed Response Unit's officers.

Commander Bradley decided to risk a look through his binoculars. *Jesus Christ, it's Maurice Holmin! How the hell did he get into the plane? Were the two pilots part of the escape plan?*

*****

Holmin was worried. The original plan was for him to stay hidden until all the boxes had all been removed to the cargo shed, where Willi Prosch would let him out when the coast was clear. Was Willi in the cargo shed now? Why hadn't he come out to watch the cargo being unloaded, like he said he would? It was worth a fortune. Surely Willi would want to make sure none of them went astray? Maybe he should go looking for him, but that would mean having to take the two pilots with him. But then the precious cargo would be unattended. No, perhaps it would be better to stay here and wait for Prosch to show up.

Holmin looked around again. The first pallet was being pushed onto the loader. Other than the two pilots standing where he had ordered them to in front of him there was no-one else around apart from a bloke in a Peugeot saloon reading a newspaper. The car carried the logo of Lufthansa, the German airline. Holmin peered more closely. In the gloom he could just make out the letters on the number plate. *Shit!* He spun round to look at two trucks parked a little further away. *Double shit! They're British numbers! They've tricked me!*

In a flash Holmin whipped the gun out of his pocket and grabbed Bishop round his neck. He pushed the barrel of the gun against his temple.

'Don't move!' he shouted. He glanced at Crowburn. 'Either of you!' Then he looked up to the loader where Cattrow and McDougal were manoeuvring a box onto the platform. 'Bring that thing down . . . now! You try anything and I'll shoot this guy's brains out.'

The two officers did as asked. Holmin made them throw their weapons out of reach and forced them to lie face down on the ground were he could see them.

'Who's running this show?' he asked Cattrow. 'Please give me a truthful answer, otherwise I'll have to start killing people.'

'The man in the car.' The sergeant indicated the Peugeot saloon with his head.

'What's his name?'

Cattrow told him.

'Hey, Bradley,' Holmin called out. 'Get out of the car with your hands up.'

The Commander had seen Holmin pull out the gun and was rapidly assessing how the situation would develop. He knew that his men would be watching on their monitors but would take no action unless he ordered it or the situation was desperate. For the moment the convict had the upper hand. His head was too close to that of the hostage to risk a sniper shot. Now Bradley climbed out of the Peugeot and stood in front of it, arms raised.

'Walk over here, slowly. Keep coming . . . keep coming . . . stop! Lie down. Okay, have you got marksmen under cover here?'

'Yes,' said Bradley, looking up from the ground.

'How many?'

'Six.' The real number was double that.

'Right, this is what you do. When I tell you, you're gonna bring that car over here. My hippie friend here and me are going for a ride. He's gonna be my driver. You're gonna phone Security and tell them to let us out of the airport. You understand?'

'Yes.'

'And please don't double-cross me because I'm itching to pull this trigger, see?'

'Okay,' said Bradley.

'I mean it. Look, I'll show you.' Holmin brought the gun down and fired at Crowburn, hitting him in the chest. The older pilot yelped in pain and crumpled to the ground. The gun being momentarily pointed away, Nathan Bishop made a snap decision and rammed his elbow back as hard as he could into the convict's stomach. He wrenched himself free, spinning round to get into position to punch him again.

Holmin grunted and doubled up but kept hold of the gun. Unsteadily he brought it round to point at Bishop's head. His finger tightened on the trigger but before he could squeeze it twelve bullets entered his body, half in his head, the others in his heart. He was dead before his knees folded.

Bernie Crowburn was in a bad way, conscious but obviously suffering. Bishop cradled his head in his arms as Commander Bradley radioed for the ambulance.

'Don't worry, Bernie. The medics are here. They'll sort you out.'

Crowburn winced. 'That's the last time I fly with you if this is how it's going to turn out.'

'Are you in pain?'

'Yes.'

'Good.'

CHAPTER 36

The dark blue Jaguar purred down the motorway at a steady 80. At six thirty in the morning traffic was building up but there were not yet the usual terrifying convoys of 40-ton trucks to weave in and out of. For the two men in the car the self-congratulatory euphoria had now settled into the more serious concern of money.

The financing arrangements for Damocles had been somewhat convoluted and it had taken Myron Winslade's personal accountant a fair amount of effort to come to a deal which satisfied all parties. Included in the complications were the advance payments into the American pilot's Zurich bank account. This substantial burden had been borne by Willi Prosch, who had also put up the front money which Winslade would now use to pay off his fellow conspirators. Other costs, including purchasing and exporting a pointless cargo of clothes to Germany, would be reimbursed to the man who had incurred them, Auberon Amberley-Kemp. And Shepherd himself had negotiated an extra payment for deflecting police interest towards the wrong brother.

'No doubt the Old Bill are grilling Giles already,' said Shepherd, sitting in the passenger seat.

Bron laughed. 'Serves him right, the creep. Everybody's darling. He makes me sick. I have to hand it to you, Michael, it was a neat idea to keep up your friendship with him. Guilt by association and all that. Shame they found the document too early, though. Buggered things up for you a bit.'

'Well, plan B ain't so bad. I'll survive. I'm rich now, remember.'

'Have you spoken to Myron? Did they pull him in?'

'Yeah, they took him down to the local nick to question him they had to let him go. He's got a good alibi of course. And expensive lawyers.'

'What did he tell them?'

'Probably a typical Myron charm offensive. *Of course, I'd be delighted to assist you, officer. That stolen plane? Shocking! Who would do such a thing? No, I only know what I heard on the news, officer. Michael Shepherd, yes I know him. Nottingham? Yes, I went to see him there because I'd bought some stuff from him on eBay.*

See that clock on the mantelpiece. Bought it from Michael. A fine piece of craftsmanship, don't you think, officer? And so on.'

Bron laughed. 'Brilliant! Put the radio on, Michael. Let's see if there's anything about us on the news.'

'. . . *crash landed at London's Heathrow airport about an hour ago. Reports say that there were two persons on board, a man and a woman. They are now helping police with their enquiries. As yet there is still no explanation as to why the aircraft circled over London for eight hours. There is speculation that either crime or terrorism are possible motives. Some reports suggest the incident may be linked to the escape yesterday of a prisoner from Stensfield Prison in Essex. A spokesman for Heathrow Airport said that with one of its main runways still out of action there might be delays to flights today . . .'*

The two men in the car were astounded. Shepherd was the first to recover.

'I don't get it. That wasn't in the plan. I thought the Yank was supposed to jump out and let the thing crash into the sea. The two other people were trapped in the cargo hold, Sarah and—' The dispatcher suddenly realised what he had said and shut his mouth.

Bron worked it out immediately. He turned his head and skewered Shepherd with hostile eyes.

'You bastard! That's my sister! You put them on the plane so they would get killed. You knew all the time I'd never see her again. You—' He slammed on the Jaguar's brakes and swerved to a stop on the hard shoulder.

Shepherd jumped out of the car and ran away as fast as he could with Auberon Amberley-Kemp in hot pursuit, screaming at him.

*****

'Did you see that?'

'Yes, I did.'

'Think we should have a look?'

'Yeah, I suppose so. Let's see what they're up to.'

The police patrol Land Rover put its flashing lights on as it U-turned on the carriageway and sped along the hard shoulder against the traffic flow towards the men fighting at the road side.

CHAPTER 37

At Heathrow it was quickly established that the boxes in the Merchantman's hold contained forty million euros' worth of high purity heroin. All four Meteor pilots were under detention. For Wilf Jagger and Nathan Bishop their incarceration meant separate secure rooms at the Heathrow Police Control Centre, located on the Bath Road just north of the airport boundary. Commander Graham Bradley had asked each of them for a brief summary of the night's activity, after which he told them they would be allowed to sleep on the beds provided. The rooms were well-appointed and comfortable, with the amenities to be found in a good quality hotel. When they woke up they could shower and change into the fresh clothes that would be provided if they wanted them. The police officer told them they could expect further interrogation by personnel from Transec and SO15. Whether or not they were released after that depended on the assessments of the reponses they gave.

'What about my aircraft?' Wilf Jagger asked. 'Being parked at Heathrow will cost a fortune in handling charges. Plus, it was supposed to be doing a Düsseldorf to Manchester later today and a Manchester to Sophia to East Midlands after that. I'm letting down customers and losing business.'

'I'm sorry about that, sir,' replied Bradley. 'Perhaps your insurers can help you there.'

'The insurers can't restore lost goodwill.'

'I appreciate that, sir, but you must understand you were involved in a serious incident. Actually, two serious incidents. We must find out the facts. That's our job.'

Jagger conceded. 'Of course. Can I make a few calls? I haven't got my phone.'

'Yes, but with us monitoring the conversation.'

'Okay, fair enough.'

Sarah Amberley-Kemp and Bernie Crowburn were in private wards in Hillingdon Hospital, a few miles north of the airport, where they had been transferred by ambulances. A police officer was on duty in the reception area, although the risk of attempted escape by the two pilots was considered low. Both were conscious but heavily sedated after emergency operations for gunshot wounds. Sarah had needed a blood transfusion. When they were sufficiently compos mentis their own interrogations would begin.

*****

Wilhelm Prosch was a disappointed man. But he was philsophical. When news came through from Winslade that Damocles had foundered his immediate response was to curse himself for wasting his money. But he soon forgave himself. The plan had been a good one and only bad luck had prevented it from coming off. And, as always, he had made sure he was insulated from just such an outcome, physically if not financially. Even the sharpest detective would be unable to connect him to the perpetrators. *Maurice Holmin, officer? No, of course I wasn't going to buy drugs off him. I don't dabble in that sort of filth any more. No, I can't think why he would ask for me before he so sadly got shot. Maybe he thought he'd try his luck. Obviously he didn't realise that now I'm a fully rehabilitated model citizen.*

So, a few euros had gone down the drain. He would soon recharge the coffers. Prosch had been one of the first into the potentially fertile eastern lands of the country after unification. Now his underlings were bringing him substantial profits from selling the magic white powder in the insatiable market. The shipment from England might have gone astray but there were other suppliers. So, he'd have to pay more. It would dent his profits a bit. There were other pleasures in life. Only the previous day his heavies had captured a minor thug from a rival gang and had incarcerated him in a disused building in the seedier end of Dortmund. Perhaps he should pay his unwilling guest a visit. His pulse quickened at the prospect as he picked up the phone.

'Kurt! Get Johann. We are going to see our friend. Don't forget to fetch the equipment.'

*****

At first Luis Dominguez was a disappointed man. Willi had sent word that there had been a hitch and the merchandise would not be available. The Mallorcan immediately began to fret about how he was going to supply his dealers, some of whom would not take kindly to being let down. Uncharacteristically he shared his problems with Kelda. Normally he kept her in the dark about his business activities. It was plain old-fashioned male chauvinism rather than mistrust. The woman's place was in the kitchen or the bed, as far as he was concerned. But this time he had broken his own rules and told her what had happened. And she had come up with the answer.

'Give up work, *cariño!* Let's have a holiday.'

It made sense, when he thought about it. How about calling a meeting. A round of golf first, then down to business. He would tell his friends in the trade that he was retiring from drug dealing. He would suggest setting up a consortium, to which he would hand over all his trading territories. The others would manage the enterprise between them and all he would ask would be a tiny percentage of the take, which, added to his legitimate profits would keep him and his *chica* in their modest life style until they grew old.

Dominguez hugged Kelda and told her he loved her, whereupon she burst into tears.

'Why are you crying, my angel?'

'Because you never told me that before.'

*****

Wilf Jagger didn't know whether he was disappointed or not. He had just woken up for the second time that Monday at the hotel in Staines he and Nathan Bishop were staying in and was now lying in bed, still trying to come to terms with the upheavals of the recent past, pondering how they would shape his future.

No doubt the phone would be ringing if he let it. The first call had come through before seven o'clock, shattering his slumbers. The media had started pestering the two pilots the previous evening, after they had been released from the secure unit at the Police Control Centre. To begin with the attention of the media had been flattering to the ego but Jagger quickly got tired of answering the same questions, especially when they were mostly irrelevant or personal. Publicity for Meteor was all very well but to one reporter who had been less than respectful about his pride and joy he had suggested that he take his recorder and insert it into one of his corporeal orifices. He was happy to let Bish face the TV news crews who had beseiged the hotel, insisting on an interview.

Now the phone was still off the hook and Jagger had no intention of participating again in the media circus, at least for a while. He would have a leisurely late breakfast and start organising the recovery of Zulu Charlie back to East Midlands once it had been released after examination by the police.

He dragged himself out of bed to go to the bathroom but then saw the slip of paper that had been slid under the door. It was a note from Bish:

Gonna fight my way thru the paps to see Sarah and Bernie. Back in time to take the Vibrator back to EMA with you. I'll give them your love.

*****

216

At Hillingdon hospital the police escort had been stood down. The gunshot victims were progressing, both out of danger, Crowburn the weaker of the two. They too were media targets but the hospital authorities had kept the journalists at bay. The ward sister was happy to let Nathan Bishop into Sarah's room, with the proviso he didn't tire her.

'You're the pilot on the news, aren't you?' smiled the nurse.

Bishop nodded. 'Waiting for offers from Hollywood now.'

Sarah was propped up on pillows, a little pallid. Her smile when she saw him betrayed her true feelings. She leant forward for a kiss on the lips.

'You're a star,' he said handing her the newspaper he had brought. Sarah read the headline:

HEROINE PILOT LANDS CRIPPLED HIJACK JET

'Well, you're a TV celebrity,' said the girl. She started to read the story, summarising as her eyes scanned the page.

'. . . plane was stolen to force the authorities to release convicted murderer Maurice Holmin, later shot dead by marksmen at Heathrow airport . . . novice copilot Sarah Amberly-Kemp—they've spelt my name wrong—who had never flown a Boeing 767 before successfully landed the plane after one engine had blown up. The plane's left wheels were also missing, broken off after colliding with fire trucks during take-off . . . blah de blah de blah . . . all four Meteor pilots now released from custody, but Sarah Amberly-misspelt-Kemp and Bernard Crowburn are still in hospital recovering from gunshot wounds . . . police would neither confirm nor deny that they would be questioned further . . . two men arrested while fighting on the M1 motorway hard shoulder might be connected to the crime . . . body of prison officer found in burnt out van ditto . . .' Again Sarah rested the paper on the bed clothes.

'It's incredible, all that stuff going on on one night, all related. Like the plot of a film.'

'Yeah, and nobody seems to know how Holmin got into Zulu Charlie. The cops asked us about the freight. We thought it was just clothes but apparently there were drugs in the boxes too. Holmin must have been hiding in one of the boxes. That's why we were under arrest, in case we were part of the set up.'

'I must call Giles. Make sure he's okay. I pray to God he's not involved.'

'No need. I phoned him earlier. The police questioned him but he's back home again. He thinks he managed to persuade them he's innocent. But he thinks Bron might have set him up, using that document you found.'

Sarah's mouth opened in amazement. 'Bron? Surely not . . .'

Bishop kept his silence, not knowing what the girl was thinking after being told that one of her brothers might have betrayed the other.

Sarah sighed. 'I must phone my parents.'

'I did that too. They're okay, relieved that you're okay.'

'Selfish me, Nathan. I should have asked. How are you?'

'Fine, heroine, how are you?'

'All the better for seeing you.'

'Yeah, whatever.'

'No, Nathan, really.'

The two looked at each other.

'Do you mean—'

'Yes, I do.'

*****

Fortunately the trailing paperazzi were unable to follow Wilf Jagger and Nathan Bishop through airport Security as they made their way to the cargo area to prepare Zulu Charlie for the flight home. The hold was empty, Jagger muttering that there would be no revenue to offset the cost of the flight.

'Want to fly left seat, Bish?'

'Thought you'd never ask,' grinned the younger pilot.

'Long as I don't get shot on arrival.'

'I'll throw my body in front of yours to protect you.'

'Deal.'

CHAPTER 38

Letting himself into his flat as night fell, Jagger strangely felt a sense of let down. Perhaps a reaction to the excitement of the last two days, he reasoned. Not to mention the depressing shabbiness of his abode. He had had to take a taxi from the airport. His defunct car was still stuck at Orchard Lea Grange.

Now Jagger's mind found itself wandering into the hypothetical. Not for the first time he found himself wondering whether he should sell the business, give himself a rest from all the hassle. Now of course there were crewing problems to deal with, with Sarah and Bernie off roster, which meant Meteor had only one captain—himself—until Bish had completed his command training. Ed Park was leaving to start his Central Airlines 777 course very soon. The two new boys wouldn't be fully qualified as copilots for some time yet and with Bernie indisposed all the training load fell to Jagger too. He was going to be working pretty hard for the next few weeks.

Should he pack it in? Now would be a good time to sell up. Air freighting was out of the doldrums, for the time being at least.

He made himself a coffee and sat down, mug in hand, while his imagination tried out various post-Meteor scenarios. Have to be flying, can't do anything else. Sell the business and work for the new owner, that was one possibility. Let some other mug take the strain. Then he would be able to get out to Washington more easily to see his son, without having to worry about who was running the show while he was away. Or there was that new Italian airline starting up that needed MD11 qualified pilots. He could fly as a captain straight away without having to claw his way up a seniority list. But that would mean living in Naples, not his favourite city. The advert had specified familiarity with the language. Jagger's Italian was limited to 'where is the bar?' and 'ham sandwich'.

The Chief Pilot of Meteor Air Express switched on his laptop and checked his emails. The usual rubbish. Half a dozen from media organisations. Got his address from the website, no doubt. He would open them later when he had the enthusiasm.

Hello . . . what's this? Subject: Purchase of Meteor VC9.

Jagger opened the message. His mouth dropped open in astonishment. A Chinese businessman wanted to buy Zulu Charlie! He owned a chain of factories making car components, including two in England, and his hobby was aviation. He was a fan of the Merch and had seen it twice during displays at air shows. Would Captain Jagger be prepared to accept five million dollars for Zulu Charlie? The plane would stay in England because the Chinese man spent a good deal of time there. He was prepared to lease the aircraft back to Meteor Air Express if required, subject to retaining fifty percent of any profits generated. He would also like to be trained to fly it under supervision. His dream was to fly the world's last Vickers Merchantman himself.

Well, that requires some thought!

Jagger sipped his coffee, mulling over the unexpected development. He stood up and wandered through to the back window. In the light from the streetlamps he could see a fox brazenly sniffing around a neighbour's garden. *Five million dollars!* Then a car door slamming in the road at the front frightened the creature away.

The door bell rang. Jagger vacillated, unenthusiastic about meeting any member of the human race at that moment. He walked quickly to the front window and peered out. The car which had scared off the fox was a red Lamborghini. Hilary. Yes, he would like to see her. He clattered down the stairs, trying to tidy his hair with his hands.

'Good evening,' she said with a smile when he opened the door. 'Hope I didn't disturb you.'

Jagger remembered he was still wearing the clothes they had provided for him during his detention at Heathrow. God he must look a sight. He mumbled his apologies and invited his caller in. Inside the flat he fluttered around like a headless chicken, finding her a chair in the lounge that wasn't full of old newspapers or clothes, dashing into the kitchen to fill the kettle and make her a drink even though she had said she didn't want one.

He removed his raincoat from the sofa where it had last been discarded in a heap and sat down, excusing the dishevelled appearance of himself and his abode. He vaguely recalled that he had invited Hilary round for a meal but his memory would not tell him which day or time. Was it now? Of course, maybe she was there in her official capacity, even though she wasn't in uniform. Pretty smart, though, navy skirt, pale blue sweater and short fur jacket. *If only I'd tidied the place up a bit.*

'Have you recovered?' were Hilary's opening words. 'I've been watching the story on TV.'

'Pretty well, thanks. Are you here . . . on duty?' asked the pilot.

'No. I'm on a day off today. I popped round to let you know how things turned out at our end. Jaipal's quite chuffed, I can tell you.

It's all over the papers, as you probably know. Sarah's a celebrity. I phoned you earlier but your mobile went to voicemail.'

'I know,' said the pilot. 'It's still at Sarah's, in my car.'

Hilary gave him a run down on some of the details he didn't know about. She told him that the police had arrested Michael Shepherd and Sarah's brother Auberon.

'A stroke of luck, Wilf. They were fighting each other on the motorway hard shoulder and a patrol car happened to see them and went to investigate. They were breathalysed negative and the officer was just about to let them go with a warning when his buddy realised that one of them fitted the descriptions that had just been circulated. So they pulled them in.'

'Have they been charged?'

'Shepherd has. Conspiracy, demanding with menaces, handling drugs. We're almost certain he arranged the theft of the 767. Sarah's brother will be more difficult to nail. He's got no form as far as we know. Winslade's a slippery fish, too.'

'And what about Giles and the rest of us? They told us to expect further questioning. Are we still suspects?'

Hilary transferred herself to the sofa and patted Jagger's arm.

'Don't worry, you're still a free man. At the moment.'

'I'm pleased to hear it.'

The woman laughed. 'Jaipal reckoned either you or Sarah were flying the plane when it was taken. He thought you were part of the plot.'

'Terrific,' said Jagger. 'What convinced him otherwise?'

'We found another suspect.' Hilary told him about the man who had been found in the middle of a road in Suffolk with a parachute attached to him.

'What, walking around?'

'Hardly. He had no head.'

Jagger screwed up his face. 'Nasty. What's the story behind that?'

'Still a bit of a mystery. But the RAF fighter that was following the plane reported hitting something. Apparently when they examined the fighter after it landed they found traces of blood on its wing, and a dent. Of course it might have been a bird they hit, but on the other hand . . .' Her voice trailed away.

The pilot grimaced again. 'And they don't know who it is?'

'Difficult to identify someone in that state, as you can imagine. They haven't found the . . . missing part. His clothes were British but the parachute was made in the USA. Doesn't give us much to go on. Last I heard they were checking his DNA.'

There was a pause. 'Changing the subject, Hilary, I can't remember when it was I invited you round for dinner.'

'Tomorrow night, you forgetful old fool.'

'Right. I'll try to get this place tidied up a bit before then.'

'I'm honoured.'

Suddenly Jagger brightened. 'What are you doing for the rest of the evening? Shall we go out somewhere? Any suggestions? Or I could order a takeaway.'

'Yes, let's do that. But first . . . we've still got some unfinished business to attend to, haven't we? Or have you forgotten that as well?'

'It would be a good way to work up an appetite.'

'It would.'

They looked at each other for a long moment, eyes filling with arousal. Their arms reached out.

'Just one thing,' said Jagger, his voice thickening.

'Yes?'

'You will be gentle with me, won't you?'

THE END

Books written by Julien Evans: Fiction

Madeleine's Quest
Chalk and Cheese
The Sommerville Case
The Damocles Plot
Flight 935 Do You Read

Non-fiction:

Handling Light Aircraft
How Airliners Fly

Printed in Great Britain
by Amazon